The Hunchback's Gift
Part 1, Voices of Defeat

Book Seven of the Stillness Series

Richard Lee Ferguson

THE HUNCHBACK'S GIFT - BOOK 7 OF THE STILLNESS SERIES

Part 1 Voices of Defeat

Book Cover by Bookfly Design, James Egan

Illustrations by Brian Bowes

Published in 2025

ISBN: 978-1-966776-13-0 (paperback)

ISBN: 978-1-966776-14-7 (hardback)

ISBN: 978-1-966776-15-4 (ebook)

"In a world of hunchbacks, a fine figure becomes a monstrosity."

— Honoré de Balzac

""A one-eyed man is much more incomplete than a blind man, for he knows what it is that's lacking."

—— Victor Hugo, *The Hunchback of Notre-Dame*

Also by Richard Lee Ferguon

The Stillness Series

Book 1: Stirring the Stillness, Part 1 Voices of Quest

Book 2: Stirring the Stillness, Part 2 Tortured Journey

Book 3: Stilling the Stillness, Part 1 Voices of War

Book 4: Stilling the Stillness, Part 2 Restless Spirits

Book 5: Becoming the Stillness, Part 1 Voices of Madness

Book 6: Becoming the Stillness, Part 2 Haunted Caves

Book 7: The Hunchback's Gift, Part 1 Voices of Defeat

Book 8: The Hunchback's Gift, Part 2 Superior Ones Risen

Book 9: Flames of Extinction, Part 1 The Last Voice

Book 10: Flames of Extinction, Part 2 Stillness is Stilled

For the full series, visit the Amazon series page: https://www.amazon.com/dp/B0F1WJ5J4N

Contents

Principal Characters

Voices – God and Goddess

Ming-huà Powers – First Superior One, daughter of Michael/Tamara Powers
Michael Powers – Intermediate, father of Ming-huà
Tamara Powers – Intermediate, mother of Ming-huà
John Powers – Intermediate, grandfather of Ming-huà
Bai Meiying Powers – Intermediate, grandmother of Ming-huà
Child of Buddha – Intermediate, mother of Tamara Powers
Zookeeper (aka Matthew Weston) – Intermediate, husband of Ming-huà
Pythia Powers – A Superior One, daughter of Zookeeper and Ming-huà
Jared Paine – First husband of Pythia Powers
Siyabonga – Intermediate, second husband of Pythia Powers
Kholwa – Intermediate, mother of Siyabonga
Tara Powers – A Superior One, daughter of Pythia Powers and Siyabonga
Abassi – A Superior One, son of Siyabonga and Tara Powers
Anne Monroe – Intermediate, granddaughter of Walter Monroe
Eleos – A Superior One, daughter of Abassi and Anne Monroe
Zhang Yen – A Superior One
Harihara – A Superior One, daughter of Eleos and Zhang Yen
Lady Oracle – Mysterious Guide, granddaughter of Buandelgereen
Scarecrow (aka Siren Rung) – Mysterious Guide
Altan – Mysterious Guide
Lance Romellion – FBI agent
Queequeg – Mongol chief
Temulun – Talking dog

Preface

Can Humans Be Replaced Peacefully?

Query: Are you one of the increasing numbers of people who think humans are irredeemably destructive and pose such a threat to the planet that their extinction would be a good thing? However, do you also abhor the massive destruction and suffering that would necessarily be the consequence of their demise? Bloody, violent dystopian novels often focus only on a few survivors of such devastation, not on the suffering that would extend to all other life forms on the planet. While there are many excellent dystopian novels, such a formulaic concentration on a small group of heroic protagonists can be narrow and unsatisfying.

So, how to unravel the ubiquitous human presence without simultaneously destroying the rest of the planetary ecosystem? Can a successor species evolve fast enough to replace humankind, or would it be extinguished before it has a chance to spread?

Such a successor species, by random chance or intentional design, must possess far greater cognitive and empathetic capacities to thwart the human proclivity for eliminating real or perceived threats. What would it be like for those first generations of advanced individuals surrounded by a sea of slow-witted but resourceful *Homo sapiens*? How would they survive the human penchant for fearing otherness and a relentless instinct to exterminate it? Whether the guiding force effectuating this change is Nature, Superior Alien, God or Gods, Goddess or Goddesses, here is an interesting way forward:

Replace *Homo sapiens* with a more advanced species, but not *drive* them to extinction through violent extermination, rather *dilute* their genes to insignificance over generations. There is precedent for such top-down genetic engineering. Human biologists eliminate dangerous pests by introducing mutant strains that breed with the targeted species to produce offspring harboring the desired genetic makeup. Generations later, the original species is superseded.

A new form of consciousness must necessarily arise—one in which strange Voices with immense cognitive power reverberate in advanced minds in the same way Voices once arose in the minds of early *Homo sapiens separating them from competitors such as Neanderthals*. Humans would initially diagnose those hearing such new Voices as schizophrenics, but they are, in fact, the incipient stirrings of a superior species. However, new Voices must be only the beginning, as this emerging species must also evolve powerful physical capabilities to overcome human weapons of destruction.

The doves must have sharper claws than the hawks . . .

The Stillness Series is the epic story of one such scenario.

Prologue

~ Dear, dear Reader ~

On a dreary afternoon, in one of the dingy back streets of San Francisco's Tenderloin district, three young men, known in the neighborhood as vicious drug dealers, are seen at various locations running and screaming as if chased by demons. This in and of itself would be odd since these men are no strangers to violence and rigidly adhere to the male ethos of taciturn stoicism.

No. What is odd is that not a one of them possesses arms.

Witnesses will testify that the day before all had arms. Now they have only stumps. And not bloody stumps. No. It appears as if the men had been born without arms, or at least had them amputated years ago.

When questioned, the men could only babble something extraordinary about a hunchbacked girl being responsible.

Along with their arms, they seem to have lost their minds as well.

All except for one . . . .

~ The Gift Comes Crippled ~

There is a shape on the horizon—bent, silent, watching.

It does not come with armies or angels. It carries no banners, makes no speeches. Its back is twisted by time, its hands scarred by generations of service. And yet it brings the final offering: the **Gift**.

To some, this gift is salvation.

To others, extinction.

To most, it is not understood at all.

The world is dying, not only its forests and oceans, but its meaning. Governments fracture. Religions feed on spectacle. Machines hum louder than children's voices. What remains of the war has bled into every system, every city, every nerve. A sickness of consciousness.

In this world, the characters reassemble, and they are older, wearier, no longer certain they deserve a future.

Ming-huà, gentle savior of the weak.

Pythia, daughter of rage and vision, rises from captivity with fire behind her eyes.

Abassi, once a cynic, now walks the razor's edge between prophecy and terror.

Tara, heavy with a child that may not be human, must decide whether birth is a blessing or a weapon.

And the **Hunchback**, long silent, finally speaks: not aloud, but through events that cannot be reversed.

This is no longer a question of belief. It is a question of succession.

What comes after humankind?

And who decides?

The Precious Object has changed form. It is no longer carried. It *carries them*. The voice John once heard now speaks to many—clearer, harsher, less patient.

A judgment has begun.

There is no war now. Only reckoning. No quest. Only consequence.

~ *Questions, Questions* ~

And so the questions gather at the edge of extinction:

Is humanity still capable of mercy, or only nostalgia?

What does it mean to be defeated—not by an enemy, but by oneself?

And when the Gift is finally opened—will it be too late to choose who receives it?

Chapter One

Part I – Ming-huà

Next Step

~ *A Secret* ~

Far out into the depths of the forest, on an isolated island off the coast of Washington State, a young hunchbacked girl lives alone in a primitive two-bedroom cabin. Though appearing roughhewn and ramshackle from without, the inside is kept clean and orderly. Few furnishings exist other than a well-stocked kitchen, crude wooden table with one chair, four-poster bed in the main bedroom and a smaller one in the guest room, colorfully painted nightstand, armoire, and assorted other chairs. One chair, an apparent favorite, squats solidly on four short, gracefully curved legs. Its faded upholstery covers an overstuffed backrest that bears a deep, bowl-like impression perfectly formed to accommodate the girl's hump. A wicker basket next to the chair contains balls of yarn and some knitting needles. Oil lamps hang from various hooks, ready to be lit when darkness makes reading or delicate handwork difficult. It is late afternoon and the young hunchback is currently on her knees, bent over an elaborately carved wooden trunk she keeps at the foot of her bed. She mutters to herself as she rummages through the contents. Occasional sighs of frustration escape her lips as she digs deeper.

"Where are you?" she asks. Often, very often, she talks to herself. Being alone for many years has honed her skills at passing the time without feeling bored or adrift. Her conversations with herself are often rather long and convoluted, but today she is more succinct in her utterings.

"There you are, silly thing. What were you doing way down there?"

She pulls out a packet of letters bound together with twine, and returns to her favorite chair. Setting the packet on her lap, she gently unties the knot and leafs through the tumbled, unbound envelopes. She scans the postage dates stamped in the corners. Some of the envelopes are addressed to her in finely scripted English, others in gracefully coiled Chinese calligraphy. All are from her mother. She closes her eyes and picks a random envelope, carefully setting the rest atop the coverlet where she has smoothed the folds to make a flat space. Afternoon shadows from the towering Douglas fir trees have enveloped the cabin in gloomy dark, so she rises and lights an oil lamp hanging above the chair, then sits again and peruses the familiar handwriting with a sigh of pleasant anticipation.

This one is dated over two years ago and the address is written in spidery English letters. Still, she waits to pull out the letter, enjoying the anticipation. Ever since that terrible incident when she was a little girl, she has learned to repress her eagerness and tamp down her impatience. These skills are not mere matters of expediency. No. To her, they are matters of life and death.

"Well, open it, open it Ming-huà!" she exclaims impatiently.

"All in good time."

Ming-huà's father died when she was a young child. She keeps a black and white photograph of her parents in the trunk, but her mother (also a hunchback) never discussed the subject of her father. Even after innumerable attempts to raise the topic, Tamara flatly refused her daughter's enquiries. Any mention of him met with strict silence. Finally, out of the blue on Ming-huà's thirteenth birthday, her mother casually revealed the shattering news that he had been a wandering businessman who suffered dreadfully from mental illness, eventually dying in a mental institution. Stunned, Ming-huà asked a string of questions, but Tamara again refused to answer or elaborate in any way, vowing that further questioning would be useless. Ming-huà continued to try, but her mother remained faithful to her vow. Further mention of him was strictly *verboten*. However, Ming-huà remained stubbornly persistent. After months of pestering, she finally learned her father suffered from schizophrenia. Beyond that, Tamara refused to elaborate. Researching the illness on her own, she woke up every day dreading to discover voices chattering unspeakable things in her head. Fortunately, this never happened. But, to her horror, she had already discovered an affliction that terrified her far more than schizophrenia. It was due to this affliction that her mother exiled them to such a far-away spot.

"Well, are you ever going to read it?" she says to herself.

"Quiet Ming-huà! Look at that silly squirrel outside running up and down the trunk of that tree. In the dusk, you can just make him out. Such a big tail! Ow!" Ming-huà instinctively puts her hand over her stomach. "That hurts. It hurts. What a hungry little fellow."

Usually, Ming-huà feels only a steady vibration from her hump, but there have been many times when a surge of electric shocks jarred her into awareness of something amiss in the surrounding world. Right now, she feels that type of jolt, one she is quite familiar with. It is the stab of hunger, transmitted through the receptors in her back by the frantic little squirrel. She immediately becomes uneasy and wants to disengage from the unpleasant sensation, but she has never been able to turn off these bursts of suffering. Only intense concentration on some other object has succeeded in alleviating the disturbing signals that so often afflict her mind. As a little girl, she puzzled over the vibrations and the surges, knowing them to be significant but always beyond her ability to fathom. Eventually, she came to accept them. Tamara, however, noticed her unique sensitivity growing in its power; and with this increased power, it correspondingly strengthened in its ability to cause Ming-huà empathetic pains. It soon became obvious these pains originated from the suffering of any creature in close proximity.

With this troubling fact in mind, her mother made the determination that being around people in a big city was the problem. They had to get away from the distressing exigencies and violent emotional swings of a dense human population. Such proximity, her mother reasoned, had overloaded the sensitive receptors in her daughter's hump and had begun exerting a morbid sway over her extraordinary mind. She watched Ming-huà sink into a mire of ever-increasing bouts with torment and sorrow, all transmitted by those unhappy souls around her. Ming-huà's mother hesitated to pack up and leave, mainly for lack of opportunity and means. Only following a first horrifying incident that left no choice did she take her daughter to this isolated place. They lived happily for a few years until, on her sixteenth birthday, her mother suddenly informed Ming-huà she must leave her daughter and travel to a magic cave where she would vanish from this existence and never return. Ming-huà would, by some unspoken, terrible necessity, be left on her own. Her mother's last act consisted of turning over a bank account that would automatically provide Ming-huà sufficient funds every month to cover expenses, and perhaps a little more if her daughter lived frugally.

Now, three years later, Ming-huà has adapted to an utterly isolated life beyond all expectations of change.

"Come on, can't see the silly fellow any longer. He's run up the tree with his treasure. Open it."

"Yes, it's time."

She slowly removes the letter, carefully unfolds it, and briefly scans the words without reading, as might a thirsty woman pause in appreciation before taking deep swallows from a cool glass of water.

~ *The First Horrifying Incident* ~

Years earlier, who would have thought her troubles began with a favorite doll? When still a very young child, Ming-huà became attached to a ragdoll sewn together by her mother. It had been stuffed with poly fiber and clothed in a dress of extravagant colors. The chubby calico face had a permanent smile painted on. Its eyes were distinctly Asian, and its black locks of coiled fabric cascaded around its head. The moment the completed doll was presented, Ming-huà held it close to her chest, slept with it, and carried it everywhere. She wanted to give it a name, but of all those that came to mind none satisfied. One bright day the solution emerged like a thunderbolt from some unknown patch of Ming-huà's imagination. Following this epiphany, the name "Miss Gladflower" could be heard repeated by the little hunchback girl with regularity.

"Miss Gladflower, time for tea."

"Miss Gladflower, let's go for a walk."

"Miss Gladflower, you seem sad today."
"Miss Gladflower, tell me about your boyfriend."
And so on. . . .

~

But one dreary afternoon, when left momentarily unattended on the lawn, Miss Gladflower fell prey to a neighborhood dog who, before being chased away, left the doll with a serious wound on her back. The pretty fabric had pulled loose and stuffing bulged out. Once the dog had been safely shooed off, Ming-huà grabbed the unfortunate Miss Gladflower and retreated to her room where she performed emergency surgery. She tried pushing the stuffing back into the body, but it would not stay and kept bulging out in a most horrible manner. Ming-huà recognized the resemblance immediately.

"Ugly hunchback!" she cried. "Ugly hump!"

Some signal from her own hump jolted her mind, and she stared at the doll in anger.

"I want you to be gone, ugly hunchback!"

It dissolved into thin air.

Completely disappeared.

Not a trace remained.

Her heart stopped and she could only stare at an empty lap where Miss Gladflower used to be.

Ming-huà heard her mother gasp from behind. "It is come!"

She watched in stupefied horror as her mother clapped her hands over her face and moaned loudly, "Now we must leave! We must leave and never come back!"

These impassioned words terrified her, but she was in a state of shock. With her mother's threat to leave and never come back, she stared at the empty place where the doll had been and wished it back.

Nothing.

She concentrated hard.

Nothing.

Her power worked in only one direction. This discovery tore something from her soul that itself, like Miss Gladflower, could never be returned. Ming-huà howled in abject terror. No matter how many times she asked what her mother meant by "it is come", no answer ever came. Following the incident, life for her became a whirl of confusion; packing, moving, stopping, unpacking, starting, resting, running, always with no particular destination except for some unspecified, isolated location. Only the desert (Ming-huà later realized it represented the most obvious choice) seemed eliminated from Tamara's list of possibilities. Ming-huà never learned why, but whenever her mother mused aloud about the desert as a solution, the dismissive words, "No, no. Too many ghosts!" quickly followed. To Ming-huà, this utterance gave an inexplicable expression of finality to the problem.

Often, when frustrated over some difficulty, Tamara would say, "I wish your father were with us now."

Ming-huà briefly passed through her mind the notion of what it must be like to have a husband, then merely smiled serenely back at her mother. How could she miss a schizophrenic father? The very word conjured visions of spooky madness. Still, he must have been an outcast, like her. This fact, at least, provided some connection to him.

Since her earliest years, in spite of possessing a quite strikingly beautiful face, Ming-huà had come to accept her self-perceived ugliness. For as long as she could remember she had given up on ever attracting a boyfriend, or being involved in any romantic affair, even a momentary one. Although many had been wonderstruck by her gorgeous features, she rejected their advances as evidence of pity. Instead, she chose to view the world like an old woman long since divested of her sexual charms, whose life is very much lived with both feet planted firmly on undeceived ground. Without unnecessary relational complications, she fully recognized the absurdity and evanescence of life's struggles. Grandmothers can afford to be wise. Ming-hua's charm lay in her utter absence of idyllic dreams and grandiose plans. Only the massive anomaly of her hump interfered with living the entirety of her young life as a self-possessed seventy-year-old.

Through a veritable maze of endless roads, cheap motels, and the byzantine movements of Tamara, they found themselves in the State of Washington. While contemplating the desirability of settling in Canada, or going farther north to Alaska, a string of obscure islands off the coast drew their attention. After researching all of them, and visits to a handful, Tamara settled on the most isolated and pristine. Persevering over the objections of a hesitant real estate agent, she insisted the choice of that distant island was irrevocable, and demanded he find a suitable plot of land with a minimally habitable structure. It took a long time to locate. Finally, on a lonely parcel in the middle of the forest, the real estate agent reluctantly showed her a rather broken-down cabin, far from any other human habitation. He tried to talk her out of it, emphasizing the dangers of a single woman raising a child alone, with no electricity and no neighbors to give comfort. Worse, there were no schools to educate her daughter.

After listening politely, her mother said, "No, it is perfect, thank you. We will do just fine."

The agent knew of a handyman that would make the cabin more habitable.

"Yes, yes, that would be good."

Had Ming-huà's mother and herself not been hunchbacks, the agent would have more strongly objected, perhaps even refused to be involved. However, he concluded hunchbacks were a species unto themselves, and like some sort of Neanderthals, could survive more readily in harsh conditions than normal people. With the deal quickly struck and arrangements made, the cabin was soon transformed into a cozy retreat by the talented handyman (who became quite close with the two odd females).

Mother and daughter prepared to move in.

~

Meanwhile, during the prior year, Ming-huà had been experimenting with her power. Alternately terrified of it, yet fascinated by it, she tested herself by focusing her attention on a variety of small inanimate objects.

"Be gone," she would whisper.

Nothing.

"Be gone!" she commanded.

Nothing.

After spending so much time trying and failing to duplicate her obliteration of Miss Gladflower on more innocuous objects, Ming-huà gave up and tried, in her clumsy way, to move on to other childish things. Nevertheless, such innocent bliss could not be recaptured. A pall hung over her, a kind of dread that colored her once open and happy view of life. Assailed by her mother's frantic quest and flailing actions, her emotions slowly migrated inward where she assiduously nurtured a self-sufficient tranquility (to such an extent she could pass muster at a medieval nunnery). Sweet and pliable, silent and contemplative, she followed her mother uncomplainingly, and spent most of her time in a state of silent contentment.

However, a second incident occurred that drastically reinforced her sense of otherness. Just before they moved to the island cabin, she sat in her motel room sewing a torn blouse the way her mother taught her. Ming-huà pricked her finger, drawing blood, so she sucked on it to stop the bleeding. Satisfied it had been staunched, she began anew but once again pricked her finger in the same spot, hurting much worse and drawing even more blood.

"Ow! Stupid needle!" she cried. "Stupid stupid needle!"

It disappeared.

Gone.

Nowhere to be found.

Stunned, Ming-huà again sucked her finger in wonder and thought to herself, *So, that's it! I must be angry to make things disappear. Anger is what does it!*

At first, this idea pleased her, as she had solved the mystery.

Now when I get angry, I can make things go away.

But after further reflection, she again felt a childish terror. *What if I get angry at mother? No, no, no, no. I must never get angry. Never!*

The thought that she might make her mother, or some other innocent being cease to exist curdled her blood and made her even more inwardly drawn. She now approached life as carefully as a person with hemophilia approaches a bramble bush. This self-imposed monastic existence only intensified when they moved to the cabin. Yet, far from feeling confined, Ming-huà was instantly entranced by the surrounding forest, and fell easily into a quiet, ascetic life. The endless green and whispering of the trees soothed her. The forest animals, abundant in their diversity and effortless in their movements, delighted her beyond words. Tamara, watching her daughter's progression like a hawk, took great comfort in Ming-huà's silent joy and rapid progress. She now planned the date when she would leave Ming-huà forever. Their parting was abrupt, heart-rending, and inexplicable. Tamara's only response to Ming-huà's pleading was that she had no choice. Thus, shortly after turning sixteen, Ming-huà found herself completely alone. Once, on a stormy night when her loneliness and anger at being deserted by her mother got the better of her, she made Tamara's picture vanish. Again, the evidence of her power horrified her and made her withdraw even farther into her own world. This was no devil-child, whipped to cruel frenzy by the unleashing of her destructive power. No. This very power terrified her and drove her generous spirit into deeper solitude lest she inflict intentional or unintentional harm on others.

She mustn't slip again. Ming-huà felt quite content to spend the remainder of her years living anonymously in a small cabin surrounded by forest. Only the letters from her mother remained as fragile, loving ties binding her to another human being.

~ *Post Office* ~

Nevertheless, unpleasant memories of her power rarely return as time passes in repetitious predictability. Now, habituated to her island solitude, Ming-huà slowly finishes reading her mother's letter, then reads it again and with a satisfied sigh, carefully refolds it and slips it inside the envelope. Retying the bundle of letters, she steps lightly back to the trunk and places them deep in a corner. She closes the lid and for a moment runs her fingers over carved scenes decorating the top.

"Tomorrow is post office day," she reminds herself, then returns to her favorite chair to spend some hours knitting before going to bed.

Once a month Ming-huà walks to the post office pulling a red wagon to collect groceries and what little mail is in her box. Her mother's letters have long ago stopped coming. The only mail of any consequence are bills and her monthly statement showing the deposit of funds from some mysterious source. After picking up the mail, she goes to the small grocery store and stocks up on food. These excursions are almost always uneventful, and the little talking she engages in with other humans is brief and awkward for all parties. Still, even such minimal human contact is welcome. Ming-huà deliberately limits her time around people so that their internal angers, frustrations, sufferings and pains merely give the white noise in her hump a somewhat grating, raspy tone.

Ming-huà awakes early, and because the walk into town is long and tiring, she makes a hearty breakfast to last until dinner. In the absence of human companionship, her thoughts are necessarily focused only on the immediate needs and observations of the moment. Preparing food, working in her garden, and alternately sewing, knitting, and quilting occupy the bulk of the day. A trip to the post office always disrupts this monotonous schedule, and so has taken on the characteristics of an adventure far exceeding its actual significance. To an outside observer, the only noticeable sign that this is a special day would be an increase in the chattiness of Ming-huà's self-directed soliloquies.

"So sorry, little eggs, that I have to put you in this hot skillet, but a body has to eat. Just know it is all for the good. I will use your nutrients for good purposes, and you will sacrifice your snug little home in the shell for the betterment of the world . . . I hope. I must remember not to get angry, especially today. I will be around people. Only people are in danger. Not my animal friends, no matter how cruel they can sometimes be. But, not to worry, I have never yet gotten angry in town. People are usually either nice or ignore me altogether . . . particularly after they see my hump. I recognize many of them now, and we always exchange pleasantries. Not to worry, Ming-huà. All will be well."

In this manner she carries on a discussion with herself throughout breakfast. However, once she steps out of the cabin, grabs the handle of her little wagon, and starts down the path, she stops chattering and attends to the sounds of the forest. Always, she first listens for the wind whispering through the needles of the fir trees. Once perceiving that familiar sound, she picks up on a variety of birds making their usual ruckus. Her hump seems alive to the various life forms, and its usual low-key hum comes alive and commences a pleasant sing-song rhythm. Only the eternal lower chords of universal hunger and the jolts of sudden, violent death contribute a slightly ominous, bass gravitas to the chorus. Ming-huà embraces her sense of belonging in this natural world, one that is devoid of human pettiness, greed, ignorance, and casual cruelty. It is that other world, that human world, where her type will never belong. Still, in spite of the satisfaction found in solitude, she does look forward to seeing her own kind again. Even the awkward curiosity her misshapen body attracts is not enough to keep her entirely a hermit. It rarely occurs to Ming-huà that she should feel sorry for herself. The few pangs of self-pity she does feel invariably arise when around loving couples or happy families. In those instances, her hump sheds its darker tones and soars in soprano majesty. However, instead of making her happy, this exquisite music elicits only sadness and depression, which Ming-huà ascribes to the deceptive feedback of her brain, not to the eternally truthful emanations from her hump.

Now, as she walks, Ming-huà feels unwelcome excitement, an emotion she is unaccustomed to, for it is always followed by disappointment and a feeling of being let down by the universe. Unfortunately, this feeling of disillusionment is an affliction she always carries back to her cabin after trips to the post office. Unwilling to dwell on such self-fulfilling prophecies, she initiates a discussion with the passing woods.

"Such a pleasant walk. All of you giants are so kind to line my stroll with your majestic presence." She bows politely and looks up at the boughs of a nearby fir where a noisy squirrel is scolding her for violating its space.

"Oh, don't be silly! I'm leaving soon enough. Be nice."

On she walks, excitement tinged with nervousness growing more palpable in spite of her self-admonishments to remain calm. As she reaches the outskirts of town, houses reveal themselves and the dirt path abruptly becomes a paved road. When the houses become more numerous, she sees a few people working outside and waves. They wave back, staring a bit longer than they normally would at a person strolling by. Ming-huà's hump remains a stable hum, and she takes no offense at the curious spectacle she must appear to those who rarely see her. Often, when subjected to surreptitious scrutiny by others, her hump will send inharmonious chords, but she has learned to pay no attention and go on with her business as if all were normal and unremarkable.

"Hello!" she calls to a person who pauses while raking a garden.

"Hello!" comes the reply.

Unknown to Ming-huà, every townsperson knows who she is. She would be surprised to know how much they talk amongst themselves about the "odd young hunchback girl" who lives alone far out in the forest. Children and teenagers, of course, have convinced themselves she is a witch with supernatural powers. There is, however, a split of opinion about whether she is a good witch or an evil one. It used to be that some brave young souls would steal at night to her cabin and watch for supernatural, "witch-things" like dancing with a broomstick and chanting covens of grotesque witches sacrificing an animal, or a human. But nothing ever happened, except she would come onto her porch and ask them if they wanted to come inside and listen to her read aloud. At first, it was assumed this constituted a ploy to lure them in and be sacrificed. A few heroes agreed, and she really did just read to them. As a result, the practice of spying on her cabin fell into disuse due to the dry content of her books and the boredom they induced.

When Ming-huà nears the one-street business district, friendly but reserved verbal niceties increase, as do the stares. Still, she is pleased. Her hump only occasionally registers the jarring emotions of a passing individual whose unhappiness or anger disrupts the placid hum, but her visit proceeds with a minimum of fuss. Ming-huà enjoys the civilities exchanged between her and the townspeople, as they are appropriately brief and non-threatening. Inside the post office, she sees familiar faces retrieving their mail, but there is one individual she does not recognize, and whose entire demeanor is out of place in this rural outpost. He reminds her of the scarecrow in a movie her mother shared many years earlier, except he is dressed nicely and wears no floppy hat. His attention is entirely focused on her and does not quickly look away like most people when she makes eye contact. She nods, and he nods in return, smiling all the while just like that movie scarecrow. Ming-huà is used to stares, but his gaze is different. Very different. Her hump is awash with confusing waves of indecipherable impressions emanating from this strange man.

Pretending to look through her mail, she waits for him to leave. But he doesn't. He just stands and stares while others walk around his deceivingly immoveable figure. She notices he does not merely stand, with arms in a normal position. Instead, he seems to be in constant movement while remaining in the same spot, as if his joints were all made of rubber. *Like the scarecrow*, she thinks. Preferring to wait until he is gone, she pretends to be absorbed in her mail but he continues to stare, his odd body atwitch with restless movement. Finally, Ming-huà forces herself to pass by him as she leaves. Instead of stepping aside, he dances a little jig and slides in front of her, nodding. The smile never leaves his face, *like the scarecrow. Like Miss Gladflower.*

"Hello, Ming-huà," he says calmly.

Her hump's receptors shift into overdrive, but the information received by her brain is garbled and incomprehensible. Neither good nor bad. Neither happy nor sad. Neither this nor that. A contradictory enigma.

She is at a loss for words and looks at him questioningly.

"Hello, Ming-huà," he repeats with a smile.

"Hello," she mumbles under her breath while continuing to move awkwardly toward the door. Her thoughts are a jumble of confusion, and to escape becomes her only imperative. She manages to slip by him and make it out of the building. He follows, and yet he does not simply follow. No. Rather, he dances after her, spinning his arms and waving his hands at odd angles. Now, for once she is not the center of attention, as a handful of people in front of the post office pause to admire his performance. Ming-huà wants to take the opportunity to hurry away unnoticed with her wagon in tow and finish shopping so she can avoid this extraordinary character. Some perverse feeling wants her to stay and demand how he knows her name, but she is far too intimidated and shy for such a bold move. As she separates from the little crowd and retrieves her wagon, she hurries to the grocery store, nervously glancing behind to make sure he does not follow.

Ming-huà is anxious to return to the safety of her little cabin, so she rushes to complete her shopping and quickly leave town with groceries in tow. Unfortunately, this is hunting season, and there are more customers than usual who have arrived on the island to shoot deer. She waits in a long line at the cash register, all the while being ogled by strangers. At last, she pays, loads her wagon, and quickly heads down the street. To her relief, the scarecrow is nowhere to be found. When the end of the paved road is reached, she relaxes and slackens her pace. Still, she occasionally looks back to make sure no one is following. Now, with the security of knowing her forest friends are all around, she falls into a comfortable stride and turns her attention to the mystery of the scarecrow and how he knows her name.

~ *A Second Terrible Incident* ~

Thus lost in thought, a sudden rush of excited yells and coarse laughter erupts some distance away, shattering her reverie. Ming-huà is aware a creek runs parallel to the path and this is where the ruckus seems to originate, but dense foliage blocks her view. Unsettled by the crude noises, she quickens her pace, intent on ignoring the commotion and assuming it comes from a group of rowdy tourists having an outdoor gathering. Somehow, an ominous rumbling from her hump indicates otherwise. Her nerves are on full alert, and she longs to put the noise far behind. But without warning, her hump sends a series of viciously painful jolts into her brain, and she doubles over in agony. As the shouting and roaring continue, she forces herself to gain control over her body and rushes off the path toward the spot where, she now assumes, a person is in distress. When she reaches the edge of the creek, a bewildering scene unfolds before her eyes.

Two young males, dressed in camouflaged khakis, are knee deep in the creek, leaning over something churning desperately beneath them in the water. Ming-huà cannot make out what is happening, so she takes a few steps closer. To her horror, she realizes the men are drowning a struggling fawn. They are laughing, probably drunk, encouraging each other to keep the poor fawn's head beneath the water and roaring playful obscenities when the tiny nose slips their hold and tries to breath in some air.

Without thinking any further, Ming-huà 's confusion turns to rage as she watches the obscene pleasure these evil men are deriving from such pointless and heartless murder. If she hesitates even a few seconds longer, the little fawn will be dead, so her entire wrath is loosed upon its tormentors.

In an instant the two men are gone.

Disappeared.

Just like Miss Gladflower.

Their bodies dissociated and the rich molecules and atoms that comprised them dispersed into the environment where they might serve better purposes.

Not a trace left. No clothes. Nothing. Only two hunting rifles lying on the bank remain as evidence the men once existed at this spot in space and time.

Ming-huà carefully lifts the exhausted fawn out of the water and steadies her on the bank, where her mother awaits at a discreet distance in alert anticipation. It is only then that the full horror of what she has just done dawns upon the shaken young hunchback.

~

As if escaping a murder scene, Ming-huà runs back to the path and stands looking down its dirt length toward the cabin. Her legs will no longer obey her commands, and she feels faint. Knowing she must get as far away from this spot as possible, she nonetheless plops stupefied on a fallen log and buries her face in her hands, heaving dry sobs (tears will not come to help wash away the guilt). She does not know how much time passes, but she must have sunk into some sort of stupor, for she awakes to the lengthening shadows of dusk and sees a man standing over her, smiling.

It is the scarecrow.

He dances a little jig and proclaims, "I know what just happened."

Ming-huà stares at him in shock.

"Believe me, I know. It was a good thing to do. That is why I followed you today. Don't worry, it is good! They did not suffer, and the suffering they inflicted on the world is over! Kaput!"

Much to Ming-huà's consternation, he again dances a jig. The smile never leaves his face. He looks up the path toward the town. "It is time we go."

"Where?" asks Ming-huà dumbly.

"To your quaint little wooden castle, of course. Those two who are no longer two will soon be missed. Sooner or later there will be people coming. When that happens, you want to be away from this spot."

"But—" Ming-huà starts to object.

"Innocence itself. You are innocence itself. Even Miss Gladflower knew that when you made her disappear."

Ming-huà trembles in the face of this absurdity. This dream. This nightmare. She can only mutter, "Who are you?"

He holds out his hand to help her up. "Come! It is late. We must be on our way. I will tell you as we walk."

She takes his hand and they start off together in silence, Scarecrow pulling her wagon. "You can't stay at my place," she finally says.

"Of course. Never intended to stay at your place. But, nonetheless, we need to talk. Oh yes, we need to talk. But certainly not here. Not at the scene of the . . . well, of your reconfiguration."

"Reconfiguration?"

"Yes, reconfiguration. You just rearranged a few atoms here, a few molecules there, and *voilà*!"

Ming-huà feels sick. "I killed them."

"You reconfigured them." He glances at her in alarm as she slows her pace. "Are you sick? Do you need to vomit?"

"No," she replies miserably. "I wish I did."

He contorts his body into a dramatic pose.

"Who are you?" she asks again.

"My name is Siren Rung."

In her misery, she dryly chuckles. "What?"

"Siren Rung."

"A funny name . . . sounds oddly familiar."

"It should." He laughs as at an inside joke.

"Why should it?"

"No reason. Let's keep walking, it's getting dark."

Ming-huà's legs move, but she feels queasy and weak. She shudders, wraps her arms around her body, and tries to erase all thoughts from her mind, but her hump reverberates with an unfamiliar, grating buzz. Her trembling continues all the way to the cabin.

~

Once inside, Ming-huà collapses on a straight back chair. She tries to keep her body rigid while her mind struggles to cope, but the shaking becomes uncontrollable. If she keeps asking questions, perhaps her nerves will calm.

"I know your name now, but who are you?" In spite of her struggles to maintain some semblance of calm, the words come out a stuttering mess.

"You are trembling. Are you afraid of me?"

"No, should I be?" Her voice is a high-pitched plea.

Siren Rung looks at her with a degree of pity. "As your father would say, it is the Time of Shaking."

"My father! You knew him?" Again, the words are staccato, as if it takes some effort to spit them out with clear enough pronunciation to make them understood.

Revelations have come too fast and furious for poor Ming-huà to absorb. Her trembling increases to an alarming degree, and she succumbs to more violent shaking, even causing her normally equable visitor to quickly grab a blanket off the bed and wrap it around her as one might do for a freezing person. Between clattering teeth, Ming-huà attempts to repeat her questions, viewing them as crucial lifelines to reality. It takes her multiple times to finally force out the words, albeit stretched loosely apart by abrupt pauses and deep intakes of breath.

"Who are you? How do you know my father?"

Apparently encouraged by her perseverance, he dances another little jig, this one far less exuberant, edged in its movements with a hint of sorrow. With one leg lifted in the air and hands raised heavenward, he freezes the pose and glares at her dramatically.

"As I told you, I am Siren Rung, and I knew your father very well. We all did. By the way, call me Sy."

Ming-huà is not listening, her attention drawn to her own suffering and the two men whose faces, cruel as they were, expressed a humanity that, to her, must have possessed some deeper quality of redemption. Surely they must have had some quality of goodness! They must have had mothers, wives and children. And to have caused them to simply vanish! The agony of having committed such an atrocity is unbearable to her.

Ming-huà tries to return her attention to the visitor's words, but she feels dizzy, and her bones and muscles melt away, no longer able to prop up her body. She feels herself slipping downward. . . .

~ *Aftermath* ~

Ming-huà is awakened by a persistent knocking at the door. She is surprised to find herself in bed, nightgown on, covers drawn around her neck, sunlight flooding the room. Her mind is sluggish and she slowly remembers certain terrible events, but is unclear how long ago they happened, or whether they happened at all. *A dream. It was a dream. Thank God!* But the knocking continues insistently, and she knows it does not arise from any dream. She quickly rises and throws on a robe.

Cracking open the door, she sees the town sheriff and a handful of men standing behind.

"Hello Mr. Turner," she says in a growly voice.

He tips his hat. "Hello Miss Powers. Sorry to bother you. May I come in?"

Ming-huà pulls her robe tighter around her neck and keeps the door cracked open just enough to see his face. "Oh, I'm so sorry, I just got up. What is it?"

"Well, we have reports of missing persons. Two men. White males. They were hunting near your cabin. We found their guns, but they are still missing. Can I come in, please?"

No dream no dream no dream oh God no dream.

She keeps the door only cracked open. "I don't know anything about it, sheriff."

"Did you see any men around yesterday?"

"No. I went to town, to the post office and shopping, and came straight back here. I didn't see anything."

"Their guns were near the creek that runs close to your place. Did you hear anything?"

"Like what?"

"Voices, gunfire, you know, anything?"

"Sorry Mr. Turner. No."

"Are you sure?"

"I'm sure."

He hesitates, then says haltingly, "Well . . . if you saw or heard nothing, I guess there is not much to say, is there?"

"No."

"Well, if you remember something, anything, please call me. Here's my card. Call me if you think of anything, no matter how insignificant you think it might be. Will you do that, Miss Powers?"

She takes the card. "Yes. Yes, I will," adding vaguely, "I have no phone."

He turns to leave and says, "Come on, boys, let's keep searching." Over his shoulder he acerbically utters, "Thanks for your time."

Ming-huà does not respond. She closes the door and moves as in a daze to the comfort of her overstuffed chair. Settling in, she replays the events of the previous day with a clear reenactment of details that are mesmerizing in their horror. She feels oppressed by the stale air and opens a window. As she does so, a squirrel begins chattering in a nearby tree.

"Silly squirrel, so early to be so talkative." These words are muttered instinctively, automatically, her thoughts now focused on something else. Something important.

"Where is the scarecrow?"

She looks down at her robe, then scans the room and sees her clothes from the previous day neatly folded on the night table.

"Who is scarecrow?"

The trembling starts again, and Ming-huà quickly goes to the kitchen and busies herself preparing breakfast. "Keep busy, Ming-huà," she says out loud. "Keep busy and focus on what you are doing. Nothing can be done now. Nothing."

She hears the squirrel again, and says, "Oh, if only I were you. If I had only hunger to think about. Only hunger! Not. . . . "

~

It is afternoon, and in her misery, Ming-huà takes to the garden and pulls weeds with single-minded purpose. The physical work feels good, and she lapses into a rhythm, unmindful of anything around her. When the faces of the two men materialize in her imagination, she doubles her efforts at pulling and tossing, pulling and tossing.

Often, when the wind rustles a branch or an inquisitive deer steps on a twig, Ming-huà stops her labor and looks around . . . for what? The sheriff? The two men who have reassembled? No. She looks for the scarecrow. *How fitting!* she thinks bitterly. *A scarecrow in my garden, scaring away . . . who knows?*

Days pass in this fashion. With an innocent conscience torn away so brutally, her quiet contentment and symbiotic relationship with the natural world seems a distant memory. *Murder is not natural,* she reminds herself daily. *My animal friends do not murder. I am the canker that now afflicts this forest.* No more does she carry on long conversations with herself, as if she shunned her own existence. An echoing remorse at her loss, and the ever-present fear of exposure, are her constant companions. Although sinking deeper in her own pain, and with a single-minded intent to exile herself even farther from the human race, there exists only one person she longs to see.

Still no scarecrow. . . .

Once, Sheriff Turner stopped by her garden and asked if she remembered anything, but she replied with a simple, "No," and he never returned. She dared not inquire about the search, or the missing men's background. Just a simple "No" and she was cleared of any wrongdoing by everyone but herself. Guilt has worked its magic and eroded even the small amount of confidence left to defend against despair. Her hump continues preternaturally silent. A barely perceptible hum the only reminder it exists at all. Proof, to her, that estrangement from the world must be permanent and inexorable. She cannot sleep nor can she eat, and gradually her strength dwindles to the point she gives up working in the garden. Her greatest fear looms just over the horizon, when she must return to town and expose herself to the living. Or, alternatively, she can simply wait and let herself die. Appropriate punishment for murder. Better yet, she tries to dissociate herself, as she did to those poor men. But, as always, her power does not work on her own body. So, she takes to her bed and wastes away as, she feels, fitting and proper for a murderess.

~

"It's time to leave."
The voice comes from some distant place, barely discernable to her ears.
"Come, come, Ming-huà! It's time to go!"
Nearer. Familiar.
She feels her head lifted and a spoon with warm soup put to her lips. "Drink. It's time to go. Drink!"
Pillows are fluffed and she is helped to sit up in bed. More spoonsful of soup. She sips. It tastes good.

"Goodness gracious, girl! You're skin and bones! That's no way to travel. Drink more!"

More is given. More is consumed. The room is warm and her caregiver remains a fuzzy smudge. She sleeps. Two days pass between sleep and soup. Her strength returns. Her hump buzzes with unusual energy. One afternoon, she focuses.

"Scarecrow," she murmurs. "I thought it was you."

"Scarecrow! No, no, no, my dear. It is Sy."

He dances a lively jig. "I'm no scarecrow. See me whirl! I keep the crows away better than any scarecrow!"

He affects an exaggeratedly deep bow. "It is Sy . . . Siren Rung, at your service. And we must leave!"

"Leave? Why?"

"*Goddess* says so."

"What?" The word makes Ming-huà freeze up inside. Her muscles tighten and her mind struggles to make sense of her reaction.

"*Goddess*?" she blurts.

"Never mind. It is enough that we must leave."

A sudden terrible thought prods her to sit up. "Are they coming for me?"

"They?" He laughs knowingly. "No, no. It is not, 'they who are coming for you'! Instead, you, my dear, are going to them!"

"I don't understand."

"Nor do I, but I never understand *Her*. Nevertheless—"

"*Her*?"

He shakes his head irritably. "Never mind! You are The Daughter. The Chosen One. Get a bit stronger. Eat. Eat! Tomorrow, we go, come hell or high water!"

"But this is my home!"

"Correction, it is no longer your house. It is your prison."

Ming-huà sinks back and assumes a sour face. "As it should be. This is where my crime was committed. The corpses of those two men were little more than a stone's throw away."

"No, little hunchback. There were no corpses, remember? You simply reconfigured the innumerable constituents of their bodies and freed them for other, better purposes. In the meantime, you stopped the terrible suffering of a poor little fawn and obliterated the animate machinery of evil that disguised itself as these men."

"I will not play *God*."

At this, Sy roars with laughter and slaps his knees in delight. "*God*? Oh, that is rich! That is hilarious! Hilarious! If only you knew what a good joke that is." He dances another jig, throwing his arms outward and craning his head heavenward. "You hear that, Great Lady? She doesn't want to play *God* while *God* plays with her! Marvelous! Delicious!"

"Stop!" cries a startled Ming-huà.

He abruptly stops and turns his fierce eyes upon her. "Do you believe in *God*?"

She hesitates. "No," she whispers.

"And *Goddess*?"

For some reason, the memory of her mother pops into her head, and the mention of *Goddess* reverberates in her hump as a profound clarion call, deafening as one of Quasimodo's bells. She is thrown into utter bewilderment and cannot say a word.

"Well?" he prompts.

Still, she remains speechless.

"Never mind! Tomorrow we leave!"

Ming-huà is shaken back to reality by his raucous behavior and loud voice.

"Look. . . Mr. Rung—"

"Call me Sy."

"Look, Sy, I don't know anything about you. I have no intention of leaving my home. In fact, I want you to leave. Please!"

Sy falls quiet and stares at her with an unreadable glint in his eyes. "What does your hump say?"

"What?"

"Your hump. What does it say?"

"What do you know about my hump?" she stammers.

"Everything. And you're supposed to be The Daughter? Ha! You are just as silly as that squirrel you always talk to. Your hump nurtures a seed that has been planted since your grandparents were around. It is now sprouting. Thus, it is time for a gardener. Me!"

Dancing another loose-jointed jig, he cackles, "Scarecrow with a green thumb! I'm beginning to like that moniker after all! From now on you can call me Scarecrow!"

Ming-huà falls silent as her last remaining willpower caves in upon itself, leaving her too weak to make further demands he leave. Observing her weakness, Sy's face suddenly darkens and all pretense at lightheartedness falls away to reveal a somber, intimidating presence. He leans over her and speaks in the harsh growl of a disturbed lion, his eyes frozen daggers unveiled now for the first time.

"Ming-huà, you have a power that is unique in the world. It is your fate to possess this power. However, no longer can you hide it away in this place; its once safe and pleasant environs are now disturbed by . . . unexplained disappearances. Humans abhor unexplained things, and they will move heaven and earth to explain them, even if incorrectly. It is time you test the limits of your power's potential. Now, misshapen child, you must venture out into the larger world of people; a world full of deadly traps and elaborate snares. You must! Unbeknownst to you, that cursed hump is a blessing, and it can make things vanish, but it can also make things be reborn, and all the while it sings the Music of the Spheres—music which it is your task in life to decipher properly. Your grandmother could decipher the taps from a Precious Object. Your mother could decipher the echoes of space and time in magic caves. Your father, in the depths of his so-called schizophrenia, never gave up his quest to decipher the wishes of *Goddess*. It is your fate to do the same. It is your destiny."

He straightens up, a mischievous smile softening the harshness of his glare. "And that destiny will be paid for. You will find your anonymous financial guardian will double and triple the amount of money deposited in your account. A dream! Enough to finance a dozen quests! By the way, your little cabin will continue to be paid for . . . just in case. And what about this clever sorcerer, yours truly Siren Rung? Ah! He is descended from other sorcerers whose life threads are entwined with those of your parents and grandparents. Siren Rung will gleefully dance ahead of you on your journeys, grabbing every opportunity to take what evil the world has to offer and in return, poke both its eyes in jest! Oh, yes, he will step back and laugh at this old world's teary blinks and sputtering outrage." He pauses for effect. "After all, you are The Daughter. The Chosen One."

Ming-huà listens submissively. "I have many questions," she says softly. "But, not now."

"No, not now," he agrees. "I will give you another day or two to rest, eat, and reflect. But then, we are off."

"All right, I will go." She can barely believe her own words.

"Good! I'll return in two days. Be packed. One suitcase only, or a backpack. Nothing else. Ah! I forget! You have a built-in backpack. No matter! We leave early. Be ready."

She watches him walk jauntily down the path, his nimble form hazy in the twilight. As he fades away, riddles, like swarms of butterflies, flutter in an undulating cloud around his lanky, scarecrow body. Oddly enough, she is not startled by this vision. Instead, the riddles act as lures drawing her into his orbit. She is her mother's daughter.

~ *Leaving the Island* ~

Later that night, lying in bed, Ming-huà struggles to understand the meaning behind Siren Rung's rather disjointed rambling. A few words had penetrated: "mother", "father", "grandmother", "grandfather", "quest", "*Goddess*", but she now has no energy to try and flesh out the portentous significance binding them into a coherent whole. She simply decides to give herself over to this decidedly outlandish man, come what may. He will relieve the burden of coping with the desiccating grind of an everyday life weighed down by guilt and murder. As she reflects on these notions, she is surprised how quickly and completely, heart and soul, she has succumbed to his siren call. She remembers saying, "All right, I will go," as if someone else spoke the words. Perhaps the response came from her hump's command, or maybe from the ghostly voice of her mother, but once spoken, the words consummated the total surrender she had been unconsciously seeking. Yet surprisingly, in the totality of her defeat, she sees an unexpected glimmer of hope. In a fleeting moment of surrender, everything in her world precipitously turned on a dime, but rather than feeling dazed, she now views the future with a degree of reawakened confidence, albeit as yet with no clear purpose. Her beloved forest would continue, but she would be gone, the awful spirits of her two victims left behind to haunt those who cannot be haunted. As of now, her old life is ended. It matters little that she does not comprehend the meaning behind the beaded necklace of shimmery words strung together by Siren Rung. What matters now is how to deal with an uncertain future. From the darkness outside, Ming-huà hears a squirrel . . . the same squirrel? . . . chattering away. *He's scolding me again, telling me to leave. I've outlived my usefulness here. No, that's not quite right. I've lost the right to live here.*

~

When Sy comes for her, Ming-huà had been sitting in her favorite, over-stuffed chair for hours, a small suitcase primly beside it on the floor, both waiting patiently. Before his arrival, she had been luxuriating in all the rich objects that inhabited what was once her comfortable universe. That universe, although now ostensibly spread before her eyes in the present, had already become a memory. It encompassed the outside, the forest, all her animal friends and confidantes—indeed her entire life—yet she remains tearless. No senti-mentality must be indulged in by a murderess! *Does it become easier?* she won-ders about murder. Through the window, she catches sight of Sy approaching in a lightheaded, dancing gait. "I suppose we will find out," she muses aloud, a sorrowful, brief throwback to her happier days of long soliloquies. Ming-huà has begun to view the world in the sulky manner of a young girl who has lost her virginity to a boy whose heartless lies have only just been discovered. Now, she stands to greet Sy with a determination borne of resignation, and calls out an invitation to enter. As he opens the front door, she is startled to see her two murdered victims peering in through a side window. Momentarily frightened, Ming-huà twists away from the sight, and notices Miss Gladflower sitting on the same overstuffed chair she had just vacated. *It seems the ghosts have taken over, and lost no time in doing so,* she thinks. Abruptly her body stiffens in protest over these uninvited specters, and swivels back toward the window. She shouts angrily, "You evil men should not have tried to kill that helpless fawn!" She is astonished at her own violent outburst, and turns her head sharply to look back at the chair. In a much softer tone, she admonishes the doll, "And Miss Gladflower, I am sorry, but you should not have lost your stuffing in such an insulting manner! I will leave you all to your own devices. Haunt an empty cabin, if you wish. I will go with this absurd man to face whatever fate has in store!" Before Sy's admiring eyes, she picks up her suitcase and storms past him out the door, leaving the little cabin in her wake.

~

It is a while before Ming-huà works up the courage to ask, "Where to?"
Without breaking stride, Sy answers, "To the mainland."
"After that?"
"After that? To a magnificent city, of course!"
Ming-huà 's spirits fall. "A city?" she asks pathetically.
"Yes, with lots and lots of people. We really must have you dive into the deepest part of the icy river. Sink or swim!"

"It is not whether I sink or swim that worries me," says Ming-huà. "What if I get angry? What if I let slip something I cannot take back? I can't face another. . . incident."

Sy assumes a tragic face. "I know what worries you, little hunchback. That's as it should be. But you are destined for greater things than the *wee sleekit, cow'ring timorous beastie* your fears make of you."

Ming-huà shakes her head ruefully. "This cursed power has plowed my own field and uprooted my own comfy house. Your foolish behavior will not make me laugh off the awful deed I have done. Shame on you! Two men are dead."

They walk in silence for a while. Ming-huà suddenly pauses and asks, "Did they have families? I have been too scared to read, or inquire in any way."

Sy closes his eyes and shakes his head disapprovingly. "Here is the paved road. We're almost to town. I suggest we stop at the post office to make sure they have a forwarding address."

"You already know the address we're going to?"

"Of course. *She* thinks of everything." He rummages through his pocket. "Here it is."

Taking Sy's proffered note, Ming-huà asks, "*She*?"

"Not now. We'd best hurry or we'll miss the next boat to the mainland!"

In spite of his entreaty, Ming-huà stops and looks back down the tree-lined path. Sy rests a hand on her shoulder and gives a gentle squeeze. "Regrets?"

She allows herself to be pulled back from her reverie. "All I have are regrets."

~

As usual, when they enter the town, Ming-huà's hump begins to vigorously hum, its intensity rising and falling as she passes people on the street. She zips into the post office and retrieves a couple of envelopes and uses Sy's note to fill out a forwarding address form, and rejoins the scarecrow figure fidgeting outside. Once safely on board the boat that will take them to the mainland, Sy visibly relaxes while Ming-huà sits on a bench enjoying the view, her mind grasping at whatever pleasing scene might offer a peaceful, soothing balm to her restless hump. She focuses only on the surface of the water, for she knows to plumb the depths, where dwell the creatures of the sea, there is hunger, violent death, and painful disease. Avoiding unpleasantness is now the singular imperative driving her actions. Sy watches her and feels pangs of regret that she will soon be forcefully dragged away from her comforts and driven into a world where her survival will be severely tested. He knows the incident with the two hunters is only the beginning of the process.

Chapter Two

Introduction to the City

Departures and Arrivals

~ First Impressions ~

It has been years since Ming-huà set foot on the mainland, and immediately her senses are overwhelmed by a frantic activity that does not exist on the island. Her hump is ablaze with the fleeting emotions of passers-by, while her mind reels at the chaotic movements of people and their machines, racing this way and that, all with cryptic purposes and single-minded obsessions. Ming-huà feels like a child on her first day of school, panic-stricken and driven by instinct to return to the safety of home. Nevertheless, in spite of her trepidation, she grits her teeth and soldiers on. But before taking many steps, she plops her suitcase on the ground and sits dizzily on a curb. Sy dances back and forth impatiently, exhorting her to breathe deeply.

"Hurry up, little one! We have places to go, people to see, a bus to catch!"

Ming-huà waves her arm weakly. "Let me rest for a minute."

"You're too young to be tired."

"I'm not tired, I'm frightened. I can't breathe. I need time."

Those passing by crane their necks and gawk at Ming-huà's hump. Sy meets these rude rubberneckers with an accusatory glare, but the hunchback is painfully aware of her otherness. Now, she rises and mutters, "Let's go," determined to escape the feeling of being a spectacle, or worse, a carnival exhibit. Sy hails a cab and she climbs into the safety of its cocoon, avoiding the eyes of the driver ogling her in the rearview mirror.

"They are not staring at your hump," says Sy. "You will never believe it, but they are marveling at your glorious beauty; your gorgeous face, luxurious hair, luminous eyes, queenly bearing. All of you! Magnificent!"

Ming-huà can only scoot farther down in the seat, unwilling to look out the window at the restless hive buzzing past. Before she knows it, they arrive at the bus terminal, jostling in a disorganized line where Sy finally makes it to the counter and purchases two tickets to San Francisco. An old, diesel-spewing bus awaits, and as they board, Ming-huà notices her fellow passengers are a rather motley-looking group, none of whom take any notice of her deformity. Most of them are exiles themselves, drab and inward-turning, left behind by the flashier members of a wealthy society. Sitting among them, she is saddened by their disappointments and failures singing an off-key, melancholic dirge through her hump. For the first time since leaving the island, she feels at home among these fellow cast-offs. Miles roll by, towns come and go, and Ming-huà falls in and out of sleep. Sy never sleeps, chattering the entire way with other passengers, speaking to each in turn by gliding effortlessly into their individual language idiosyncrasies as easily as slipping on and off a cloak. As for Ming-huà, low-key pain and isolation are the sad chords that reverberate in her hump—chords she has long recognized and made peace with. Perhaps, she thinks, it is the reason she feels comfortable with the people riding in this mournful bus.

Once, in the midst of a long, desolate stretch of scrubland, she awakes just in time to see a coyote loping in the distance. Sharp pangs of hunger and a fierce determination to find prey double her over in pain. How different the desperate, never-to-be-satiated craving for food by non-human animals, compared to the slow burn of human suffering! Agony quick and agony gradual—everwhere!

"No, Ming-huà, not so," says Sy.

"What?"

"There is a notion among many that one cannot experience joy without first experiencing suffering. Many of your grandmother's comrades often discussed this conundrum. Do you believe it?"

Ming-huà shakes her head, still feeling the coyote's bitter knot of starvation. "I don't know."

Sy shrugs, but she feels a tremor deep within her hump. "How do you know about my grandmother?"

He breaks into a raucous laugh. "If you only knew!" he cries. He jumps into the aisle and assumes a ridiculous, twisted, operatic pose. "If you only knew!"

His antics elicit a smattering of applause from the passengers.

As Ming-huà watches, she briefly questions Scarecrow's sanity, but remembers her own father had suffered from schizophrenia, and must have also acted crazy. She recalls Sy mentioning something about her grandfather being part of a quest. *Like my grandfather,* she wonders, *is Sy embarked on some mysterious quest? But what kind of quest? And what kind of quest was my grandfather on? Mother knows. Why won't she tell me? What spectacle did papa make of himself? Was he viewed as a freak, like me? Like mother? Sy is also a bit of a freak. Am I truly a freak? I hear no voices, see no hallucinations, suffer from no delusions. Or do I? No, I am worse! My condition is worse! My hump and its ability to detect things, things that are suffering, is worse. My destructive power is worse. My deformity is worse! Oh, yes yes yes. My condition is much worse!*

In her distress, Ming-huà remembers her mother once described her as a "one-trick pony", born with a saddle on her back, but no rider. Yes, she circles the carnival ring riderless. Around and around. But now, Sy has grabbed the reins and has ridden her out of the comfy cozy cabin that now seems so distant. For better or worse, she is inexorably moving toward some unknown fate. Visions of disaster flood her mind, and she feels helpless to turn back. Yes, she decides, her condition is much worse than her father's or grandfather's must have been, and trembles at her powers. Certainly those powers will unleash something terrible on the world. They will lead to her life and those of unknown others to come crashing down in a death-spiral.

When the bus enters the outer suburbs of San Francisco, her hump comes alive with a surge of confusing signals—a mishmash of conflicting human sensations, all overloading her ability to process. At the central bus terminal, she staggers to a waiting taxi with the help of Sy, who supports and guides her protectively. He barks the address to the driver, clearly anxious to reach their destination for the sake of his protégé's increasingly debilitating condition. The taxi pulls in front of their destination at the top of one of San Francisco's most prestigious hills. Sy pays the driver and helps Ming-huà step out. She looks up to behold a magnificent Victorian house rising in stately grandeur. Multiple turrets loom majestically against the sky, while a gorgeous wraparound porch accentuates the inviting nature of the building's charms: swirling curves, fish-scale shingles, and lovely bays, all providing an intimate allure that to Ming-huà seem irresistible. The house proudly stands atop a steep hill overlooking San Francisco Bay. To her further delight, the grounds are a luscious mix of shrubs, flowers, and ornamental trees that seamlessly merge to form an organic extension of the architecture itself. A wave of familiarity passes over Ming-huà, though she had never seen this place before. Her anxiety falls away.

Sy produces a key from nowhere and unlocks the front door. Passing through the ornate foyer, Ming-huà is overcome by the regal grandeur of the house. She turns to Sy in wonder.

"Is this where we will stay?" she asks in a hopeful voice.

His concern for her state of mind melts away in a paroxysm of relieved laughter and spontaneous dance.

"Yes! Yes, little hunchback! You are home! All the ghosts that inhabit this place are rooting for you. In fact, here you are loved by spirits and spooks alike!"

She blinks in disbelief. Even her hump vibrates soothingly, as if corroborating Sy's words. After a brief tour, Sy escorts her to a magnificent bedroom on the second floor.

"Don't worry, my room is at the other end of the hall. For purposes of propriety, in case anyone asks, I am your uncle. Now, unpack, wash up, and come down to the little anteroom I showed you. We will have tea and discuss plans. In future, that is where we will meet to discuss the day's events. It is the favorite of all our ghost friends."

"Who are these ghosts?"

Scarecrow contorts his body in the most absurd of poses. "You'll see. Yes, you'll see! Now, unpack, unwind, wash up, and join me downstairs to detoxify, demystify, reoxify, and—dare I say it—deify."

In spite of herself, Ming-huà has to laugh. "I have no idea what you are talking about."

"Of course not! Nor could certain dead psychiatrists and aged detectives. But that is neither here nor there. Do you drink?"

"What?"

"Drink! Drink! You know, alcohol, booze, spirits, nectar-of-the-gods, liquor, demon drink, grog, hooch, firewater?"

Ming-huà remains dumbstruck.

"Well, girl?"

Nothing.

Sy assumes a tragic face. "Whiskey, whiskey!"

"No," she finally blurts.

Scarecrow crumples to the ground in a heap and moans. "Not your father's daughter! Woe is me. Not your father's daughter! Ah well, tea it is." He half rises and slinks crestfallen out of the room, calling over his shoulder, "Half an hour, downstairs, we talk!"

Not even Sy's bizarre antics and strange words hinder the feeling of comfort and safety this house conveys. She shudders at the sea of suffering and anger in the surrounding multitudes that must even now be crashing against the outer walls of this sanctuary, trying to reach her hump. But all is quiet. *It seems the house projects some sort of membrane or force-field that protects my hump from being assailed,* she thinks. *No need to overthink it. Just enjoy while I can!* Still, beneath the calm, she has never been more cognizant of the latent power that she fears will, at some point, demand release. Never has she felt more frightened, yet strangely exhilarated at the knowledge. With these turbulent thoughts, she showers and goes downstairs to talk with Scarecrow.

~ *The Plan* ~

Sy stands with a drink in his hand and invites Ming-huà to sit.

"Not as comfy as your favorite chair back on the island, but hopefully it will do."

As she sits, he gulps the last of his drink and pours a cup of tea.

"Here you are," he says, looking slightly disgusted at its contents. "For what it's worth."

"Thank you."

"Now, Ming-huà, we must talk."

"Okay."

"Are you listening very carefully?"

"Yes."

"And your hump?"

She smiles. "It is content."

"Good, because it will soon be tested."

Ming-huà visibly tenses. "How?"

"Starting tomorrow, we will go for long walks together. We will go to different parts of the city. We will pass many people. There will be many, many emotions flooding your hump. Some happy and joyous, to be sure, but most full of stress, anxiety, fear, hatred, anger, suffering, suffering, suffering."

Ming-huà recoils. "Why must I do this?"

"Conditioning, my dear. You are in training."

"For what?"

He waves his hand dismissively. "Later. Now, as part of your training, I want you to do something else."

She waits.

"This is the most important point: every day you must spend a great deal of time . . . well, how do I put it? . . . you must spend hours each day practicing, like a concert pianist . . . like your grandmother."

"My grandmother?"

"Yes, on your father's side."

"She was a pianist?"

"The best."

"Did she have . . . I mean, was she. . . . ?"

"No, but her beauty was unsurpassed even without a hump."

Ming-huà chews on this revelation for a while. "What must I practice? I can't play the piano."

"No, but you can perform a different kind of music. You carry a piano within. Your hump, a part of you, is like a grand piano. It interprets the music of the masses. That makes you the instrument itself."

"What must I practice?" Ming-huà asks again, this time with suspicion hardening her tone.

Scarecrow pours a drink for himself and dances a lively jig without spilling a drop. "Did you notice what I just did?"

"You danced about quite foolishly, like you always do."

"No, no! What else?"

"I don't know."

"The Daughter," he says dismissively under his breath. "Look, I controlled this glass while cavorting about. Not a drop spilled. Control! That is the key!"

Ming-huà waits patiently for clarification.

"You see," he continues. "Your power is like my dance. All movement. But if not controlled, it disturbs everything around . . . like a tornado: undirected and destructive chaos. Your job, little one, is to learn how to control your power."

"Fine. How?"

"We know it is triggered by anger. Now we must teach your power to temper the anger with justice. As the Bard said, 'The quality of mercy is not strained.'"

"I don't understand."

"In short, Ming-huà, you must develop your current ability to . . . reconfigure . . . with the ability to tailor the severity of the sentence to the severity of the crime."

Ming-huà shakes her head in confusion.

Sy gives a snort of impatience. "I'll be blunt. You must learn to remove a hand . . . or a finger, rather than all-or-nothing obliteration."

Ming-huà's eyes grow large. "But I don't want to reconfigure anyone, as you put it. Not anyone at all! I never want to use my power again."

"This is why you are The Daughter. Look, the fact is you will use it. Inevitable. Anger is fundamental. Even you can't escape it. Ask those two hunters. Anger has driven revolutions, rebellions, murders, divorces, and any number of untold suicides. No, you are not immune. Even with your kind and gentle nature, anger is a major pathway in your brain, inexorably connected to your hump."

"What if I never get angry?"

"Ah, that is why we will go for walks. It marks the beginning of your training."

"Leading to?"

Scarecrow pirouettes, but this time angrily, emptying his glass in a prodigious guzzle. "Leading to very dark places, places where *She* has made a vow to . . . never mind! Leading to you being as much a virtuoso as your grandmother."

"Sy, I cannot control my anger, let alone my power. I've tried."

"I know, but that was then and this is now. Our task is to merge anger with justice. You see, a judge should not let personal anger interfere with a just verdict. So you must elevate injustice to anger, and then direct the anger back to the injustice by imposing justice."

"I think you have had too much to drink."

"Not enough. Anyway, that is our mission. Our mission starts now!"

Before Ming-huà can react, he grabs her hand and forces it onto the table. As she struggles to free his grip, a hammer appears, raised in his other hand, poised to come down with a terrible blow.

"First!" he shouts. "First I must break the bones in your hand!"

"Don't!" she cries, but to her horror, he viciously brings the hammer down on her outstretched hand. Her eyes instinctively close at the coming blow.

~

When Ming-huà opens her eyes, Sy is smiling. He releases her unharmed and waves his empty hands in her face.

"See? The hammer is gone. You made it go away. It is reconfigured. Kaput!"

"But . . . but I was not only afraid of the hammer," she stammers. "I was more afraid of you."

"Ha! You see, little hunchback, fear and anger are Siamese twins."

"But why didn't you . . . disappear. I wanted you to!"

His expression darkens. "I am here for a reason. You can no more reconfigure me than you can reconfigure yourself. But the hammer . . . well, that is a different story."

Ming-huà, heart still pounding, shakes her head wonderingly.

"Now, imagine I was a murderer," says Sy. "Imagine the hammer was a knife, or a gun. We will train you not to remove the entire person, but his hand only, as well as the knife or gun. Doing that, you now have achieved justice with mercy."

"But—"

Sy holds up a cautionary hand. "And just as importantly, there is no pain associated with the removal. Just *a priori*—gone! Now the perpetrator is not a murderer, but is nonetheless *ex post facto* punished for his intent."

Ming-huà can only continue to shake her head. Numbed by the entire scheme. Yet, her hump remains quiescent, a vessel filling with his words, containing them as they deepen. She resists.

"Mr. Rung, I am not fit for this. I'm just a deformed girl who wants to go home in peace."

His face transforms into a fierceness reminiscent of when he raised the hammer. "Peace! No, hunchback! You will never have peace! Not even on your precious island. You left behind the obliterated remains of two men. Fool!"

Ming-huà cringed back in her chair.

Sy continues in a calmer voice. "Imagine if you had the power to only remove their hands. They would still be alive, the fawn would be alive, and their families still whole. Justice served. Worse suffering averted."

This constitutes the first indication Ming-huà has that the men had families. She closes her eyes, horrified at the consequences of her unthinking deed.

Oh, if I could be rid of this curse! she thinks.

"You will never be rid of it, little one," says Sy in a soft, sympathetic tone.

"You can read minds?"

"You can read Charles Dickens?"

"Who are you, really?"

He slips back into his operatic clown routine and leaps gracefully. "A scarecrow! Nothing much more to me than to Miss Gladflower!"

"But I could make Miss Gladflower disappear."

"Ah, I am made of stronger stuff! . . . or should I say stuffing?"

"Mr. Rung—"

"Ah ah," he wags a finger. "Sy, if you please. Or Scarecrow. Whichever."

"Sy, unfortunately I am not. I would like to go back to the island."

"To the island?"

"Yes."

"It is gone."

Ming-huà blinks uncomprehendingly.

"It is gone," he repeats.

"How? Oh my *God*! Did I. . . . "

Sy laughs. "No, no. I mean, it no longer exists for you."

"Sy, I'm over eighteen. I can decide. You cannot stop me."
Scarecrow is silent for a long moment, then says, "Come with me."
"Where?"
"Just come."
She follows him to the front door. He opens it and steps out, inviting her to join him. She hesitates.
"Come on, I'll be right here. I won't push you down the steps or close the door on you. Come on."
She steps out. . . .

~ *Into the Depths* ~

Ming-huà finds herself back in the anteroom, sitting in the same chair. Sy stands over her with another drink in his hand.
"What happened?" she asks.
"I see you're still a bit dazed."
She rubs her forehead. "Yes. What happened?"
"You fainted."
Her hump is faintly vibrating in clashing, discordant, and ugly notes.
"Here," says Sy, handing her a fresh cup of tea.
Slowly, the unpleasant, scratchy noise from her hump subsides.
"It will be that way from now on, and even worse on your island," says Sy nonchalantly.
"Why worse on the island?" she asks.
"You are exiled. A stranger in a strange land. Adrift. The island is now beyond the horizon, and the currents carry you farther and farther away even as we speak. Your only hope to see it again is to sail all the way around the Great Sphere. Only then, when your journey ends, will you return to its beginnings."
"When I die," she says in disgust.
"No, when you are reborn."
He prances around in circles. "Enough of this philosophical rubbish! Enjoy the night, because tomorrow we start!"
Sy peers at her expectantly. "Now do you want a drink?"
"Sy, it is still morning."
He shakes his head. "Look out the window."
She does.
It is dark.
Scarecrow laughs. "You were out longer than you think."
Next morning, Sy calls her to breakfast.
"Ready?" he asks after she takes her last bite.
"Yes." Her voice is strong, determined.
Sy jumps up and pirouettes. "I see sleep has fortified you! Let's go then!"

When they step outside, her hump remains quiet, and she suspects Sy had something to do with yesterday's overwhelming cacophony. Without time to think further, they start walking.

~

At first, Ming-huà feels no discomfort. Although the San Francisco wind is chilly, the sky is an iridescent blue, and the reassuring warmth of the sun penetrates her hump. Birds are happily chirping and she assumes there must be ample food available to satiate their hot-blooded appetites. But as they descend the hill toward the bowels of the city, familiar echoes of dense human crowds prick her consciousness. Her hump stirs to the innumerable discords of big-brained passions. A kaleidoscope of conflicting sensations builds steadily when they commingle with the mass of humanity packed together in the busiest streets; tourists, workers, shoppers, cops, transients, homeless, couples, families, and the full panoply of every other category of person. Her hump goes almost silent, as if a giant breaker switch had been tripped. Now she feels almost fully anesthetized to her surroundings, dazed and numb to the throngs who appear propelled in all directions by giant, intricately elaborate conveyers designed by a mad architect. Sy keeps glancing at her blank stare, but his pace never falters. Periodically, intense emotions such as sharp pain, violent anger, bleak sadness, hopeless depression, unbounded joy, euphoric love, even ecstasy, penetrate like jolts from a pinched nerve. When this happens, she lets out a cry, but Sy keeps steadily on.

Eventually, as they enter the Tenderloin district, one of the most dreadfully run-down parts of San Francisco, he instinctively slips his arm through her elbow. His caution is not unwarranted. They pass by many alleyways, all dark and strewn with trash and feces, sheltering every manner of tattered person, male and female, young and old, all aware they constitute the disposable detritus of a rich society reeking of perfume and deodorant in disposable excess. Here, the mix of despair, hopelessness, anger, and hostility, break through the discomforting but endurable white noise from her hump and brutally assail what little is left of her resistance. It is too much to bear. She stumbles around a corner and leans over to vomit. Still registering no emotion, Sy tells her to let it come. After spitting the last tendrils of mucous, she issues a long, piteous moan.

With this sad sound, his cold distance breaks down and he rubs her hump sympathetically.

"All right, little hunchback, let's go home now," he says. "Besides, it will be dark soon. We have walked enough. We're done for the day."

"Sorry," she whispers. "I am not strong enough."

"No worries. You just vomited up the undigested remains of the world's psychic gristle. We'll be home soon. Eh? Okay?"

"Yes, please. Let's go."

Sy continues to rub her hump with his healing hand and she feels a soothing release; a grounding that mercifully dissipates the stomach-churning toxicity that has collected. On the way, they pass a few street performers. Ming-huà signals Sy to stop, and she watches them with childlike pleasure.

"Yes, that's right," he says. "Not all is bleak and desolate. There is joy in the world. There is hope. It is the needless suffering that must be confronted. That is why you are here. You are truly The Daughter."

"Shhh," Ming-huà scolds him. "Just listen to the music. I already feel better. No more of that nonsense about The Daughter. I don't even know what that means."

"Yes, well—"

"Shhhhhh!"

"Okay, okay."

~

Upon entering the comforting shelter of the house, Ming-huà rushes upstairs, seemingly rejuvenated.

"I must bathe," she calls from the top of the stairs. "But afterward, we should sit and . . . how do you say? . . . debrief."

Sy stares in astonishment as she disappears into the bathroom. "How is it possible she is so resilient?" he says aloud. "She recovers so quickly! Maybe she is The Daughter after all." He dances a jig and looks upward. "Eh, *Goddess*? Maybe You're right! Another few days and she will be ready to meet Lady Oracle, right?"

Sy cranes his head as if to hear a voice from far away. "Yes, I see," he says. "No rest for her, eh?" he shakes his head doubtfully. "Okay, I'll make her tea and set her to work. But be careful Great Lady. If my intuition is correct, *You* need to lighten up a bit. Give her time. She is, after all, *Your* vessel, but she may crack, as did *Your* previous . . . designee."

~

At the same time Sy is having his conversation seemingly with the air, Ming-huà stands under the shower and wonders at her state of mind. While vomiting in that alley, she vowed never again to follow Sy. Never! Her sole desire centered on immediately returning to the comfort of her island, regardless of the consequences, and live out her life in some semblance of peace. But on the way back, something happened to make her change. Perhaps it was Sy's magical hand soothing the restless beasts in her hump, perhaps it was the hump itself, perhaps it was the street musicians, perhaps something else. Whatever it was, she now felt resolved to see Scarecrow's . . . what to call it? . . . experiment, to its conclusion. Ming-huà reacted to this new found resolve in amazement, and no small amount of suspicion. It ran counter to her most cherished disposition—that of spiritual and physical solitude.

Still engaged in pondering these mysteries, Ming-huà suddenly realizes she has been standing like a statue under the shower, holding a bar of soap. Focusing all her attention, she orders it to disappear.

Nothing.

Try again.

Nothing.

She smiles sheepishly. "Guess I'm not mad enough at you. Or afraid of you enough."

She lifts the soap close to her face. "Go ahead, threaten me."

Then she has an alarming thought. "What if I eat you, and you taste so disgusting, I make you disappear?"

The thought briefly intrigues her, but she places it back in the dish. "No. Can't do it. Foolish foolish girl!"

With this last bit of silliness, she steps out of the shower, gets dressed, and goes downstairs to join Scarecrow.

When she joins him in the anteroom, he looks up with bleary eyes, already having quaffed any number of bourbons.

"No need for a long discussion," he says. "We will continue our walks tomorrow. Meanwhile, continue your exercises."

"Okay. For how long do we go on these walks?"

"Until you're ready."

"For what?"

"Until you're ready." He coughs and mumbles, "That's all I have to say. Tomorrow we leave at the same time. Good night."

~

And so, for over a week, Sy and Ming-huà walk through all parts of San Francisco, her reactions remaining a mix of nausea, horror, and pleasure. But as each day passes, Sy seems to grow more distant. There are times he reverts to his old, clowning self, but she grows suspicious that something dreadful hangs over him. Each night, he insists she "do her exercises" and try to make objects disappear, which she is never able to accomplish. When she informs him of her failures, he shrugs and says, "Just takes time." But one day, after a particularly strenuous walk, he tells her to meet him in the anteroom as usual.

~

As she enters, Sy is sitting with a drink in his hand, looking quite glum.

"There's tea in the pot there," he says. "Help yourself. I'm too comfortable."

"Thank you."

"Ming-huà, you still have work to do."

"I know, but I'm tired and want to sit for a minute."

"Well, you need to do your exercises."

"Not now."

"Have your tea first. Rest a moment, then I want to show you something."

Ming-huà notices he is nervous, something she has never seen in him before. She tenses. "What?"

"Well, remember our little discussion about the purpose of your exercises, of controlling your powers?"

"Of course, you want me to take off an arm rather than the entire person, or something like that."

"And remember I said you must practice, you must train like a pianist to be able to . . . well, control what you reconfigure?"

"Yes."

"Wait here."

Sy slowly leaves the room, shaking his head as he goes. He returns cradling a rabbit.

Ming-huà jumps up in alarm. "I'm not going to make a rabbit disappear! Never!"

"Of course not. That is not what I'm asking."

"Then what?"

Before she has time to think, he brutally pins the rabbit on the table, holds its head down, and brandishes a knife.

"No!" she shrieks.

As the rabbit struggles and squeals, he raises the knife.

"*God*, no!" she cries again, knocking over an end table as she rushes to save it.

Sy plunges the knife down.

She hears the rabbit emit a high-pitched scream.

Chapter Three

Awakening

Novice

Ming-huà stands trembling, arms wrapped around her body, watching Sy carry the healthy rabbit out of the room. Tears of relief roll down her cheeks. When he returns, a wide grin lights up his face, and he prances joyfully around her, crying out, "New life, no knife! New life, no knife!"

"I don't know how I did it."

Sy chuckles. "Of course not, but you did it! You did great! Now, you're Peter Rabbit's best friend!"

"Would you have done it?"

"Done what?"

She shoots him a look of impatience. "Would you?"

He turns solemn. "What do you think?"

She shakes her head, unwilling to play. "Would you?"

"If I say 'yes', you'll hate me for being so cruel. If I say 'no', you won't believe I'll do it next time."

"Next time?"

"Ming-huà, when the knife disappeared, my entire body tingled. If I had been a normal person, I would have been . . . you know, reconfigured. We must work harder to control your savior impulses. Next time I want only my hand to feel pinpricks."

"How can I? There is no time to think."

"Wrong. Train yourself. Remember your grandmother's gift. She could play the most difficult compositions by musicians like Liszt and Beethoven because she had trained her fingers not to hesitate."

"But I am not her."

"Her blood and the blood of your father are in your veins. You are The Daughter. The ability is there. Hidden. You must learn."

"The blood of a concert pianist and a schizophrenic flow through my veins? It can never be. I am simply a deformed woman with a deformed power. Best left to die out."

"Tell that to Peter Rabbit! Tell it to that fawn you saved."

Ming-huà shakes her head doubtfully.

"I may have a solution that will speed up the process, if you're willing to take the place of our furry friend."

Her eyes widen. "You mean threaten me with a knife?"

"No, of course not, just threaten you with pain. We know pain can trigger the power."

"Pain leads to fear, or anger."

"Exactly. We know your power is triggered by both. Believe me, Ming-huà, I don't want to spend the next few weeks or months threatening cute animals. Besides, we have bigger fish to fry, and you need to be ready. Do you trust me?"

"No."

Sy jumps skyward and clicks his heels, then pulls his best operatic pose and roars with laughter. "Smart girl! Smart girl!"

She remains unamused.

"Seriously, Ming-huà, my plan will not entail much pain. Just a little, but hopefully enough. Enough. Let's see if it works. Even if it doesn't, it won't leave you permanently damaged, just a little pain is all."

"I'll think about it."

~

That night, Ming-huà evaluates the complex mix of emotions roiling her mind. On the one hand, she feels a new and unfamiliar tinge of pride in her power. What if she really could control it and use it for good? On the other hand, she remains horrified at the possibility she might inadvertently snuff out an innocent life. Unable to sleep, she creeps downstairs to the room where Sy keeps the rabbit. She pulls a chair close to the cage and stares into the dark interior. Its huge, luminous eyes reflect the dim light and stare back at her fearfully.

"I won't hurt you friend," she whispers. "In fact, I saved your little bunny life. Tell me, what does it feel like not to have so many complicated worries? You're just like my friends in the forest. Food, shelter, a mate—you require so little, but you fear so much. We humans require so much more, and fear so much more. Our fears are endless, stretched out over time and space in a thousand different ways. Your fears are so limited, but oh so deep! Your lives are richer for it, little friend. Every second you feel deeply; every second you survive the impossible; every second you live on the knife edge, all the time dreadfully suffering from gnawing hunger or fear of a predator. Believe me, I know. My hump tells me all. It's telling me that now. You are so afraid."

Ming-huà shivers. *So afraid!*

Maybe that's why you want to live so badly, fewer the worries, the worse they are? No, no. Non-human animals don't commit suicide. Do you little fellow? Suffering is suffering. All around.

"Yes, that's right," comes Scarecrow's voice whispering close to her ear. "Suffering everywhere. That is why you're here. You are The Daughter."

Ming-huà jumps at his words and looks at him with her hand over her heart. "Sy, you have to stop scaring me like that. If you can read my mind, keep it to yourself, or better yet, explain to me what this Daughter business is. No more deflections."

"You're not ready. Have you thought about it?"

"It?"

"My experiment? Remember, pain?"

"I need to think about it."

"I thought that's what you were doing."

"In a way, I suppose."

"And?"

"I don't know, Sy. I haven't decided."

"You know, in the basement, I have a boa constrictor."

Ming-huà's heart flutters.

"I had planned to use it for the next step."

"Boa constrictors eat rabbits," Ming-huà murmurs.

"Yes."

"You wanted me to make the boa constrictor disappear?"

"It was a thought."

"No! Are you crazy! I will not kill living things. Period. I want to go back to the island. Now! This is too much."

"Which is why I suggest we try my pain idea. The object that would give you pain is not alive."

"How does it work?" As soon as she asks the question, Ming-huà is furious with herself for letting curiosity weaken her resolve.

"Well, the trick is to make the object that would cause you pain only half of the total object. Remember, the point is for you to develop the ability to reconfigure only part of something. So, I have rigged up a very primitive object. If it works, no experimenting on living creatures."

"What is it?"

"I have to finish it first. Tomorrow I will show you. Time for us both to sleep."

"How can I sleep after this?"

"Try. At any rate, I am going to bed. You can stay and continue your conversation with Peter if you want."

"I will." She looks at him significantly. "He's better company than some I know. But, Sy, I warn you now. If you refuse to clue me in on this 'Daughter' business, I will leave."

"If we succeed, think of the good you can accomplish—the suffering you can relieve."

Ming-huà shakes her head. "No, Scarecrow, there is an old saying that perfectly applies here: the road to hell is paved with good intentions."

Sy laughs humorlessly. "You have it backwards, hunchback. The road to good intentions is paved with hell. Good night."

Ming-huà watches Sy leave, then turns to the rabbit. "I will take the pain, little Peter. I'll never let him sacrifice you to a snake. But I will sacrifice myself." She looks deeply into the rabbit's bright eyes. "Question is, why am I willing to do this? Why? I fear it is pride, little one. Pure pride. Still, what if I actually can use my power to make a difference? To reduce suffering? Is that not reason enough? Achilles' *hubris* or Buddha's compassion? Perhaps they are just two sides of the same coin."

~

Next morning at breakfast, Sy announces they will remain at home and perform the experiment.

Ming-huà has spent the night steeling herself, and she is prepared. "Okay, how does it work?"

He rises quickly, afraid of giving the hunchback time to change her mind. On the way out of the room he calls, "Let me show you."

Sy returns carrying something hidden in his palm. Holding a fist out to her, his fingers unfold to reveal a strange object. She peers more closely. One half is an oblong shaped, rather sharp stone, and the other half is a broken egg shell. One rounded end of the rock is seated inside the shell, and the other sharper end sticks out, as if it was in the process of being born.

Ming-huà looks at him questioningly.

"You will be laying down and I will hold this high above your forehead. Once I let it go, it will fall far enough for the stone to cause quite a bit of pain. If the stone disappears, the empty egg shell will do no damage whatsoever. Primitive, but effective, I think."

Ming-huà objects. "Sy, I will never be able to make either the stone or the shell disappear."

"Why do you say that?"

She shrugs. "I don't know. It just seems too silly."

"But painful if you fail."

"Yes, but I don't think my power works like this."

"Won't know until we try. We already know your power works when you suffer pain, but here is the key: you must keep your eyes open until the moment I drop it. Then you will know it is on its way. I count on you to react. You must direct your power only against the stone, not the shell, otherwise we will be back to square one. Understand?"

"Okay, but let's get it over with so we can move on."

Sy has her lay on the couch and holds the object high above her head.

Ming-huà begins to realize how much the stone will hurt falling from such a distance.

"That's too high," she objects.

But the words have hardly left her mouth when he suddenly lets it go.

She instinctively closes her eyes.

Nothing.

The entire object has disappeared mid-flight.

Ming-huà stares up at Sy speechless, while he claps his hands. "Okay!" he cries. "Partial success! We know you can reconfigure the entire object. Now you must learn to reconfigure only the stone."

She sits up woozily, feeling drained, as she always does after using her power, so does not respond.

"You're tired," Sy observes. "Rest a little, then we try again. The world contains an endless supply of stones and eggs. We repeat for however long it takes!"

Ming-huà wants to object. She wants to call off this entire absurd nonsense. She wants to tell him she is unwilling to continue. Instead, she hears herself saying, "Yes, let's keep trying."

"That's the spirit! You are The Daughter! Truly! I have already prepared more of these strange little objects."

"You knew I would fail?"

"Quite the contrary! You succeeded. Now you simply have to learn not to succeed so much!"

"I can try."

Sy runs out of the room and returns with another object, this one almost identical to the last. "I'm calling these little gems stoshells. Now, lay back down. Lay back down. Let's try again."

Again, he holds it above her head, only this time, he asks, "Are you ready?"

"Yes."

It drops.

It disappears.

Nothing is left.

"It's okay!" cries Sy. "I have plenty more where those came from. Again!"

"No," she says. "Each time, I get more tired. No more today."

"Okay, you're right," he replies.

"Give me your hand." He helps her rise and directs her to a chair. "I'll pour myself a drink and yourself some nice, hot tea."

As he walks across the room to the decanter table and reaches for an empty glass, he suddenly whips around and savagely throws another stoshell directly at her head, shouting, "Only the rock!"

She screams.

It disappears.

All of it.

"Damn!" he exclaims. "I thought maybe. . . . "

Ming-huà collapses in the chair. "No more, Sy, no more."

"Yes, yes, no more today. Tomorrow we start again. We'll go for a walk and when we return, we'll try again."

"For how long?"

"As long as it takes."

A week passes during which Sy repeats the experiment multiple times a day. Every time, the entire stoshell vanishes. Ming-huà is exhausted and discouraged, but Sy seems more and more enthused.

"Closer! We're getting closer!" he exclaims after each failure.

And after each exclamation, Ming-huà objects with a weary reply. "No, we're not. I cannot control it."

Then, one day, a breakthrough.

~ *Graduation* ~

Sy is holding another stoshell over her head as usual, rambling on about her mental state and whether she is more effective when surprised or when given a little more time to prepare. In the middle of a sentence, he unexpectedly drops it.

When Ming-huà opens her eyes, a half eggshell wobbles on her forehead.

Sy dances around like a madman, clapping his hands and shouting, "You did it! You did it!"

Ming-huà is stunned. She sits up, letting the shell fall into her hand, and rotates it curiously. Even the part of the stone that had been seated inside the shell is gone! How is that possible? Her power seems attuned to something more refined than the gross outcome of simply wishing half an object gone. *How can it be so discriminating? Impossible!*

Even as she ponders these conundrums, Sy whirls and throws another stoshell at her head.

She lets out a shrill cry and reacts.

No stone.

Shell remains, having fallen harmlessly to the floor in mid-flight.

Once more Sy prances about. "Success again! Again! Pianist reborn! Virtuoso! Magnificent! You are ready! Ready!"

Ming-huà slumps back on the couch, watching Sy with a mix of pride and fear. What have they unleashed? Can she turn it off? A vision of Pandora's box flashes through her mind. No going back. No toothpaste back in the tube. On a whim, Ming-huà looks at Sy's collection of stoshells and wishes them gone.

Nothing.

She is not surprised.

Ming-huà closes her eyes and thinks, while Scarecrow's celebrations fade in the background.

She realizes her power is limited, or perhaps has a universal safety catch. Unbridled reconfiguration of atoms and molecules directed mainly by the amygdala is too dangerous. However, curbing this power would be like a bus fitted with a governor; the driver is prevented from going faster than a predetermined speed, no matter how hard the accelerator is pushed. Yes, that must be it. Fear and anger, those are the ingredients of suffering. Fear of failure, fear of poverty, fear of hunger, fear of pain, fear of ridicule, fear of powerlessness, fear of losing power, fear of predators, fear of love, fear of losing love, fear of being fearful . . . the list is endless. When fear is triggered, so also is anger. Anger at failure, anger at those who succeed, anger at poverty, anger at pain, anger at ridicule, anger at powerlessness, anger at those who exercise power, anger at predators, anger at rejection, anger at withdrawn love, anger at being angry . . . the list is parallel to fear, and equally endless. No wonder her non-human friends live their lives far beyond human capacity to understand. The equations that govern their lives are far simpler, and far deeper than the Rube Goldberg equations that mimic complexity but elude efficacy. Yes, humans are lesser beings with greater capacity for fear and still greater capacity for anger. As Nietzsche pointed out, humans are the only species to make promises, and the only species to break them.

All of these thoughts, and many more, pass through Ming-huà's brain, and eventually her thoughts turn to the linage that flows backward to her father and grandmother. *Father was a schizophrenic, so was he more than human, or less? If I am The Daughter, as Sy insists, my father must hold the key. Or mother? Or both? Or is it grandmother?*

Ming-huà's perplexing questions become too much. She opens her eyes and looks at Scarecrow, who in turn is openly staring at her.

"What are you thinking?" he asks.

"Tell me about my father. Tell me about my grandmother. Tell me about this title you have given me—The Daughter. I deserve to know."

"Ask your mother."

"She always refused to tell me anything. Now she is gone. There is only you."

"No."

Ming-huà is startled by his bluntness, and manages to croak out the question, "Why?"

"We have passed a milestone. We must move on. No looking back. It is about time for you to meet someone."

"Who?" Ming-huà is irritated with herself for asking. Scarecrow is diverting her once again. Why does she continue to put up with it? She fears it is nothing more complicated than pride. When she realizes he has not answered, she asks again. "Who?"

"Lady Oracle."

Ming-huà laughs in spite of herself. "Silly name. Is she some sort of old hippie? I mean, we are in San Francisco, right?"

"No, she is not exactly 'an old hippie' as you say. But she is someone quite special, in spite of the silly name."

"Will she throw more things at my head?"

Sy laughs. "Actually, yes, just not stoshells."

"What then?"

"Once you meet Lady Oracle, you will visit the saddest, the poorest, the dregs of humanity."

Ming-huà lets out a groan. "I am not interested in visiting this type of humanity. I have already experienced extreme poverty and isolation. I do not need to see more."

"It is important to continue your exercises."

"I am too frightened at how my hump will react."

"Exactly!"

"No, I do not want to visit the saddest people."

"Then we will visit the cruelest."

"No. That is much worse!"

"Well then, we will visit those most passionately interested in the salvation of humanity."

"Salvation?"

"Do you not want to save yourself?"

"I have no idea what you're talking about. I want you to answer my questions."

"Or you'll leave?" Sy says these words in the form of a challenge, or a dare.

Ming-huà takes no more than a second to respond. "No."

"Good. You were right when talking to Peter Rabbit. Pandora's box is open. You will visit the saddest and the cruelest of humans. Lady Oracle will show you the way. Now that you are released from the box, you must by necessity go where the winds blow."

"I don't understand any of this."

"You must go where *She* directs."

"*She*?"

Sy throws up his arms. "No more questions!" His words are harsh. "You are no longer a novice! It is time to leave the cloister."

"Lady Oracle?"

He nods affirmatively.

"I don't want to see her," says Ming-huà with firmness.

"*Goddess*, you are stubborn!"

They argue. Back and forth they go. Ming-huà eventually admits she is terrified of being subjected to such sensory abuse.

Sy cuts her off with a scornful laugh. "Don't you see, foolish hunchback! Humans are infested with vermin. Their so-called higher emotions—love, intellect, altruism—are neural parasites. Diseased. Once the disease spreads and infects others, love turns to hate, intellect becomes the curse of all life on earth, and altruism is extended beyond its intended purpose in order to justify holocausts! Thus suffering. Suffering of an immense scale. That is where you come in. *His* addiction must be broken once and for all!"

"Whose addiction?"

"Never mind. Forget I said that. All you need to know is that you have a chance to relieve some of the suffering. Can't you get that through your thick hunchbacked skull? Damn it!"

Ming-huà listens with head lowered as if savaged by violent winds. Her mind focuses on the two men drowning the fawn. *Sy is doing the same thing to me*, she thinks. *Except I'm powerless to make him disappear.*

"What are you doing to me?" she asks weakly.

"Ming-huà, what would you have me do? Should I take you to evangelical Christians to expunge your demons, or to Catholic priests to exorcise them? Perhaps neurosurgeons to remove them, or psychiatrists to make contact with them? They all share the same misconception: condemn that which they do not understand! Same nonsense they did to your father! Same to your mother! Why? Fear, of course."

"But my animal friends are also fearful, and they are not bad for being afraid."

"And your human friends?"

"I have none."

"That is not true."

"If you were my friend, you would support my returning to the island and forgetting all this."

"But I am not your friend."

Ming-huà is taken aback by this naked admission. "You see?" she mutters.

"Reducing universal suffering is more important than relieving the individual sufferer."

"How can you achieve one without the other?"

"Such is life's paradox. Such is science's power. Such is *God*'s lie. And such is *Goddess's raison d'etre*."

"What does all this have to do with me?"

"You are no longer a novitiate. Time to go out into the world and confront the paradox. Increase the power of science. Expose *God*'s lies. Obey *Her* wishes."

From his pocket, Sy suddenly pulls out a stoshell and flings it viciously at her head. An empty half-eggshell falls harmlessly to the floor.

"You have the means. Now use it to save all the fawns of the world."

~

Lying awake in bed that night, Ming-huà feels herself slipping into an abyss so wide and deep that she loses sight of the rim on which she stood just hours ago. Hurdling through space, her psyche, her sense of self, stretches like a bungee cord to the breaking point, and she breathlessly waits to hear the final snap.

~ *Lady Oracle* ~

A few days later, after many dreary excursions and a plethora of successful experiments with a variety of objects, Sy makes an announcement at breakfast.

"Today we visit Lady Oracle."

Ming-huà's heart skips a beat. "When?"

"Now. You can finish your coffee later."

Ming-huà takes a last sip and they are out the door. The wind whips her scarf and as she secures it, she sees a taxi waiting. She looks questioningly at Sy.

"This time we travel in style," he laughs. "No time to lose."

Ming-huà feels a sharp pain in her hump and pauses. "I don't think I'm ready for this."

"You let me throw stoshells at your head but you're too afraid to meet an old lady?"

"She's old?"

"Older than you know."

After they enter the cab, Ming-huà asks him about Lady Oracle. "She is what you might call a social worker. She owns two apartments in the worst sections of town—Chinatown and Tenderloin. First we go to the Taylor Street apartment in the Tenderloin district."

"What does she do?"

"Like I said, she is a sort of social worker. She uses her apartments as bases of operations."

"What kind of operations?"

"You'll see. Enough questions."

The cab drops them at a run-down neighborhood where the buildings appear not much more than ruins. Walking a couple of blocks, signs of deterioration worsen. The ground is a veritable garbage dump across which every manner of human rubbish is blown about by the wind, where sidewalks are stained, gutters are brimming with trash, and the air itself reeks of malodorous stench. Seedy looking people are scattered about, some walking, some leaning against buildings, all scary to Ming-huà. Her hump is flashing a thousand hostile sensations.

"Not far now," says Scarecrow cheerily.

When they reach Lady Oracle's apartment building, Ming-huà looks at a very bleak exterior of stained concrete defaced by grotesque paint dribbles and obscene graffiti. At least the inside will partly insulate her from the awful sensations and intimidating bystanders. Sy opens the door without knocking and she enters quite willingly. Her first impression is of darkness, cloaking the room in portentous shadows of black and gray. A single candle burns on a distant mantlepiece, casting a weak glow that illuminates only the closest objects. She looks at Sy with raised eyebrows.

"That's right, Lady Oracle does not like light."

"She never goes out?"

"Of course she does. But, for whatever reason, when she is in this home, she prefers darkness. Oddly enough, in her other apartment, she prefers bright lights all day and night.

While Ming-huà puzzles over this curious eccentricity, Sy calls out, "Lady Oracle! Are you home?"

A tall figure looms quickly in a doorway, indirect light silhouetting her flowing black hair and flashing eyes. When she flips on the lights, Ming-huà is dazzled by the sight. The woman's bronze skin has a magic sheen, and even the colorful fabric of her resplendent Mongol *deel* cannot hide a svelte musculature underneath. A vital, thirtysomething with a gorgeous face, she peers intently at the hunchback. The presence of this magnificent woman stuns Ming-huà, and she blurts out, "But you said—" stopping herself in time.

Sy laughs and twirls playfully. "I exaggerated!"

He performs a deep bow and Lady Oracle merely smiles. "Still playing the clown for your wards, Siren Rung?"

"It is a lamentable habit."

Lady Oracle moves gracefully to Ming-huà and takes her hand. "Come in, Ming-huà, you are welcome here."

Only now does Ming-huà notice the abundance of jewelry adorning this intimidating woman. She is speechless and allows Lady Oracle to lead her into another room, much larger and with a bit of sunlight slanting in from a partially shuttered window.

"I am letting in some light for you, my dear, to make you more comfortable in my . . . concrete yurt."

The woman offers Sy and the hunchback chairs. "Tea will arrive in a moment."

Sy moans.

The group remains silent for a short while.

"You are Mongol," says Ming-huà softly.

Lady Oracle seems surprised. "Siren told you?"

"No, he tells me very little. I just know."

"How?"

"I don't know, perhaps the mention of a yurt?"

"Your intuition is correct. I am Mongol."

Sy fidgets and twirls his hands. "Not intuition. Not this one. Her magical hump told her."

A self-possessed young boy brings a tray containing a steaming teapot and cups. He leaves without a word being spoken. Lady Oracle pours tea in two of the cups and looks at Sy inquisitively.

"No, thank you. Too early for me. A shot of whiskey would be nice."

Lady Oracle laughs. "Old habits die hard. How about *airag*?"

"Perfect." He glances in amusement at a puzzled Ming-huà. "Fermented horse milk," he explains.

"Bataar!" she calls. When the boy enters, she speaks in Mongolian and he rushes out, only to quickly return with a bottle of *airag* for Sy.

Lady Oracle says, "You can use the teacup, Siren. No reason to stand on ceremony."

"None at all."

She looks penetratingly at Ming-huà. "Now, dear young lady, I expect you are curious."

"Very."

"Instead of my guessing what you find most curious, I will answer your questions."

Ming-huà hesitates.

"Feel free," prods Lady Oracle.

"I hardly know where to begin," stumbles the hunchback. "Sy brought me here for some reason. As usual with him, I am offered no real explanation. I would like to know what it is."

"I'm afraid it is a test."

"What kind of test?"

"A test of your powers. A test involving real people rather than stones and eggshells. Through me, you will meet many different types of people, and those people are certainly not the most pleasant of people."

"And?"

"And we will see."

"What do you do?" asks Ming-huà after digesting this last, unsatisfying response, but too timid to pursue the subject.

"I used to tell fortunes for a living. They were mostly wrong, but I was paid. Then I met my husband, and I gave up fortune-telling until he died. Now I do not tell fortunes from the past, but rather I try and make futures from the present."

"What did your husband do?"

"He was strong. Magnificent! A great man who could move mountains with his muscles and move multitudes with his words. He was a longshoreman. A union organizer."

"I see. I am sorry."

"You must be curious how he died so young?"

"I admit I am."

"He was murdered."

This unexpected information sets Ming-huà back in her seat. "Oh, I'm so sorry."

"My work is to reach out to his murderers, or people very much like his murderers."

"Yes, Sy told me you are a social worker."

"Oh, no no no, my dear young lady, I am definitely not a social worker."

Ming-huà does not respond. Instead, her hump is receiving the most hauntingly sad vibrations; long, drawn-out chords of great suffering.

"You are in pain, deep pain," whispers Ming-huà, reluctant to offend.

"It is true," replies Lady Oracle.

"If you don't practice social work, what is it you do?"

"Irrelevant. What I have been doing is ineffective. You represent a chance for me to succeed."

"At what?"

"You know, my grandmother Buandelgereen knew your grandparents."

Ming-huà catches her breath. "Really?"

Lady Oracle nods. "Also, your parents."

Ming-huà realizes this is a diversion from the subject at hand, but the revelation astounds her. "How?"

"That was a long time ago, and the story is very very long and involved. Some day when we have fewer pressing issues, I will tell you what I know. I think you are aware your father left manuscripts, very detailed manuscripts, of his parents' quest as well as his own trials and tribulations."

"My mother mentioned something about them," says Ming-huà excitedly. "Can I see them?"

"Perhaps, some day. But, for now, we have somewhere to go."

"Can't we stay here a while. I really must know more."
"Not possible," Lady Oracle says firmly.
"Where are we going?"
"To a crack house," says the Mongol woman with a grim smile.

Chapter Four

Trial by Fire

Oracles and Zoos

~ First Visit ~

Before she has a chance to make further objections, Ming-huà finds herself tramping down a host of San Francisco's sordid back streets, struggling to keep up with Sy and Lady Oracle. The Mongol woman wields a heavy walking stick which resembles the staff of some Biblical prophet. Ming-huà's hump jars her mind with a succession of painful vibrations that signal danger. At last they reach a stand-alone, dilapidated house. Increasingly powerful waves of anger and desperation cause her hump to rebel against any further agony. She stops in her tracks.

"Come on," says Lady Oracle.

"We're going in there?"

"Of course."

"I'm not sure I can," utters a miserable Ming-huà.

"None of that!" scolds Lady Oracle. "You must. Be brave."

Approaching the front door, an unholy stench of defecation, rotten food, vomit, urine, and a host of other noxious odors fill the air.

"I can't go in there," Ming-huà whispers urgently to Sy.

"You must!" he snaps.

Lady Oracle uses her stick to bang on the door. A small crowd of nasty-looking characters gathers around to watch, some laughing, some muttering obscenities, and others issuing warnings to, "Get the fuck outta here, bitches."

Lady Oracle ignores them and keeps banging. Finally, the door is partially opened by a skeletal man with nothing on but a torn T-shirt discolored by a multitude of stains. He is young, but appears as skeletal as an Auschwitz inmate. The foul smells roll out the door like a thick fog and envelop all of them in a miasma of reeking stink.

Ming-huà covers her mouth and nose with the scarf and turns to leave, but Sy grabs her arm and pulls her back.

"You again, bitch!" snarls the half-naked skeleton.

Lady Oracle remains unfazed, and replies placidly, "You told me to return today. You said he would be in today."

"Fuckin'? I did? Fuck me! Who are these two shits?"

"Friends."

"Why're they here?"

"To help."

"Fuck! Help with what?"

"Is Zookeeper in?"

"Yeah."

"Can you call him?"

"Fuckin' bitch! Go on in and find him yourself. I have to take a shit."

When they enter the wretched house, Ming-huà watches the young man go into another room and squat. She hears him grunt, and a runny stream of defecation squirts out onto the floor and splatters against the wall. She feels faint and presses her scarf harder against her nose. As they go from room to room, they must pick their way through piles of trash and debris that cover the floors. Passing a bathroom, she sees the tub is full of rancid, black water with unidentifiable garbage floating on top of the scum. The toilet is backed up to the rim. One room has a baby crib, empty, surrounded by garbage. Occasionally, she sees a person lying on a stained mattress or on top of mounds of trash. Ming-huà is on the verge of running headlong out of this nightmare when she hears Lady Oracle say, "Ah! There you are, Zookeeper!"

Another young man, just as grubby and thin as the first, rises to meet her. He is covered in tattoos and has a scraggily beard. However, something about him is different than the others. He has a coiled energy, striking features, and a burning, feverish glare that harbors a mixture of extreme viciousness and exquisitely angelic charisma. Even through her scarf, Ming-huà notices he has probably not bathed for months. He catches her looking at him.

"Where'd you dig up the hunchback? She might be pretty but for that beetle-back."

"And you might be handsome except that you're butt-ugly," replies Lady Oracle.

Zookeeper ignores the comment and continues to stare at Ming-huà. "It's got a pretty face if you get past the 'foul bunch-back'd toad' look."

Sy suddenly leaps in the air and pirouettes, striking an exaggerated operatic pose. "Sooo! The young crackhead speaks Shakespeare! Wonder of wonders!"

"Holy shit, Lady Orgasm!" exclaims Zookeeper in a richly modulated voice, gaping wide-eyed at Siren Rung. "You've brought two freaks today."

"Yes," she replies, ignoring the insult. "You must be used to freaks by now."

"She speaks who never utters a lie," he replies. "Zookeeper is the keeper of zoos. This zoo is full of exiles from Doctor Moreau's bestiary. I am their keeper. I love all of them, but they must be fed."

"Better and better!" enthuses Sy, rubbing his hands together. "More evidence of an educated derelict."

Zookeeper glares at him contemptuously. "Be careful little man, I am the Zookeeper and you're here at my pleasure."

Lady Oracle abruptly turns her attention from Zookeeper and asks Ming-huà, "What are you feeling now?"

Ming-huà is taken off-guard. "What?"

"Your hump, your hump. What's it telling you?"

"It is telling me I am in a bottomless pit of suffering."

Zookeeper looks at her curiously.

"Yet," says Lady Oracle. "You have not run away. Not from the stench. Not from the desolation. Not from the pain. Not from the suffering. What has prevented you?"

Ming-huà looks perplexed. "That is a good question. I should. I would have before. My hump is burning with a thousand painful sensations, yet I remain. I don't know."

"Is that why you brought hunchback here?" asks Zookeeper. "To observe us derelicts . . . the walking-dead . . . the bestiary?"

"Of course. This is a zoo, correct Zookeeper?"

"Ha-ha! You got me there, Lady Clitoris. Now, did you bring money to pay the entrance fee?"

Lady Oracle silently digs out of her pocket a one-hundred-dollar bill and hands it to him. "As per our agreement."

He takes it, hands shaking. "When rich villains need poor ones, poor ones may make what price they will."

"Lordy!" exclaims Sy. "This boy continues to amaze!"

Lady Oracle turns to Ming-huà. "Tell me what Zookeeper is feeling."

Ming-huà hesitates, but Lady Oracle nods her head and smiles encouragement.

"He is a congealed mass of anger, pain, fear, and . . . something else. It's unclear . . . fury, cruelty, vengeance . . . maybe kindness, compassion? Unclear. He must have spent years compacting his feelings into such a tight ball. Hard to see. Opaque."

While Ming-huà is speaking, she perceives Zookeeper closely examining her with undeniably perceptive and intelligent eyes.

When their eyes meet, Zookeeper laughs and turns his attention back to Lady Oracle. "What the fuck? Are those brilliant observations worth one-hundred-dollars to you, Lady Tits? Jesus! You got fuckin' cheated! Hey, hunchback, it's you who needs analysis, not Zookeeper."

"Yes, I am sure I do," says Ming-huà meekly.

This makes him pause, but he quickly tries to recover his bravado. "Look, hunchback, you're curtailed of fair proportion, cheated of feature by dissembling nature. You're deformed, unfinished, sent before your time into this breathing world, half made up."

Tears well in her eyes.

Zookeeper seems stricken. "But look, hunchback, you're not so bad looking. Not at all. Shit, you've got a nice face. The rest of you is nice also."

He turns on Lady Oracle. "Why the fuck did you bring her here? This shithole ain't no place for her. Freak or no freak, she's a different kind of freak." As if to himself, Zookeeper adds, "Very different."

Sy claps his hands and leaps in the air. When he lands, he looks at a surprised Zookeeper and cries, "A wicked conscience mouldeth goblins swift as frenzy thoughts!"

Zookeeper starts to reply, but two seedy looking men skulk into the room and stand threateningly. Each carries a knife. "What about us, Lady What's-Your-Name. Hand over our fuckin' shares."

"The agreement was between the two of us," says Zookeeper leering at Lady Oracle. "But my exhibits deserve a fee also. How else is a keeper to keep them fed?"

Lady Oracle, with a shake of her magnificent long hair, tosses them ten dollars each.

"Not enough," one of them says.

"More than enough," replies Lady Oracle calmly. "Let's go."

She starts to walk out of the room with her two companions when the men block the door.

"Not enough, bitch."

Sy digs in his pocket and says in his usual supercilious manner. "Let's see, I think I have a couple of quarters here."

A knife presses against his neck. "Funny man! Look, bitch, hand over or this piece of shit gets his jugular cut."

The other man also brandishes his knife.

Ming-huà is terrified and directs her attention to the men's hands, but before she can act, Sy turns to her and shouts, "No, not yet! This is not the test!"

Confused, she takes a step back. Meanwhile, Lady Oracle has produced two more hundred-dollar bills. "Here you are, gentlemen. Take it. We will leave quietly."

Zookeeper whistles. "Damn! I should have asked for more. Fuck me!"

The two men grab the bills and lower their knifes.

As they are leaving, Ming-huà hears Zookeeper say, "Let witchcraft join with beauty, lust with both! By damn! I've got the hots for that hunchback!"

"Then go fuck her," says one of the men.

By the time she hears these words, Ming-huà and her companions are out the door and moving rapidly down the street toward home.

~ *Refractory* ~

The next few days pass without incident. Ming-huà no longer takes walks with Sy, and he has given up throwing things at her, as she is always successful. However, he does return late every night after visiting Lady Oracle. He is never drunk, only tipsy from her *airag*, but he makes up for that deficiency by downing any number of whiskeys before turning in for the night. Ming-huà begins to suspect the entire knife incident at the crack house was a set-up. A test to see her reaction. Why did he stop her then? Of course, the three men were in on the conspiracy. That is why they were paid so exorbitantly. Nevertheless, the motives of Lady Oracle and Sy are suspicious, even malevolent. What is their next step? Ming-huà now knows she can at least partly succeed in controlling her reactions to extreme environments. In the past, she never would have been able to enter that crack house, let alone stay for so long. She is becoming hardened. That, she is certain, is their goal. But to what end? Go around the world seeking out evil and making the perpetrators, or parts of them, disappear? How will that end suffering? Will it not create more? Maybe one of those hunters she 'reconfigured' on the island would have invented a cure for cancer if he had lived longer. The suffering of a fawn weighed against the suffering of millions? It makes no sense. The more she thinks, the more confused she becomes. *What of Lady Oracle? What does she know about my parents and grandparents? What is her connection to Sy? So many questions!* She goes to sleep that night determined to force an explanation from Sy the next day before he leaves to meet Lady Oracle. *He must! Or else? Am I truly willing to leave? I'll cross that bridge when I come to it.*

~

Next morning after finishing breakfast, both sit together quietly sipping their coffee. Ming-huà gathers her courage and is about to make her demands when Sy holds up a cautionary hand.

"No need! I know. You want a full explanation of everything I know, annotated and with footnotes. Or else? Well, you never got that far in your thinking. I'll save you the trouble of having to make that decision. This morning you are accompanying me to Lady Oracle's other apartment in Chinatown, where there's abundant light. She will throw some of it on your demands. Satisfied?"

Ming-huà stares at him admiringly. "Yes."

Sy leaps up in his most loose-jointed scarecrow manner. "Then, let's go!"

Ming-huà is not enthusiastic about returning to another run-down, dangerous neighborhood.

"Wait. Could we maybe invite her to come here?"

Scarecrow looks askance at her. "You are the one seeking the information. It's your obligation to go there since Lady Oracle is willing to provide some clarity to your family's . . . history. The seeker must seek the one who is sought."

Ming-huà reluctantly nods agreement.

Once again they tromp through the helter-skelter crowds and trudge up and down San Francisco streets, this time moving in an unfamiliar direction. Chinatown is bursting with activity. Multitudes of tourists mix with local residents, shopkeepers, and street vendors who cater to them by accentuating stereotypical Chinese humility. Sy leads her off the main artery of Grant Street and down a dizzying array of small side streets and alleys to an apartment building designed in traditional Qing dynasty style. Ming-hua's hump has been busy, but in a very different way than she experienced in the Tenderloin district. The sensations seem as mysterious and menacing as if she were penetrating the lair of an ancient secret society.

"Scared?" asks Sy as they look up at the facade.

"A little."

"You should have met her grandmother! Whew!" Sy shakes his hand as if it had been burned.

"You knew her grandmother?"

"Of course. In her heyday, carried a rifle strapped to her back. Wow! What a woman!"

"Sy—"

"Shush!" He knocks on the bright red, dragon-carved front door.

A moment passes and Ming-huà blurts, "She's not in. Let's go."

But even as the last words leave her mouth, the door opens and Lady Oracle stands majestically before them.

Ming-huà's hump is instantly alive with unfamiliar vibrations that defy translation.

Lady Oracle's flashing eyes settle on her. "Come in."

The apartment is almost blindingly bright, with an array of huge, round windows pouring fierce sunlight into the rooms. Supplementing this natural radiance, innumerable electric lights and lanterns add to the excess of brilliance.

"Yes, I see your reaction, Ming-huà," says Lady Oracle. "This is my yang to the other apartment's yin. Although, contrary to popular opinion, they are not opposites. When I am here, I am the dark spot in the light yang, and when I am there, I am the light spot in the dark yin."

"I see," says Ming-huà, thinking of nothing better to say.

They enter a room full of traditional Chinese furniture, scrolls, calligraphy, books, lacquerware, and all manner of bric-a-brac. Pungent incense from an ancestral shrine fills the air.

"Sit and Bataar will bring tea," says Lady Oracle. She turns to Sy, "And you come with me."

Ming-huà is left alone for a long time, amusing herself by looking at all the intriguing objects that fill the room to bursting. A Mongol boy enters holding a tray. When Lady Oracle returns, she takes it saying, "Thank you, Bataar," and sets it on a massive Chinese table. She offers tea. Ming-huà accepts.

"So many beautiful things," says the hunchback. "They take my breath away, but most are Chinese. Aren't you from Mongolia?"

Lady Oracle chuckles. "Yes, but remember, we conquered them. I believe the saying goes, 'to the victors go the spoils."

Ming-huà smiles back. "The Yuan dynasty was a long time ago."

"True, but my linage also goes back a long time. However, that is not why you're here. Sy told you I would provide explanations. He is only partly correct. Last time we spoke, you expressed an interest in your past. I will tell you what I can, but reserve the right to be brief and not provide too many details. In some cases, I will provide no details. Where do you want to start?"

"My father."

"A schizophrenic, so humans thought."

"And?"

"A lawyer."

"Lady Oracle, I already know these facts. This will take a very long time if all I get are such short, almost monosyllabic answers."

"It is all you will get."

Ming-huà sighs. *More games, more deflections.* "He was in the war?" she asks.

"Yes."

"Vietnam, I know," says Ming-huà impatiently.

"Yes."

"But something happened to him there?"

"Yes, as war does to young men . . . women also. . . . "

"No, I think this was different."

Lady Oracle pauses and looks at Ming-huà in a new light. "How different?"

"That is what I am asking you."

"Your mother didn't tell you?"

"All she has told me is that Michael Powers was a schizophrenic, a lawyer, and a soldier in Vietnam. He had a first wife who was killed in an auto accident and a son who lives in the East Coast, I don't remember where."

"That's all you know?"

"Yes, mostly."

"That is enough," says Lady Oracle sharply.

"No, it is not enough. What happened to father in Vietnam?"

"There was a battle."

"Yes?"

"His comrades all died."

"And?"

Lady Oracle narrows her eyes. "Did your mother tell you about his voices?"

"No."

"The Precious Object? . . . the Great Warrior?"

"No."

"Then better to leave well enough alone."

"No."

Lady Oracle looks at Ming-huà curiously. "Then how do you know his experiences in war were different from other men?"

"Because my hump does not stop working when I talk with my mother. Every time she mentioned his name, every time she mentioned the war, I felt weird pulsations I have never felt before. Like tremors. Something about him was different. Something happened to him that was different. What was it?"

"He survived. His comrades died."

"Yes, but there is more to it, isn't there?"

"Next question," snaps Lady Oracle.

"You're unwilling to explain?"

"Yes, for now. Perhaps later in the course of our conversation."

"But—"

"Next!" snaps Lady Oracle.

"All right, my grandfather."

"On your father's side, I presume?"

"Yes, John Powers."

"A businessman. Very bright. And like your father, also a misdiagnosed schizophrenic."

"Really?"

"Go on, ask."

"My mother mentioned something about a quest?"

"Yes."

"To China?"

"Yes, and Mongolia."

Ming-huà's eyes widen. "What was the quest?"

"Your mother did not explain?"

"No."

Lady Oracle sighs deeply, resignedly. "To find someone."

"Who?"

"*Her.*"

"What?"

"*Her.*"

Ming-huà blinks in confusion. "I don't understand. He went on a quest to seek a woman? Was it my grandmother?"

Lady Oracle laughs. "No! The person he sought is a very special person. A very powerful person. A very mysterious person. It was during the quest he met your grandmother on your mother's side."

"My grandmother. . . Child of Buddha?"

"Yes, Chinese. Like your mother, also a hunchback. She helped your grandfather."

"My grandmother was also on the quest?"

"Yes."

Ming-huà buries her face in her hands. "This is all too confusing. Your answers are too short. I need clarification. Explanation. I don't know the correct questions to ask. Please!"

"Your grandfather met a young Chinese pianist—Bai Meiying—on the quest. It was during the Japanese invasion. Later, they married and escaped from China. Eventually, they made it to San Francisco. That is where your father was born."

"And my other grandmother?"

"Child of Buddha stayed in China, in a mental institution, where your mother was born."

Ming-huà shakes her head in frustration. "This is too confusing. It is like some unsolvable puzzle."

"Not at all," says Lady Oracle calmly. To cut through the maze of facts, think like a Mongol."

"How is that?"

"What is the common thread connecting your grandparents, your parents, and you?"

"I don't know."

"Yes, you do. Think."

"The quest?"

"Bingo!" cries Lady Oracle.

"What was the quest about?"

"As I told you, to find *her*."

"But who is *her*?"

"Well, to make a long story short, *her* was a small part of . . . well, a larger *Her*, and as it turns out, the larger *Her* was also on a quest. In fact, the larger *Her* is still on a quest."

"To find what?"

"You."

Chapter Five

Trials

Scarecrow's Stuffing

~ *Tangled Webs* ~

Ming-huà stares at Lady Oracle dumbstruck. All she can manage to utter is, "Me?"

"Yes."

Lady Oracle turns to Sy. "Siren, take her home. It is enough for today."

"No!" cries Ming-huà. "Please! I need to know more. I . . . cannot . . . fathom. . . . "

"Take her home!" snaps Lady Oracle.

Scarecrow jumps. "Yes! Indeed, you're right. She needs time to think." He looks askance at Lady Oracle. "However, use caution Great Lady. We do not want another broken one."

"Ha! This one will not break!" Without warning, the Mongol woman grabs a small statuette and flings it at Ming-huà's head.

It disappears.

"You see? Even in her muddled state, she will prevail. Even the unexpected will be dealt with. She is tougher than you think, Siren. Now, go!"

Ming-huà stands dazed. "But, I have so many questions!"

Sy takes her hand. "Come, there will be time enough later."

As they step outside, Lady Oracle calls from the doorway, "Questions are mother's milk! Build up your hunger, my teat awaits! Now rest and ponder what lies in wait for you. All will be revealed in good time."

~

Making their way home, Ming-huà feels worse than if she had never visited Lady Oracle. Her mind grasps at straws, trying to decode the paltry hints she had been given. Distressed at her overwhelming confusion, she briefly entertains the idea of turning around and storming into Lady Oracle's apartment demanding answers.

"Don't even think it!" cries Scarecrow. "It is enough for today. Going back will only incur her ire, and I have seen the results of her wrath. No, keep walking!"

Sy reverts to his usual skipping, dancing, parading shenanigans, but Ming-huà will not be distracted from her thoughts and remains grim the entire way home. Once inside, she retires upstairs, but Sy calls as she ascends the staircase, "An hour, in the usual place! We have things to discuss. Perhaps you may find them interesting! I will be waiting, drinking my own mother's milk!"

When she joins Sy, he has already downed several whiskeys, but hardly shows any effect. Nonetheless, she soon realizes his tongue is loosened, and sits in anticipation.

"Look, little hunchback, there are things at play here that are far beyond your comprehension. Forces are at play. Forces you cannot imagine."

"Are they dangerous?" she asks, alarmed.

"Well, that depends. Yes and no."

"I don't understand."

"You're caught between two . . . opposing . . . oh, how do I put it? Two opposing powers. So was your father."

"How?"

"Remember what Lady Oracle told you; the one common element in this entangled web is the quest?"

"Yes, I remember."

"Well, the quest is certainly the key."

"What was it?"

"You mean, what is it?"

"Yes, what is it?"

"You see? That is the key, and it is a key I cannot give you. Not on my life."

"Do you know what it is?"

Sy capers about. "Do I know what it is? Of course I know what it is! *Goddess* knows I've been around it long enough!"

"*Goddess?*"

Sy turns serious and puts his finger to his lips. "Shhhhh! Do not mention *Her*. Too soon."

Ming-huà lets out her breath in frustration. "How am I ever to make any sense of all this when I am forever given hints and innuendos, but never straight answers!"

"Truth is curved, like spacetime."

"Never mind!" she cries in anger. "I'm going back to my room."

"Wait!" he exclaims.

"Either tell me straight out what this is all about, or leave me alone!"

"Okay. Are you mad?"

"What?"

"Are you crazy—do you hear voices?"

"No."

"Do you see things that are not there?"

"I don't think so."

"Is the crack house we visited real?"

"Too real!"

Sy empties his glass in one big gulp. "We are going back."

Ming-huà shudders. "Oh, no! I will not return to that place. Ever!"

"We are returning in two days' time. Meanwhile, we will return to Lady Oracle's house in preparation."

"No."

"Do you want to learn more about your past? About the quest? About your future?"

"Yes."

"Then we will go. There is no turning back."

Ming-huà leans forward and looks deeply into Sy's eyes. "Who is Lady Oracle?"

He laughs. "You mean *what* is Lady Oracle?"

She blinks. "Okay, now please explain."

"On the surface, she is a woman. A woman who never talks about herself. But there is something far deeper behind her physical appearance. She has a secret, a very deep secret, never revealed to any human. I dare not reveal it now, for she always says humans talk too much. Fortune teller? Perhaps, but if so, that is why she tells others' fortunes and never her own. I remember she told me once, 'I have learned that words chattered by most people are nothing more than threads cleverly stitched together in an embroidery to hang on a wall for public consumption. It is intended to display their life's tapestry; but the tapestry is actually created for the purpose of hiding unsightly stains on the wall behind.'"

Ming-huà shakes her head. "Are you telling me she is not human?"

Sy continues. "Yes, in a way. Oh, she is deep. Very deep. But remember, dear hunchback, her mother and your grandmother were friends. Co-conspirators, if you will. Your grandmother Child of Buddha, and Lady Oracle's grandmother Buandelgereen, shared the quest. It is the quest where your answers lie. And to get to those answers, you must follow where Lady Oracle and I lead. You must trust us."

"Sy, I will not go back to that crack house."

His face contorts into a rage she has never before witnessed. Fury envelops his entire form, and his body flashes shock waves that make her hump quake. "You will go back!" he thunders. "By damn, you will, else you will end up a pathetic wretch in some back alley! You will!"

Shrinking back in the chair, Ming-huà stares at him in a mix of amazement and fear. Speechless.

Instantly, his entire demeanor changes, and he reverts to the loose-jointed scarecrow she is familiar with. He freezes in a comical stance and flippantly says, "So, you see, we will go."

She finally gathers enough courage to speak. "You won't hurt me, will you Sy?"

He maintains his pose, but she sees tears roll down his cheeks. "Never! Don't you see, Ming-huà, there is something deeper here that you mustn't know too soon. Others have been broken. I do not want to see you broken as well."

"What others?"

Like his scarecrow namesake, every joint in his body seems to liquify and he plops in a chair. "Well, your father for one," he says wearily.

"What? Sy—"

Scarecrow stiffens and holds out an arm as if fending off an attack. "No! I said too much already. Remember what Lady Oracle said, your questions are like mother's milk. She will answer them."

"But when?"

"In her own time. When the time is right. But even Lady Oracle is the lesser *she*. When that greater one, the one I refer to as *She*, determines the time is right. No sooner."

"*She*?"

"Shhhhhh! Mustn't go there yet. Suffice to say, keep asking questions, but do what I say, and what Lady Oracle says. It is the only way. Do you believe me?"

"I wish I could, but you scare me. Lady Oracle scares me. But what scares me the most is this *She* who keeps coming up."

"Mum's the word, for now," he says smiling. "All in good time. First, we must return to the crack house."

"Why?"

"That you will discover. Now, will you go?"

Ming-huà's answer is firm. "Yes."

As soon as the word leaves her mouth, she is shocked at having said it.

~ *A Nightmare* ~

Lying in bed that night, Ming-huà finds it impossible to sleep. Images of that horrible crack house haunt her, and she cannot make herself reconcile her agreement to return with the revulsion she feels at the prospect. What force drives her to these awful decisions against her own will? All along her journey, from the death of those two hunters—to San Francisco—to this apartment—to Lady Oracle's—to a crack house where she would normally never consider entering; some compulsion makes her agree to the unagreeable. Where does this compulsion arise? Does it come from Lady Oracle? From this mysterious *She*? From Scarecrow himself? It is all too much—and all too real. Hump ablaze, she drifts in and out of sleep. Finally, a deep canyon opens beneath and she falls over the edge, plunging deeper and deeper. . . .

~

In freefall, she panics and wildly tries to grab projections from the cliff face, but to no avail. Although the bottom is black, she knows it is rushing up to meet her. Suddenly, she stops hurtling downward and finds herself floating above a sterile, white room where a group of people shuffle back and forth aimlessly. They act in odd ways, some talking to themselves, some with violent tics that snap their heads up and down, back and forth. Their clothes are loose-fitting pajamas. Ming-huà abruptly realizes she is in some sort of asylum. Hovering above the inmates as they pace back and forth, she sees a familiar face. . . .

~

No! She wakes up with a silent scream and labors to get out of bed, half-asleep but fully terrified. Free of the covers, she begins to rant, "Mother mother mother! . . . Crazy, mad, insane!"

Ming-huà runs to Sy's door and bangs as hard as she can. The door opens immediately, as if he had been waiting. Taken aback, she retreats a few steps and shouts, "My mother, Sy! She was crazy! She is crazy! A mad woman!"

Scarecrow swiftly rushes up to her and holds her head in his hands. "No, no, no, Ming-huà. No. She was not. She is not. It was for the sake of your father."

"But I saw her in the mental institute! Don't tell me she wasn't there! My hump tells me the dream is true!"

Sy leads her downstairs and fixes them both hot tea. As they sit, he continues to speak a string of soothing words until her composure returns.

"Now," he says gently. "Are you ready to listen?"

"Yes."

He takes a sip of tea and makes a face. "Awful stuff! Anyway, I can tell you this much: your mother checked herself into that asylum to be with your father."

Ming-huà shakes her head in perplexity.

"You see," continues Sy. "She was a gift, so to speak, from the greater *Her* to your father."

"A gift?"

"Um, yeah."

"What are you talking about? A gift? A slave?"

"No, not that exactly. Not at all. Perhaps a better word to use is not gift, but vessel."

"Vessel? Speak clearly, Sy."

"Yes, I cannot make it clearer. A vessel."

"For what purpose?"

"Isn't it obvious?" Sy tilts his head, waiting.

"No."

"To give birth to you, of course."

Ming-huà lets that statement sink in, but this time she refuses to be shocked into muteness. "Sy," she says as calmly as her taut nerves allow. "I want answers. If the quest is about me, and my mother was used as breeding stock, then it must be important. Correct?"

"Correct."

"So, if I am important, I am entitled to clear, unambiguous answers."

"Agreed."

Ming-huà lets out a deep sigh. "Then tell me, who, or what, is Lady Oracle?"

"Who's on first?"

Ming-huà blinks in confusion.

Sy leaps up and capers about the room. "Who is on first! That's what I asked! Who's on first? Who, of course! Who? That's what I just said! Who's on—"

"Sy, stop!"

He stops and mutters, "Well, you get the picture. Don't you see, little hunchback, you're asking the wrong question of the wrong person."

"Then who should I ask?"

"Who's on first!"

"Sy! I—"

"No, no, just listen. You must ask Lady Oracle, but she will ask the greater *Her* and only then decide which question to answer. Their answers may be circular, but to really get to the bottom, you must return to the crack house."

"But why? Why a crack house? In all this vast world, what's so important about a crack house?"

"It is not the crack house that's important."

Ming-huà snorts in frustration. "Then what is?"

Sy laughs. "Who's on first?"

This time, Ming-huà refrains from getting angry and furrows her brow in thought. *It is code, foolish girl!* she chides herself, searching her mind for a solution. But it won't come. Not yet.

Sy smiles complacently. "Give it time. You'll figure it out. More tea?"

~ *Return to Lady Oracle* ~

"Sy tells me you have agreed to return to the crack house," says Lady Oracle.

Ming-huà sits nervously with Sy back at Lady Oracle's Chinatown apartment. The lights are ablaze, exacerbating Ming-hua's headache, but she is determined to remain quiet and let this strange Mongol woman take the lead.

"Yes," she says curtly.

There is a drawn-out moment of silence. Lady Oracle seems to be waiting in anticipation. Sy, not as patient as either woman, pipes up.

"Lady Oracle, I think she deserves answers before continuing."

The Mongol raises her eyebrows. "Answers to what?"

"You know very well. I am powerless, and can only give clues. Ming-huà knows about her mother and father—how they met—and is anxious to learn more."

"You are now her advocate?"

He strikes a dramatic pose. "In a manner of speaking."

"Remember what happened to your . . . predecessor . . . in China?"

"Bullet in the head," says Sy nonchalantly.

Ming-huà stiffens.

Lady Oracle quickly interjects, "From a Japanese rifle."

"Yes, but directed by *Him*," says Sy accusingly.

Ming-huà is stung by these insider references that so clearly mark her as an outsider. Not understanding what her two companions are talking about, she can only sit and wait, hoping to discover a few familiar, explanatory shells on the desolate beach of their shared allusions.

Lady Oracle falls silent and gazes at Ming-huà. "Last time you were here," she says. "I told you questions are mother's milk and my teat awaits. I await."

"Both of you refer to *Her*, and now a *Him*. Who . . . or what . . . are they?"

"Voices in your father's head."

Sy coughs and casts a skeptical glance at Lady Oracle.

"I will ask again," says Ming-huà, taking the hint. "Who, or what, are they?"

Lady Oracle smiles appreciatively. "You have grown backbone along with your strengthening powers. *He* is *God*. *She* is *Goddess*."

~

"*God* and *Goddess*," repeated Ming-huà reflexively. "Those were his voices?"

"Yes. Your mother didn't tell you?" asks Lady Oracle.

"No. But if those were the voices in his head, what does it signify? As I understand it, schizophrenics hear all sorts of voices and see things that aren't real."

Lady Oracle nods agreement, but does not reply.

Ming-huà looks at her two companions. "Well, what do they signify?"

Sy fidgets and leans forward in his chair. "What if they were more than voices?"

"You mean if they are real?"

Lady Oracle casts a cautionary glance at Sy. "Let's not get ahead of ourselves. All of us here are aware that the belief in supernatural deities, ancient and revered as it is, cannot be more than mere superstition. Suffice it to say your father, or part of him, believed they were real. He was a very conflicted man."

"So, we know he was ill," says Ming-huà. "What about both of you? Do you believe the *God* and *Goddess* in my father's hallucination, or delusion, or whatever you call it, are real?"

"To your father they were real," says Sy.

"I'm asking about your beliefs!" she exclaims.

Lady Oracle rises and stands haughtily. "Ming-huà, reality is a tricky proposition. You ask us to explain the unexplainable. Now, tomorrow morning we visit the crack house again. It is already arranged. Sy, have her here at ten."

"Wait a minute!" cries Ming-huà rising from her chair to confront Lady Oracle. "You can't just leave it at this! Why why why must we go to this crack house?"

"Dear," says Lady Oracle softly. "Crack usage causes hallucinations and delusions."

"And?"

"And a person who resides there may very well be . . . how do I put it? May very well be pertinent to our discussion."

Ming-huà's face registers a dim awareness. "Zookeeper?"

"Yes."

Chapter Six

Hell Awaits

Devil Dealers

Since the unexpected visit of the hunchback woman, Zookeeper's voices, long dormant, have returned and now plague his every waking moment. To him, it is as if she disturbed a hive of bees whose angry buzzing foretells existential danger. But in this case, the imminent threat is posed not by flesh and blood enemies, but by a reanimation of the once-lifeless demons in his head, unless . . . unless what? Bees will attack intruders in stinging fury, but what weapon does he possess to defend against such an airy, otherworldly menace as the hunchback? The drug-addled but fiercely loyal exhibits he nurtures in his zoo can swarm and sting any intruders from rival gangs, but this hunchback presents an entirely different challenge. He laughs inwardly at the notion that a fragile snit of a girl can represent such power. Yet, he knows it is a power to rival his own.

On the surface, Zookeeper's life story is not unusual, at least not for the Tenderloin: father unknown—abandoned by a drug-addicted mother—in and out of foster care—beaten, mocked, and discarded—in and out of juvenile hall—in and out of brutal street fights with other castoffs—and finally in and out of jail, where he endured the in-and-out humiliation of soul-coring rape. Spiritual death by a thousand cuts. Yet, early in his young life, Zookeeper recognized he had one powerful advantage over all the others. That advantage he could not put in words, but it resided in his ability to exercise the skill of a coroner and surgically peel back the layers of forensic clues that reveal the inner minutiae of what makes an individual tick. More than that, he could plumb the deepest motivations of people, and for what goal they will kill or die to achieve. As he grew older and more street-wise, he quickly learned the desperate craving for drugs represented a goal that made its addicts especially vulnerable to his power. As a student of history, he calculated his own armies, unlike those of Napoleon and Alexander, would be recruited from the most reviled and wretched of outcasts. In this, he felt more a kinship with Hitler and his hypnotic ability to attract psychopaths. A limited pool, he admits to himself, but the sad trajectory of his brutal existence reveals to a scarred mind no other path. Throughout his life, many have referred to him as charismatic, but he knows his power far exceeds that inadequate adjective. Just as his own demons have been reanimated by the hunchback, so he has reanimated the demons in others by substituting his will for theirs. At least, until now. Therein lies the problem; the hunchback!

Zookeeper, fully aware of his own power, feels it crash like a wave against the unbending breakwater of the hunchback's own mysterious force, and shatter harmlessly in spattering fragments. Far from repelling him, that force exerts a fatal attraction that draws him as inexorably as he draws others. *Immovable object?* he wonders. *We shall see.*

Zookeeper is unsure how to categorize the hunchback. She is not an enemy, nor friend, nor snotty bourgeoise female, nor a hypocritical do-gooder, nor a curious onlooker like Lady Oracle. During the hunchback's visit, he felt the psychic probing emanating from her extraordinary hump, projecting its delicate tendrils of awareness into his brain. To his all-perceiving eyes, her hump burned as powerfully as the churning core of a nuclear reactor. An enigma. *Queen Mab?* he wonders, *or parasitic wasp?* More importantly, does she represent a threat? Such questions he ponders from the inner sanctum of the crack house while waiting for her next visit, arranged for whatever reason, by Lady Oracle. This inner sanctum is off-limits to all residents of the house. The door is always locked. Inside, it is as clean and pristine as that of the most assiduous housekeeper—an island of spotless paradise amidst the ocean of filth that surrounds it. Perfumed air freshener and joss sticks mask the all-pervasive stench. Books line its walls, and Zookeeper sits meditatively in an easy chair, sifting the cascade of thoughts and barrage of newly arrived voices that assault his sanity. What puzzles him the most is that the revivified voices triggered by the hunchback's visit are completely different than any of those he experienced in the past. Still distant and growlingly hazy, their rumblings scare him in ways he cannot define. His concentration is directed at the connection between these new voices and the hunchback when he hears a knocking at the sanctum's door.

"Hey! Zookeeper! You in there, motherfucker? We got a juiced-up nigger-boy cravin' apple jack."

Zookeeper calls toward the closed door, "Got cash?"

"Fuck yeah! Wouldn't bother you if he didn't."

"How juiced up?"

"Big time."

"Weapons?"

"Shit, didn't check."

"Fuck you, Angel Cake! Is he inside the fort?"

"Naw, left his cock hangin' outside. He's fuckin' jumpy though."

"Strong boy or weak?"

"Looks fuckin' strong to me."

"Hang, I'll be there. Shit! He wearin' gang colors?"

"Not that I can tell, but, damn Zookeeper, get your ass out here, I got to weasel in my shit. You handle the cash; I handle the blood."

By the time Zookeeper has dispensed with the "client" by accepting cash for crack, he sees three figures approach, one of whom bears a quite distinctive hump. Immediately, his senses are on full alert. He discards his pusher persona and assumes the mantle of Shakespeare to project a defensive shield against non-addict intruders. The Bard almost always works to captivate even the most resistant of them. When they approach near enough for his voice to be heard, he assumes a lavish bow.

"Good morrow, Mistress Oracle!"

"What are you doing out in the fresh air and daylight so early Sir Zookeeper?" she replies. "Aren't you afraid of being desiccated by too much time in the sun?"

"Business. I see you bring your two freaks. Well, two freaks among my other exhibits will cause no particular disturbance. Nature teaches beasts to know their friends."

Again, a small crowd has gathered to make various obscene comments. One skeletal man, whose tissue-thin white skin seems to sag so much his tattoos give the impression of running down his arms like melting wax, shouts, "Shiiiit! Listen to that fucker Zookeeper talk fancy shit. That's dope, motherfucker!"

Zookeeper grins and bows low in recognition. He turns to Ming-huà and says, "Welcome back to my zoo. The animals inside do bite, so don't try to feed them. And definitely don't stick your hand through their cages. You hear?"

Ming-huà submissively nods assent, while Lady Oracle rolls her eyes. "Ming-huà, this boy is just trying to scare you. The only danger in that house is from slipping on rotting garbage and breaking your neck."

Sy laughs and dances a little jig. "Guess I'd better be careful!"

Zookeeper has kept his eyes on Ming-huà, and feels the tingling pressure of some inexplicable power flowing from her body to his. He shakes it off and leads them into the house. With no intention to show them his inner sanctum, he wades through the trash, past the nervously suspicious stares of his addicts, to an abandoned room where the stench is slightly less overwhelming.

"We can talk here," he says. "Now, what do you want this time?" he asks Lady Oracle.

"Before I tell you, I want you to have this." She jams a folded piece of paper in his shirt pocket.

"What the fuck's that?"

"My address. After our meeting today, you will want to come and talk with me."

"About what?"

"You'll see. Now, you asked what I want. This time I want to ask you some questions about yourself."

Zookeeper gives her a cold stare and his eyes flash with hostility. "What the fuck for?"

"What happened to Shakespeare?" chuckles Sy. "Discarded for more pressing business?"

"Shut the fuck up, freak, I'm talkin' to Lady Clitoris here."

He notices out of the corner of his eye the hunchback's reaction. She stands awkwardly, clearly uncomfortable and skittish. *This is definitely not her idea*, he thinks. Just as Lady Oracle opens her mouth to speak, the same two men who threatened them before enter the room brandishing the same knives. The stink from their bodies cuts through the already foul-smelling atmosphere.

"Zookeeper, you fuckin' failed to inform us the bitch would come back. Does she have enough bread to pay all of us?"

"I dunno," says Zookeeper. "Don't even know what the fuck she wants." He looks at Lady Oracle. "Well?"

"You will be paid."

"And my exhibits here? They are my two palace guards, and whew! They get mean when deprived of their daily sustenance. Bring enough coin to keep them happy?"

"Perhaps," says Lady Oracle. "Depends."

"On what, bitch?" asks one of the men.

She glares at him with a fierce smile. "On whether you are good boys."

"Shiiiit! Give us the money first, then we leave you alone," says the other man.

"You have to forgive my friends," says Zookeeper. "They haven't been properly introduced. This is Pepper Spray and Amygdala. I named Amygdala myself because of his emotional nature. Clever, eh?"

"I'm impressed," says Lady Oracle.

"Shit!" barks Pepper Spray. "What about it, Lady Fuck! Prepay or get out. Cash up front in this house. Right, Zookeeper?"

Lady Oracle looks at Zookeeper. He shrugs. "Exhibits got to be fed, appetites appeased, you know? Peace in the zoo is essential for the well-being of our . . . rarer exhibits."

She pulls out five one-hundred-dollar bills and holds them up. "This is yours if you do something for me first."

Amygdala smiles maliciously. "Shit, lady. We can just take the money."

"Let's go!" she says to her two companions, turning on her heel to leave.

Both men flash their knives and block the door, but Zookeeper holds up his hand. "Wait a minute! She might want something simple." He turns his attention to Lady Oracle and bows slightly. "What the fuck do you want us to do, Mistress Oracle? I mean, you've still not explained why you're here."

"You have been around a lot of violence, right, Zookeeper?"

"Yeah."

"Also committed quite a bit of your own violence on others, correct?"

Zookeeper snorts. "Hell, yes! Goddamn right I have! War gives the right to conquerors to impose any condition they please upon the vanquished." He pauses and narrows his eyes suspiciously. "Why do ya ask?"

She nods toward Ming-huà. "I want you to kill this girl."

A collective gasp comes from everyone in the room except Sy and Lady Oracle. Ming-huà lets out a shocked squeal and cringes in terror.

"You're shittin' me!" says Pepper Spray.

Zookeeper tries to recover from his shock. "Why?" he asks.

"That's my business."

"No fuckin' way!" shouts Zookeeper. "What kind of a set-up is this?" He looks out the window. "You're setting us up for the cops!"

Lady Oracle takes out five more one-hundred-dollar bills. "Will a thousand convince you?"

The eyes of the palace guards widen as they greedily ogle the cash.

By this time, Ming-huà is clawing at Sy's arm, crying, begging him to get her away, but he pushes her down.

The men stare at her in confusion.

Lady Oracle waves the money. "Well?"

Zookeeper's brain is suddenly exploding with commands from the new voices. "Do it! Do it!" they scream. "Kill her! Do it!"

Ming-huà is on her knees, begging hysterically. Sy stands above her, harshly squeezing her shoulder to hold her down.

"Do it!" Zookeeper shouts to Pepper Spray and Amygdala. "But don't kill the hunchback! Kill her! Mistress Oracle!" In a momentary flash of insight, Zookeeper knows his words are not his own, but is helpless to stop them. "Kill her! Do it!"

Even with Zookeeper's frantic orders ringing in their ears, his two comrades hesitate. "Just fuckin' give us the money, lady!" cries Pepper Spray.

"Kill her!" commands Zookeeper. "Kill her! There's more where that came from!" Furious at his henchmen's reluctance, he gestures wildly. "Do it! Kill her!"

The two men pause for a brief instant and glance nervously at each other. Then, in some unspoken agreement, rush toward her with their knives, Zookeeper urges them on. "Do it! Do it!" He still does not recognize his own voice, and realizes with horror the demons in his head are forcing their own words out. "Kill her! Do it!"

Lady Oracle stands perfectly still and waits.

Pepper Spray and Amygdala, are upon her, knives gleaming in the light as their blades tear into her body.

Ming-huà screams.

~

A sudden and horrifying silence grips the room in a death-like moment of frozen shock.

Lady Oracle stands tall, unharmed.

Pepper Spray, Amygdala, and Zookeeper stagger in speechless disbelief.

No longer do any of them have arms. Mere stumps emerge from their shoulders. No blood. No pain. No open wounds. The skin was as smooth as if they had been born armless.

Not a word is spoken for an agonizingly long moment, then Amygdala screams and runs out of the room, followed by a babbling Pepper Spray. Zookeeper stares in shock at Ming-huà. The voices in his head are quiet. He feels her probing him and he collapses in a chair, stupefied.

"Let's go," says Lady Oracle smoothly.

"But we can't leave them like this!" objects Ming-huà.

"Yes, we must. They are in no danger of dying. It is best if we leave and let them come to terms with their situation."

Lady Oracle motions to Sy, who forcefully lifts Ming-huà by the arm and leads her out of the house.

Zookeeper, still in shock, watches them leave and reaches down to push himself out of the chair when he realizes to his horror that he truly has no arms.

His mind goes blank.

~ *Zookeeper Faces His Demons* ~

Zookeeper sits in the chair, stupefied, unwilling to acknowledge what just happened. Looking around absently, he spots a pack of cigarettes and a lighter on the end table. Instinctively, he reaches for them, and is again confronted with reality. No arms. No hands. No fingers. No sense of touching. Nothing—not a cigarette, a woman, an enemy, a weapon, a tissue to wipe his nose, change his clothes, pour a drink—nothing ever again! Life without arms unfolds before his horrified imagination, and it appears impossible. Others of his "exhibits" wander in and stare at him with uncomprehending eyes.

"Shit, man!" cries Angel Cake, utterly befuddled. "What the fuck! Shit! What the fuck happened to you, man! Fuckin' shit! I saw Amygdala and Pepper Spray runnin' like hell outta here with no arms, man! Fuckin' insane! What happened? What happened to the two bros? Shit! Fuckin' speak to me, man!"

There can be no response from Zookeeper, whose face reflects severe shock and disbelief. He does not hear or comprehend the questions thrown at him from Angel Cake. One thought, and one thought only, pushes its way through the fog—seek out the hunchback and reverse the process. Make her give him back his arms! Find the hunchback! Where is she? Lady Oracle! He'll take a gun! But he becomes sick knowing he can't even hold a gun, let alone point it. Nonetheless, his only salvation is to go find Lady Oracle and the hunchback. Now! Now!

He reaches for his shirt pocket to retrieve the paper with her address, but again the grim reality hits him.

"Angel Cake! Shit, no time to explain, man! Reach into my shirt pocket and pull out a paper!"

"What?" asks his confused exhibit, whose dull mind is already making its laborious pivot from abstract incredulity to material enrichment—de facto inheritance of the crack house.

"Goddamn it, get it outta my pocket!" He thrusts his chest toward Angel Cake, who pulls out the paper.

"Read it to me!"

Angel Cake reads the address.

"I know that fuckin' street!" cries Zookeeper, now running past a visibly astonished but coldly calculating Angel Cake.

Before he knows it, he is in the street, stumbling awkwardly. With no arms it is difficult, and he often veers and careens wildly. Dimly aware of the stares from passers-by, he makes his way toward Lady Oracle's apartment in the Tenderloin.

~

By the time he stands at Lady Oracle's front door, he is gasping for breath and cursing the horrific exertion required to run and keep his balance. His legs ache, muscles cramp with excruciating pain, and shooting pains rack long-neglected parts of his body. Zookeeper's mind continues to reel at the unreality of his situation. He tries to knock, but again the inconceivable reality slaps him in the face. Inflamed to a new level of desperation, he uses his foot to kick the door, but without arms as counterweights, he flies backward and lands heavily on the concrete. For the first time, tears of frustration and helplessness flow in rivulets, blurring his view of the bright San Francisco sky. He is literally a helpless babe, and like a babe teetering on the edge of a well, he loses his balance. Zookeeper free falls into the deep well of anguish, watching the sunlit rim of the world race away, receding so far only a tiny round patch of blue remains—so distant it is beyond reach. So lost is he, the figure of Lady Oracle helping him into the apartment does not register. Once inside and sitting in the dark of her "yin apartment," he regains some semblance of reason and gathers his inner resolve to make the most important plea of his life.

He tries to force a sentence out of his mouth, but the only word he can rasp under his breath is, "Hunchback!"

"What about her?" asks Lady Oracle nonchalantly.

How can she be so calm? he asks himself. How in the fuck can she be so fuckin' calm! "Hunchback!" he screams.

"Zookeeper, she is not here."

"You fuckin' bitch! Such goddamn calmness . . . and me. Look at me! At me!"

"I see. Let me get you a drink."

"I can't . . ."

Lady Oracle smiles. "No problem."

She calls a name. A boy enters the room and she tells him to bring a glass of whiskey, no ice, no water. He nods and returns carrying a tray. "Thank you, Bataar." She picks up the glass and holds it to Zookeeper's mouth.

Zookeeper turns his head away.

"You might as well get used to it," she says smoothly.

"How can you be so fuckin' calm?" he says in wonder, still clearly in shock.

"Tilt your head back."

He does.

Lady Oracle lifts the glass to his lips and gently lets the whiskey trickle into his mouth. He sucks greedily.

"Bataar!" she calls.

"Yes?"

"Another."

And so it goes until Zookeeper is numb enough to sleep.

When he wakes, he is on the couch. How much time has passed is a mystery to him.

Lady Oracle sits across from the couch.

"Well?" she asks. "Can you talk now?"

"The hunchback," he rasps.

"What about her?"

"I need her to replace my arms! Put them back!"

"She can't."

"Bullshit! Where is she?" He looks around wildly.

"Zookeeper, she is not here. You are. You are still in shock, but it is slowly wearing off. Try and remain calm, or I will kick you out."

Zookeeper starts to fly at her in a rage until he realizes he is no longer in a position to make any threats.

"Okay, okay. I want to see the hunchback. I want her to return my arms. I don't give a fuck how she does it. Just have her do it!"

"No, Zookeeper, you and I must talk first."

"Go fuck yourself! I want the hunchback!"

"I can put you back out on the street."

"I can call the cops."

Lady Oracle laughs. "That's rich! And tell them what? A crack dealer's arms were somehow removed by a hunchback without leaving any blood or scars? Go ahead."

"I . . . I . . . don't know what the fuck to do. Help me, or if not, I'll do harm to you. Somehow, some way, I'll do you harm."

Lady Oracle shakes her head in pity. "Zookeeper, as your Bard wrote, 'Diseases desperate grown, by desperate appliance are relieved, or not at all.'"

"What do I have to do?"

"Stay here with me for a few days. I have a number of things we need to talk about. You will be looked after by Bataar."

"What about the hunchback?"

"Later."

"I want her now!"

"You're slipping again, Zookeeper. I cannot help you unless you get past this shock and help me."

"How the fuck can I help you?"

"By talking to me?"

"About?"

"The new voices in your head. Especially one particular new voice."

"These fuckin' voices are driving me batshit crazy! How do you make them stop?!"

"Bataar!" calls Lady Oracle. "More whiskey!"

Zookeeper tries to rise from the couch, but without arms as counterweights, he slumps back in defeat. "And a fag!" he shouts in helpless rage.

Bataar somehow produces a cigarette as if from thin air, places it between Zookeeper's lips, and lights it. Without being asked, he hovers over Zookeeper, pulling out the cigarette and putting it back. Although just a boy, he performs this service as if he had been a servant for a lifetime.

Zookeeper looks at Bataar quizzically. "Thanks, kid," he says resignedly.

Even as he speaks, a voice emerges as a low, ominous growl deep within his mind. It gets louder. It gets nearer. Its words are spoken in the deep timbre of creation. Zookeeper's face is rendered immobile in a mask of trepidation.

"You hear it, don't you?" asks Lady Oracle. "It isn't multiple voices; it is one voice—a composite of all voices."

Zookeeper remains still. The voice reverberates like an approaching locomotive.

"Zookeeper!" shouts Lady Oracle.

He remains frozen in terror.

"You're here, aren't you, God?" she says.

Chapter Seven

God's History Revealed

First Principles

~ Ming-huà is Confronted ~

Zookeeper struggles to keep the terrifying voice at bay. Its words dampen his normally radiant spirits. Like rain dousing a campfire, it splutters and sizzles, spreading an all-pervasive dreariness. To bring back the light requires reversing the rotation of earth itself. Faced with such impossibility, his psychic core curls its flowery petals inward and retreats from the approaching night. Lady Oracle can only watch Zookeeper slip into unconsciousness.

"He is fighting *You*," she says aloud toward the ceiling. "He is strong. Yes, he will do . . . perhaps. Now that he is defanged, the task can begin. Bataar, help me get him into the spare bedroom and tuck him in. I am leaving and will not return for hours. If he wakes, give him the special tea . . . no, better make it decaf coffee. He's definitely not a tea man. If he asks for booze, give him that. So long as he sleeps and does not leave. Understand?"

Bataar nods.

~

Lady Oracle stands resolutely before the front door of the old Victorian house and knocks. When Sy opens it, she pulls him outside and whispers, "How is Ming-huà?"

Sy looks away. "Terrible."

"Good."

"It is according to plan?"

"Yes, now let me see her."

"Are you sure—" Sy starts to object.

"I'm sure." Lady Oracle interrupts, her voice severe.

"In that case, let's meet in the room where Ming-huà feels most comfortable. You know the way. Go ahead and I'll bring her down."

Lady Oracle smiles. "Lots of ghosts in that room."

"Lots. Maybe that's why she feels so comfortable. Friendly ghosts. Kind of comforting."

"I'll heat up some tea."

Sy lets out a long groan. "I'll get her."

Lady Oracle waits patiently, but eventually begins to wonder what is taking so long. Just as she moves toward the door, Sy returns with an apologetic expression.

"She won't come."

"Why?"

"Doesn't want to see you. Really doesn't want to see me either, but she's stuck with me. But you . . . well, after all, you did sic those druggies on her."

"For the sake of humanity."

"She doesn't know that. She views it as a set-up. A callous exercise. An immoral experiment."

Lady Oracle chuckles. "Of course she does. So much the better. Her resistance is the next hurdle. Bring her down."

"I'm telling you; she won't come."

"Then I'll go to her."

"Door's locked."

"Unlock it."

Sy shakes his head doubtfully. "Okay. I won't be responsible for whatever happens."

"She can do nothing to me."

"I know, but. . . ."

"So?"

"Okay, let's go."

Sy and Lady Oracle ascend the stairs, keys jingling in his hand. When they stand outside Ming-huà's door, Sy knocks.

"Go away!" she calls.

"Ming-huà, open up. Lady Oracle needs to talk with you."

"No! I'm going back to the island. I'm packing now. Don't want to see either of you! Leave!"

Lady Oracle nods.

Sy unlocks the door.

Ming-huà is leaning over her suitcase, packing some clothes. Surprisingly, she does not bother to look up. "I know you have a key. I knew you would unlock the door regardless of my wishes. As you can see, I am serious. The farther I get from the two of you, the better. The non-human animals on my island have more morals than the entire human race. I want to be with them. There's a certain squirrel . . . anyway, nothing you can say—"

"Your mother is on her way."

"What?" cries an astonished Ming-huà.

Even Sy is surprised, and shows his amazement by croaking out in tandem with the hunchback, "What! Really?"

"Your mother will be here tomorrow," says Lady Oracle in an infuriatingly placid tone. "She wants to talk with you, as I do now. There are many things you do not understand."

Ming-huà is speechless and slumps in a nearby chair, waiting.

"Tamara Powers, your globe-trotting mother, has returned from a very long trip, visiting many different places in many different times. She is aware of what happened at the crack house, and wants to speak with you about it."

"What do you mean, 'many different places and many different times?'" asks Ming-huà. "The last thing she told me was that she was traveling to a magic cave from which she would never return. Naturally, I chalked this up to a mother's clumsy way of breaking to a young girl that she was leaving and would never return. Probably with some man, but who knows? I never really questioned it."

"She did go to a magic cave located in a vast desert," says Lady Oracle.

"I never once believed it was real," murmurs Ming-huà.

"That cave," Lady Oracle continues, "Is why taking you to the desert was out of the question. Your mother, your father, your grandparents, all of us in this room, are in many ways connected to that cave. Now, do you want to hear what I have to say?"

"And those men I mutilated because of you? Are they connected as well, or are they innocent victims?"

"All connected. Do you or do you not want to hear?"

Ming-huà reluctantly nods.

"Then let us go down to the room of ghosts, have tea, and discuss the situation without theatrics."

"Ghosts?" asks Ming-huà.

Lady Oracle smiles. "You know very well."

Ming-huà's silence speaks volumes.

Once they settle in the anteroom, tea is poured and an eerie quiet prevails.

"Well?" says Ming-huà, determined to maintain her frigid disapproval.

"Are you aware of how your mother met your father?"

"She never told me."

"And you were too young when your father died to ask about it," confirms Sy.

"Obviously," says Ming-huà. "What does this have to do with anything?"

"Well," says Lady Oracle. "Your parents' marriage was arranged."

"Arranged? Like in medieval times?"

"Sort of."

Ming-huà shakes her head in frustration. "Just explain it to me. Dispense with the Socratic method."

"True," chimes in Sy. "Humans are hard-wired to respond to a story. You know, once upon a time. . . . " He garnishes his observation with a comedic pose.

"Good idea," says Lady Oracle. She takes a deep breath. "Once upon a time, a *Goddess* instructed *Her* representatives on earth to arrange a marriage between Michael Powers (once fated to be *The Son*) and Tamara, daughter of Child of

Buddha (now fated to be the mother of *The Daughter*). You are the product. You are *The Daughter*. Brief enough?"

Ming-huà furrows her brow. "Too brief. I don't understand any of it. *Goddess*? The son? The daughter? Magic caves? Really, this is too absurd!"

"Is it more absurd than your ability to remove objects and people from existence and scatter their atoms to the four winds? Is it more absurd than blinking two hunters out of existence? Is it more absurd than leaving three men without arms?"

Ming-huà looks down in silence.

"Is it?"

"No. Tell me more."

"You are to . . . get together . . . with Zookeeper."

Ming-huà looks horror-stricken. "Are you out of your minds! How can you even suggest such . . . such . . . such an atrocity? Do you think I'm completely stupid? Me? A brood mare? Is the atrocity committed on my mother to be repeated on me?"

"No, not that. Your mother was selected, as was your father. They were happy together."

"Selected!" Ming-huà is laughing hysterically. "I see! Who selected them?"

"*Goddess*."

"And you are . . . the breeder?" asks Ming-huà sarcastically.

"No. I, like my mother, am the facilitator."

"Facilitator! Is that another word for murderer? Is *facilitator* in the same absurdly euphemistic category as *reconfigure*?"

"This is why your mother is coming. It is to explain. You do want an explanation?"

Ming-huà looks out the window, her eyes misty. "She is my mother."

~ *Zookeeper is Confronted* ~

When Lady Oracle returns to her apartment, Zookeeper is awake, sitting on the couch—brooding and angry—his eyes watery red from being plied with whiskey by Bataar.

She sits across from him in her favorite chair. Zookeeper stares at her with murder in his heart.

"No need to make such an ugly face, Zookeeper," she says. "You can't kill me, but I can kill you easily enough. You are a victim, like all the innocent people you victimized. How does it feel?"

"Fuckin' bitch! Mocking me is fucked! Go to hell!"

"Go to Shakespeare."

"What?"

"Go to Shakespeare—and respond properly."

"Fuck you!"

"That is not Shakespeare. Do it properly."

Zookeeper looks at her in wonder. "What kind of a fucked-up bitch are you?"

"Shakespeare, Zookeeper."

"Fuck!"

"Reconnect, Zookeeper."

He pauses, letting her words percolate. "Oh, I see. Therapy."

"Therapy."

He bares his teeth. "You have a kid, Lady Oracle?"

She tilts her head in mock confusion. "A goat?"

"A child, damn you!"

"No."

"Want one?"

"Perhaps."

He looks at her with a malicious gleam in his eye. "You want Shakespeare?"

"Go ahead."

"'Hear, nature, hear; dear *Goddess*, hear! Suspend thy purpose, if thou didst intend to make this creature fruitful! Into her womb convey sterility! Dry up in her the organs of increase; and from her derogate body never spring a babe to honor her! If she must teem, create her child of spleen; that it may live, and be a thwart disnatured torment to her! Let us stamp wrinkles in her brow of youth; with cadent tears fret channels in her cheeks; turn all her mother's pains and benefits to laughter and contempt; that she may feel how sharper than a serpent's tooth it is to have a thankless child!'"

He pauses, then continues in a low, growling voice. "And may her child fall into the clutches of a pusher, who will make it an addict and live in its own shit! *Goddess*, may thee remove its arms and legs so its mother will cry in agony!"

"Excellent, Zookeeper!" cries Lady Oracle clapping. "You never disappoint! Deep does your genius go. Now, how much deeper can it go?"

"Deep enough to find a way to get revenge!"

"On me?"

"On that fuckin' hunchback! You wanted her killed, didn't you? Don't tell me you didn't! Pretend as you will, you are afraid of her. That much I know!"

"Well then, what do you think of her?"

Zookeeper is rendered speechless.

"What do you think of her?" repeats Lady Oracle.

"She is fuckin' evil! Look at me! Take me to her so she can put my arms back on."

"If she is evil, why would she?"

He has no answer.

"Zookeeper, look at me."

He does.

"She is not your enemy; she is your salvation."

"What?"

"She is your salvation. She will be your wife and together you will have a child."

"What the fuck are you talking about? That's complete bullshit! If I see the little mutant, I'll kill her!"

"What you don't understand, Zookeeper, is that you are also a mutant."

~

His face darkens. "I may have had . . . certain powers once, now, I'm just a freak, like your little hunchback."

"You just called her a mutant, not a freak."

"Slip of the tongue."

"Do you want to know her name?"

Zookeeper doubles down. "It has a name?"

"Same as you."

"What's her fuckin' name?"

"Ming-huà. Ming-huà Powers."

"What kind of fuckin' name is that? She's Chinese, right?"

"It is a quite beautiful and quite rare name, just as she is quite beautiful and quite rare."

"She's rare all right!"

"As are you."

"Hell!"

"Her mother had magical powers."

Zookeeper laughs sarcastically. "My mother had magical powers all right! Magical junkie powers. She would steal my baby teeth for money."

Lady Oracle looks at him compassionately. "Zookeeper, your mother did have magical powers, but they were hijacked by drugs. Nonetheless, she unknowingly passed them on to you, just as Ming-huà's mother passed her powers on. Now, you both need the power the other possesses."

"Bullshit! She's the one who took my arms! The only thing I need from her is to put them back!"

"But she will, don't you see?"

Zookeeper's eyes widen. "She will?"

"In a manner of speaking."

"Shit! I know what that means. Fuck her!"

Lady Oracle smiles. "That is the goal."

"Christ! You people are crazy!"

"Even now the wheels have been set in motion. All we have to do is bring you both together, leave you alone with each other, and you will find that miracles do happen."

"Fuck!"

Lady Oracle groans. "Zookeeper, do you possess any useful words between the glorious poetry of Shakespeare and the gutter variations of 'fuck'?"

Zookeeper is at a loss and fails to dredge up a suitable response.

Lady Oracle stubbornly continues, "Even you have admitted she is pretty."

Zookeeper starts to blurt an obscenity, but hesitates, still smarting from her insult to his carefully built façade of esoteric intelligence. Finally, he says, "Maybe her face—but that fuckin' hump!"

"And your armless body? Who will have you now?"

"Not looking for anyone."

"You have no choice. No way you can care for yourself."

"So, she is to be my nurse?"

"No, she is to be your savior."

Zookeeper shakes his head ruefully. "Not in the market for a savior."

"But, Zookeeper, you are also to be her savior."

He bares his teeth. "You want us to get married and live happily ever after?"

"No, we want you to get married and have a child. It is the child that we are most interested in. Whether you live happily ever after is up to the both of you. Being a savior is not being happy."

"First thing you've said that makes any sense!"

"So . . . if not a savior, how about a father? What do you have to lose?"

Zookeeper begins mulling the possibility. First and foremost, what could he gain out of it? A hunchback wife? No bargain. But . . . but. . . .

"Does she have bread?"

"You mean an income?"

"Fuckin' right that's what I mean!"

"Yes."

"She has a place to live?"

"Yes."

"Okay, she's got money and a place to live. What else does she offer me? Pity?"

"No, your life."

Zookeeper shakes his head. "Lady Oracle, you gotta understand, this hunchback took off my arms. How am I supposed to forgive her? You fuckin' think we both just trip merrily on our way?"

"Zookeeper, she took off your arms to defend me. Think, boy! She can also defend you."

This possibility opens up an entirely new dimension to Zookeeper's thoughts. Not only could she defend him, she could do more, so much more. She could help him rebuild his drug empire. Who needs an enforcer? Who needs palace guards? With her powers, anything suddenly seems achievable.

"When can we meet?" he asks.

"I'll let you know. In the meantime, you will stay here until arrangements can be made."

Zookeeper feels his power surging back—but that terrible voice still growls menacingly in the background.

Observing the blank look on his face, Lady Oracle asks, "You hear *Him*, don't you?"

"What?"

"You hear a voice, correct?"

"What, you think I'm some sort of schizo?"

"You hear a voice, correct?" she repeats firmly.

"If I do?"

"It is *Him*."

"Who?"

"*Him*."

Zookeeper looks at her askance, but the voice keeps dragging his attention back. He tilts his head sideways and violently shakes it, as one might do with water in their ears.

"Zookeeper, you can't rid yourself of *Him* that way," scolds Lady Oracle.

"Who are you talkin' about? Who is *Him*?"

"*God*."

"Christ! Here we go again with your crazy talk! Why go and talk to me that crazy way?"

Lady Oracle ignores the question. "Do you believe in *God*, Zookeeper?"

"Shit no! *God* has done nothing for me."

"Are you a junkie, Zookeeper?" asks Lady Oracle.

"Used to be. Got smart. Sold it, not snorted it."

"But you were an addict?"

"Goddamn it, told you so! Fuckin' while back, took forever to get myself clean. Went through hell, but I did it."

"Yes, that was due to your power. Remember when you were addicted?"

"Shit, yeah."

"Do you know *God* is also an addict?"

As if a lion had been prodded to fury, the voice from the depths of his mind roars to life; pulling at him, tearing at him, like some monstrosity buried alive trying to claw its way out. Zookeeper closes his eyes, rocking his head side-to-side. "No! Fuckin' voices! Get out! Out!"

Lady Oracle's face is inches from Zookeeper's. "*God* is also an addict, only *His* crack house is the entire world, and *He* wants you to give *Him* a high!"

Tears of frustration pour from Zookeeper's eyes. "What the fuck does *He* want! Make *Him* stop!"

"*He* craves suffering, and only the hunchback can make *Him* stop the shouting in your head."

"How?" cries an anguished Zookeeper.

"She can make *Him* disappear—or at least *His* voice—the same way she did your arms. Are you ready to see her?"

"Yes, yes, yes!"

"Bataar!" shouts Lady Oracle.

The boy instantly appears.

"Bring Zookeeper a special whiskey."

Lady Oracle goes into a back room reserved only for herself and sits in a chair behind a massive desk covered with papers. She picks up one of the papers and whispers, "Tamara arrives tomorrow. We'll see."

~ *Hunchback Converses with Scarecrow* ~

Ming-huà wakes up very early the next morning at the Victorian house and sits in the kitchen sipping tea. She nervously fidgets with whatever objects are within reach. Her mother is scheduled to arrive sometime in the afternoon. *Why so nervous?* she asks herself. Answering her own question is easy enough: her mother has become an unknown quantity. This business about a magic cave renders her a riddle, an exotic stranger to explore—and exploration of riddles is always danger-ous. Nonetheless, mixed in with the nervousness is a deep yearning to reconnect with the loving mother of her childhood. Such conflicting emotions complicate her anticipation. While impatiently mulling these conundrums, Ming-huà also ponders the power she inherited from her mother. According to Lady Oracle's telling, Ming-huà's power flows from her mother, although during her entire childhood, she had not seen any evidence of it. Only the "magic cave" exists as a tantalizing hint of some supernatural ability. She recalls her mother mentioning something about her grandmother during the war in China. It was something about a quest, and her grandmother being a woman possessed of unique powers. Typically, her mother refused to answer questions that would clarify the story. Her mother—always evading the past. *Yet,* Ming-huà remembers—*not just the past, but how the present also made her restless and jittery.* As a girl, her mother's presence always seemed evanescent, as if the merest wisp of a breeze would carry her away. This maternal, transitory figure was thus made all the more precious to a young Ming-huà.

No less precious now, she thinks. *There are so many questions!* She tries to catalog the plenitude of questions she wants to ask, but her thoughts are sidetracked by the unavoidable catastrophe of her actions at the crack house, not to mention the distressing problem of Zookeeper. *Is that why she's coming?* wonders Ming-huà. *To take Lady Oracle's side and convince me to . . . be with that horrible addict, or pusher, or whatever he is? Never! Not even my mother can convince me to take that path!*

While engrossed in these thoughts, Sy bounds into the kitchen, pours himself a cup of coffee, and sits across from her with a sly look on his face.

"Thinking about your mother?"

Ming-huà frowns, still angry with him. "Trying to."

"Remember I mentioned a predecessor?"

"Yes."

"My predecessor's predecessor knew your grandmother in China during the war."

Ming-huà is captivated. At last she murmurs, "Go on."

"She had the power, in spades."

"Go on."

"She could decipher taps from inside a statue."

"Taps . . . statue?"

"It was called the Precious Object. They found your grandmother, Child of Buddha, in a mental institution."

"They?"

"People on the quest—including your father."

"Quest for. . . . "

"*Her*, of course."

"Go on."

"*She* is *Her*, is *Goddess*, is the Precious Object, is. . . . "

"A quest for *Goddess*?"

"Yes and no. Up and down, I can tell you no more. What I can tell you, is that this junkie, Zookeeper, holds a key to something else."

"What else?"

"*God*, of course."

"I don't understand."

"Look, I am only able to give hints—hints I myself don't fully understand. Yin and Yang, *God* and *Goddess*, Light and Dark, Male and Female, Suffering and . . . what would you say?"

"Joy?"

"No, not that. Ask your father."

"He is dead."

"Exactly. Death is not the logical opposite."

"Yes, it is. Life and death."

"No, that is the key. Symmetry is broken. As *She* would so often say: 'fate starves at probability's door.'"

"How is the dialectic opposite broken?" asks Ming-huà. "Life and death. It works."

"No. All that comes before and after life is stillness—not death. Furthermore, all that comes before and after life is also motion—also not death. Stillness and motion. You see, death is not an opposite at all. Perhaps that explains—" he abruptly pauses.

"What?"

"Riddles. Your own mother is a riddle, as was her mother, as was your father, as are you . . . you and Zookeeper."

"Funny, I was just thinking that my mother is a riddle."

Sy leaps into the air. "There! You see? Riddles everywhere. But I do know your grandmother could read the taps."

"And?"

Sy wags his finger. "Ah, ah, ah! Your grandmother is the key to your mother, your mother is the key to you, you are the key to . . . what?"

"I don't know."

"Your own child, of course, but only with Zookeeper."

"What? . . . why?"

Sy collapses back onto the chair. "I do not know. I am only told so much."

"By?"

"*Her.*"

Ming-huà shakes her head in frustration. "Now we're back to the beginning!" She pauses; a light flickers on in her mind. "Or is Lady Oracle *Her*?"

Sy laughs uproariously. "No, no! Not at all. Are Beginning and End dialectic opposites?"

Ming-huà groans and holds her head. "I don't know. This is too much!"

"Would you prefer too little?"

Ming-huà stands and stomps angrily out of the room, calling over her shoulder, "I'd prefer to return to my island with my mother and leave the rest to your . . . dialectics! And that is precisely what I intend to do!"

Sy watches her bound up the stairs and smiles smugly.

Chapter Eight

A Fateful Meeting

Can Suffering be Stopped?

~ Mother and Daughter ~

When her mother walks through the front door, Ming-huà's heart skips a beat and she blinks back tears of recognition. At first glance, Tamara Powers looks almost the same but for greyer hair and deeper cracks in her already leathery skin. But on closer inspection, her mother's hunchback seems more pronounced than ever. A cane projects before her, tapping on the hardwood floor as she walks. Ming-huà rushes to her, and they embrace in a heartfelt hug emblematic of two people deeply in love. Lady Oracle and Sy stand aside and let mother and daughter bask in the moment. No words are spoken for many moments. Finally, Lady Oracle coughs and guides Tamara into the anteroom. Bataar follows with the suitcase. Sy conducts the Mongol boy to the guest room, while the others find seats. Ming-huà and Tamara sit in adjoining chairs, refusing to let go of each other's hands, their arms forming a chain between them.

A few words pass between mother and daughter when Lady Oracle turns her attention to Ming-huà and interjects. "Your mother cannot stay long, and we have many things to discuss. I must soon return to my apartment and my . . . guest."

Ming-huà's heart clenches. She feels her mother's hand tighten in her own. "Can we have some time to catch up?" she asks.

She is surprised when her mother says, "No, daughter, it's best to face this now rather than later."

"But—" Ming-huà starts to object, but stops when she sees her mother frowning.

"We'll have time later," reassures Tamara. "But now"—she turns to Lady Oracle—"the issue is this young man."

"Yes," agrees the Mongol woman. "Zookeeper is his assumed name. His real name is Matthew Weston. Parents dead. No siblings, as far as we know. You have been informed of the circumstances, correct, Tamara?"

"Correct."

Lady Oracle looks at Ming-huà with a placid expression. "Your daughter here is adamantly opposed to the idea of . . . union."

Ming-huà stiffens in her seat, forcing herself to remain quiet, intent on listening to her mother's response.

"I understand she is opposed," says her mother. She gazes at Ming-huà and squeezes her hand tighter. "Will it surprise you to know the same arrangements were made for me and your father?"

"I have been told something about it," replies Ming-huà.

"Yes, the same arrangements. Exactly the same. Lady Oracle's grandmother, Buandelgereen, acted as the . . . facilitator. The goal, or purpose, or intent, was to have a child. A special child."

"But, Mama! You don't—" Again Ming-huà tries to voice an objection, but her mother pulls her hand from her daughter's and holds it up in a cautionary gesture.

"No, just listen." Tamara starts to continue, but pauses when Sy returns and sits quietly. She nods and turns back to face her daughter. "That special child turned out to be you. Now, I am told you have many questions. Not all can be answered, but some can. As I was saying, Buandelgereen came to me with a long, complicated story. The details do not concern us here. Suffice to say, she knew your grandmother, Child of Buddha."

"My grandmother Child of Buddha," Ming-huà repeats in wonder.

"Yes, your grandmother—Child of Buddha—participated in a quest—"

"To find *Her*!" blurts Ming-huà.

"Correct . . . sort of. At the end of Buandelgereen's long story, I was told to marry Michael Powers, an American who supposedly suffered from schizophrenia, but also possessed some unspecified power. Not being a good Chinese girl, I strenuously objected, but Buandelgereen explained the purpose, so I eventually agreed. Long story short, I ended up marrying your father, and here you are."

"Faced with the same decision!" exclaims Ming-huà in disgust.

"Yes."

"Did you love father?" presses Ming-huà.

"Eventually."

"Were you attracted to him?"

"Eventually, yes."

"Well, there's the problem!" snaps Ming-huà. "I don't love Zookeeper, I am not attracted to Zookeeper, he is a disgusting, filthy, horrible person, a drug dealer, and probably much worse. Speaking of worse, the purpose of this . . . union . . . has not been explained to me."

"Suffering," says Lady Oracle.

"What?"

"The world is full of unnecessary suffering. *God* is addicted to suffering. *Goddess . . . Her . . .* wants to cure *Him* of *His* addiction."

Ming-huà is speechless.

"Of course, it is far more complicated, dear," says Tamara, again taking hold of her daughter's hand. "We all speak in metaphors, don't we?"

"You may have married father, but you certainly wouldn't have married this Zookeeper character!" exclaims Ming-huà. "Have you seen him?"

"No."

"Not only is he a bad person, he now has no arms, thanks to me! Would you marry him?"

"If I were responsible for his . . . disability," says Tamara. "Remember, as far as I knew, your father suffered from schizophrenia when I married him."

Ming-huà falls silent for a few moments, then says, "That's different."

"No," says Lady Oracle. "Zookeeper is not what you make him out to be. He is actually a very worthwhile person, and his power makes him a very valuable person. He has lost his way."

Ming-huà laughs derisively. "I should say so! But I am not going to lose my way."

"You have not met *Her*," says Lady Oracle.

"A *Goddess*? You must be joking. Mama, she is joking, right?"

"No, she is not joking. I met *Her*. I would never have agreed to marry your father if I had not."

"Well, I haven't met *Her*, nor do I intend to. Mama, let's go back to the island together and live peacefully and simply! No more San Francisco. This is madness!"

"But, dear," says Tamara. "All of us sitting here are mad—your grandmother was mad, I am mad, and you, dear girl, are the maddest of the lot."

~ *Zookeeper Again Faces His Demon* ~

The more Zookeeper thinks about Lady Oracle's offer of sacrificing the hunchback's future to him, the more he likes it. All sorts of fantasies pass through his mind, spurred on by the voice howling at him to kill her, or kill himself, or kill someone, anyone! All of those shouted proposals to commit homicide have attracted him. Revenge on the human race is appealing. In his current state, the thought of revenge on any person, regardless of who it is exacted upon, is supremely satisfying. But revenge on those responsible for his current condition elicits the most graphic images. He envisions drawing the hunchback into his good graces, then finding a way to cut off all her limbs, not just her arms. He dreams about torturing Lady Oracle, maybe cutting out her tongue and forcing it down her throat until her smug superior attitude ends in a pathetic death rattle. He relishes pulling the intestines out of the skinny friend of Lady Oracle who dances around and insults with sarcastic humor. These delicious reveries are urged on by the voice—a brother sadist who understands the erotic excitement of inflicting pain and suffering. Lady Oracle has hinted the voice is that of *God*. That idea has him in stitches. How fitting! *God* is addicted to pain and suffering! Who knew? *God* is the greatest sadist in the universe! Zookeeper fancies himself a graduate student in search of a mentor. Steeped in pain himself, he understands how sadism works. This voice, this *God*, sure as hell does. Let the voice rant on; *God* will become Zookeeper's master, and Zookeeper *His* apprentice.

Yet, Zookeeper has an inkling that these sadistic fictions he so relishes are not the true temper of his steel. If the horrific voice is *God*, it is a false *God*. Try as he might, Zookeeper's self-image as the disciple of a sadistic deity is tainted by some deeper skepticism that, if he is honest, arises from more virtuous roots. Such roots have always been his downfall, preventing him from taking that extra step of cruelty that would lead him to triumph over his enemies. It is, paradoxically, a vexatious compassion and annoying empathy that, try as he might, cannot be expunged from his mind. These weaknesses of compassion and empathy always prevent him from fully implementing actions that he otherwise must perform to succeed. How else could he rise to the top of a streetwise hierarchy? As if he wore an electrified collar, he cannot murder or rape without feeling a painful jolt from his soft core. Often, he has faced brutal choices, but in the end, could never pull the trigger or bury a knife in someone's stomach, or rape a pretty junkie in need. He has tried. He has failed. A weakness only the power of projecting his will onto the dull-witted is able to camouflage. Using Shakespeare is merely an amateur's parlor trick when dealing with intelligent people. He intrigues intelligent people long enough to temporarily use them, but can never hold them long enough to truly satisfy a conqueror as, say, Hitler could. Shabby indeed.

Zookeeper aspires to be a vicious killer, leader of an empire, but the soft core of his soul is more angelic than anarchist. Up to now, he has succeeded in clipping the wings of his inner angel, but this latest disaster cries out for him to once and for all pull the wings out by their roots so they never grow back. Unfortunately, deep down he knows he can't. Truth be told, he won't. An infernal beatific soothsayer deep within warns him not to abandon the last chance he might have for redemption. What if the hunchback is truly his chance at salvation? After all, when they first met, Zookeeper's power clearly told him she is good. Very good. And she does have a nice face. No, a beautiful face!

In the midst of these reveries, Bataar enters the room and asks, "Need anything?"

Looking at him sideways, Zookeeper's face reflects distrust and puzzlement. "What do you get outta this, kid? She pays you a lotta bread? Teaches you about sex?"

Bataar's expression does not change; it remains a mask of imperturbability. "Need anything?" he repeats calmly.

"Yeah, pour some whiskey down my gullet, but first come wipe my ass. I gotta shit."

Bataar nods and follows him into the bathroom. In spite of his crude bravado, Zookeeper is sick with embarrassment. He feels humiliation, but also a nagging curiosity at this boy's odd comportment, so much Mother Theresa in one so young—especially a boy. When he was a boy—

"Are you finished?" asks Bataar.

"Yeah, Goddamn it! Just do it!"

Bataar ignores his outburst and quietly wipes Zookeeper with placid detachment.

The boy is just as unruffled as when he pours a whiskey or helps Zookeeper puff his cigarettes. This puzzles the armless man immensely. Faced with unstinting kindness from others, he feels disoriented and self-doubting. That very kindness triggers the unwanted softness which, in turn, makes him rage even more insistently against it. If he had a psychic scalpel, he would cut out the malignancy.

Back on his comfortable couch, Zookeeper is assailed by the voice urging him to kill Lady Oracle, or Bataar, or himself.

Do it! Do it! screams the voice in his head.

"Shut-up!" Zookeeper bellows in futile rage.

Bataar, apparently unmoved by his distress, calmly puts a cigarette between Zookeeper's lips, then patiently pulls it out after he takes a long drag.

Do it! Do it! the voice keeps insisting.

Zookeeper laughs mirthlessly. "How?" he barks.

Bataar ignores the non-sequitur, somehow knowing it is not directed at him.

As if noticing the Mongol boy for the first time, Zookeeper asks, "Where the fuck is Lady Oracle? I want to talk with her."

"She will soon return," he replies serenely.

"Well," grumbles Zookeeper. "I hope she gets here soon. I want to talk to her. How about that whiskey, kid?"

Do it! Kill her! Do it! It you don't, she will poison you! the voice persists.

"Damn it, shut up!"

~

Lady Oracle strides into the room after her visit with Sy, Ming-huà, and Tamara. She abruptly stops before Zookeeper, her face still flushed from the long walk. "Who are you talking to?"

"Bataar."

"You told Bataar to shut up?"

He points to his head. "No. That was directed at the fuckin' voice."

"It is one of the little demons in your human DNA. Ignore it."

"Whatever. I want it to go away."

"We will see Ming-huà soon."

"Oh, yeah, the hunchback," he says derisively. "My savior."

Bataar pulls out the last stub of Zookeeper's cigarette and crushes it in an ash tray. "Anything else?" he asks.

"No, thanks buddy," says Zookeeper. "Uh, for everything, you know?"

Bataar flashes a rare smile. "Still want whiskey?"

"Naw, thanks. I need to talk with Lady Oracle."

The boy nods and leaves.

~

Lady Oracle and Zookeeper do not speak for a long while. He breaks the silence. "When do I get to see this bitch?"

Lady Oracle shakes her head as if disappointed in an unruly child. "Zookeeper, you needn't keep up this ridiculous vulgarity. It is beneath you. Any man who can recite Shakespeare needn't revert to gutter language. Not only that, your entire behavior is beneath your power."

"What is this power you keep talking about? I mean, I know how to manipulate stupid people, but that's nothing special."

"Oh, Zookeeper, if you only knew! The power you exercise on 'stupid people', as you call them, is merely the tip of an iceberg. The vast bulk of your power remains submerged."

"Ha! I'm just waiting for a Titanic to sink!"

"That's just it, Zookeeper. Your default view of life is one of brutal struggle, violence, and death."

Zookeeper smiles sardonically. "Well, ain't that the way life is? Natural selection, Lady Oracle. This *God* crap you keep talkin' about is a ruse. It's survival of the fittest."

Lady Oracle moves her eyes across his armless stumps. "How are you doing on that score?"

"Winners and losers," he sulks.

"Have you ever experienced joy?"

"What's that?"

"Only suffering?"

"More or less. Screwing a woman, jacking off, drinking—there have been moments." He looks at his stumps and his expression reflects seething fury. "Suffering! Is there no pity sitting in the clouds that sees into the bottom of my grief! Suffering is my boon companion. You nailed it. I said I suffer, more or less. Well, lately, more!"

"What if you could help stop suffering?"

"Not possible."

"True, not all suffering, but what if you could prevent unnecessary suffering?"

"Still not possible."

"Let me ask you a question."

"Shoot."

"Do you believe your two friends—Pepper Spray and Amygdala—have caused others to suffer?"

"Sure as shit have."

"Can they still cause suffering to others now, without arms?"

Zookeeper scoffs, "Sure as fuck be a hell of a lot more difficult!"

"So, the incident at the crack house—did it prevent greater suffering in the future in exchange for inflicting lesser suffering in the present?"

Zookeeper mulls this over. "I don't know. Can't read the future."

"Yes, you do know. And yes, you can read."

"No."

"Yes. Why do you know? Because you know Pepper Spray and Amygdala. You know what they're capable of with arms, and you know what they are not capable of without them."

"Look, if you so all-fired keen about preventing suffering, why not just kill them? Cut to the chase. Eliminate the middle-man. In the long run, that would have caused less suffering, because I can fuckin' *God* damn assure you, they are suffering now. Just like me. And it's a long, drawn-out suffering, like torture."

He hears his inner voice burst out in a deep, coital moan of pleasure. "Jesus Christ!" he mutters under his breath.

"*God* liked that description," says Lady Oracle.

"Okay, enough of that *God* stuff. It scares the shit outta me. Anyway, you haven't answered my question. Why not just kill them and get it the fuck over with?"

"You know the answer to that."

"Let me guess; bleeding heart."

"No; redemption through suffering."

Zookeeper's face glows with excitement. "Ha! You just contradicted yourself! No redemption without suffering? So how can it be you want to eliminate suffering? That would screw up your whole premise."

"Not at all," says Lady Oracle calmly. "Redemption for those who cause suffering, not those who are the victims of suffering. Eliminate the ability of those who unnecessarily inflict suffering to do it, then you eliminate the need for redemption."

"In other words, if you don't cause suffering, there's no need for redemption?"

"Correct. Suffering by non-intentional, non-directed means—fire, disease, flood, predation, famine—will continue. But what of suffering by intentional, directed means—murder, war, rape—what if that ended?"

"Impossible."

"True, that is what *He* banks on to feed *His* addiction. What if some new, inexplicable power arises that stops intentional, directed suffering?"

Zookeeper laughs mockingly. "By removing the arms of all those millions who inflict suffering on others?"

"Yes, figuratively." Lady Oracle stares at him unblinking.

"You're mad! There will always be at least psychologically-induced suffering!"

"That is the next step."

"To what?"

"Erasure of the human race as we know it."

Stunned at this completely absurd statement, Zookeeper looks upon Lady Oracle as a woman needing to be institutionalized. "So, a pathetic ex-junkie with no arms and a kind hunchback with no clue will change humanity? You really are fuckin' crazy!"

"True, but so are you and the hunchback."

Zookeeper hears the voice stirring ominously.

Lady Oracle leans forward, eyes sharp like a bird of prey. "Look, Zookeeper, you are an intelligent young mutant with untapped power who has suffered much and, in the process, has abused your mind and body in the most wasteful and tragic of ways. Therefore, you have mutilated the pristine core of your power. Think back, over two hundred thousand years ago. Think! You were there, in the genes of a woman who gave birth in Africa. Out of her womb came the first modern human. Out of Ming-huà's womb will come . . . something similar, and yet something not. After many, many false starts, the birth of this child has been carefully arranged over multiple generations. Multiple generations of people considered mad. People who simply needed nurturing and protection from an uncomprehending world bent on destroying them, or burying them in institutions."

Zookeeper chuckles. "All this trouble just to end up creating another generation of fucked-up crazy!"

Lady Oracle stares at him unfazed. "It has already begun. It began many generations ago; it began two hundred thousand years ago."

"Yeah, and only a few hundred thousand generations to go! Fuck, don't you get it?"

"Look around you, Zookeeper. Tell me what you see? Fancy apartments, high-rises, electricity, automobiles, jet airplanes, computers, men on the moon. Which of these miracles of science do you think those first humans, living brutal, savage lives, anticipated? What if you tried to tell them in their own language? I can only imagine the looks they would give you."

Zookeeper remains silent, but shakes his head doubtfully.

Lady Oracle continues. "You may be among the first ancestors of a new race of humans."

"But they won't be human anymore," he says.

Lady Oracle says with chilling finality, "No, they won't."

~

Zookeeper decides to stop objecting to these nonsensical notions. He will go along with the madness and use these wackos for his own purposes. Let them indulge in whatever fantasies make them happy. As long as they feed him, give him booze and cigarettes, wipe his ass, and provide him a place to crash, he'll stick . . . at least until he gets his shot at the hunchback. He is convinced that Lady Oracle lies, and that the hunchback really has the power to replace his arms.

You are right, she lies! screams his voice. **She lies! Kill her!** Zookeeper shudders and calls Bataar.

He appears from nowhere. "Yes?"

"Get me a whiskey, okay, kid?"

Bataar hesitates and looks at Lady Oracle. She nods.

Lady Oracle watches Bataar leave to fetch the whiskey, then turns to Zookeeper. "It is a demon created by your own human DNA," she says firmly. "Metaphorically speaking, that voice is a distorted interpretation of *God*, and *He* feels threatened again." Unexpectedly, she claps her hands, looks toward the ceiling, and beams. "Good!"

~ *Mother and Daughter Alone* ~

Shortly after Lady Oracle finishes her meeting at the Victorian house and leaves to attend to the impatient Zookeeper, Sy also withdraws, trailing the wake of his burdens up the stairs after him. Ming-huà and her mother are left alone to discuss their problems with a privacy desired by only one of them. More tea is poured.

Ming-huà takes a sip and, as if afraid to wait and weaken, quickly says, "I won't marry him. I won't have anything to do with him, let alone have a child by him. Nothing you can say will make me. Oh, Mama! Let's go back to the island and live a quiet life!"

Tamara stays quiet for a while, then says, "Let me tell you a story. It is the story of a young, beautiful Chinese pianist. Oh, such a pianist! She was asked to marry an American and have a child by him, same as you have been asked."

"I've heard this," Ming-huà says resentfully. "It won't matter."

"Just listen, child. Be patient and let your mother have her say. Now, you can guess the identity of the American in my story; your grandpapa, of course. Like your father, he believed he suffered from schizophrenia. Now, this beautiful Chinese pianist who accompanied him on the quest, Bai Meiying, had great compassion for him, but certainly not love. Not love at all. Oh, Ming-huà, it was much worse than that. For this beautiful Chinese pianist, this Meiying, was also a lesbian, and could never see the American as others wished, including him. Your grandpapa wanted her to love him so much! But there could be no possibility of her agreeing to conceive his child. Absolutely none. Sound familiar?"

"Mama," says an exasperated Ming-huà. "Grandpapa was no Zookeeper!"

Tamara lifts her eyebrows. "How do you know? You know nothing about him! He heard voices, like your papa. Terrible voices. His mental illness scared Meiying terribly, and it made even the idea of marrying him and conceiving his child impossible. As a lesbian also, the thought of it made her physically ill. You are not facing that."

"And what about you, Mama? What did you have to face when they told you to marry Papa and conceive a child?"

"At first, I objected strenuously, but I owed Buandelgereen my very life. Without her, I would have been forced to grow up with your grandmama in a mental insitution in China. Still, I initially refused. I was adamant with Buandelgereen. After all, the man was mentally ill. And, although I am not a lesbian like Meiying, the thought of having sex with him petrified me and made me completely unwilling to go along."

"So, what convinced you?"

"*Her.*"

"Is that all?"

"No, there was much much more. But, now is not the time to go into that."

"Magic caves in the desert?"

"Yes."

"Well, Mama, I have not met *Her*, have not visited any magic caves, and am now confronted by a disgusting man whose violent temperament and brutal ways terrify me. Being schizophrenic would be his least worrisome trait."

"You know, Ming-huà, he looks at you in the same way."

"I am not schizophrenic!"

"No, you only removed both his arms, are a hunchback, and possess powers that terrify him as much as his power terrifies you."

"Okay, neither of us is marriageable material."

"Daughter, you must marry him and conceive this child!"

The vehemence of her mother's words startles Ming-huà and she blurts, "Mama, no! Why?"

"Because not to do so would render all the sacrifices of your parents, your grandparents, and many others, futile!"

"How?"

"Girl, haven't you figured it out? The child you must bear will be unlike any who came before. Its powers, male or female, will far surpass your grandparents, your parents, and yourself. This power has been carefully nurtured and protected. By doing so, it has increased in potency through the generations."

"But—"

"No, daughter! You must go through with this! The future of the planet and all living things depend upon it. I will not have all those lives that went before wasted because of your squeamishness, and that includes my own life. Lady Oracle tells me this boy, this Zookeeper, is not who you think he is. Trust me, she knows. He is actually quite remarkable himself. It is your duty to obey, and it is imperative that you find in him the goodness he possesses. Your father, I discovered, was good. A good man. A haunted man, like Zookeeper, but at the core, someone quite different from the run-of-the-mill person. You will discover Zookeeper to be similarly worthwhile. Besides which, you owe him. Always remember, it was you who took off his arms."

"But that—"

"No! Do you want all your friends on the island, all life on Earth, to have no future? Do you want this catastrophe to come about simply because you mistakenly find this man frightening, or disgusting? Ming-huà dear, you both need each other, and the rest of life needs both of you together. The result will be a crucial step to salvation for all of us—for all living things."

Ming-huà's eyes widen in amazement. "You're saying that the entire human race must be replaced?"

"Exactly, replaced by a superior, more empathetic species—the descendents of your union with Zookeeper."

Ming-huà buries her face in her hands and sobs.

Chapter Nine

A Fatal Flaw

Zookeeper Rebels

"It's been three fuckin' days since you told me I would see the hunchback," Zookeeper complains to Lady Oracle. "When do I see her? I mean—shit or get off the pot."

"Her name is Ming-huà. You will see her when I say so."

Zookeeper has a sardonic glint in his eyes. "Got a problem with your plan, Lady Oracle?"

"She is not ready."

"Can't blame her. But I'm ready."

"You can help."

"How?"

"Perform major surgery on your personality. Connect with the better part of your soul and jettison the rest. There is a very worthwhile person inside you—let it out. If you do, then the sooner life will get easier, and the sooner your power will fully bloom."

"You keep talkin' about this power of mine. Well, what do you think it is? I mean, shit, it must be a hell of a lot more than I think it is, so what is it?"

"Do you see this object?" Lady Oracle holds up a stoshell.

"Yeah, I've been wondering about that."

Suddenly, she throws it at Zookeeper's head. He ducks and it sails harmlessly past.

"Ming-huà would have made it disappear before it hit her. You anticipated the throw and ducked. Two different kinds of power."

"Shiiit! Anyone would have ducked."

"No, I threw it very fast. An average person, even an athlete, would have been hit. You don't know it, but you read my mind and reacted before it was thrown."

"You're telling me I can read minds? That I'm a fuckin' mutant like the hunchback?"

"Yes, but you have wasted the power and corrupted it with drugs. It is like a withered muscle, slack and next to useless. It will require intensive therapy to rebuild. Are you willing?"

"First, I want my arms reattached!" he shouts.

"That can never be."

"Well then, take your bullshit theories and stick them—" Zookeeper abruptly stops, remembering his plan to go along with their madness until he can reach the hunchback. "Oh, well . . . maybe you're right. I always felt I had a certain power to influence people. Yeah, you're right. Help me." He hopes his words sound sincere enough.

Lady Oracle smiles. "You may be able to read minds, but you are terrible at reading mine. What am I thinking right now?"

"I don't know."

She grabs his shirt front and pulls him forward. "You do! Think! If you cannot tell me, then you are out on the street! No use to me!"

"I don't know!"

Lady Oracle stares deep into his eyes. "Calmly, now. Think."

Images fly through his head. Crazy images. Images of deserts and caves and jungles and iron doors and *Goddess* statues; a mishmash of exotic fragments. None make any sense. But then the fragments suddenly come together—a broken mirror run backwards in time—becoming whole. He sees Lady Oracle clearly in the mirror.

"You're thinking I'm a liar, a cheat, a thief—a fool who has the audacity to think he can so easily deceive you. You know I'm lying about wanting help. You know I want to use you. You know I want to use hunchback."

"Yes," replies Lady Oracle. "All that is easily surmised. Now go deeper—deeper!"

"You know I think you're lying about the hunchback's inability to return my arms. You know I've often thought of murdering you, if I could. You know I think you are insane."

"Too easy. Deeper!"

Zookeeper shudders, locked in the grip of the mesmerizing mirror that is Lady Oracle's mind. "You think I'm worth something. You think that underneath my façade, I have extraordinary powers which have yet to be freed. You think that I'm worth the aggravation and the effort. You think my power can be used for good purposes. You think I'm destined to be with the hunchback and conceive a child with her."

"And?"

"And you think I will cease to exist if your plan fails."

"Correct."

As if snapping out of a hypnotic trance, Zookeeper quavers and shakes his head to clear it, muttering under his breath, "Well then, I must make sure your plan succeeds."

~

Lady Oracle excuses herself. Zookeeper sits for a while feeling the worst kind of dread. There will be no fooling this woman, no deception. She sees through him as clearly as one sees through a window. Never has he been in such an exposed position; naked and helpless before her searching mind. His one thought now is not that of revenge, or acquiring advantage, or even of comfort, but of flight. He wants to run out the door and flee back to the crack house, to submit to others and fill his body with enough drugs to find oblivion. That is where he belongs. In reading Lady Oracle's mind, he realizes she is not lying about the hunchback. His arms are gone for good. Now there's nothing left but to pour the strongest drugs he can find into his body. And then. . . .

"That is not a good idea, Zookeeper," says Lady Oracle, appearing at the doorway. She glides into the room and sits across from Zookeeper. "Not a good idea at all."

"How did you know . . . ?" His head sinks. "Never mind."

"Tomorrow we go to see Ming-huà."

This news stirs no joy in Zookeeper. "What's the point now?"

"Remember? Salvation?"

"I need a whiskey."

"No, not this time. You can wait. If you prefer not to wait so you can fill your body with drugs, the front door is unlocked. If you leave, no one will stop you."

Zookeeper glares fiercely but keeps his mouth shut.

"Tomorrow morning, if you are still here, we leave after breakfast at nine o'clock. If you are gone—" She shrugs.

The next morning, Zookeeper is gone.

Lady Oracle views his absence with her typical nonchalance.

"He'll be back," she remarks aloud.

~ *Ming-huà's Decision* ~

That night, Sy, Lady Oracle, Tamara, and Ming-huà all sit together in the ante-room of the Victorian house gloomily silent. Outside, the swollen San Francisco fog rolls in from the dark night and presses its wet obesity against the windows. Zookeeper's disappearance has been discussed, but now there seems nothing more to say. Suddenly, Sy jumps up and dances a jig. "Look! I know what you've said, but just let me go get him! Getting him back here will be easy!"

"No, Sy," says Lady Oracle resignedly. "He is gone."

"He's only gone if we let him go!" exclaims Sy.

Ming-huà notices her mother ignoring Scarecrow and staring at her.

"Dear daughter, you can go back to the island now," says Tamara. "There is nothing holding you here any longer."

"And you, mama?"

"I return to the place from which I came."

"Can I go with you?"

"No, dear."

Ming-huà looks down. "I know that." She thinks of her squirrel friend scolding from his perch in the branches of a Douglas fir.

Lady Oracle stands abruptly. "I have to go."

Everyone mumbles their goodbyes and silence again descends on the group. Now Sy rises slowly from his chair, his movements uncertain, drained of purpose. He walks out of the room without a word, as if something inside him has quietly come undone.

Tamara watches him leave, then turns to Ming-huà. "Well, daughter, this will be our last evening together."

"Oh, mama, must you leave so soon? We haven't had enough time."

Tamara smiles enigmatically. "Time is plastic, bending this way and that, even bending back upon itself. We will visit with each other again, but I must return to my own . . . duties."

Ming-huà wants to ask about the nature of her duties, but some inner warning stops the words before they leave her lips.

"Duty. . . ." her mother repeats. "I must also go to bed." She chuckles. "The older I get, the more easily I tire. Goodnight, dear." She kisses her daughter and, on the way out of the room, picks up a stoshell, turning it in her hand as if it was a strange object she had never before seen. "Life is indeed a mystery."

Ming-huà rises and walks her to the foot of the stairs. "Good night, Mama. Sleep well."

"Thank you, dear."

As Ming-huà watches her mother ascend the stairs, she makes up her mind.

Tamara stops halfway up and looks back at Ming-huà. "Good! You will not regret it!"

The next morning, Ming-huà has already left for the crack house by the time Sy and Tamara meet downstairs for breakfast.

~ *At the Crack House* ~

Upon his return to the crack house, Zookeeper is greeted rudely by Angel Cake.

"Well, look who the fuckin' cat dragged in!" he exclaims.

Zookeeper ignores the tone. "I need a place to crash."

"Well," says Angel Cake imperiously, "Find a corner with soft garbage to lie on. I have your old sanctum room. Remodeled it, too. Got rid of the fuckin' books. Did that bitch Lady Clitoris give you bread?"

"No."

"Shiiit. What you gonna do?"

"Stay here. Get myself pumped with crack."

"Not if you don't contribute. Go back to that bitch and get money, man, else you ain't welcome. You ain't Zookeeper anymore, you is just kept—another kept addict." Angel Cake laughs at his own joke. "Now *you* is an exhibit!"

Zookeeper stares into space, listening to the voice demanding he kill Angel Cake.

Surveying Zookeeper's two stumps, Angel Cake says, "Guess you in a world of hurt, man. I sympathize, but, shit, we all gotta do what we gotta do to survive. Like you said, survival of the fittest."

"Yeah. What about Pepper Spray and Amygdala?"

"Ain't seen their sorry asses since . . . since when that weird shit went down. Find that hunchback chick?"

"No."

"Find out how she done it?"

"No. Say, man—got any candy? I'm sorely in need."

Angel Cake's face hardens. "So, you lower yourself down to our level, eh? No, man, not unless you got bread. Tell you what I'll do though, you can crash here a couple days for old times' sake, then you gotta go, unless you put the touch on that bitch woman. Cabbage is always good here."

"Thanks," says Zookeeper sarcastically.

"Hey, man, don't blame me for your troubles. Brought 'em on yourself, man, for letting those freaks in to the sanctuary."

"Yeah."

"Poetic justice, man. Now you're a freak. Now, you're one of them."

These words hit Zookeeper hard and reverberate like Quasimodo's bells.

"Yeah," he says submissively.

"Go find your corner," sneers Angel Cake over his shoulder as he walks away.

The stench makes Zookeeper queasy, and he chalks it up to being gone so long breathing fresh air. *Have to get used to it again*, he thinks, and finds himself an unoccupied corner where he lies down on a pile of trash and sleeps.

~

While Angel Cake sits in the sanctum, his feet on the table, peering at a collection of crack chips and rocks, a sky-high junkie who looks like a somnambulant zombie knocks feebly on the door.

"What!"

"Someone at th' front," croaks the zombie.

"Ain't th' cops?"

"Fuck no. Just some hunchback girl."

Angel Cake jumps up. "What?"

"Hunchback girl."

"Shiiiiit!" screeches Angel Cake. "What she want?"

"I dunno . . . ah, go fuck yourself Angel, I'm gone back to my hootch. Ask her yourself, shithead."

Angel Cake is scared. He knows she is the one who somehow made the arms of three people disappear. *Some kind of fuckin' witch*, he thinks. Spurred by the images of that awful day, his fear turns to terror and he hesitates, even considering skipping out the back door, but he hides the rocks and gathers his courage.

"Yeah?" he says at the front door, staring down at the hunchback.

Ming-huà has her scarf pulled over her mouth and nose, and speaks in a muffled voice, "I want to see Zookeeper."

"Shit!" cries Angel Cake anxiously. "You wanna take off his legs now?"

"No. Is he here?" She looks threateningly at his arms.

"Yeah, yeah," says Angel Cake apprehensively, backing away. "He's here."

Ming-huà feels emboldened by his fear. "Show me."

Angel Cake quickly finds where Zookeeper is sleeping, points him out to the hunchback, and scurries back to his safe room. Ming-huà wants to wait for him to wake up, but the smell is making her sick, so she leans over and calls his name. He does not stir. She calls again. Nothing. Finally, unable to stay longer, she makes a last attempt and shakes him awake. Startled, he tries to rise, but lack of arms is still new, and he flops back like a fish out of water. She struggles to help him up and steadies his swaying body.

"Let's go outside and talk," she says urgently, as the stench has now made her nauseous.

"Can you put my arms back on?" asks Zookeeper with the hopeful look of a puppy.

Ming-huà's heart aches for what she has done, but replies simply, "Outside." She hurries him out the front door and down a few blocks, where she knows there is a bench. As they walk, she frequently glances at Zookeeper, and realizes he has a nice face, quite handsome actually. His vulnerability has softened his features and makes him more appealing, and certainly much less frightening. On deeper inspection, the emerging lines in his face project the somber mien of a lonely sufferer. Maternal instinct aroused, Ming-huà is stung by pangs of guilty compassion and spiritual empathy. She notices he keeps his eyes lowered to avoid passers-by gawking at the sight of an armless man.

The instant they sit, Zookeeper again asks, "Can you put my arms back on?"

"No."

"Why not?" he snaps.

"I don't know why not. I've tried."

"Try again."

"Zookeeper, it doesn't work that way."

"Try!"

"I have. My whole life I have tried."

"So, you've done this to other people before?"

Ming-huà lowers her eyes. "Yes."

"How many fuckin' people are running around out there without arms because of you?"

"Zookeeper, you and your friends are the only ones."

"Then what the fuck do you want with me?"

His harsh words frighten her, but she presses on. "To explain."

"Guilty conscience?"

"Yes."

Zookeeper's voice softens. "Why did you do it?"

"Zookeeper, I was just trying to defend Lady Oracle from being hurt. I'm so sorry. I did not think." Tears roll down her cheeks, unimpeded.

Zookeeper seems unmoved. "Look, what do you want? Want me to forgive you? Make you feel better? If you want to feel better, give me some br . . . ah, money, so I can find comfort."

"That's not why I'm here," she says, wiping away the tears.

"Well?"

"I want you to come back with me."

"Hell no! I'm not going back to that crazy-ass woman Lady Oracle!" He shudders and murmurs, "That fuckin' woman scares the hell out of me. She's crazier than you."

"I don't mean back to her place. I mean, come back with me to the house I'm staying at. Let me help you."

He looks at her suspiciously. "Charity?"

Ming-huà ignores his question. "What did Lady Oracle tell you about me?"

"Some shit about us having a kid."

"For what purpose?" Ming-huà asks, though she knows the answer.

"I don't know. Couldn't figure it out. Something about a magical kid who could end suffering . . . just crazy shit like that."

"Yes," Ming-huà sighs. "Crazy to think someone as ugly and misshapen as me could even consider such a thing."

At first, Zookeeper thinks this remark is an invitation to flatter, but his powerful insight tells him she is utterly sincere. In spite of his resistance to gushing "naïve, romantic shit", he sees her for the first time as not fake, or clueless, but someone possessing a deep and profound goodness of a type he has never dared expect to encounter. But this realization scares rather than inspires him. In response, he forces himself to recall his plans to use her for his own purposes.

"You're not so bad," he says.

Ming-huà smiles sadly. "Thank you."

Zookeeper realizes he said the wrong thing. Her melancholy washes over him with such a sweet sorrow that he is anxious to repair the damage.

"Hunchback, I actually think you are quite beautiful." He locks his eyes on hers. "If I could write the beauty of your eyes, and in fresh numbers number all your graces, the age to come would say, 'This poet lies; such heavenly touches ne'er touch'd earthly faces.'" He is shocked to realize his words are spoken with undeniable sincerity.

Ming-huà, with her own powerful faculty, knows his words come from the heart. She blushes and says, "First things first. My name is Ming-huà. I understand your real name is Matthew Weston. May I call you Matthew?"

He laughs acerbically. "No, no! That name is *verboten*! I'm Zookeeper. Forever Zookeeper." He pauses. "Ming-huà—did I say it right?"

"Yes, perfectly. So, will you?"

"Will I?"

"Come with me."

Zookeeper mulls over his options. A crack house full of junkies and filth, or a nice house with Ming-huà? The decision is a no-brainer.

"Yes, I will. But, Ming-huà, you know I need help with . . . personal things. Do you have anyone who performs that sort of service?"

"I am perfectly willing to—"

"No!" he cries. "Not you! No. I would be too . . . embarrassed."

"But—"

"Absolutely not. If that's the case, then I'm going back to the crack house."

Ming-huà thinks aloud. "Maybe we could borrow Bataar's services."

"That's the ticket! That kid is amazing. I'll feel more comfortable with him wip—I mean, helping me."

"Then let's go," says Ming-huà cheerfully. "Do you need anything at the crack house?"

"Not a damn thing—except distance."

As they walk, Zookeeper feels inexplicably happy. For the first time since he lost his arms, there is some light pulsing dimly through the dark night. He feels his spirits rise, Phoenix-like.

In this jocular mood, he quips, "Well, what the hell. You and me are gonna change the world. None of these rubes around us knows they are passing two saviors. Ha ha! What a joke!"

"Zookeeper," says Ming-huà. "I do not believe it is a joke."

"You don't really buy all that shit Lady Oracle is selling, do you?"

Ming-huà suddenly chuckles, taking Zookeeper by surprise.

"What?" he asks.

"There are more things in heaven and earth, Horatio, than are dreamt of in your philosophy."

Zookeeper roars with laughter. "You got me there, hunchback!"

Ming-huà frowns.

Zookeeper stops abruptly. "Oh, shit! You don't mind me calling you that, do you?"

"No, that's not it," she says. "I was just thinking how much you and I both have to learn."

"You got that right. Listen, Ming-huà, what do you get outta this gig really? I mean, I get a place to stay, food, all that shit, but you?"

Ming-huà cannot answer that question, even to herself. She had come to Zookeeper with no plan beyond convincing him to return so he could be cared for. But the idea of them actually getting together, let alone having a child together, is a thought she will not allow access to her conscious mind as even a remote possibility.

"It is enough that I know you will be cared for," she says.

Again, his insight tells him that Ming-huà's words are reliably true, but his old scars and prejudices will not admit such a possibility. There has to be some angle he is leaving out. Maybe she just wants to have a kid, and he's the only one she could ever hope to have sex with. But when he looks at her face and scans her body, he sees a very beautiful woman, and knows his notion is absurdly fallacious.

"Ming-huà, do you actually think we should have a baby together for these people?" he asks in the form of disbelief.

Again she blushes, this time all the way down her neck. "Of course not," she whispers.

"What?"

"Of course not."

Zookeeper feels oddly let down by her response. "Don't get me wrong, I mean, you're pretty and all that, but . . . but the whole idea seems too weird, even for someone as weird as me."

"Yes, I agree."

Something in her answers make him uncomfortable. "Come on, Ming-huà, tell me the truth. Could you ever conceive a situation where we could . . . get together?"

"Yes," she says boldly.

This takes Zookeeper as much by surprise as it does her.

"Really?" It is a silly reply, but the best his confused brain can produce.

"Yessss," she says, tentatively. "But I think that is one of the reasons why I want you to return with me. If you do not, then neither of us will ever find the answers."

"Answers?"

"We will never see *Her*."

"Oh, come on Ming-huà, now you're sounding like Lady Oracle!"

As they walk, Ming-huà speaks more to herself than to Zookeeper, trying to sort it all out in her mind before they reach the house. "The truth lies very deep in the past, even before my ancestors, my grandfather, my grandmother, my mother, my father, even before them. *She* holds the key. I must see *Her* to understand, just as my parents and grandparents did. I cannot do that without you."

"Why?"

"It is the plan . . . you and I. If not the plan, then no *Her*."

Zookeeper shakes his head. "But that's crazy."

Ming-huà says nothing.

"Ming-huà, look at me. I can barely walk. I can't wipe my own ass or put on my own trousers. Christ! Why do you even look at me?"

"Hush!"

"Okay, okay. Let's change the damn subject. Jesus, how much farther?"

"Not too far. Up that hill."

"Oh, shit, that's fuckin' steep."

"Yes."

"Forget I said that. So—where are you from?"

"All over. Mainly from a beautiful island where I lived a beautiful life with a beautiful. . . . "

"A beautiful?"

"Never mind, you'd only laugh at me."

"No, I wouldn't."

"Sometimes you are cruel like that."

Zookeeper falls silent.

After walking a while longer, Zookeeper says, "Let's sit on that bench. I'm pooped."

"Okay."

They sit for a few moments, giving him time to gather his courage. "Ming-huà, I'm crude and cruel. Actually, can be quite vicious. My mother taught me to be prepared to say or do anything to get what you want. Beg, borrow, steal, kill. You're from a different world." Tears well in his eyes. "I . . . I just don't understand you, or Lady Oracle, or any of this shit. Why me? That's what I can't get through my noggin. Why me?"

"I don't know. Let's find out."

"Tell me more about this *Her* you keep harping at."

"Wait till we get to the house. Save your breath. One last big hill and we're there."

"What's that weird guy's name again?"

"Sy." She chuckles. "Sometimes I call him Scarecrow."

"Yeah, fits. What's he gonna think?"

Ming-huà just laughs. "You'll see."

When they reach the front door, Ming-huà finds it locked. She knocks and Sy cracks it open. At once he throws it open wide and hugs Ming-huà. "Thank *Goddess* you're back!" he cries.

Ming-huà looks around. "Where's mama?"

Sy makes a whistling sound. "Gone! Gone while you were away, like the ghost she is. Said to tell you she would be waiting for you at another place and time. A ghost woman!"

He looks over Ming-huà's shoulder and sees a ragged man standing in the doorway—a man with no arms.

Chapter Ten

Stormy Weather

Armless Maneuvers

~ Greetings and Salutations ~

Zookeeper stares in wonder from his seat on the couch as Sy dances jig after jig and whoops like a madman.

"How'd you do it, Ming-huà?" he shouts. Mohammed to the mountain! All is well! All is well! I'm going to call Lady Oracle. That cagey old fox knew this would happen!"

"Not now, Scarecrow!" scolds Ming-huà. "It's late and we need rest, don't we Zookeeper?"

"Shiit! Right now, I need a fuckin' whiskey and a smoke!"

Ming-huà glares.

"Sorry. Old habits die hard. Hey, Scarecrow—or Sy—or whatever your damn name is, got some whiskey? Prithee?"

Sy places his hand over his heart. "A man after my own heart! Do I have whiskey? Can I dance?"

He rushes to the cabinet and pours a row of shot glasses.

Ming-huà laughs and takes a glass to Zookeeper. He rolls his head back and opens his mouth greedily. She hesitates.

"Give it to me, baby!" he cries. "Straight shot straight down the hatch! Do it!"

She empties the contents into his throat. Zookeeper swallows, then smacks his lips. "Ahhhhh!" he bellows in pleasure.

After this ritual has emptied all the shot glasses, Zookeeper is flushed and garrulous. "Hey, Sy good buddy!"

"Yes, my friend?"

"Tell me about this chick Ming-huà keeps talking about . . . this *Her* person."

Sy's demeanor instantly transforms from clown to raging prophet of Biblical proportions. "*She*? *She* is *Goddess*! The Great Deity who dares to challenge *God*! That old addicted bastard of a *God* trembles before *Her* wrath at *His* abusive ways! And both of you are tiny parts of the Great Plan, as am I."

Ming-huà, already having some knowledge of this Great Plan and accustomed to Sy's usual histrionics, remains meekly silent, but Zookeeper is drunk enough to flap his tongue in derision. "Shit, man! You're just as crazy as Lady Oracle! Ha, ha! Well, I'll play along. Just keep the whiskey flowing and ol' Zookeeper will be right there with you, buddy!"

Embarrassed by Zookeeper's outburst, Ming-huà stares at the floor.

But Sy leaps backward startling everyone, and shouts in outrage, "You scum! You dare . . . !?"

He suddenly grabs a small bronze statue from the end-table and throws it as hard as he can at Zookeeper's head.

Before a shocked Zookeeper has time to react, it disappears inches from his face.

Stunned silence.

Instantly sober, Zookeeper quickly turns his astonished eyes on Ming-huà who meets his gaze with a placid expression.

Sy surveys the scene, relaxed and smiling. letting the moment sink in so a shocked Zookeeper can adequately recover his scrambled senses. He then says in a genial manner, "You see, Zookeeper, it is best to keep your mockery to yourself, or else next time I will do something similar without your protectoress nearby."

Zookeeper's first reaction after his astonishment fades is to suspect a set-up, but when he sees Ming-huà's face, sad and weary, looking at him with relief, he knows the truth and it burns deep into his heart.

"I'm sorry, Zookeeper," she says. "I didn't know Scarecrow would do that. You've had too much to drink, and your lesser self came out a bit. My Scarecrow friend here is very fond of sudden, unexpected, and dramatic demonstrations."

"My *God*!" sputters Zookeeper. "You really . . . I mean . . . it actually . . . Jesus! . . . to see it again! Fuck me!" He looks at Ming-huà in awe. "Christ! You ain't human, girl! Christ almighty!"

"She saved you," says Sy gently. "I would show some respect."

"I . . . I know, Sy. It just takes time to get used to . . . to her power, you know? My *God*, Ming-huà! You are . . . are . . . magnificent! The icy precepts of respect have frozen in my veins!"

"That's better, young man," says Sy. "Shakespeare in a pinch. There is indeed hope for you! Now, it's time to go to work."

"Huh?" grunts Zookeeper.

"It's time to get to work! To be useful to yourself and to the rest of the world, you must learn to use your feet."

Zookeeper shakes his head, thoroughly confused. "Feet?" he repeats.

"Come over here," says Sy.

Zookeeper stands next to Sy whose computer screen is open and displays a website showing armless people performing a variety of activities one would think impossible without arms.

"You see?" says Sy. "Driving a car, eating, cooking, playing music, writing, painting, dancing—all using only their feet! You can do just about anything!"

Zookeeper experiences his second revelation of the day watching the videos.

"How do I learn?" he asks.

"By doing," replies Sy with a little jig. "However, I have a close friend who was born without arms. He will visit tomorrow and help you get started."

"Why are you doing all this?"

Sy laughs. "Still so suspicious? We must remove your distrust just as your arms have been removed—painlessly."

"So I'm part of this Grand Plan you all have, right?"

"Correct."

"I still don't get what my contribution will be, other than"—he looks diffidently at Ming-huà— "sorry babe, sperm."

"If you actually think you know what your contribution will be, you would not be here because you would not be contributing."

Zookeeper wrinkles his brow. "I think I understand what you just said, but it doesn't answer my question. Since I don't know what my contribution will be, why don't you tell me?"

"You won't know until we have completed our journey."

"What journey?" asks Zookeeper.

"Yes, what journey?" echoes Ming-huà.

"Why, the journey we three, maybe four, are gonna take."

"To?"

Sy assumes his best operatic pose. "A quest. Yes, Ming-huà, a quest, like your parents and grandparents. The same quest. A quest to finish the quest."

Ming-huà is struck dumb, but Zookeeper plows ahead. "Where to, goddamn it!"

"To a different place and time."

"What the fuck does that mean?"

"It means, Zookeeper, that we cannot even consider going on this quest until you learn to use your feet. So, the quest starts tomorrow with your first lesson."

Zookeeper wants to object, curse, threaten, stomp out, throw something—but within his mind, the voice stirs and thunders with ominous vibrations of unmistakable threat. A low, rumbling earthquake warning, **No, no, no, never, never, never....**

Zookeeper turns pale and feels faint.

Sy shouts, "Ignore *Him*! It is only *God* trying to frighten you. Ignore *Him* and embrace your destiny!"

Zookeeper jolts—something deep within him snaps loose. A break, sudden and final, severs the weight he's been dragging: the haze, the filth, the false bravado. It falls away. What remains is clean, fierce, unburdened. A self he had forgotten rises, clear and unstoppable.

"Yes, yes!" he shouts as if he were at some evangelical come-to-Jesus meeting, except the reverse. "Go to hell, *God*!" he roars. After this emotional release, Zookeeper collapses onto the couch and says in a hoarse voice, "I need whiskey, Scarecrow."

~ *Toe Maps* ~

The next day Zookeeper spends hours with Ben Solokov, a man born with no arms. Solokov demonstrates amazing dexterity by using his toes for a variety of tasks, and explains how the brain will remap its neural structure to signal organized commands to the feet and toes just as it normally does to the hands and fingers.

"But you were born this way, man!" objects Zookeeper. "You've had your whole life to adjust. Look at me. This shit just happened and I can't even think of making my toes work the way yours do."

Ben shakes his head. "No, you're wrong. I have helped many armless people right after they suffered accidents, and it did not take nearly as long as you think. It just takes practice. It just takes doing, over and over, till the brain remaps. Look, we'll start with simple exercises."

Zookeeper complains, but reluctantly tries, at Solokov's direction, to manipulate his toes in completely novel ways. They are uncooperative. Somewhere, deep within him, a power begins to stir. Dormant for a long time, his stubbornly creative nature asserts itself, and the unused potential of his true capabilities emerges.

"Here, try and pick this up," says Ben. "Do it like this." He curls his toes around the handle of one of Ming-huà's hair brushes, leans his head down, bends his leg at an impossible angle, and combs his hair.

Zookeeper whistles. "Shit, I couldn't do that in a million years!" In spite of his protestations, it's clear he wants to try.

"Oh, yes you can. I've been watching you. Get some practice . . . no, not some—practice all the time. It'll take hours, not years. Now, try it."

Zookeeper makes a clumsy attempt. He fails.

"Try again."

He fails again, cursing all the way.

Ben chuckles. "I know how you feel. Again."

And so it goes.

For days.

For weeks.

For months . . . of agonizing progress. But progress he makes. His skills develop in fits and starts, but to the amazement of everyone, Zookeeper perseveres with a stoicism that arises from some deep well of inner strength, surprising even himself.

One day, Ben pulls Sy aside. "That kid is amazing. Never seen anyone make such progress so fast."

Sy winks knowingly. "It's his power."

"Power?"

"Yeah, power. Hard to explain, but he's special."

"Well," says Ben. "Don't know about that, but he sure learns quickly."

"That's why he's here," quips Sy, who dances a jig in celebration.

"Why is he here?" asks Ben.

"Ben, that one is not for you to know. Suffice to say, he's here for the same reason the hunchback is here."

"Which is?"

"To save the world."

Ben takes a moment to soak in that statement. "Well, that's a big task. He gonna do it with his toes?"

"Ben, wait and see. That's enough talking. You've been a big help. Someday, historians will write about your role in all this."

"All what?"

"Never mind. Just keep doing what you're doing."

And Ben he does, with Bataar as his constant assistant helping with the most thankless of chores. Over many months, Zookeeper is able to perform most of the daily tasks he needs to function. Then, one day, Ben doesn't return, and Zookeeper is left to his own devices. The next day, Lady Oracle pays a visit.

~ *Ming-huà Struggles* ~

During the time that Zookeeper has striven to develop his skills, Ming-huà has undergone an extended internal dialogue, alternately berating herself for continued collaboration with Sy and Lady Oracle to implement the Grand Plan, and justifying her participation in such a potentially violent scheme. In the process, she has suffered a crisis of confidence in her own ability to recognize right from wrong. Wild swings in her mood have characterized this process.

Recognizing it for what it is, Sy has left her alone to work it out.

Ming-huà remembers reading about pilots flying over cities during wartime, dropping bombs on thousands of civilians without having to witness the carnage, and she feels equally disengaged from the damage she inflicts. After all, she never sees blood, just a cauterized, clean nothing where there should be gore and intense physical pain. In fact, she may be in a worse position than the pilots, because she actually witnesses the resulting mental anguish caused by her actions. Somehow, this seems worse than the pilots' situation.

Dwelling on thoughts like these, she often dips into black depression.

Yet . . . yet, on the other hand, the news recently reported a kidnapper being arrested for sexually abusing a little girl. Ming-huà realizes that if she witnessed such an atrocity, she would remove the man's penis, or arms, or legs, without compunction. While dissociating him entirely would be horrifying, simply and painlessly erasing his organ seems the epitome of justice. Or is it? Her life is getting more and more complicated, and she fears her moral compass no longer points true north. No human should be in this position. Human? Is she even that? Were her parents and grandparents human? She is aware of some scheme to replace the human race with Superior Ones. So, is she human or not? If not, is that good or bad? Ming-huà's default position is to think of her difference as bad. Letting her power be developed and used by others has driven her into a daily crisis of self-doubt and uncertainty. In the course of her seeking assurance, she has undergone an intense period of reading about the legal, religious, and philosophical underpinnings of justice.

The subject of vigilantism has particular shaken her. Mob violence and public hangings tear at her conscience.

How can one be both judge and jury? What punishment could ever be fair? How can *she*—a mortal woman—remove parts of people, or erase their existence entirely, and still dare to speak of justice? *What if she is wrong?* What if she misreads the signs, overreacts, or fails to grasp the pain and history behind someone's unforgivable act? Lady Oracle and Sy have given her no guidance. None. And yet they ask everything of her. She is no cloaked executioner sweeping through the night on a steed of vengeance, no faceless arbiter meting out punishment by divine fiat. Or is she becoming that? What right has she? Justice . . . or vigilantism?

She remembers the two men on the island. Gone. Forever. Their families—wives, children—left with nothing but absence. All to save a *fawn*. *A fawn*. Is that enough to justify their annihilation? Shouldn't it be? Or is this the first step down a path to madness?

But the fawn lives, breathes, suffers. It, too, walks this earth. Does it deserve to be tortured without consequence, simply because it belongs to a different species? *Because it lacks the words to cry out?*

One day, lost in this storm of doubt, she finds herself speaking aloud, as if possessed by a voice not entirely her own: "Kant argues, as an extension of his categorical imperative, that all people must act in a morally correct manner at all times. Failure to do so must result in 'just deserts,' and the perpetrator must suffer punishment proportionate to the crime committed." She doesn't know where the words come from, but they explode inside her, filling her heart with a terrible fire. Her mind races to finish the thought: *Is tearing off someone's arms proportionate to attempted murder? Is total dissolution fair punishment for drowning a fawn?*

Has *She*—that silent, unseen Power—crafted Ming-huà to be some kind of *übermensch*, beyond morality? If so, she swears: *she will not become Raskolnikov.* She will not rot beneath the weight of her own self-justified murder.

But is it murder if she acts to protect the innocent? If no one else can—or will?

"No . . . no!" she cries. It's too much. Her heart is breaking under the weight of it all. She is being pulled in two directions—torn between the unyielding, inhuman rigidity of black-letter law and the raw, touching sensitivity of Nature's braille. Back and forth the dialectical underpinnings of her emotional conscience and her cold logic battle within her, each drawing blood, each scoring victories, each suffering defeats.

Behind this furious storm of conscience, her power waits. It does not counsel. It does not judge. It simply waits—for release . . . or for chains. And somewhere, not far from the battlefield of her soul, Scarecrow watches in silence, waiting too, for the verdict only she can deliver.

~ *Anteroom Discussion* ~

Sitting in the anteroom one evening, Ming-huà sips tea while Sy and Zookeeper drink whiskey. Bataar, as always, helps Zookeeper, who has not quite mastered using his feet to lift a cup and drink. He is close, but often spills the liquid while lifting it to his lips, so he insists Bataar help him with whiskey, as it is "too valuable to waste on practice."

Sy sets a mug half full of water on the floor in front of Zookeeper. "Come on, lad!" he booms. "Give it a shot. Got to keep practicing."

Zookeeper is in unusually good spirits. He nods toward Bataar holding a full glass of whiskey and winks. "I'd rather just keep giving shots to my poor, overworked stomach."

"Do it," says Sy with a low warning in his tone.

"All right, all right." Zookeeper wraps both feet around the mug and works it so that his big toe grips the handle. Holding it steady, he carefully lifts his foot over his knee and leans down so his lips can meet the mug being slowly lifted by his foot. Only a little spills as he succeeds in taking a sip. He carefully sets it back on the floor.

"Excellent!" chirps Sy and Ming-huà simultaneously.

"Just before he left, Ben showed me how to open a pop-top beer can with my feet. Once I get this easy shit down, that's my next project."

He gives Bataar the sign, leans his head back, and the Mongol boy carefully pours whiskey down his gullet.

"Aaaahhhh! Hits the spot!"

Sy turns to Bataar. "Pour some whiskey into a beer mug, Bataar. Let's see him do his stuff with a little incentive."

"No, no, no," says Zookeeper. "Not now."

"Yes, yes, yes, now," says Sy. "Do it, Bataar."

The boy fills the mug a quarter full of whiskey and sets it on the floor. Zookeeper sighs, but seems to relish the challenge. As he wraps both feet around the mug and grasps the handle with his big toe, he carefully lifts it over his knee and pauses. "Shit, this fucker is heavy!"

"You can do it," encourages Ming-huà. "Think of the reward."

This time, he doesn't quite make it and the mug is listing to the side where Bataar saves it from spilling the contents.

"Crap!" cries Zookeeper.

Sy waves his arms in dismissal. "Next time. Keep trying. Every day you get better."

"Another shot, would'cha kid?" asks Zookeeper.

Scarecrow turns to Ming-huà. "And how about the weight you've been lifting? Reached your lips yet?"

She assumes a puzzled look, though she assuredly knows what he is driving at. "Sorry?"

"The weight you're carrying. Found a way to lift it and drink from the pure well of serenity?"

"No. I am far behind Zookeeper."

He sets an empty glass before her. "For you, it is not to fill, but to empty."

She looks at it with a knowing suspicion. "Empty what?"

"Your doubts. These concerns of yours have already filled the glass and you are just pouring more on top, so the whole thing is just an overflowing waterfall going down the drain."

"Chinese philosophy, Scarecrow?"

"Absolutely. It is your heritage. Use it. You're wasting your time on Immanuel Kant. Read Zhuang Zi."

"I have."

"Read him again. You are not of their world, Ming-huà. You follow your own Way now, your own Dao. Old Lao Zi had it right; 'the Dao that can be spoken is not the eternal Dao'. Ming-huà, I would also argue that the Dao that can be understood is not the eternal Dao. Don't try to understand."

"But Sy, I have to understand. How can I go on if I don't understand?"

"Remember your squirrel back on the island?"

"Of course."

"He understood."

"How can you say that?"

"Didn't he scold you?"

"Yes, for what I did to those two men."

"No, for hesitating to leave the island and fulfill your destiny."

"That's just nonsense. I mean—"

"The fawn also understood. Still does. Still understands. As we speak, she is happily cavorting in the forest, feeling the sun, enjoying the abundance of fresh grass, full of bounteous life! And a mother now to boot!"

Ming-huà scrutinizes Scarecrow. "And the two men?"

"They are in everything, living or not. The fundamental constituents of their being continue on, diffused throughout the world in a billion different ways."

"Cold comfort to their loved ones."

"Hot comfort to Bambi."

"But—"

Sy interrupts harshly. "No more! You're pouring more useless guilt in a glass already full to the brim. Empty it and let the future have room to grow."

"What is my future, Sy? Removing body parts from the human race?"

"No! The opposite! Removing their tumors. That means their viciousness, their sadism, their blind hatred, bigotry, cruelty. In other words, removing injustice!"

"Removing these things from billions of people?"

"You are the start. The beginning. The ancient mother of mothers in Africa two hundred thousand years ago."

~

"Hey!" cries Zookeeper, well into his cups. "What about the father?"

Sy laughs. "Without the father, there is a dead end."

"Okay, well, if Ming-huà can do all that with her fuckin' power, what can I do to contribute to this Grand Plan of saving humanity?"

"We are not saving humanity," says Sy. "We are changing humanity."

"Evolution?"

"If you wish."

Zookeeper is suddenly quite excited. "Well, shit! Tell *Her* to give me the power to put stuff back on . . . I mean, you know, reassemble the parts Ming-huà removes. She removes bits and pieces from bad people so they are punished; then they see the error of their ways and change and become good little humans; then I step in and replace the parts they lost. You know, it's like your fuckin' yin and yang idea. Perfect! Father takes away and Mother gives back . . . or rather, Mother takes away and Father gives back . . . ah, fuck! You get the picture."

Sy chuckles. "I'll pass that suggestion along to *Her*."

"Do it, man! We've got this nailed! Shit, give me another shot, kiddo! Man am I smart or what?"

Ming-huà shakes her head and looks at Sy. "He has a point. The whole thing is absurd, so one additional absurdity won't hurt."

"You and I both know it doesn't work that way," says Sy. "Maybe two hundred thousand more years into the future and. . . . "

"Shit, I'll wait!" cries Zookeeper. "Just keep the whiskey coming and I'll stick around like some old Egyptian mummy."

In spite of the silly banter, Ming-huà remains conflicted. Words alone cannot allay her fears. To her dismay, she realizes a definitive answer will never come. With power comes burden, and with burden comes doubt, and with doubt comes wisdom. This—at least—is her hope.

Chapter Eleven

Announcements

On to Bigger Things

~ News ~

At breakfast one morning, Sy gives his announcement in the most ostentatious manner. He bangs his spoon against a coffee mug and rises. Ming-huà and Zookeeper, accustomed to his eccentricities, await whatever he has to say with composure.

After clearing his throat numerous times, Sy assumes a solemn demeanor.

"This announcement is one we have all been waiting for. It's time."

The others wait, but he abruptly sits down.

"Okay, I'll play the game," says Zookeeper. "It's time for what?"

"To leave, of course."

"Okay, I'll keep playing. Where to?"

"A place that is many places and a time that is many times."

Zookeeper roars, "Shiiitttt! Quit fuckin' around, man. Tell me straight. Where are we going?"

Ming-huà speaks softly to Zookeeper. "He won't tell you."

"Why the fuck not?"

Sy leaps up and holds an operatic pose. "She's right, I won't tell you. Why? Because I don't know myself."

"Well, you must know something," insists Zookeeper.

"I do know a little. As I said, we are going to many places; we will go to the American desert, to a cave in Mongolia, to a mental institution in China, to a tunnel in Vietnam, to a cemetery in Rhode Island. Furthermore, we will visit these places at different times in the past and future. Does that satisfy you?"

"Sure . . . if it was true," laughs Zookeeper. "Now, where are we really going?"

"We are going into the minds of a thousand people. We are going into the past lives of a thousand people. We are going to the future lives of a thousand people."

"Christ!' Zookeeper grumbles. He looks at Ming-huà. "Do you know what the fuck he's talking about?"

Ming-huà shudders. "Every word he says vibrates in my hump. He speaks the truth." A painful ache encircles her head as if barbed wire were being tightened. The ache quickly penetrates deep inside her brain.

"What truth? We ain't going to all those places!" scoffs Zookeeper.

Sy sits again. "You'll see."

"Where do we go first?" asks Ming-huà.

"You know," he replies.

Again, she shudders. "The desert?"

"Yes."

"My mother. . . . "

"And your father," adds Sy.

"What's the point?" asks Zookeeper, now quite concerned.

"Don't worry, Zookeeper," says Sy. "It will only take a short time to cover thousands of miles, all those countries, and tens of thousands of years past and future. More coffee?"

Ming-huà's headache becomes unbearable. She pushes her coffee cup aside and quietly announces, "I have a bad headache. I must go back to bed with a cold cloth. Sy, when do we leave?"

Scarecrow gives her an enigmatic glance, and says in a clipped voice, "Tomorrow."

"Thank you." She leaves the kitchen abruptly with no further words spoken.

In her wake, Zookeeper looks at Sy quizzically.

In response to his questioning stare, Sy's face darkens. "She suffers. She, who hopes to help ease suffering in others, is herself suffering. We shall see."

"You look worried," says Zookeeper.

"We shall see."

~

The next morning, Ming-huà has disappeared. Sy discovers a note on her bed. It reads: *I am going to the most dangerous parts of town and invite attack. It may take a few days, but I am resolved to avoid using my power regardless of the consequences. I MUST know I can control it, even when provoked. If not, then I will return to the island and live the happy life of a hermit.*

~ *The Fatal Test* ~

The first night Ming-huà sneaks out of the house and sleeps in an alley with other street people, there is no incident. She carries a bedroll, and those around her show no interest in the arrival of another occupant in their narrow domain. A few grunts of acknowledgment are all she receives. The stench is heavy, but the cold San Francisco wind dulls its edge. During the day, she roams the streets, searching for the most neglected corner of the city.

The next night, she finds an alley in even worse condition. Again, nothing of consequence happens. Ming-huà, frustrated, considers returning to the crack house but hesitates. She fears Sy or Lady Oracle might track her there, so she stays. *Maybe I went too far trying to look like I belonged,* she thinks. *Cleaner clothes might've drawn attention.* But it's too late now.

She continues wandering and settles into another alley, filthier than the two before. This time, the stench is dense and unmoving. Only two others share the space—both men, both worn down in different, unsettling ways. It is late afternoon. The shadows stretch across the walls, pushing the alley deeper into darkness. Ming-huà is already there, staking her spot by rolling out her bedroll. The two men sit against the opposite wall, legs out, passing a bottle back and forth. A nearby neon sign flickers on and off, its red glow filling the space with an unnatural rhythm.

Ming-huà feels unease rising in her gut, but forces herself to meet their eyes, daring them with her gaze. The more they drink, the more twisted their voices become. Their words decay into cruelty. Their laughter turns harsh, jagged. Each time they glance her way, they let out a fresh burst of mockery.

Now her fear sharpens. Still, she stays. She watches. She waits.

Then her hump stirs with unmistakable sensation. It is not imagined. These men mean to do her harm. The intention is clear, laced into the heat moving through her spine. They are drunk, volatile, filled with the kind of rage that demands a target. And her body, alone and silent in the corner, is the nearest one.

The men begin to move toward her.

Their steps lack coordination. Their bodies sway. The air around them thickens. The smell hits her before they reach her—a mix of alcohol, sweat, and something more sour, more human.

She pulls herself inward, lowers her body, draws the blanket around her shoulders and up to her neck. But they are close now. She feels the pressure of their presence.

Though their forms are dim in the failing light, her hump registers bursts of intensity—sharp flashes of violent desire rising from whatever is left of their will. One man reaches down and yanks the blanket away. The other circles behind her, fumbling at the buttons of her coat.

She clutches the fabric to her chest, voice firm but controlled. "No."

"Come on, girly!" slurs one of the shadows. His shaky hands jerk her upward.

"Look at this!" cries the other. "A hunchback!"

"Don't matter," slobbers the first. "It's got a pretty face and a wet cunt. Don't give a shit about her back."

Ming-huà gives a sharp kick and momentarily frees herself from their clutches. Now half standing, her back against the wall, she wants to run, but is blocked by the two men. The pulsating red throb from the sign gives the scene an ominous blood-like quality. Reflected in its rhythmic pulse, a knife appears. She feels it pressed against her throat. Both men are now excited, and they renew their fumbling efforts to remove her clothes. Ming-huà briefly struggles, but the blade cuts into her flesh and she stops.

Closing her eyes, she repeats aloud to herself, "Now is the test. Now is the test."

"Shut up, bitch!"

She's jerked fully upright and her pants are pulled down.

Ming-huà whispers, "Now is the test. Now is the test."

She focuses on the pulsing red glow, willing herself not to wish harm to these sad, desperate men.

Increasingly terrified at their frantic efforts, she again closes her eyes. "Now is the test. Now is the test."

They are pulling at her panties. She opens her eyes and is roughly thrown to the ground on her back. One man continues to hold the knife to her throat, the other straddles her, his penis now visible in the throbbing light.

"Now is the test!' she cries, trying to focus on graffiti scrawled in white paint on the opposite wall. Oddly, her hump transmits hunger pangs from a bird perched on the lid of a dumpster squatting in metallic disinterest at the back of the alley.

The man with the knife calls out, "Do it! Do it!"

Ming-huà feels her legs roughly spread apart.

"Do it! Fuck her good!"

In a flash, the knife is gone.

The hand holding it is gone.

The other man's erect penis and scrotum are gone.

All three figures are frozen in a bizarre tableau of horror. Only the pulsations of light convey movement.

Then, the screams. The blind terror. The running. She is alone.

The light throbs in disregard of the ugly violence that just happened, providing an almost soothing beat to the now incongruously quiet alley.

You are The Daughter. A voice in her head. Its first appearance. She knows the owner of the voice. Now, she knows she is as insane as the others. Or, perhaps. . .
.

"Is there no escape from this? I don't want to be the daughter, whatever that means."

No escape. Go back to Scarecrow and do as Lady Oracle says. You have just wasted your power on two fools unnecessarily.

"They were once innocent boys."

There is no innocence.

"Even in the womb?"

Especially in the womb.

Ming-huà feels the tears roll down her cheek. "Then there's no escape," she mutters in resignation and defeated acceptance.

There is no escape. It is your fate.

"No. There is always hope. Lady Oracle told me there is an old saying: fate starves at probability's door."

Ha, ha! Yes! You are learning, Daughter. Now, go back unless you want others to suffer as those two are.

~

It's early morning when Ming-huà walks through the front door, to be greeted by Sy, Zookeeper, and Lady Oracle. Her face speaks volumes, and Lady Oracle says simply, "Go to bed. We will leave in two days, after you have a chance to recover. Meanwhile, stay in bed. Food will be brought."

Without replying, Ming-huà slowly ascends the steps to her room.

~ *A Conversation* ~

Two days pass. Ming-huà can't get out of bed. She suffers from a complete breakdown; raging fever; conscience in freefall; unquenchable desire for the liberating painlessness of death. Sy, Lady Oracle, and Bataar all take turns at her bedside. Visiting doctors have no solutions. Zookeeper, now facing his own existential crisis, has withdrawn to an inner sanctuary invulnerable to penetration by anyone. Ming-huà's condition declines with such inexorable rapidity that Sy is obliged to suggest the unthinkable to Lady Oracle one morning. He says, "I fear we must return her to the island or else all is lost."

Lady Oracle glares with imperious severity. "Foolish man! Once back on that island, she will never leave!"

Sy shakes his head sadly. "Then, she dies."

"No! Call Zookeeper. I want to see him."

"Why?"

"He's our only hope."

"But he refuses to come out of his room except to eat."

"I know, but he will not refuse me!"

Sy disappears and returns after a long time with a recalcitrant Zookeeper in tow, whose mood for days has not strayed beyond snarling resentment and silent fear.

As soon as he sits, Lady Oracle admonishes him, her mental finger figuratively wagging at him like a strict mother scolding a naughty child.

"Do you know what will happen to you if Ming-huà leaves?"

"Yeah."

"Then we need your help."

Zookeeper scoffs. "She's practically on her deathbed. What do you want me to do?"

"Get in touch with the one reason we have taken so much trouble with you."

"What's that?"

"The seed of empathy and kindness that has yet to fully germinate in your barren soil."

"I feel so badly for her!"

"No! You're terrified for her and for yourself. You love her and are afraid to learn she does not reciprocate. We know you weep for her, Zookeeper. We know!"

"What do you want me to do?"

"Go to her."

"And?"

"Go to her. Now."

"If I don't?"

"She will be gone, and so will you."

"Let her go back to her island. That's the best thing for her."

"Even if it means you're on your own?"

"I can manage."

"Well, Zookeeper, that's a fine sentiment, but that's not what I mean when I said she'll be gone."

Zookeeper feels a sudden and frightening chill. "I'm waiting," he says.

Lady Oracle shakes her head. "You know. If she does not resolve this crisis now, she will die. The power inside her is now beyond her ability to direct, or ours."

"Who says she'll die? Send her back to the island. She can recover there."

Lady Oracle stares at him in heartfelt pity. "She will die, Zookeeper."

His extraordinary power can leave no doubt of her sincerity.

Shaken, he mutters, "What do I say to her?"

"Zookeeper, you will know what to say when you say it."

"I don't—"

"Go!" Lady Oracle commands.

And so he does.

~

"Ming-huà, are you in?"

"Go away, Zookeeper," she says weakly.

"Come on, I want to talk to you. Open the door."

"Leave me alone. Go away!"

"You owe me at least this, Ming-huà. I've already told them to let you return to the island."

"I don't need their approval."

"Then let's go. Let's go together to the island. Take me with you. Gotta be better than this shithole."

The door slowly opens and Zookeeper sees an alarmingly weak Ming-huà stagger back to bed.

"You mean it?" asks Ming-huà, pulling the blanket up to her chin.

"You bet."

"Come in and sit."

Zookeeper sits uncomfortably in a straight back chair.

"Tell me, Zookeeper," begins Ming-huà with a non-sequitur. "What do you think of suffering in the world?"

"You mean, do I think you can help remove it?"

"No, not entirely, but lessen suffering. Can I do it?"

"We can all do it."

"No, Zookeeper! You know what I mean."

"Okay, be more specific."

"Can I lessen suffering in the world by using my power?"

Zookeeper looks down toward his missing arms. "I'm not the one to ask."

"If you had my power, what would you use it for?"

"You know very well what I'd use it for."

"Money."

Zookeeper chuckles. "Not money at all. Power. With power anything is possible, including money."

"Is there no one you would use your power to save, even it didn't benefit you directly?"

"No."

Ming-huà is not deceived. "You lie."

"Really! I have no one!"

"You lie, I tell you. I can see into your soul, Zookeeper."

"Ha! Who would I protect?"

"Me."

This takes him aback. It's true, and he knows she knows it. *Stupid,* he thinks, *to hide it.* "It's true, I would," he admits. "I do care for you."

"Even with what I have done to you?"

"Why ask? You know the answer."

"I want to hear it from you."

"Yes, even with what you have done to me."

"Why?"

"You really want to make this hard, don't you Ming-huà?"

"Sorry, I don't mean to. But it's important to me."

"Because I think I'm falling in love with you."

"I have thought so for a while," sighs Ming-huà. "Is it because of my power? Is it because you can use my power for your own purposes?"

"If you believe that, you're not much of a mind-reader."

"Both of us can read minds, Zookeeper."

"It's true, but in this case, your thoughts are unclear to me. I'm certain you just despise me, or feel some sort of pity. But no real feeling for who I am."

"Did you know I can also recite some Shakespeare?" asks Ming-huà playfully.

"No, tell me."

"Love looks not with the eyes, but with the mind."

"Yes," says Zookeeper. "Now finish it."

"I can't remember the rest," admits Ming-huà.

"And therefore is winged Cupid painted blind."

Ming-huà laughs. "Then are we both blind?"

"Maybe," says Zookeeper. "But, seriously Ming-huà, can you love me? I mean, look at me! Look at who I am! Fucked-up junkie with no arms."

"I don't know if I can love you, Zookeeper. But I know I need your help."

"That's a joke," he scoffs. "What can I give you?"

"Grounding."

"Grounding in what?"

"Ugly reality."

"So, that's my role?"

"Partly. Tell me, is suffering necessary for life?"

Zookeeper sighs. "That again?"

"Must there be suffering to experience joy?"

"Certainly."

"Then, if I lessen suffering, I lessen joy?"

Zookeeper's demeanor suddenly changes. His face morphs into that of a thoughtful, serious man. "Let me ask you this, did the fawn you saved feel joy after you saved it?"

"Yes, I assume so."

"So, its joy was not lessened?"

"No, but the men—"

"You always return to the fate of those who dispense suffering, never to those who escape it."

"And you? Would you have killed Lady Oracle if I had not removed your arms?"

"No, but I would have let the others do it, encouraged them even, which is worse. Now, let me tell you a little secret. If you had not stopped me, I would be a murderer, would not have met you, and spent the money robbed from a dead woman on more drugs to addict more people and thereby increase suffering many times over. However, by doing to me what I deserved, I'm experiencing joy. Why? Because now I can see there's another way in this world . . . and I would not have met you."

"We live in a strange world."

"You possess a strange power." Zookeeper peers into the distance, as if observing some far distant object. "You know, your power is untested. What I mean is, we don't really know whether it's for the ultimate good, the ultimate bad, or just more random gyrations. But if Lady Oracle and Sy are correct, it's not just you and me that are involved here, it's your parents and grandparents too. Not only that, Lady Oracle and Sy, or"—he points skyward—"*She*, are talking about us making sure your powers are passed on, for the good of the human race. Now, I don't know whether it's good for the human race or not, but if your power is not a beneficial adaptation, natural selection will take care of it soon enough. Mr. Darwin was very clear on that point."

Ming-huà looks at him in a new light. "Where did you get your education, Zookeeper? When you're not talking like a drunken sailor, you certainly don't sound like some low-life junkie scrabbling for existence among the world's castoffs."

Zookeeper guffaws. "That's rich! Ming-huà, we're the world's castoffs! Don't you get it? Either your power will work for the greater good and give us an adaptive edge, or we'll be goners. Ground under by a vengeful mob of lesser humans. Question is, will we end up like the Neanderthals? . . . or, I should say, will you end up like the Neanderthals, since I'm merely a lesser member of the mob. Or, on the other hand, will they be the Neanderthals and you be the successor species to *Homo sapiens*?"

"I plan to be neither."

Zookeeper shakes his head. "Don't think that will be a choice."

"Stuck with you, am I?"

"Ha! I'm beginning to think you are. Still want to go back to your island?"

"Zookeeper, that's what they assume. That is never what my intention has been."

"But I thought—"

"You thought wrong."

"Then what's your intention?"

"For the time being, to do as they say."

"Locked in your room?"

"For show."

Zookeeper gives a deep snicker. "You're pretty amazing."

"You're pretty amazing yourself. You have learned so quickly how to use your feet. You know, I was wrong about you."

"How so?"

"I assumed—there's that word again—you would be forever angry and bitter. That you would want revenge, or worse, go back to drugs and just give up. But I was wrong."

"Almost did, but you came visiting, remember?"

"Yes, I remember. Now, let's get down to business, Zookeeper."

"Okay."

"I propose we go along with Lady Oracle and Scarecrow. I have become some-what familiar with these places and times they talk about. The journey will be long and definitely dangerous, but I need you beside me."

"Why?"

"For show."

Zookeeper grunts with displeasure. "So that's all I am to you? For show?"

"Don't be offended, Zookeeper. I use the words in a special way. Will you listen without getting all huffy for a minute?"

He grunts again, this time in accord.

"Once I'm ready, they will take us first to the desert. To a cave. A special cave."

"How do you know this? They told you?"

"No, my mama told me."

"I thought she left before you really had a chance to talk."

"We talk in many different ways, Zookeeper. Not always with our voices."

"Um. Okay. What's so special about this cave?"

"Did you know Lady Oracle has a grandmother still living?"

"Well obviously she has a grandmother. I just assumed she was dead."

"No. Her mother is dead, but her grandmother is very much alive, although very old. Yes, she is very very old and lives in one of Lady Oracle's apartments. In fact, she lives in the yin apartment."

"The dark one?"

"Yes. Not just dark. Yin represents everything hard, cold, wet, and feminine."

"Yeah? I've never seen her."

Ming-huà chuckles. "Of course not. Neither have I."

"What about her?"

"Her name is Buandelgereen. Lady Oracle told me she is an old Mongol woman whose powers are beyond even my ability to fathom. She is bedridden now, barely alive, but very very active in other worlds."

"Shit, Ming-huà, this is getting too deep for me. What do you mean *other worlds?*"

"Don't you remember? Lady Oracle said we're traveling to a place that is many places and a time that is many times?"

"Yeah, and I still don't get it. What does it mean?"

"What it says."

Zookeeper groans. "Oh, don't you start with that mystical crap! Just tell me straight out. What does it mean?"

"It means something happened to me after that last incident in the alleyway. I mutilated two men whose fates I will never know. I brought it on them. I asked for it. I thought I could control the power. I couldn't. They paid the price. This devastated me even more than I already was. But, in my depths of pain, *Her* voice came to me. Those men were on a path to harm many more people before they die. Now, they're rendered harmless. Is that good or bad for the world?"

"Well, I've been thinking about that. Suppose you had removed Hitler from the scene before he took power, or even when he was in power. Or Himmler, or any of those guys. What then?"

"No one knows."

"Exactly. It could lead to worse things."

"Yes, I am aware. It could. Now, what if a thousand years in the future, the entire human species has this power?"

"No longer human. Either way, they would have a near-perfect society, or they would wipe themselves out."

"How is that different from today?"

"It ain't."

"Like you said, Zookeeper, natural selection will determine the right or wrong of it. Not us." Ming-huà's voice is reduced to a rasping whisper. "Now we understand each other. Go, please. I need to rest."

~

As Zookeeper takes his leave, his intuitive perception tells him there is a flaw in Ming-huà's thinking—an imperfection or defect she has missed. He can't quite put his finger on it, but he suffers a nagging fear that this failing is potentially catastrophic.

Chapter Twelve

The Eve of the Journey

Ancient Buandelgereen

~ A Vision from the Past ~

"Before we leave, you must first meet my grandmother," says Lady Oracle two mornings later.

Ming-huà is excited but maintains her poise. "I want to meet her. Mama tells me she is a legend. Almost a deity. Is there something you wish me to say to her?"

"No. It is she who wants to see you before . . . well, before the opportunity passes. She knew your grandmother and your mother."

"Yes, I know."

"She's very old now, well over a hundred, and cannot leave her bed. But her spirit is as strong as ever. You are someone special to her."

"I think I understand," says Ming-huà nervously. She remembers her mother giving brief glimpses into the extraordinarily adventurous past of this woman whose life is so entwined with that of her own. Her mother described Buandelgereen as a fierce Mongol warrior In her day—one whom even Genghis Khan would envy. This woman warrior used her skills to help protect her grandparents during their quest. "But, is there anything I should refrain from saying?" Ming-huà asks.

"She will ask you questions," replies Lady Oracle. "You will have a very hard time understanding because of her frailty. Her voice is barely perceptible. She often unknowingly reverts to speaking Mongolian. I will help you understand the questions."

Ming-huà feels painfully intimidated. "But, really, is there anything I should not say? Any subject I should avoid?"

"Why should you?"

Ming-huà turns quite solemn. "Memories."

"Dear girl, the only threads that hold her together comprise the thinnest, most precarious strands. This threadbare life force is as fragile as the web spun by an ancient spider, and its silken fabric is otherwise known as memories. Without memories, she would blow away at the lightest of breezes. You are her forward memory."

"Forward memory?"

"You are one of those precious remaining threads that hold her together, and she has teased it out of her threadbare soul to cast it forward like a fisherman at the end of day harboring one last hope."

"And Zookeeper?"

"Yet another thread. There are none left to spare. She is now naked to the world."

"Yes, I know. I am The Daughter," says Ming-huà bitterly.

"Don't make light of it. *She* will not be happy."

"Buandelgereen?"

"No. *She*."

"*Goddess*?"

"Yes."

"*She's* spoken to me only once. You may believe in *Her*, but I believe in schizophrenia, and voices in my head lead me to only one conclusion: I suffer from a mental illness."

"Have it your way. You'll see."

"Yes, I'll see. Why else would I be going with you?"

"Oh, I can think of other reasons. Come! It is time!"

~

Lady Oracle flies through the busy San Francisco streets, as if Buandelgereen would die before they made it to her bedside. Before she knows it, Ming-huà enters the dark yin apartment and pauses to let her eyes adjust. From outside, it seems a normal apartment building with a Chinese facade, but once inside, it somehow mushrooms to appear impossibly cavernous. Yet all that space swallows light, and only the muted glare of sun squeezing through covered windows reveals the clutter on floors and walls. Ancient furniture, faded scrolls, dusty paintings, colorful vases, statues, and assorted bric-a-brac leave almost no space for navigating around. It is the eerie repository of ageless artifacts.

When Ming-huà enters Buandelgereen's room, she can barely perceive the withered body beneath great folds of bedding. Her ancient head is propped on a pillow, white hair in wild disarray, spread out explosively to form a circular halo around the wrinkled face. Her eyes are closed. It seems to Ming-huà that the sheer weight of blankets has crushed the life out of this old woman. Near the bed stands an oxygen tank with mask at the ready. Lady Oracle leans close to her grandmother's ear and whispers something Ming-huà can't hear. Buandelgereen's eyes flutter open. Her lips move, but no one can hear. Once more Lady Oracle leans close, but Buandelgereen suddenly speaks in a surprisingly strong voice.

"Welcome, daughter of hope."

"Thank you."

Ming-huà's hump is awash with conflicting signals. Buandelgereen's mind is a mad swirl of passionate loves, deep regrets, angry grudges, unbending hates, boundless joys, warrior belligerence, and so many other deep emotions that are mixed up and enigmatic. *This woman is powerful*, thinks Ming-huà. *Very powerful. Her portends are confusing and unclear. What does she really think?*

There is silence while Buandelgereen gathers her strength. Finally, she says, "Granddaughter?"

"Yes?" replies Lady Oracle.

"Have you told this child about the cave?"

"A little. Too much too soon might be overwhelming."

"Come closer, child," says Buandelgereen to Ming-huà. "Closer, so I can warn you."

Ming-huà walks to the side of the bed and leans close to Buandelgereen's ear, whispering, "Yes? A warning?"

The old woman's voice is again very frail and hard to understand. "There are ghosts in that cave. Many, many ghosts. If you are not careful, they will take you places you do not want to go. *He* has minions there. Terrible demons who will lead you down the wrong pathways. Those bad pathways will take you to different times, past and future. You must always be on your guard."

Ming-huà realizes with shock that Buandelgereen must suffer from dementia. "Who is *He*?"

"*God*, of course."

"Oh."

Buandelgereen's voice again gains strength. "Your grandmother, Child of Buddha, could read the taps."

"From the Precious Object?"

"Exactly. She had a gift."

"So does my mother."

Buandelgereen manages to lift her head a bit, and speaks with emphasis, "And so do you, child. So do you. In spades, as Americans like to say. Nonetheless, you are afraid?"

"I am afraid of the consequences."

"Go on."

Ming-huà feels disinclined to humor this old woman who clearly suffers from delusions. "That's all."

"No, that is not all. It is the issue of suffering that bothers you, isn't it?"

"Well, yes, in a way."

The old woman asks for water and Lady Oracle starts to put a glass to her lips when Buandelgereen pushes it away and demands to sit up. Pillows are brought and once in the sitting position, she takes a moment to catch her breath, then says, "Now, we must talk about suffering. What are you worried about?"

Ming-huà is so taken with the apparent insight of Buandelgereen, she speaks truthfully. "Madame, if I use my power, I am afraid I will only make suffering worse, not better. Already, I have caused great suffering."

"How much have you prevented?"

"That's just it. I don't know. I'll never know! It might take a thousand years for some terrible result to occur because of what I did a thousand years earlier."

"We'll all be dead in a thousand years, dear. Still, here's what you're forgetting: eventually, you will not be alone. Like all evolutionary adaptations, either this works for the better or it does not, and it will not take a thousand years. In point of fact, the human world has unknowingly seen thousands of intermediates throughout history—ones whose powers are great, but not equal to yours. Some of these intermediates are famous, some not—some lived lives for good, some not. Most procreated with their own kind, so in this lengthy process of mate selection, became a relatively isolated population. Therefore, over time, genetic drift has accelerated the acquisition of powers you now possess."

"That is precisely what Zookeeper said. Natural selection decides. Not some deity. Have you ever considered the possibility that this experiment should end now, and I be allowed to die in peaceful isolation so this 'adaptation' is snuffed out before it does too much harm?"

"Yes. However, believe it or not, there is someone addicted to suffering who will not allow natural selection to do its work."

Ming-huà sighs. "Yes, so I have been told. *God*."

"And, all this time, your parents, your grandparents, and yourself, have all been, shall I say, protected. All of us around you, and many others in the past, have been protectors."

"Others?"

"There are many. However, the intermediates they protected never reached the evolutionary stage you are now at."

"But what interest do you have in creating this new species of human?"

Buandelgereen coughs and gasps for breath. Lady Oracle quickly turns the dial on the oxygen tank and places a mask to her face. The old woman takes shallow breaths, but holds up her hand indicating they should wait. Several minutes pass until her breathing stabilizes and the mask is removed. Buandelgereen turns her attention back to Ming-huà.

"You see me as a delusional old woman. You see yourself as having a mental illness. You see your gift—your power—as . . . what? A curse?"

"None of those things are definite in my mind," says Ming-huà. "That is why I stayed. That is why I'm here. To find out the truth of those propositions."

"Are you aware, child, how many sociopaths, narcissists, antisocial psychopaths, and serial killers are out there?"

"No. Are you?"

"I see a world where they increase every day. I have lived in an age where they controlled much of the world. I see no future for the human race as long as *He* receives the drug *He* so craves."

"I do not believe there is a *He*," says Ming-huà. "You yourself talked about natural selection. There can't be both."

"What if *He* is simply another word for Nature? Another word for the universe? Or, consider this, *He* and *She* are metaphysical terms for two conflicting schools of thought among those who oversee the protectors. After all, even Einstein—intermediate that he was—used *God* as a metaphor for the natural laws of the universe."

Ming-huà does not reply.

"Don't you see, child? They're interchangeable. *He* represents all the idols humans have fashioned and nailed to a giant tree as personifications of the mystical unknown. When the tree continues to grow it absorbs the idols, forming gnarled tumors as it engulfs them, their mystical features sealed into the bark itself. After a while— perhaps still barely recognizable by their protruding visages as objects of worship—the idols become a part of the tree; an unnatural part of the natural world. *She* represents One who would remove the foreign objects before they become fatal, and let the tree revert to being simply a tree. Which is which? Whichever you choose, the underlying truth remains."

With this long speech, Buandelgereen is wheezing for breath. She slumps down a bit and closes her eyes. The oxygen mask is applied again, and she does not resist. Soon, she raises her hand to signal there is more to come. Everyone waits while she regains her energy. During this interval, Ming-huà's mind is racing ahead to questions she wants to ask. No longer does she see this old Mongol woman as demented. A new vista has been opened to her, and she feels the urgent need to explore it.

Buandelgereen opens her eyes and peers at Ming-huà. "Where were we, my dear?"

"Deities and Nature are interchangeable. One is not distinguishable from the other."

"Only to humans, child. Only to humans. On the other hand, perhaps, to that fawn, you are a *Goddess* with supernatural powers."

Lady Oracle speaks for the first time. "She does have supernatural powers."

Buandelgereen holds up an ancient, cautionary finger. "Ah, not at all. Ming-huà's power is as natural as flight to a bird. True, it has been nurtured, but more in the nature of caring for a beloved plant, not bowing in supplication to an unnatural . . . idol. If the concept of *God* enters into consciousness, is *He* not raised to substantive existence by virtue of Nature's myriad neuronal pathways, like the idol in the tree. Do you still hear the voices, girl?"

Ming-huà is startled. "Only once. Not since."

"And what did *She* say?"

"The voice said I am The Daughter and there is no escape from my fate."

"Ah, true, true. But fate starves at Probability's door."

"I know that phrase! That's what I told *Goddess*!" exclaims Ming-huà.

"Who taught you that phrase?"

"My mother."

"I see," whispers Buandelgereen. "And what did *She* say in response?"

"*She* laughed and said I was learning."

"Ha! So like *Her*."

"Does *She* ever give a straight answer?" asks Ming-huà expectantly.

"Never, child. Spacetime is warped, as are *Gods* and *Goddesses*. Their singular-ities are beyond us."

"What is it you want me to do?" asks Ming-huà with an urgency tinged with frustration.

"To start a world where, figuratively speaking, no one's without arms—except those caused by accident."

"Or a world where, figuratively speaking, everyone's without arms," mutters Ming-huà.

"That is what we will find out," says Buandelgereen. "Now, go. Too tired."

The grand old lady turns her head and shuts her eyes to the troublesome present.

~ *Aftermath* ~

On their way back to the Victorian house, Lady Oracle says, "You and Sy be ready to leave tomorrow morning at nine o'clock. In the meantime, we will both think about what grandmother said."

Ming-huà has a sudden thought. "Before we leave, I want to find out what happened to the other two men whose arms I took off at the crack house."

"Why?"

"I need to know."

"I already know," says Lady Oracle.

"Tell me."

"One is dead, suicide. Jumped from a tenth story window. The other is in a halfway house. Also suicidal, but he's got help."

Ming-huà feels as if she has been punched in the stomach. "So, this is the brave new world we're building?"

"No, it's the bad old world we're leaving behind," snaps Lady Oracle gruffly. Too gruffly for Ming-huà not to recognize a kernel of doubt. "Be ready tomorrow morning."

~

Morning reveals a bright day, with the San Francisco wind blowing them out of the city southward. Sy drives, Lady Oracle beside him in front. Ming-huà sits in the back seat, jammed in with Zookeeper among a pile of suitcases. Ming-huà is distracted, appraising and reappraising her conversation with Buandelgereen. Since the trip began, Zookeeper has remained steadfastly silent. Sy, easily bored, reverts to his natural state—royal jester.

"Look," he chirps. "If I'm going to be betwixt and between two women, I expect some compensation, like conversation maybe."

Neither responds.

"You two belie the stereotype of chattering females. Well, chattering is politically incorrect these days. Wasn't back in my day of medieval concubinage. But today!" He bangs on the steering wheel. "Good *Goddess*! Never met such a pair with X chromosomes so damn mute!" He mutters beneath his breath, "Or however many your kind has."

Neither of the women respond.

"Whew, still mum! I mean, if you're both so good at reading minds, what is mine telling you both right now?"

"It's telling me you want to get out and walk," says Lady Oracle. "And I will happily let you and do the driving myself."

"Well, that's a good guess, but unfortunately for you, incorrect. How about you, Ming-huà? Want to take a crack at what I'm thinking?"

"You're nervous, scared really."

"What?"

"Nervous and scared."

Sy laughs. "About what?"

"About this trip we're taking. I know your predecessors and their predecessors before them died doing the bidding of . . . whoever is in charge of this experiment. When my mother was a little girl back in China, staying at a mental institute, my grandmother mentioned a Mr. Feng shiren. He—"

"Not an experiment," interrupts Lady Oracle, clearly wanting to change the subject.

Sy laughs nervously. "Whoa!" He locks Ming-huà's eyes with his in the rear-view mirror. "You're actually partly right, hunchback. But it's the wrong part! I'm not scared or nervous, I'm anxious."

"No difference," says Ming-huà.

"I beg to differ. Scared and nervous means hesitation. Anxious means the opposite. Speed it up! Let's discover how this works out—better than the movies!"

"*Goddess*," says Lady Oracle.

"What?" asks Ming-huà.

"I said *Goddess*. *She's* the one in charge of this . . . quest, not experiment."

"Another quest?"

"What else is life but a series of quests?"

Though Ming-huà is secretly gratified by the label being placed on this trip (a quest—just like her mother and grandmother embarked upon so long ago), she feigns hard-headed detachment and presses. "Look, if we're on a quest, then we're working together, else it's not a quest. And if we're working together, tell me about this cave in the desert we're heading to."

"Your mother knows all about it," says Lady Oracle matter-of-factly. "She didn't tell you?"

"I've already said my mama told me very little, and what little she did tell me, I didn't understand. Didn't understand your grandmother either."

"My grandmother was vague on purpose. If I tell you, you won't understand. Got to see it to believe it. After all, you already consider yourself mentally ill.

When we get to the cave, you will be confronted with either the fact you truly are mentally ill, or . . . something else. A different reality. By the way, have you heard the voice again?"

"No."

"*She's* not ready, which means you're not ready."

"I'm as ready as grandmama was! As mama was!"

"Are you? They were in regular contact with *Her*."

"Please be clear, Lady Oracle. I've got doubts about this entire . . . quest idea. I also have doubts about the existence of any deity—*God* or *Goddess*—even metaphorical ones. On the other hand, I cannot ignore my own power. I've tried, but it doesn't work to ignore it. Now I can somewhat control it, which is good. Therefore, I follow along with you on this trip. You might find what you're looking for, but it may not be what I'm looking for. Understand what I mean?"

"Perfectly."

Zookeeper suddenly cries, "Pull over!"

"Why?" asks Sy.

"Gotta pee. All this talk makes me wanna pee. We're in the middle of nowhere. Just pull over."

It is late afternoon and the desert stretches to infinity on all sides. Distant mountains cast long shadows.

"All right. Nearest town is still sixty or so miles away," says Lady Oracle.

"That where we're going to stay?" asks Ming-huà.

"One night only, then to the cave."

Sy pulls over and Zookeeper gets out to pee. He walks some distance, and finds a spot behind a little rise. Wearing loose-fitting suspenders, his fly already open, Zookeeper slips off a shoe and uses his toes to tug down on a trouser leg to expose his penis. He leans forward and relieves himself, then lets the trouser leg ride up with the tension of the suspenders. Satisfied, he ambles slowly back to the car, but it eats at him to know defecation would be a different matter entirely. For that he needs help. It was always Bataar before, but now Ming-huà has volunteered, and the thought makes him shudder. A new and unsettling feeling of helplessness has set in all over again, almost as strong as when he first lost his arms. That's why he won't talk. He wants to be invisible, especially to Ming-huà. Anger and depression gnaw at him—bearing down the hardest when natural functions are necessary.

When they arrive at the nearest town, they check into a motel and stay in two separate rooms, Sy and Zookeeper in one, Ming-huà and Lady Oracle in the other. Almost immediately, Ming-huà's hump is alive with signals, many of which are echoes of past guests whose traces still linger.

"Where's a good place to eat?" Sy asks the clerk.

"The restaurant here is closed," she replies. There are a couple of good restaurants in town, and one farther out."

"Which has the best food?"

"Locals prefer the one farther out."

"How far?"

"Few miles."

"What's it called?"

"El Fantasma."

Ming-huà is standing close, and the mention of that name suddenly overwhelms her with a rush of images that obscure awareness of the moment. Flashes of long dead presences burn through her mind. Dizziness and weakness overcome and she sways unsteadily.

"Ming-huà, wake up girl!" exclaims Sy. "We're going to drive a bit more to this El Fantasma place and eat where the locals hang out. You okay?"

"I ain't going," says Zookeeper. "Need shuteye, but can someone help me get situated in bed?" He looks at Ming-huà.

"I'll stay," says Lady Oracle. "I can help."

Zookeeper casts his gaze on Ming-huà with a bit of hang-dog look in his eyes. "You gonna stay here or go?"

Go! Do not stay. Go! roars a voice in her head. Deafening. Commanding. Not to be denied.

Ming-huà is rattled. "No, I'll go with Sy. I'm pretty hungry."

"Okay," says Zookeeper hesitantly. He would be more comfortable with Ming-huà as a helper, but can offer no plausible reason why Lady Oracle will not be suitable.

~

Sitting next to Sy in the front seat on the way to the restaurant, Ming-huà realizes something that surprises her because she had not thought of it before.

"Sy, you say you are protectors, yet you do not have my . . . I don't know, power or ability."

"Ha! Nor do we have the power of your parents and grandparents!"

"But without these abilities, how do you. . . . "

"Understand? We don't. However, beware Ming-huà, we have other powers unavailable to you."

"I have always suspected that. Can you share what these powers might be?"

"Ming-huà, you are going to find that out tomorrow when we go to the cave." He gives a shrill cry. "Oh, yes! You'll find out! Ah, here's the restaurant."

Even before entering, Ming-huà's hump is buzzing with messages, all swarming in an indistinguishable electric buzz. After they find a booth, menus are delivered by a tired-looking waitress clearly unhappy they have arrived so close to closing time.

"This place is full of ghosts," says Ming-huà to Sy.

"I'm not surprised," he retorts enigmatically. "See any you recognize?"

Before she can answer, the waitress returns. "Decide?"

"Tonight's special," says Sy. "And decaf."

"Cream?"

"No."

The waitress looks at Ming-huà, her eyes passing quickly over her hump. "You?"

"Same."

"Something to drink?"

"Just water."

"Okay."

Once the menus are collected, the waitress turns and quickly calls out, "Two specials!" to the cook without bothering to attach the order to the wheel. She plunks down the water and decaf, then disappears into the kitchen.

"Recognize any?" asks Sy.

"Any what?"

"Ghosts."

"Hush!" whispers Ming-huà. "Let me concentrate."

The sullen waitress delivers dishes to a nearby table. Ming-huà fights through strong signals from the woman's unhappy but commonplace mood to focus on a clattering tangle of background noise from previous lives whose shadows must have hovered in this place from some distant past to intersect with her in the present. It is remarkable these echoes from the past remain so strong after so much time (their spirits appear more like ancient parchment than crisp paper to her). It is an unmistakable message they have been waiting to convey for so many years. *Waiting for what?* wonders Ming-huà. *And why?*

"For you to arrive," says Sy. "But I do not know why."

"I'm still not quite used to your reading my mind, Sy, but the ghosts are here, and strong, and they want me. But what for?"

"I may be of some help. Your parents worked here when you were a baby."

"What! Why didn't you tell me earlier?"

"So you could find out for yourself. Seeing for yourself is better than second-hand reports."

"But Mother is still alive. She is no ghost."

"Well, yes she is. You see—"

The sullen waitress brings their food and refills their drinks with the alacrity of a person in a hurry. "Anything else?" she asks.

"No," Sy and Ming-huà chime in simultaneously.

Both ignore their meals. "Ming-huà," says Sy with gravity, leaning forward in his seat for emphasis. "Your mother exists in many places and many times, even those times when she has already died."

"Are you saying she is dead?"

"I'm saying . . . well, I don't know what I'm saying. It's up to you now."

"What is?"

"To decipher what these ghosts want of you."

This statement makes Ming-huà quiver. The signals are confused, contradictory, weak. However, one word rises clearly above the whispering chorus of the spirits: cave. All the rest is undecipherable. Nevertheless, the word itself cuts to the heart of her fears. Somehow, the voices are warning her.

"Sy," she says wearily. "It is something about the cave. These voices, these phantoms and their signals, all these years, are trying to tell me something about the cave. I'm afraid."

"Come," says Sy quietly. "Let's go get some sleep, for tomorrow it is the cave you must face."

That night, one very impatient waitress sighs with relief when the hunchback and Scarecrow leave without eating a bite.

Chapter Thirteen

The Cave

Changing Equations

~ Desert Stillness ~

Breakfast that morning is tense, conversation sparse, every mind turned toward their desert destination. Ming-huà's hump becomes strangely silent, merely a low background hum which strikes her as quiet before the storm. But her brain is a different story.

Do not go!

Those words had been repeated in her head all night, spoken by a male voice. A swampy voice. A deep, dank, gritty rumble that filled her mind with a corrosive slag of wet soot and harsh sulfur—a nineteenth century furnace bellowing smoke from a thirteenth century hell. The voice is not of her hump.

"I hear a voice," she announces.

"I think I can tell," says Lady Oracle. "Male or female?"

"Male."

"Probably *God*, although *He* and *She* can switch one to the other. What does *He* say?"

"Not to go."

"Of course!"

"I'm afraid. Yesterday at the restaurant, my hump was crazily alive. Sy will tell you. Wasn't it, Sy?"

"Oh, yes."

"Today, it's silent, but now this voice."

"*He* is nervous," says Sy.

"Where's Zookeeper?" asks Ming-huà.

"In his room," says Sy. "I took care of him. He's eaten and taken care of business."

"Isn't he coming?" asks Ming-huà. "He shouldn't be left alone."

"I offered but . . . best he stays here today," says Lady Oracle.

"But who will take care of him?"

Sy laughs. "That kid is amazing. Said he would be fine until we return. Don't worry, I got him set-up. Left him practicing opening a pop-top can with his toes. Amazing."

"Lady Oracle, I hear the voice," says Ming-huà evenly. "Male. It is *God* trying to talk me out of going to the cave. Correct?"

"More or less."

"This frightens me, but I am also concerned about why you think Zookeeper should stay here. Why? Is my life in danger, or his?"

Lady Oracle frowns. "Let's not get too dramatic, Ming-huà."

"It is not I that am being dramatic. This cave for example, and your unwillingness to explain. . . . "

"Zookeeper's role in this entire affair is unrelated to the cave. Your role, however, is."

"Then tell me what I am about to find."

"Actually, I can't," sighs Lady Oracle.

Ming-huà's hump perceives sincerity.

Do not go!

"The voice scares me, Lady Oracle. It keeps at me. Why can't you tell me?"

"Very simple. Because I don't know myself. This is *Her* doing, and *She* will be the one to decide what happens at the cave, not me."

"You honestly don't know what to expect?"

"Correct."

Do not go!

"That scares me even more."

"Which?" asks Sy. "The voice or the cave?"

Ming-huà shakes her head dolefully. "That is a question I cannot answer . . . at least not yet."

"Are you ready?" asks Lady Oracle.

Ming-huà takes a deep breath. "Yes."

Sy dances ahead to the car. "Whew! Already hot!"

~

The road stretches endlessly in front and behind. Sand and rock extend on all sides; a monotonous landscape only broken in the distance by a necklace of purple hills. Ahead, Ming-huà sees a dust devil swirling madly, locking its frenzied grains of sand in violent bondage, twisting and contorting to form a tortured column spiraling upward, like one of Michelangelo's agonized slaves struggling to free himself from the marble. The voice has ceased for the moment, and she enjoys a brief respite from reminders of what she will soon face. No one interrupts the quiet. Even the voluble Sy has nothing to say, but grips the steering wheel and stares straight ahead. Ming-huà nods off for a few minutes, and when she awakes, they are driving on a dirt road spewing plumes of dust behind. Sharp dips and deep rills violently shake the car and cause enough strain on the shock absorbers to trigger a moaning, grinding metallic protest from the suspension system. Still, no one says a word. At last, Sy pulls off what little dirt road there is onto a sandy flat area where a lonely acacia tree leans mournfully in their direction, but casts no shade on the car.

"From here we walk," says Lady Oracle, stepping out and pulling on a wide-brim straw hat.

Sy hops from one foot to the other pretending as if the ground is a griddle. "Desert just made for dancing!" he exclaims. From his pocket, he snatches a crumpled little hat and dons it in a grand gesture, though it does nothing to shade his face.

Ming-huà stands next to Lady Oracle and breathes in deeply the scorched air, then adjusts her own straw hat to provide the best angle for shade. "I'm ready," she says.

"Hold on," says Sy, reaching into the car and pulling out his backpack. He checks to make sure the flashlights are packed and there are adequate water bottles. "Okay, let's go! Onward and upward!"

Ming-huà fancies the three of them look like a scene from *The Wizard of Oz*, surrealist style. Hunchback Dorothy, Scarecrow Sy, and the odd one out—Lady Oracle, who to Ming-huà is a combination of the Good Witch and the Wizard himself. They start off down what appears to be an animal trail.

Do not go!

The voice again, this time much louder and more desperate. She pushes it aside and concentrates on what might await at the cave. It is her firm intention to not be shocked at whatever happens. For her, it is essential she remain calm and draw from her own resources to deal with whatever occurs. When they reach the mouth of the cave, her hump signals nothing more dramatic than a constant, droning hum. Sy juggles a couple of flashlights while they sit on rocks just inside the entrance, enjoying the cool interior and sipping water. Still, few words are spoken. Lady Oracle and Sy seem to be waiting for something.

But nothing happens.

Ming-huà grabs a flashlight. "I'm going to explore," she says.

"No!" exclaims Lady Oracle. "It is not time."

"For what?"

"I do not know. All I know is that it is not time."

Ming-huà snorts in frustration. "This is crazy!"

Sy stands in front of her. His malleable face changes again, to an expression of firm determination. "You will not go, hunchback."

Before she has time to respond, a shrill cry floods the cavern, sending chills up Ming-huà's neck.

Lady Oracle rises from her seat and says, "Now we can go."

~

Before they can take a step, a figure emerges from the black depths of the cave. It is a young woman, quite beautiful, wearing a backpack and carrying a walking stick. *Her* eyes are luminous, and shine as if *she* had been crying. As *she* approaches, no one moves. Ming-huà consults her hump and draws a complete blank. No messages. No signals. Not even the usual low static. When the woman draws near, it is as if all the air had been sucked from the cave and only *her* breathing keeps them alive. Ming-huà notices *she* has no flashlight, yet *she* had just come from a lightless world. Lady Oracle and Sy remain speechless, evidently waiting for instructions. Now, Ming-huà's hump is suddenly buffeted by a flurry of messages as if her mind has been tossed into a mental wind tunnel. One message resonates clearly through the storm: this is no young woman. This woman is as ancient as the wind itself. *She* looks at Ming-huà and speaks.

"You alone, come with me."

Her few words carry an odd, ethereal quality: a handful of miniscule snow crystals tossed to the wind, leaving in their wake the impression of a glassy film suffused with the cold purity of ice.

Ming-huà looks at Lady Oracle and Sy. Although they remain silent, both nod in acknowledgement of the woman's words.

"Would you hand me a flashlight, Sy?" asks Ming-huà.

Sy dances one of his patented jigs and pretends to point a flashlight in multiple directions. "You won't need it, hunchback dear!"

As Ming-huà opens her mouth to respond, the woman has turned and is heading through the icy film into the black void. Ming-huà takes a deep breath and follows.

She is determined to ask no questions for fear of appearing to this formidable woman a panicky child. Onward they walk in complete darkness, yet fully aware of their surroundings in some manner which is a mystifying wonder to Ming-huà. Miraculously, she sees without seeing; rock walls, rock ceiling, side tunnels, jagged quartz protrusions that erupt downward, reminding Ming-huà of misshapen gargoyle faces fiercely scowling. Still, they walk. They walk down endless corridors and across narrow stone bridges formed naturally by the bottomless gorges that fall away on either side. From the depths of these bottomless pits, Ming-huà fancies she hears distant wailing arise in sorrowful lamentations. Still, they walk. After what seems an eternity, the woman finally stops and stands as motionless as the surrounding stone. They remain frozen for such an indeterminate amount of time that Ming-huà momentarily thinks they both have solidified and exist merely as fossils. The only perceptible movement comes from Ming-huà's own hump that vibrates in anticipation.

As if a switch has been flipped, the vibrations stop completely, and by the time Ming-huà casts a startled glance at the woman, *she* has disappeared. A black veil drops, black curtains close, and Ming-huà can see nothing. Now, the fanciful sensation of being fossilized is replaced by the gruesome reality. Ming-huà's racing thoughts slow to long, drawn-out meanderings, then to dim awareness of the barely perceptible thumping of her own heartbeats, until they too are doused.

When she awakes from the black void, she sees faint outlines of unidentifiable shapes, and feels crushing weight from above and resistance from below. She is suspended, her body disoriented and splayed sideways at a peculiar angle. Panic strikes and she tries to move, but in struggling, she feels the weight bearing harder down upon; the more she squirms, the more suffocating the weight. She rubs against cold, corrupted flesh that also moves and shifts in reply to her futile efforts; arms, legs, heads, feet. She hears male deep-throated groans, female agonized sighs, whimpering children, and infants whose cries are little more than pathetic, hoarse squeals. As her struggles become more desperate, the surrounding body parts likewise thrash about, as if she transferred to them sparks of animated life. Somehow, from outside this decayed mass, her disembodied gaze floats above, and she sees mountains of bodies stacked so high they disappear into the sky. Layer upon layer of decaying human flesh; African, Asian, European, American, and more, of every shape, size, and color. So great is the mound that all the victims of the Holocaust comprise but a miniscule stratum. To her utter horror, Ming-huà realizes her struggles to disentangle herself from the writhing mass is a hopeless endeavor, as every moment new layers of dead are stacked atop the multitudes of existing corpses. With each passing minute, no matter how hard she struggles upward, she is pressed farther down into the lower realms where the endless bodies become liquified.

"Get me out!" she tries to scream. "Get me out!"

But the words are muffled by the press of bodies. Trying to push limbs and torsos and heads aside, desperate to find an airhole, her arms are trapped by the sheer bulk, the pressure from above mercilessly push her into the ocean of corruption below.

"Get me out!"

Never has she felt such absolute, unthinking, mad panic. Ming-huà tries to remove the bodies entirely by using her power, but nothing happens, only the irreversible downward slide to a deeper hell, not of bodies, but simply an endless ocean of putrefaction.

~

"Well?"

Ming-huà is back in the dark cave, standing unsteadily next to the woman with the backpack whose one-word question has just entered her consciousness. The question somehow slices through the stifling air to Ming-huà's ears.

Without responding, Ming-huà's knees buckle and she drops to the ground. She wants to answer, but her shaking is intense, and her mouth will not work properly. Words form deep inside, but are twisted beyond recognition when they reach her lips.

"Well?" repeats the woman.

Ming-huà takes a few deep breaths and clenches her fists in tight, painful balls, but still the words will not come.

"Well?" echoes the woman.

A sudden feeling of outrage lashes Ming-huà's mind. How can this woman put her through such humiliating horror? How can this woman strip her so bare of humanity and expose the raw animal instinct to survive that lurks in her soul? Finally, after struggling with her rage, she weakly stammers, "How could you?"

"You have been given a glimpse," comes the terse answer.

"Damn you!" Ming-huà blurts with an uncharacteristically bitter tone.

The woman assumes a rather tragic expression. "No, child, do not damn me. Damn *Him*. The entire mass of dead humans you experienced all died in great suffering. Furthermore, all those bodies surrounding you died at the hands, directly or indirectly, of their fellow humans; war, murder, torture, genocide, and all the rest. All for the express purpose of satisfying the addiction of *God*."

"I do not believe there is a *God*," says Ming-huà weakly.

"Call it what you will, humans have given it a name. In fact, they have given it multiple names. Those that died of natural causes; disease, old age, flood, fire, and the like, occupy a separate pile. No pile of human or non-human corpses reeks of such perverted injustice as the pile in which you found yourself. Humans wreaking havoc on humans (and non-humans). Why? One label is Human Nature, another is Natural Law, another is Evolution and Natural Selection, another is *God*, another Allah, Shiva, Satan, and a multitude of other names circulating among humanity. All are the same."

Ming-huà feels her strength returning, and with it, the old objections. "I have heard this argument before. It is as ancient as the earliest hominins whose brains began to swell. What do you want of me?"

"You can start the long process of changing things—of scaling back the immensity of this suffering . . . this pile."

Ming-huà has no intention of backing down. "How? By removing arms?" She intends the question to be sarcastic, but it comes out as a plea to have it not be so.

"Yes, to remove arms, figuratively," responds the woman to Ming-huà's surprise.

"With this power to 'reconfigure' as Sy calls it, we would soon kill each other."

"No. Imagine if you had been around to remove Hitler's arms? In his case, the supremely delicious irony."

"Yes, and imagine a world where jealous spouses could remove the arms of their betrayers, real or imagined. Or drunken fathers who remove the arms or legs of a disobedient child. Of course, the potential for much worse exists, like the two hunters I murdered. I could go on. This idea is madness."

"Daughter, as this power evolves, so does the human brain. The acts you mention would be performed by the current species. As tools brought power and the abuse of power, so too did the concept of compassion and forgiveness. Thus it will be in the future. Absolute power to all beings brings absolute compassion for all beings."

"And if you're wrong?"

"Then large brains are inevitably an evolutionary dead end. Your prediction is true. *Voila!* The stage is cleared."

Still sitting on the ground, Ming-huà is unwilling to stand for fear her shaky legs will not hold her upright. She absently fingers a rock and says, "And if I just return to my island, live a quiet life, and die an anonymous death?"

Sparks flare from the woman. "I can force you down all those side tunnels we passed where you will emerge into the heart of every holocaust, large and small, that have afflicted the human race from the beginning."

Ming-huà trembles. "I have seen enough."

"Enough to do what you know you must?"

"With Zookeeper?"

"For a start."

Ming-huà speaks as if to herself. "And once started, no going back."

"Dear girl," says the woman. "It is already started."

Ming-huà has a sudden thought that quickly transforms into an unanticipated compulsion. "I want to see my father."

"He is a shade."

Ming-huà forces her voice to project unbending insistence. "I want to see my father."

"Why?"

"Did he suffer from schizophrenia?"

"You know he did, at least according to humans."

"And the humans were wrong?"

"Of course."

"Did he have a . . . power like mine?"

"Absolutely, dear girl. But he never came to grips with it, even when guided by it."

"What was his power?"

"Turns out to have been the ability to create you."

~ *A Question of Taste* ~

This last comment of the woman makes Ming-huà pause, but she is determined to get clear answers she can make sense of.

"Why have you chosen Zookeeper?"

"One of his sperm is the key to a lock that opens the future."

Ming-huà scoffs, "I'm no biologist, but I know enough to understand you are talking about one sperm among millions. How—"

The woman explodes in a burst of sparks burning red trails in the dark. "We know!"

Ming-huà instinctively cowers, but remembers something said to her in the past. She is not even quite sure what it means, but says it anyway. "Fate starves at probability's door."

At this non-sequitur, the woman laughs appreciatively. "You are smart, very smart. It is true, there is uncertainty. All his sperm will have the power to create, but each in its own unique way."

"In other words, it is an uncertainty that could equally give birth to a monster as well as a saint."

"Bluntly, yes. At this stage, anyway."

"Speaking of which, what is to prevent a mutated baby or toddler to simply make everyone disappear unintentionally?"

"You did not. Others will not. The power builds slowly."

"You're losing control of the variables."

"Welcome to the universe," says the woman evenly.

Ming-huà shakes her head. "I have read many cautionary tales."

"Risk is the only path forward for the human species. Look where they are headed now."

During this entire conversation, Ming-huà has been sitting on the ground, arms wrapped around her knees. Now she stands and looks deeply into the eyes of the woman.

"No, I refuse," she says with all the authority she can muster.

As if expecting these words, the woman does not blink. "Do you wish to return to the pile?"

Ming-huà staggers back. "You threaten?"

"Not a threat. That is where you will end up—a victim."

"So, you offer the choice of accepting your theory with the hope it turns out for the best—keeping in mind the benefit of removing Hitler's arms—or accepting your theory knowing it may just as easily be an unparalleled disaster—keeping in mind the horror of removing millions of arms and legs and bodies of innocent people who happen to be in the wrong place at the wrong time? Is it to be only the limbs of evil people, or the limbs of everyone?"

"Time will tell. And time is running out for the human race as presently configured; a species sacrificed on the altar of *His* addiction."

"Sorry, I still do not believe in *Him*. We are a species sacrificed on the altar of Natural Selection and the unfortunate long-term inadaptability of big brains."

"That has yet to be determined. This power will change the equation from the inevitable extinction of humans to the enormous potential of a new, more peaceful age."

Ming-huà is too weary to argue, and the mention of *Him* jogs her memory. "I want to see my father."

"You are stubborn."

"I want to see my father."

~

Ming-huà finds herself sitting on a chair in some nondescript, antiseptic-smelling room painted white and green. One small window in the door breaks the monotony. All else is sterile and bathed in dull, fluorescent light. An older man in pajamas sits disconsolately on a rumpled bed, looking down at the tile floor. Ming-huà recognizes her father from old photos her mother often shared.

"Father?" she ventures.

He blinks at her, and says nonchalantly, "Hello daughter. You've grown. Of course, hallucinations can do that. Quite suddenly, for that matter. How are you?"

Before she can answer, he adds, "Of course, it is my motto that one must always be polite to hallucinations, especially family ones. I was even polite to myself when I appeared as a young soldier crashing perfectly good dinner parties. Anyway, I ask again, how are you?"

"I am well, father."

"So, the future is not as bleak as we sometimes picture it, eh?"

"No."

"How is your mother? Oh, I miss her horribly!"

"She is well. How are you, father?"

"Not well, as you can see. Sacrificed myself for you and your mother. Glad to see she raised you to be a strong young woman."

Ming-huà thanks him, and says, "There is this question of *God* and *Goddess*."

Michael's face reddens. "Are *They* after you too? I had hoped *Their* voices would end with me."

"Not quite, father. Are *They* real?"

"As real as you."

"Am I real?"

"Of course not. And since you're not real, I can tell you. This afternoon, I intend to murder Dr. Wang."

Ming-huà's mother never told her the details of how her father died, and when asked, gave the curt reply, "Heart."

"Father," says an alarmed Ming-huà. "You can't do that."

"Of course I can. And I will. A fitting act of desperation for a total failure."

"You are no failure. Mother and I love you very much."

Michael's eyes tear up. "Yes, yes. Tamara is a remarkable woman. Ha! Look at how well she's taken care of you, hunchback and all. No, I can't continue this way. The ending is already written."

"Change it, father."

"Too late, daughter. Your strong, healthy presence before me, hallucination or not, is proof my decision is correct. You have done perfectly fine without a father."

"Then at least give it an alternate ending."

"Once the deed is done, I can't leave behind two endings to my story."

"Okay," says Ming-huà. "Then just change it."

Michael chuckles. "My girl, I have been pulling your leg. It is already changed. You see, I anticipated your visit"—he leans forward and whispers confidentially—"as I can see into the future. You're not the only one with powers. In fact, this meeting has already been written, the manuscript hidden away. It is all down. Lord how that used to drive the psychiatrists crazy. Literally did."

"What do you mean?"

"I mean, daughter, the book of your life has already been written. The knife I hide in my robe will not harm Dr. Wang. No, the blade will not violate her flesh. It will enter my own heart."

Ming-huà's head reels at the tectonic shocks colliding into her psyche one after the other; the cave, the ancient young woman, the titanic pile of corpses, her father, the institution, his confession of murder, and the intimation of suicide. All that sticks in the miasma of revelations is that her father had the power to see into the future. Even her own future. That was his power!

"Father, how will it end?" she cries.

~

"But he squandered it," says the young woman.

Ming-huà is back in the cave. Minutes, hours, decades might have passed. She is unsure. Her head is spinning with a million thoughts and questions elbowing each other for priority. As a result, she says nothing. The woman continues.

"Your grandfather John and grandmothers Meiying and Child of Buddha prepared the way, and Michael was to be The Son. Unfortunately, the organic severity of his presumed schizophrenia ultimately made him unsuitable."

"And I am suitable?" asks Ming-huà.

"Only if you agree to be suitable."

Ming-huà sighs with the tragic gravitas of a Greek chorus. "I think it will be a total disaster. I see a holocaust of proportions larger than the pile you showed me. It must be in father's writings."

"Ming-huà," says the woman, addressing her by name for the first time. "Your father had the power of prophecy, not you. Have you considered the future if it works? A world where unnecessary suffering caused by unscrupulously evil men and women will be eliminated? A world where *His* addiction to suffering is withered on the vine? A world where heinous acts that cause such unnatural agonies are not tolerated?"

"I have. And I have also considered its opposite."

"One way to find out."

"Natural selection?"

"As always."

"Father's writings?"

"Gone missing for a long time, but now found. I already told you what they contain. You have heard the stories."

"Only briefly. Little snatches about quests and Precious Objects and Superior Ones. These snippets do not satisfy."

"They will be made available to you."

Ming-huà pauses. "Somehow, I don't believe you. Are you the deity my ancestors saw? Are you *Goddess*?"

The woman shoots back. "Are you human?"

~

Ming-huà is escorted in silence back to the cave entrance. Then, without a word, the woman turns and walks back into the gloomy darkness. Sy and Lady Oracle rise from their rock seats to greet Ming-huà.

"Is it decided?" asks Lady Oracle.

"Yes."

"The verdict?"

"I have reluctantly agreed to carry-on, for now anyway. But I reserve the right to quit anytime and return to my island."

Lady Oracle laughs. "No such right exists, my dear."

Sy leaps from boulder to boulder. "She is correct, Ming-huà! Even if you go back, the authorities will follow!"

"Authorities?"

"Once you become known, the chase is on! You—the fox, and them—the hounds!"

Ming-huà looks to Lady Oracle, whose rather cold demeanor conveys the beginnings of a changed relationship.

~ *Zookeeper Balks* ~

Alone in the motel room, Zookeeper feels increasingly frustrated. Although he agreed to stay behind while they went gallivanting off to the cave, their obvious relief at his absence reminds him that his position in this little group is entirely secondary. Do they think of him simply as breeding stock? Is he to be kept on hand but out of the way until his services are needed? At least, in the heyday of the crack house, he occupied a position of power. Here?—an afterthought. Yet, he is fully aware he cannot simply leave and survive in the outside world alone. Trapped. This knowledge, long since understood, has buttressed a renewed sense of impotence now that he is abandoned so readily within the four walls of a cheap motel room.

Zookeeper toys with the idea of leaving just for the satisfaction of imagining them scramble to get him back. However, in his current state of development, he would not take ten steps before he would be confronted with unmanageable difficulties. He tries to gauge his true feelings toward Ming-huà, and can only come up with respect tinged with a healthy fear of her awesome power. *And love?* he asks himself. That feeling lacks solidity, reality, and appears to him a mystery he has never experienced, an impenetrable fog of confusion and conflict. Truth be told, he knows that being married to her would forever cast in stone his inferior status. He knows quite well it is his ability to get into the heads of others and manipulate them that gives him pleasure and purpose. Just as bad as her superior role, he knows he can never give her the type of sexual pleasure others could. With his limitations, she would soon seek in other men what he cannot provide. He feels resentment, self-loathing, and anger all rise in his gut.

In the midst of these thoughts, his companions return.

~

Sy bursts into the room and waits impatiently while from the open door, Lady Oracle and Ming-huà take their leave by addressing Zookeeper with half-hearted greetings before they wearily disappear to their own rooms.

When the door closes behind them, Zookeeper looks at Sy with raised eyebrows. "Well, how'd it go?"

Sy, unlike the others, is wired from the trip and twirls like a Dervish. "As well as could be expected! On to the next step!"

"Which is?"

"Do you need anything?" asks Sy, ignoring Zookeeper's question.

"I will soon."

"Just let me know," chirps Sy.

"Are you going to answer my question?" asks Zookeeper.

"Which is?" Sy asks with a balletic twirl.

"What is the next step?"

Scarecrow stops his clowning and sobers immediately. "Tomorrow, we return to the cave."

"With me?"

"Yes."

"And then?"

Sy lets out a deep sigh. "A place has been set aside."

Zookeeper rolls his eyes in disgust. "This is like pulling fuckin' teeth! Set aside for what?"

"You and Ming-huà, of course!"

"Oh crap!" moans Zookeeper. "A special stall for the brood mare?"

Sy leaps about and mimics vigorous masturbation. "And you're the stallion!"

"Fuck you, Sy!" growls Zookeeper.

"No, not me. It's Ming-huà you're to fuck!"

Zookeeper wants to react angrily, but only a chuckle is released from his lips. "*God*, you're a fuckin' idiot!" he jibes.

Sy makes an exaggerated bow. "Thank you, kind sir."

"Now," says Zookeeper, his tone a harbinger of serious words to come. "Once this kid is born—if Ming-huà and I hook up—what happens to me?"

"Easy. You're a husband and a father."

"Who's to marry us, huh? Lady Oracle? You? Is some preacher waiting at the cave?"

"Details," says Sy dismissively. "We are on the verge of changing the destiny of humanity, and you worry about bureaucratic scraps of paper. Don't worry about it!"

Zookeeper glares. "Look, I wasn't born yesterday. If I'm to breed like some damn bull, I want protection. I want compensation." He assumes a malicious smile. "My sperm is valuable, is it not?"

Sy affects shock. "You don't trust us?"

"Not on your life! I've been screwed over a thousand different ways, upside down and inside out. I'll not put myself in a position to be tossed aside without a second thought."

"And humanity?" says Sy tilting his head as if puzzled.

"Fuck humanity!"

Suddenly, shockingly, Sy's jester guise disintegrates and out of the ruins comes a maniacal killer. He thrusts one powerful hand around Zookeeper's neck and viciously pushes him against a table, bending him backwards so violently Zookeeper's vertebra is in danger of cracking apart. Helpless, the back of his head pressed against the tabletop, Zookeeper is choking to death under Sy's vise-like grip.

"You will do this for the love of humanity! Not sex! Not drugs! Not money! You will do this to facilitate the metamorphosis of humanity from crawling caterpillar to soaring butterfly! True, you are just a grub among billions of grubs!

And like human grubs everywhere, you spend your lives navel-gazing at your own pathetic life stories. Love, you fool! Love Ming-huà and what you and she can do together!"

During this tirade, Sy has progressively loosened his grip so as not to kill Zookeeper. Now he releases the neck entirely and stands back.

Zookeeper clumsily tries to rise, but the combination of gasping for air and lack of arms for balance compels him to collapse on the floor in a heap. He wants to cry out, "Bastard!" but only a sad croak is emitted from his scorching throat.

Sy is unmoved. "Who you once were is the type of human I would not object to Ming-huà making disappear, or, as I prefer to say, reconfigure. No loss to the world, but a gain of rich molecules and atoms with which to make other things. You, and others like you, are the hunters and people are the fawns you delight in drowning. Look at you now! Worthy, at least, to continue living and contribute to something better. Are you going to squander your second chance, fool?"

Zookeeper has managed to stand and stumble to the bed where he sits with head lowered. "I want out of this fuckin' madness!"

"No. You will go with us to the cave tomorrow."

"Don't you understand, Scarecrow? I'm scared. Very scared."

"Now we're talking sense," says Sy. "What are you scared of?"

"Her, the child, Lady Oracle, you, everything! You're right, I belong in the trash heap where I came from."

"Nonsense! None of this maudlin self-pity. In terms you understand, go shit. I'll wipe your ass. The earth turns. Eat. The earth keeps turning. Then sleep. Tomorrow, you will see wonders! The earth will continue turning."

Sy leans over Zookeeper and gently kisses him on the forehead, then leads him to the bathroom.

Chapter Fourteen

Lessons In Time And Space

Perfect Flaw

When they return to the cave the following morning, no one is there to greet them. The entrance yawns before them, its throat dark and portentious. Within, the cave is just as one might expect of an untouched cavern—dark, desolate, and bare. Lady Oracle maintains her air of detachment from Ming-huà, speaking only when necessary and allowing Sy to carry the weight of conversation. Her responses to Zookeeper are similarly clipped, reduced to the occasional monosyllable.

The group lingers uneasily near the mouth of the cave, unsure of what awaits.

Zookeeper pipes up. "Well, this is a great welcome. We gonna just sit around and wait?"

Sy says, "Waiting is good for the soul."

"Yeah, sure," Zookeeper grumbles.

Then, without warning, Lady Oracle speaks: "Come. We will travel to the very end."

This time, flashlights are essential. The cave appears utterly changed to Ming-huà—stripped of the enchantment it held the day before when she had walked these tunnels with the young woman. Then, it had seemed alive, pulsing with quiet magic and hidden warmth. Now it feels cold, hollow, and inert. A mineral tomb. Side passages beckon as before, but Lady Oracle passes them without pause or even a glance. Ming-huà, by contrast, finds herself strangely drawn to them. They call to her in ways that are both alluring and unsettling.

Sy stays close to Zookeeper, steadying him whenever an uneven stone causes his armless frame to teeter. Lady Oracle glides ahead, impervious to the terrain, untouched by distraction.

At last, they reach the cave's end: a wall of solid rock enclosing them on three sides. Lady Oracle extinguishes her light and instructs the others to do the same.

Darkness envelops them.

The silence takes on a life of its own, becomes oppressive—yet no one dares speak.

~ *Goddess Schools Zookeeper* ~

A woman appears as if from nothing—*ex nihilo*.

"I wish to speak with Zookeeper alone," she says calmly. Without waiting, she nods toward him and begins to walk. In a daze, he follows.

To his surprise, as it had been for Ming-huà, the darkness offers no impediment—his flashlight remains unused. Dim illumination, born of her presence, seems to guide the way. Still, his mind reels with conflict. To be chosen, singled out, stirs a fluttering hope, a sense of purpose. Yet that hope is paired with fear—sharp and intimate—as he becomes acutely aware of his own vulnerability, his smallness in the vast unknown.

She leads him deep into the cave, far from the others. When he stumbles, some invisible force steadies him. The further they go, the more his anxiety mounts. They enter a great chamber, its breadth slowly revealed in the faint radiance she emits. An armless alien in a vast alien land. Zookeeper summons all his will to remain calm, to quiet the storm rising in his chest. He has always taken pride in his composure, in never succumbing to the mindless irrationality of panic.

But when she stops and turns to face him, her gaze steady and her presence overwhelming, something in him yields. His courage falters in the brilliance of her awareness. It is just as well.

He is no longer himself.

He is now a vessel.

The woman radiates a glowing blue light. Zookeeper is momentarily blinded. When he cracks open his eyes, he squints into the intensity to see an image beyond his imagination. *She* sits in the lotus position on a huge, dazzling white flower floating above the ground. *Her* sad, contemplative face gazes from beneath an elaborate crown glimmering a kaleidoscope of colors. A cinder-bright jewel embedded in *her* forehead burns brightly and an intricate necklace lays cradled between *her* breasts. *Her* left hand rests on *her* thigh, the upturned curve of *her* fingers resembling the albino legs of a gracefully dead spider. *Her* right hand is poised in the air, index finger and thumb touching to form an almost perfect circle while the other fingers radiate outwards. The hypnotic power of *her* stare makes him quiver.

Unversed in the iconography of this incomprehensible vision, he sinks to his knees, completely overwhelmed. Normally able to handle extraordinary situations that occur in the world of the ordinary, he is incapable of dealing with such supernatural pyrotechnics. Somewhere deep inside, his rational mind fights against the onslaught, but it is overmatched. He closes his eyes against the brightness and awaits whatever will happen next. A voice booms out from the luminous vision, but he keeps his eyes tightly shut.

You are a scrubby crackhead who has dealt in despicable acts. You are smart, but not the smartest. You are good at what you do, but not the best. You can manipulate the weak and vulnerable, but are not in the same league as successful demagogues. You are cruel, but not the cruelest. You are kind, but not the kindest. You are a fool, but not the most foolish. However, Zookeeper, you have something else, something hidden deep within your genes, not yet fully expressed because it lacks the proper analogue. That is why you stand before Me. Be not afraid.

He feels the words inhabit every cell of his body, vibrating so powerfully that he fears his constituent parts will simply break apart.

"Zookeeper." It is the melodic gentleness of the strange woman's voice. "Open your eyes. Calm yourself."

With these soothing words, he cracks open his eyes again and peeks out.

She stands before him, still beautiful, still remarkable, but after the astonishing vision he just experienced, *she* is blessedly normal in a human way. Zookeeper straightens and tries to diminish *her* power by thinking of *her* as another junkie begging for relief. His fantasy is destroyed by *her* next words.

"Zookeeper, it is true you are a walking mediocrity. However, there is one precious nugget you possess that makes you the most valuable man on the planet."

Zookeeper reddens at this unexpected statement so close on the heels of his comeuppance from the vision.

"Hey!" he exclaims. "I didn't ask—"

She cuts him off with a flick of the wrist, and continues, "However, you do possess that nugget—that one hidden nugget tucked deep inside your DNA. As just explained to you, it lacks an analogue to be fully expressible. Ming-huà is that analogue. Upon such a union are species transformed."

"Great," he says weakly, trying to regain the comfort of belligerence.

"In other words," *she* says, ignoring his sarcasm. "In you we have the perfect flaw."

~ *Zookeeper Broods* ~

"The perfect flaw," Zookeeper repeats as if unable to believe it had been spoken. Nonetheless the words give him renewed energy; he puffs up and continues. "Fuck! It's nice to know I'm useful as a mediocre idiot." His face morphs into a cunning smile. "I'll agree to this bullshit if you replace my arms."

"Impossible," says the woman.

"Not for a *Goddess*."

"What you call *Goddess* is illusion. A parlor trick. Natural Law, as always, prevails. What you call *God* . . . and *Goddess* as well, are shiny rocks polished by humans to sparkle, but ultimately boil down to nothing more than physics and chemistry. Humans and their big-brain imaginations collect deities like bower birds collect trinkets."

"Very interesting, but irrelevant," says Zookeeper. "If you can't help me, why should I help you?"

"Dear boy, you have already been helped."

"By removing my arms and making me half a man?"

"You were already half a man. This will make you whole."

Zookeeper knows these debates are utterly useless. He changes tack and probes. "What will this kid I am supposed to have with Ming-huà be like? I mean, what power will he offer to the world?"

"He?"

"Okay, he or she."

"That is the question."

"How do you know he . . . or she, will be other than a normal person?"

"That is the only thing we know for sure."

Zookeeper shakes his head in defeat. "Shit, I don't know," he mumbles.

"Do you not want to be a new Adam?"

At first, he misses the reference, then picks up on it. "To Ming-huà's Eve? Like she's pointed out before, what if we're creating a race of monsters?"

"Monsters? What do you call humans now? Besides, what have normal humans ever done for you?"

"Good point."

"Have you ever been in love?"

Zookeeper's eyes grow large. "Funny, I was just thinking about that. Shiiittt! What a stupid question. I've never known what that meant—except as a kind of addiction which destroys people worse than crack cocaine."

"Can you love Ming-huà?"

"Told you, I don't know what that means."

"Can you have sex with her?"

"That I can do. Now you're talkin' my language."

"In exchange for food, drink, lodging, toilet assistance, training, companionship, and all the rest . . . in exchange for those things, having sex with her is all we ask you to do."

"And marriage? I want protection."

"And marriage."

"Well, if you hold up your end of the bargain, I can screw like a rabbit. You prepared for multiple monsters?"

"We're counting on it."

A dark pall falls across Zookeeper's face. "Are you sure you know what you're doing? Are you prepared to unleash upon the world such potential havoc?"

"No and yes. Fate starves at probability's door."

"Ha! Heard that one before. At least you're an honest *Goddess*!"

"I am no *Goddess*."

"Sure, if you say so."

The young woman points at *her* back. "Zookeeper, *Goddesses* do not carry backpacks."

"What's in it?"

"Cruelty. I pick it up wherever I see it and stuff it in here like trash to dispose of later."

"Awfully small backpack for an awful lot of cruelty."

"It is actually a black hole. Voracious. Always happy for more."

"I can be cruel," laughs Zookeeper. "Will it suck me in?"

She looks at him severely. "Without a burp."

He thinks it best to change direction. "Heavy?" he asks.

"Heavy as *God*."

~

Zookeeper knows he will go along with these people. His options are nil. Besides, he likes Ming-huà, perhaps could even learn to love her, so long as his love is not returned by pity. However, the cunning part of him growls displeasure in the background, and he secretly tells himself to bolt when a propitious opportunity arises—besides, he does not believe his arms cannot be replaced by 'these people'. *If they're holding out on me, I'll hold out on them*, he reasons.

He turns to the woman and says, "Well, all I have to say is—"

But when he blinks, *she* is gone. Once alone, the ordinariness of their conversation is overtaken by the magic, and again he feels overmatched and inadequate to make any serious decisions. Question is, will these fantastic people do more harm to him than they have done already if he bolts?

For all his laborious mining efforts, trust is the gold he has never found in his life, only fool's gold. This corrupted vein pollutes the bedrock of his beliefs and cannot be surgically removed, either by heaven or earth.

With a mix of conflicting thoughts, he returns to the group, muttering obscenities the entire way.

~

"We sleep here tonight," announces Lady Oracle.

"And then?" asks Zookeeper.

"And then you and Ming-huà make a baby."

"What?" shout Ming-huà and Zookeeper simultaneously.

"You will make love tonight." She looks at Zookeeper. "Don't worry, a formal marriage will be arranged later. Follow me to the bridal chamber."

"It's too soon!" objects Ming-huà. "I'm not ready! Not here! It's too soon!"

"No shit!" adds Zookeeper.

"No time like the present. Sy is unloading the rest of the gear, but your room is ready. Let me show you."

They reluctantly follow Lady Oracle to a side chamber, and when she steps through the opening, the drab rock walls miraculously transform into a gorgeous bedroom, complete with a magnificent bed, antique furniture, and a massive chandelier bathing it in soft light.

"You see?" says Lady Oracle. "We can perform our own magic."

"But—" Ming-huà starts to renew her objections.

"Not to worry," interrupts Lady Oracle. "Just an illusionists' trick. Neverthe-less, it will do." She gazes from Zookeeper to Ming-huà. "You have all night. It must be this night, in this room. Don't worry about oversleeping. No one will bother you."

When Lady Oracle leaves, Ming-huà approaches the objects in the room care-fully, putting out her hands to make sure the furniture, including the bed, is solid.

Zookeeper laughs when she pats a chair to test it. "I really thought your hand would just go straight through."

"Hard to believe," marvels Ming-huà. "How do they do it?"

"Good question. I wonder, with their powers, why they need us at all?"

Ming-huà glances at the bed. "Should we do this, Zookeeper?"

He shakes his head. "It's really up to you. I'm afraid my limitations prevent me from . . . you know."

"Yes, I know. Give me a few moments. Just a few moments to collect myself. I was not prepared for this to be . . . so . . . soon."

"Am I that ugly?"

"No! That's not it at all. You're really quite handsome, you know. I am the ugly one." Ming-huà utters these words in the sincerest humility, but she is reeling under the harsh reality of what before had been only speculation.

How can she sleep with this man with a horrific past who now presents an armless conundrum? Is she even attracted to him? His face is quite handsome, and his body trim and muscular, but she considers the guilt of what she did to him. . . his arms. And his care? Can she deal with that?

The idea of sex with anyone is frightening, let alone this strange, mutilated man. Yet, in the background, she feels intrigued by her power and the idea of having a child whose own powers will be unpredictable, but so fascinating to watch develop. Besides, Zookeeper is considered by many to be a freak, like her.

His image fades into the background when she thinks about having her own child, one to whom she can give unconditional love—and, hopefully, receive it in return.

Oh, it is all so confusing!

"Hello, Ming-huà! You're drifting. I said you are not ugly. No, not at all. You are actually quite beautiful."

"No, thank you but I know what I am."

"Hell!" exclaims Zookeeper, evidently out of patience. "Are we going to con-tinue chattering these meaningless niceties like . . . snobby prigs? Are we going to have sex or not?"

"That is no way to light a woman's romantic fires."

"Ha, ha! Very good! How about this: graze on my lips, and if those hills be dry, stray lower where the pleasant fountains lie."

Ming-huà blushes in spite of herself, a brittle chuckle escaping her lips, though inwardly she reels—agonized, frozen by indecision. The abruptness of the mo-ment disorients her; words elude her grasp, and she stands awkwardly, fingers ner-vously twisting in her hands. Convinced that others see her hump as a grotesque deformity, a wave of shame washes over her—deep, instinctive, and raw. Yet even through this fog of self-consciousness, she detects Zookeeper's rising anticipation and, to her surprise, feels a flicker of warmth awakening within her.

His voice becomes gentle. "Have you ever made love before?"

"No."

"Look, Ming-huà, you're going to have to initiate this. Before we start, turn off that damn chandelier. Firstly, I want you to remove my clothes. After that, I will lay on the bed. Then I want you to strip naked and follow your instincts."

"I'm not sure—"

"I will help. Come on, Ming-huà, let's make a remarkable baby that will surprise even these creeps who have put us here. First, let me kiss you." Zookeeper leans down.

Ming-huà moves forward to meet his lips, and feels a wave of pleasure that builds into a series of delightful tremors as their lips touch again and again.

She unbuttons his shirt, and guided purely by feminine instinct, moves sensuously lower.

~ *Next Morning* ~

When Zookeeper awakes, Ming-huà is nowhere to be seen. Worse, everything is gone; the bed, chandelier, furniture. He is lying on the ground inside a sleeping bag. Only a kerosene lantern casts a faint, flickering light. He wants to get up, but his armless state makes it difficult to extricate himself from the mummy-like bag. Zookeeper is happy to stay warm for a while longer, but now he has the urge to pee. To distract his mind, he replays the night with Ming-huà in his head, smiling at the memory and marveling at her perfect instincts and dormant skills. When he made suggestions, she responded willingly, skillfully, and eventually, passionately. But now he begins to worry. What if they have all left? What if he's alone? Abandoned.

"Ming-huà!" he shouts.

Nothing.

"Hey, anybody here?"

Nothing.

"Hello!" he shouts louder.

Nothing.

Now he feels a bit panicky. He kicks off the sleeping bag and struggles to stand. "Hello! Anybody here?"

Nothing. He cannot grab the lantern unless he holds the handle in his teeth.

"Hey! Somebody answer!"

Nothing.

After a number of tries, he manages to clamp the handle of the lantern in his teeth and awkwardly moves toward the main tunnel, cursing to himself the entire way. Once he reaches the main tunnel, he starts to put down the lantern and shout again, when he sees a glowing light in the direction of the cave's end. Like a moth, it calls to him. As he approaches the light, he has no further need of the burdensome lantern, so he sets it down and moves on. He strains his ears hoping to hear voices, but silence is total and oppressive. The light brightens and begins to pulse rhythmically. Again, he tilts his head to hear better.

... Tap. Tap. Tap....

Zookeeper hears a series of tapping sounds echoing through the stone corridor. A wave of fear rises in him—sudden and total—but he forces himself to stay calm. He tells himself it must be the others, engaged in some strange ritual.

Slowly, cautiously, he moves forward, each step deliberate. When he reaches the mouth of the final chamber, he stops and peers around the edge.

Inside, the others are gathered, their eyes fixed on a statue at the center of the room.

He has never seen anything like it. The figure emits an intense white glow, as if lit from within. It appears to be made of gold—a goddess, perhaps, though whether Hindu or Buddhist he cannot say. She sits in meditation, her posture composed and still. Her legs are folded, hands resting above the knees. The right hand is turned upward, thumb and forefinger forming a perfect circle.

The tapping grows louder. It is coming from inside the statue.

... Tap. Tap. Tap....

Sy and Lady Oracle are standing on either side of Ming-huà, who is kneeling in front of the statue, evidently concentrating on something. Oddly, Sy and Lady Oracle are both looking at Ming-huà, not the figurine.

This frozen tableau lasts a long time. Zookeeper is mesmerized, unwilling to show himself and break the spell. Finally, someone speaks.

"Do you understand what it means, Ming-huà?" asks Lady Oracle.

"Every time I think I have found the pattern, the key, it slips away," replies Ming-huà.

"Your grandmother could read it like a book," says Sy. "Child of Buddha was the Great Interpreter. None of the rest could decipher it."

"And my mother?"

"I don't think she can," says Lady Oracle.

Sy laughs. "Don't underestimate Tamara! She—"

"Hush!" snaps Ming-huà. "Let me listen."

Sy cups a hand to his mouth and whispers to Lady Oracle. "Her pride is at stake."

Zookeeper is not sure what aspect of this scene is more intriguing; the tapping coming from within the statue, or Ming-huà's efforts to decipher it.

While still staring at the figurine, Ming-huà calls out, "Might as well come in, Zookeeper, can't stand there all day."

She sounds like nothing happened last night, he grumbles to himself, somewhat deflated that she is not more . . . more what? Shy? Embarrassed?

"Yes, come on, Zookeeper," encourages Lady Oracle. "Join us."

"What is it?" he asks as he walks up to the group, awkward in his nakedness.

Sy jumps and makes a complete spin in the air. "What do you think it is?"

"A statue."

"Bingo! Do you have a more intelligent question?"

Ming-huà abruptly stands and orders them out of the chamber so she can concentrate.

They retreat farther up the tunnel and huddle in silence, waiting. Zookeeper, awkwardly exposed, gives a discreet signal to Sy, and together they slip away in search of his clothes.

… Tap. Tap. Tap.…

Ming-huà channels all her concentration into detecting the subtlest shifts in rhythm. As faint, near-imperceptible variations begin to surface, she attunes herself to delicate changes in tone, texture, and timbre. Slowly, almost imperceptibly, a pattern begins to coalesce—fragile, yet distinct. Immersed in this evolving tapestry, she traces the nuanced variations as they unfold, like the unfolding movements of a concerto.

… Tap. Tap. Tap.…

Soon, a sense of meaning begins to rise from the tapping—not in the form of words or sentences, but as a figure might slowly emerge from the shifting contours of a cloud. The taps now resonate in unison with her hump, their vibrations amplifying the urgency of whatever presence stirs within the statue, straining to be understood.

… Tap. Tap. Tap.…

What is conveyed strikes directly at her heart, reaching the innermost core of her being, imbued with the gravity of first principles. A murky, primordial sense of origin saturates the message—a resonance from before language, when meaning was felt rather than spoken.

Suddenly, the tapping stops.

"I understand," she whispers.

"Do you?" Lady Oracle now stands behind Ming-huà.

"I do."

"Care to tell me what it means?"

"You don't know?" Ming-huà asks. "I thought this was a test."

Lady Oracle frowns. "Dear girl, what we are doing here, what we intend to do, our plans, your future, the future of humanity—all of it is twisted and contorted into an incomprehensible multidimensional maze: a fantastic phantasmagoria of ghostly specters, deceptive paths, phantom snares, and deadly pits. In short, I do not know."

"Ah," sighs Ming-huà.

"However, I do know what this statue is called. Do you?"

"Well, I think it is some Buddhist or Hindu goddess. I don't really know it's name. Should I?"

"Indeed you should."

"Why?"

"Because it has crossed paths many times with your grandparents and parents, from China to Vietnam to Mongolia to here."

"What is it called?"

"The Precious Object."

"Yes, the name sounds familiar—something I have heard my mother mention—but it's not clear."

"Now tell me."

"What?"

"What does the tapping mean?"

"No, I will not tell you. I cannot tell you. At least for now."

"I understand."

"What next?" asks Ming-huà.

"Return to San Francisco. Rest for a week. Then, to Baltimore."

"Baltimore!" cries Zookeeper. "What the fuck is in Baltimore?"

"A trial by fire," replies Lady Oracle grimly.

Chapter Fifteen

Into The Shadow Of Death

Fear No Evil

~ Destination Hell ~

A musty Baltimore motel room: corners steeped in gloom, blinds broken and yellowed with the grime of forgotten years. A flickering neon sign outside hurls jagged spears of light through the slats, catching cockroaches mid-scurry in erratic, strobe-lit bursts. The wallpaper hangs in shreds; the bed reeks of mildew and despair. Ming-huà sits slumped in a splintered wooden chair, eyes fixed on Lady Oracle, who delivers her speech with the solemn gravity of a senator on the chamber floor.

"In the world to come," proclaims Lady Oracle, "there will be no cruelty born of race, ethnicity, religion, politics, philosophy, or desire. These primitive prejudices will be discarded into the dustbin of evolutionary memory. No one will care whether you are black or white, yellow or red—or even green. No one will care where you came from, what god you serve, or how you speak. Every novel, film, poem, and play ever written about human suffering will stand as an artifact of a brutal and extinct past. Mutually assured destruction will no longer threaten us—it will compel us to evolve toward peace. Upright walking came first, then came the brain. And now, at the corner of North Monroe and West Lanvale Street, in one of the most dangerous slums America has to offer, you will take the next step."

Ming-huà has, over time, begun to entertain the seductive promise of what her power might offer the world. Lately, she finds herself daydreaming about thwarting the cruel, protecting the innocent, and intervening at just the right moment to spare the helpless. In her heart, she is sure there are too many like that trembling fawn on the island—tormented by the few who revel in cruelty. Yet even as these heroic visions take root, a quieter voice within begins to whisper doubts, boring through her savior fantasies like a worm through sweet fruit.

Whenever the melodrama becomes too intoxicating, she throws on the brakes of reason. But the fantasies return—more vivid, more frequent—unbidden and relentless.

"That is a very nice speech, Lady Oracle, but how does a lone hunchback girl achieve this grand shift in the world's paradigm?"

"A journey of ten thousand miles starts with the first step, which we have already taken by honing your skills to become both more powerful and more discriminating. Now we take another step."

Ming-huà looks about the room with distaste, and says, "Given the neighborhood you have chosen to take me to, I can guess. However, I want to hear it from you since until now you have evaded my questions. What exactly is the next step?"

"Every night, you will walk out alone, inviting attack. We will see if your skills can cope."

"If not?"

Lady Oracle shrugs. "You will."

"What if I'm pregnant? What if I lose this precious child you are so keen on?"

"You won't. Look, Ming-huà, we must test your ability. Let us say this is a field test. Whoever attacks you will be a predator, a person who has attacked before and will attack again. Your job is to give him whatever punishment is appropriate, what is deserved."

"What is it to be?" asks Ming-huà, tapping the brakes of sarcasm to slow Lady Oracle's headlong presumptions. "Arms? Legs? Head?"

"In every legal system, the punishment must fit the crime. This is your test. You will decide."

"If I make a mistake? If I maim someone for life because I have a false impression of their intentions or motivations? What then? And how do I live with that?"

"Dear girl, you know the answer to those questions. You simply won't make a mistake. You have the gift of insight into the heart of others, and Zookeeper will accompany you. He is intimately acquainted with the darker side of human nature and human behavior. He will stop you if you are mistaking something for what it is not."

"I thought you said I would be alone!" exclaims Ming-huà.

"You will. Zookeeper will be close by."

"How can he help?"

"He is like your silent guide. If an incident occurs, he will be your advisor. He is familiar with slum dwellers. He can also shout."

"So, a hunchback and an armless man are dropped into the most dangerous area in the country and told to . . . to do what? Entice evil to fight evil?"

"In short, yes."

Ming-huà is in the middle of shaking her head dubiously, when Sy and Zookeeper walk into the room. Sy struggles with multiple bags of takeout food while Zookeeper plops on the bed and bellows, "I'm starving! Had to smell this stuff all the way here."

As Ming-huà surveys the grungy room and its bizarre cast of characters, she marvels at the absurdity of it all. *What a paradigm shift for evolution and the world! A timid hunchback girl, a disjointed clown, an armless ex-crackhead, and a good witch overseeing the whole ridiculous business!*

Zookeeper has become quite adept at eating hamburgers with his feet, and he sits contentedly munching on a thick one when Ming-huà asks, "When do we start?"

"Sooner the better," says Sy.

"I agree," says Zookeeper. "I used to thrive in dumps like this, but you all have spoiled me. Sooner we finish, sooner we go back to that nice apartment with unlimited whiskey and the pleasant company of Bataar."

"Tonight?" asks Ming-huà.

"Do you want it to be tonight?" Lady Oracle asks.

"I agree with Zookeeper. Sooner the better, before I get too nervous and fly back to San Francisco."

"Damn!" bursts Zookeeper. "At least let me finish this burger."

"No hurry," says Lady Oracle glancing at the clock on the nightstand. "The bewitching hour is not yet here."

~

Ming-huà, at the suggestion of Zookeeper, has put on a nice dress and carries a distinctive handbag, but he nixes the idea of donning an expensive looking necklace. When she appears surprised at his objection, he calmly points out, "If we go overboard, they'll think you're an undercover cop." Zookeeper is decked out in rags.

Both stand in the middle of the shabby room, hesitant to leave. Finally, Ming-huà says, "Well, let's go. Now or never."

"Yeah," replies Zookeeper. "You have to go first. I'll follow in a couple of minutes. Walk slow. Remember, I'll be close by."

Ming-huà says goodbye to a miserable looking Sy, who has difficulty suppressing the compulsion to be with her for protection, but his hang-dog demeanor clearly conveys the trouble he is having grappling with the urge to follow anyway.

In contrast, Lady Oracle looks on with a stern countenance. Only a certain softness in her gaze reveals the turmoil within.

Ming-huà slips out of the motel and moves down the sidewalk with as much steadiness as her nerves can manage. The night breathes unevenly around her. Every other streetlight appears extinguished, and those still lit cast a jaundiced glow that seems to nourish the shadows rather than dispel them. The alleyways hum low songs—half invitation, half warning—as though ancient spirits had taken up residence in the cracks and gutters.

She keeps walking. The air shifts with each block—carrying the sharp tang of rot, then the damp trace of rain, then both layered together. It seeps from the alleys she passes, threading in and out of her breath.

Somewhere nearby, she imagines Zookeeper might be following, keeping watch. The thought gives her little comfort. If danger came, she knows he would be more symbol than shield. But even that carries weight. Symbols, even hollow ones, can become anchors in moments when logic fails. In the theater of fear, the name of a friend can feel like a line drawn in the dirt.

The city remains silent. She walks through it as though wrapped in a loose net of stillness—never fully held, never fully free. Every few steps, a soft sound brushes past her, but never resolves into anything clear. Movement comes from just beyond reach. The unseen spaces between trash bins, fences, parked cars, seem aware of her presence. The city is not empty. It's simply not speaking.

Eventually, she crosses the street and loops back in the direction of the motel. Nothing has changed. The silence holds. The alleys remain charged with something she cannot name. The darkness inside them no longer feels like a lack of light—it feels like a presence, as if something waits behind it, older than anything born of wires or circuits.

She glances toward the rooftops, searching for Zookeeper, but the street offers no sign of him. She turns back, walks the same path again. The repetition steadies her. Every faded doorway and dented dumpster feels less threatening now. Familiarity is its own kind of defense, not against harm, but against panic.

Four blocks on, she pauses. One alley draws her attention. It doesn't shout. It doesn't threaten. It simply waits—with a quiet that reaches toward her.

The wind shifts. A soft rustle dances across the ground. Somewhere inside the alley, a piece of paper skates across pavement. The air feels different here—thin, intentional. She tilts her head, listening. Not just with her ears, but with the deeper sense that lives in her back. The faint hum of her hump activates. Signals trickle upward—delicate, but insistent.

Voices rise from the darkness. Not loud. Not close. But present.

She moves to the edge and looks in.

The alley offers no shape, no form. Just depth. Just waiting. Blackness without contour. She scans the street again, one last time. No movement. Zookeeper is gone, or never was. She pulls in a breath and holds it, letting the silence settle across her chest.

Then she steps inside.

The darkness takes her without struggle. It needs no effort to envelop. She moves forward slowly, careful with each step. Her eyes search for detail, but the blackness does not yield. There is no adjustment. No horizon.

The ambient sound from the city disappears behind her. What remains is something quieter—not silence, but vibration. It travels up from the concrete into her feet, moves through her legs, and settles in her bones. Her hump pulses again, more urgently now. The sensation is not threat, not exactly. It's older than that. A warning built into her body before language was born.

Then the light comes.

No warning. No origin.

It flashes behind her, clean and blinding. The alley is revealed all at once—sharp lines, rigid shadows, details thrown into impossible clarity. She doesn't turn toward the source. She doesn't need to. The force of it moves through her spine.

And then, from the far end, a scream.

High. Raw. Not animal. Not fully human.

She turns, heart hammering, breath locked somewhere between throat and mouth. The light fades in staggered flickers. In its wake, the shadows seem to hesitate, as if uncertain. They shift—not randomly, but with shape. They cling to the walls and then pull away, moving in patterns her mind can't decipher.

For a moment, everything halts. The air becomes dense, the silence taut. Meaning hovers nearby but refuses to settle. Her body stands caught between understanding and rupture.

"It's me," comes a voice. She makes out the figures of Sy and Zookeeper behind the glare.

"Step aside," barks Sy roughly. When she does, he directs the flashlight toward the end of the alley where the scream originated. Two bundles of rags form the vague outline of a pair of figures huddled together. Drawing nearer, Sy's beam reveals two people, one tiny and the other full grown, cowering before them.

"Careful," says Zookeeper. "One of them has a knife."

Closer still, and the figures become discernible. Two faces stare out from hooded jackets that rise from under a patchwork of torn blankets; one an adult woman with a skeletal face, the other a child in wide-eyed terror. The woman brandishes a knife but says nothing, while the child quivers against her body.

"Don't worry," says Ming-huà, greatly relieved. "We won't hurt you."

Neither figure responds, remaining motionless and huddled together in their filthy coverlets. The knife blade glints menacingly in the glare of Sy's flashlight.

"Say," says Zookeeper. "You know where a guy can get some fuckin' crack around here? We're new to the neighborhood."

The woman shakes her head and raises the knife.

"All right, we're leaving," says Sy. "No problem."

But Ming-huà walks up to the two figures holding out some cash. Still brandishing the knife, the woman snatches it.

"Let's go," says Sy.

Ming-huà lingers, her gaze infused with compassion as she turns to the woman. "Is this your daughter?" she asks gently.

In response, the woman waves her knife threateningly.

"Okay, I'm leaving," sighs Ming-huà.

~ *Another Sortie* ~

"Of course she doesn't trust us!" exclaims Zookeeper back in the motel room. "We, you, could be anybody with evil intentions. She's probably a crackhead herself, or hooked on some other drug of choice. Anyway, as far as she knows, we want her little girl for some child pornography scam, or worse."

"But, the money?" asks Ming-huà.

"To her, probably a ruse to get close. Rule number one in this jungle is never to get close to anyone, especially junkies. No one offers something for nothing in this world."

"My hump still vibrates from their terror," says Ming-huà. "I also sensed real hunger. I'm going out again."

"Now?" asks Zookeeper.

"Yes."

"Enough for tonight," says Lady Oracle. "There's always tomorrow."

"No, I want to go out tonight . . . alone."

"But that's crazy!" exclaims Zookeeper. "Gonna get yourself killed, or raped!"

"Let her go," says Lady Oracle calmly, her gaze never leaving Ming-huà. "Her choice."

"You going back to the same alley?" asks Sy.

"Maybe, maybe not. But I'm going."

"Why the hurry?" asks Zookeeper.

"I don't know," replies Ming-huà.

"Well, shit. If you have to go, now's the time 'cause it's so fuckin' early in the morning. Past the bedtime of most murderers and rapists. Nay, but make haste; the better foot before."

"Geezz, you and your Shakespeare, Zookeeper!" says Sy. "I'll follow you out, Ming-huà."

"No!"

"Why not?"

"I don't know that either. Give me the flashlight."

"But—"

"Enough!" bursts Lady Oracle. "I said let her go! Give her the flashlight!"

With Lady Oracle's final words still echoing in her ears, Ming-huà steps out into the night and returns to the familiar stretch of sidewalk. Her nerves remain taut, but this time, resolve steadies her stride. The air is damp and raw, the hour still locked in the hush before dawn. Her destination is no longer in question. The memory of the two pitiful figures huddled in the shadows—and the unearthly scream that still reverberates in her mind—pulls her forward as would an undertow, unseen but irresistable.

Her hump stirs, crackling with garbled signals, a scatter of unreadable impressions. Then, without warning, a sharp spike shoots into her consciousness, and her gaze is drawn across the street. Two men lean against a lamppost, watching. As she continues down the sidewalk, they fall into a slow, deliberate saunter, keeping pace on the opposite side—distant but undeniably present. Their movements radiate a simmering threat. Waves of warning rise through her hump, and old fear returns—an old ache.

The alley draws near—the same black mouth into which she vanished before—but now a new dilemma gnaws at her: to lead them there would be folly. To turn back would be worse. She searches for an escape route, but the streets are empty, their intersections stretching in a cold, geometric bleakness. Traffic lights blink through their meaningless cycle—red, yellow, green—beacons to no one.

Then comes the laughter. High, mocking, void of joy—like the cruel mirth of the hunters who once drowned the fawn on her island. The memory stings. Yet, inexplicably, Ming-huà laughs too. The sound startles her. It rises from somewhere deeper than defiance. In that moment, something ancient and immovable stirs inside her. She is no longer the sheltered girl who lived in silence on an isolated island. Something has changed—fundamentally, irrevocably. Her time with Lady Oracle and Sy has shaped her, carved new chambers in her spirit. Fear, once her master, now bends to her will. Yes, part of this strength flows from the power that hums beneath her skin, but something more elusive bolsters her now—a strange calm, as though she has made peace with the storm ahead. Perhaps she even welcomes it.

At the mouth of the alley, she halts only briefly, then steps into the darkness without hesitation. Before she has taken four strides, she hears their footsteps close behind, their voices whispering, low and intimate. Her hump flares with alarm, but this time she does not flinch. She presses on, toward where she hopes the mother and daughter still linger. With a flick of her hand, she clicks on the flashlight. Its beam slices through the shadows. The whispers behind her grow louder. And then a revelation—a strange, electric pulse of clarity: she wants them to attack. She wants to teach them what it means to stalk prey in a world that is no longer helpless. She wants to—

"Hey, lady," one of the voices says in a low, gravelly drawl. "You don't wanna be wanderin' deeper into this here alley. There's a mama bear back there, and she don't take kindly to strangers. She'll mess you up real bad if you keep on goin'."

One of the men flicks on his own flashlight and directs its beam past Ming-huà to the two figures at the end of the alley. She sees the knife clearly gleaming in the light. The scene is being played out again, but with different actors.

Ming-huà turns around to confront the men, and is greeted with two smiling faces, white teeth bursting from the dark cave of their hoods, one short, the other tall.

"Oh," she mumbles.

"What's you doin' here anyhow?" asks the taller one.

"I was just walking," replies Ming-huà, still wary.

"No need to be scared. Julian and me, we're kinda like a neighborhood watch, you know what I mean? We look scary, but . . . well, we just wanna make sure you're okay. Don't see many women . . . leastways, respectable women, walkin' around here in the middle of the night. You're quite the sight. Anyways, what you doin' here?"

"Just walking. Well, actually, I saw this woman and her child earlier and couldn't sleep, so I wanted to see if I could help."

They both laugh. The shorter one says, "Ol' Crazy Jasmine here is a bit off, keeps her daughter real close so no one can get near without havin' a knife pulled. Gets her food from dumpster diving and begging in daylight. This here alleyway is her home. You're trespassin', you might say. Yup, she's a real mother bear, sharp claws 'n all, so I suggest you turn around."

"Can I give her money?"

"Oh! She'll take that all right!" exclaims the taller one.

"Hey, Jasmine!" shouts the short one. "She's got money for you. Don't do nothin' you'll regret."

Silence. Ming-huà looks questioningly at the two men.

"Oh, she don't talk. Go on ahead, but be careful. We'll stick around."

They keep the flashlight on the woman and her daughter. Ming-huà gingerly approaches and holds out a twenty-dollar bill. Crazy Jasmine stares in disbelief, then lightning quick grabs it while still holding up the knife with her other hand.

When Ming-huà rejoins the two men, they chuckle. "You're a brave woman," says the taller one. "Where you stayin'? From the looks of you, it ain't in no alleyway."

Ming-huà consults her hump and continues to receive vibrations that can only be interpreted as threat. *Something is wrong with this picture,* she thinks. "Lamplighter Motel," she says.

"We'll accompany you there," says the tall one. "Jesus Christ! I still don't get why you're walkin' out here alone like this. You ain't lookin' for drugs or anything like that, are you?"

"No."

The short one takes a stab. "You for sale?"

"No."

He shrugs. "Okay."

Trying to ignore the warning vibrations from her hump, she starts walking with the two men back to the motel. Still on high alert, she suspects they will shove her in every alley they pass.

"What's your name?" asks the short one.

"Ming-huà," she replies. "And yours?"

"I'm Micari and this is Julian."

"Thank you for your concern," she says.

"Ain't nothin'. You know, this is a crazy-ass place to be for a woman like you, even if you are a hunchback, no offense."

"No offense taken. Here we are."

A neon light displaying "Lamplighter Motel" casts a pale glow on the three figures.

Ming-huà pauses, trying to find words, but they do not come.

"Okay, you're good to go," says Micari, looking perplexed.

Ming-huà is still at a loss, considering the peculiar way the evening has unfolded. Somehow, her hump failed tonight, and this failure has thrown her off balance. Having given her false information, what if she had acted on it prematurely?

"Thank you both," she says, and watches them walk away, conversing and laughing until they disappear around the corner.

Walking back to the room, Ming-huà finds herself deeply troubled by the entire evening's events. Sy, Lady Oracle, and Zookeeper are all waiting in her room, and when she enters, Zookeeper is the first to speak.

"Well? Leave any armless, headless, legless people out there?"

"Don't even joke about that, Zookeeper."

"I assume there were no incidents?" asks Lady Oracle.

"No."

"You go again tomorrow night," says Lady Oracle, clearly disappointed.

~

Ming-huà sleeps as best she can during the day, but her bumpy journey from doubt to confidence has shifted back to doubt. How had she so misread Julian and Micari? Far from being threats, they had actually protected her. If she cannot rely on the accuracy of her hump, how can she be confident she won't take some irreversibly erroneous step and ruin lives?

She wakes in the glare of the afternoon light to find food ordered by Lady Oracle waiting. Both women eat in silence, broken only by a few monosyllabic niceties. This quiet time suits Ming-huà, whose thoughts of the previous night are rekindled by a disturbing low-key buzz from her hump. Jarring sounds of the inner-city filter into the room: sirens, trash-talking passersby, homeless mumbling to themselves, shouts from balconies, muffled screams behind windows, loud hip-hop music, and squealing tires. *At least there are no gunshots*, thinks Ming-huà glumly. The memory of a certain chatty squirrel runs through her mind, and she is hit with nostalgia for a more serene life on the island, yet her newfound confidence and independence continue to assert themselves and again she looks forward to testing herself tonight. These back-and-forth emotional swings are noticed by Lady Oracle.

"You're changing," she says bluntly.

"Yes. I know."

"You're like a young butterfly squirming in the cocoon, struggling to burst out and spread your wings. That is part of the process. Back and forth. Does it bother you?"

"The process?"

"Everything is a process, including evolution."

"I'm still human, you know," says Ming-huà.

"Well, that may be a bit of a technical issue," replies Lady Oracle with a sly smile. "You see, we might call *Homo erectus* and *Homo heidelbergensis* and *Homo Neanderthals* and the rest of your ancestors human, but they represent a different species under the same genus—*Homo*. Well, it's the same with *Homo sapiens*."

"Are you saying I'm a different species?"

"Maybe. Does that bother you? It is all part of the process. Rest assured, you are still genus *Homo*, so all is not lost. We may categorize you as *Homo minghuasis*." Lady Oracle laughs at this last little *bon mot*. "Being of the same genus must be of some comfort to you."

"Thanks," says Ming-huà sarcastically. She tries to be insulted by this paleontological musing, but is surprised to find herself pleased by the possibility. *Imagine being a different species!* she marvels, throwing in the cautionary, *If it is true.*

"Do you want to go out alone tonight, or do you want Sy or Zookeeper along? You know, on a Saturday night there will be much more activity."

"Definitely alone."

"Why? You know it is very dangerous out there."

"Because I don't want to be distracted by worrying about someone else. If something bad happens, I want to make sure I don't make any mistakes. I have come so far and—" She abruptly stops, dismissing such a thought as brash.

Lady Oracle smiles but says nothing.

The rest of the day passes quickly, and Ming-huà waits impatiently for night.

When it arrives, she leaves the motel and steps into a very different environment.

~

Misty darkness has settled over the neighborhood like a shroud. The sidewalks teem with restless figures—mostly young men prowling for mischief—while streetwalkers lean into car windows, drawn by the slow crawl of traffic. The dim streetlamps cast a sickly pall, their jaundiced glow only deepening the gloom. Ming-huà has barely walked a block when every eye turns toward her: an Asian-looking hunchback gliding silently across their well-worn terrain, spectral and out of place. A voice calls from the rolled-down window of a dented Chevy—an indecent offer she ignores without pause.

What nerve, some think. What kind of twisted arrogance drives this malformed woman to walk so boldly, so shamelessly, as if the shadows themselves owe her passage? To some, she is a curiosity. To others, a provocation. And to a few, unmistakably, a target.

"Hey, bitch, need some comfort?" says a junkie sidling up to her. "Got what you need. Just say the word."

"No, thanks."

He laughs. "So polite! Baby, hunchbacks turn me on. I can give some for cheap, whatever suits your fancy."

"No, thanks."

Mercifully, he shrugs and moves on. Ming-huà continues walking, her footsteps steadier now, her breath more certain. It strikes her as strange—this rising sense of confidence. All around her are the fractured and the forgotten, broken lives drifting through broken streets. And yet, in their midst, she feels something stir: a power long buried, coaxing her to believe it might still be used for good. Strangest of all, she feels invulnerable. The sensation is familiar, though each time it resurfaces, she's tried to push it down—to suppress the rush, the dangerous calm. But it only grows stronger. Tonight, she walks farther than the night before, turning down a narrow side street that radiates menace. The air is thick, unmoving. The silence feels rehearsed. And yet, to her astonishment, she finds herself wanting the worst. Some hidden part of her longs to be tested, to be attacked, to see what happens when the leash is severed.

A voice—quiet, instinctive—warns her she's gone too far. But before the thought fully forms, a sudden, explosive force hurls her to the ground. The impact leaves her gasping. Disoriented, she lifts her head, only to be kicked brutally in the stomach. The pain claws upward, forcing a bitter surge from her throat. She tries to focus, but hands—many hands—grip and tear at her clothing. A blunt object cracks against her skull. The world tilts and fades.

When she regains consciousness, her body is exposed. Her purse is missing. Her dress hangs in torn fragments, barely covering her. Hands continue to press against her skin—rough, invasive, without identity. The air vibrates with laughter, loud and erratic, filled with slurs and threats and the satisfaction of power unchecked. Her legs are forced apart. In the corner of her vision, glints of metal flicker in the darkness—one a pistol, others the edges of knives. The alley contracts around her, trapping sound, scent, and motion in a single, closing grip.

Something within her breaks loose.

No warning. No words. Just a flood of internal force tearing outward, silent but unstoppable. Her mind does not form the intention. It simply erupts.

Then—stillness.

Complete and sudden. The noise stops as if the world has been cut. No sound, no motion, only the residue of shock. And then, without transition, the screaming begins.

Not anger. Not agony. Not dominance. These are the screams of fear. Deep, unraveling fear that comes when the order of things collapses.

Ming-huà rises. Her limbs tremble. She gathers the shredded fabric of her dress against her chest, shielding what remains of herself. The cries bounce off the alley walls, filling the space with a rising confusion of sound. It builds without shape, without rhythm, pushing itself into her ears and nerves.

Now her vision sharpens.

There are four of them.

Two still stand, though barely—rocking unsteadily, balanced on what's left of their lower bodies. Their arms flail uselessly, stripped of control. Their eyes hold no comprehension, only panic. The other two lie scattered across the ground in pieces—flesh and bone severed from form, limbs dislocated, torsos torn apart. No breath, no sound. Just silence where bodies used to be.

She stares, unable to move. The horror is not just external. It lives inside her now, written into muscle and memory. Her stomach tightens. Her hands won't unclench. Her feet begin to retreat on their own, step by step.

She turns. She runs.

The screaming follows, rising again behind her, clawing at the walls, chasing her down the narrow path between stone and shadow. It does not fade. It multiplies. Every surface throws it back at her, reshaping it into something larger, something harder to forget.

She does not look back.

In her flight, she fails to see the figure standing further down, half-wrapped in shadow.

Still.

Watching.

A knife gleams faintly in one hand. In the other, a child sleeps without stirring.

~ *The Watcher* ~

She does not flinch when the violence erupts.

From the far end of the alley, she watches without blinking, her body motionless, eyes trained on the girl. One hand holds the knife—not raised, not at rest. The other cradles the child whose breath remains even, eyes closed, limbs relaxed. The child does not stir. She does not expect it to.

Then, silence.

A deep, unnatural silence, the kind that follows not noise but a shift in the order of things.

And then, the screaming.

Not all at once. One voice, then two, then four, each finding its terror in its own time. Not pain. Not outrage. Something more elemental. Something pulled from the marrow and forced into sound.

She waits until the girl flees. Watches her rise, stagger, clutch what's left of her clothing, and run without looking back. She tracks the direction, notes her gait, the angle of her retreat, the exact moment when her outline vanishes from the frame of the alley. She listens until the last echo of her footfalls fades into the dark.

Then, slowly, she steps forward.

The alley reeks—filth, sweat, bile, the staleness of bodies kept alive too long in darkness. But no blood. Not a single drop. The scent of violence is here, but it carries no stain.

The remains are scattered—arms, legs, torsos. Heads angled at strange degrees. The separations are clean. No tearing. No exposed tissue. No pools beneath them. As if the bodies had been taken apart gently. As if they had been designed to come apart. The limbs lie where they fell, quiet, still, unbleeding—waiting to be reattached or discarded.

They look less like victims than abandoned pieces. Dolls in need of purpose. Tools emptied of function.

One of them is still breathing. She moves closer and crouches. His chest rises and falls unevenly. His eyes are open, wide, trying to find her. The mouth twitches, tries to speak. But there is no tongue. No sound.

She leans in until her face is inches from his.

There is no rage in her. No pity. She is only here to observe.

He is already finished. The rest of his body just hasn't accepted it yet.

She stands.

She moves without hurry through the remnants, careful not to disturb them. There is nothing to clean up. Nothing to mark. No evidence, no weapon, no blood to trail. The alley will forget quickly.

She adjusts the child in her arms and retreats back into shadow.

She will not speak of this. She will not send a warning. The world will continue to turn, unaware that something has shifted.

But she has seen what lives inside the girl now.

Not rage.

Not trauma.

Not human.

Something far more precise.

Chapter Sixteen

The Purge

Hitting A Wall

~ Collapse ~

Ming-huà has scarcely stumbled through the apartment door, breathless and shaken, before stammering out a fragmented account of the night's horrors. The words are barely coherent, but they're enough. Lady Oracle issues a swift, unwavering command: pack up and leave at once.

While she settles the bill with practiced calm, the others scramble in disarray and tumble into the rental car. Sy sits behind the wheel, engine idling, drumming his fingers with thinly veiled impatience. The moment Lady Oracle slips into the passenger seat, he pulls away from the curb and speeds into the night—no destination in mind, only the urgent need to escape.

"Slow down," says Lady Oracle calmly. "Now is not a good time for a ticket."

"Where to?" asks Sy.

"Airport."

In the back seat, Ming-huà begins to hyperventilate, and Zookeeper does his best to soothe her panic.

"No sweat," Zookeeper says. "All the cops know is that a hunchback was attacked. The fact that there will be no blood or any evidence of a crime being committed will confuse the shit out of them. Besides, how could a hunchback woman take out four kick-ass men?"

Ming-huà moans in agony.

"Now is not the time, Zookeeper" says Lady Oracle.

"Ming-huà, dear girl, try and calm yourself," says Sy. "You acted in self-defense. You did what you had to do. You did what we came here for."

"To kill two men and maim two others?" She barely gets the words out without choking on them.

"Zookeeper is right," says Lady Oracle. "This has been anticipated. I was hoping to keep it not quite so . . . extreme. But we will return to San Francisco and do further work."

"No!" exclaims Ming-huà. "I'm going back to the island. Enough of this madness! No more!"

"Ming-huà, you defended yourself from being raped and very probably murdered. You did nothing wrong. In fact, you have proven the point, albeit quite dramatically."

"What point?" cries Ming-huà.

"You are not of their kind. Like it or not, you are the next step. All that remains is to learn to exert more control in extreme situations. Just as consciousness, self-awareness of their inevitable mortality, and conscience evolved, humans had to learn to somehow tame them—thus, legal codes. Your legal code will be imprinted into your brain. Your verdict will be instantaneous and just. It will be passed down even more precisely. Thus, your child."

"Is this enough justification to kill two men and maim two others?"

"Control, Ming-huà. We will work with you so you learn to control your power more . . . well, as I said, more precisely. And you will learn to do it in extreme and fluid situations that leave almost no time for thought. In any case, those four predators will not again prey on innocent people."

"No. I am returning to my island. This has to end. I can't survive this."

"You will have to deal with a child whose powers will likely exceed yours. Or do you want an abortion if you're pregnant?"

"That will be my decision, not yours."

"Granted. Let me ask you this, why do your powers not work on me or Sy?"

"I don't know. Something to do with this *Goddess* business."

"We're here," says Sy, stopping in front of the terminal building. "Go on in and get the luggage checked while I park. I assume we all have our open return tickets?"

With a unanimous confirmation, Lady Oracle mutters, "I hope so. It was next to impossible to get them."

Ming-huà has calmed, but the tears will not stop. "So that's why you went to such trouble to get open return tickets—you knew this would happen! I'm warning you that when we get back to San Francisco, I'm leaving for the island. No amount of argument will convince me otherwise."

"We shall see," says Lady Oracle grimly.

During this conversation, Zookeeper has kept silent, but his anger now bursts out. "Shit! No one in this fuckin' car is thinking of me! It's also my baby that might be cooking in Ming-huà's belly! Mine! If she goes, I go with her! I fuckin' like the idea of being the father of a new species."

Although Ming-huà is clearly distressed at his words, she says, "Of course, you are welcome to come with me."

Zookeeper laughs. "Wonder what those poor cops are thinking now? They're probably shitting their pants."

"Please, no more," pleads Ming-huà.

"Yes, be quiet Zookeeper!" snaps Lady Oracle. "From now on, try being more Shakespeare and less Zookeeper. And speaking of the police, let's go now!"

~

The flight back to San Francisco is wrapped in silence, dense and impenetrable. No one speaks. Each soul spirals inward, caught in a quiet reckoning of hope, fear, and unanswered questions. All except one. Lady Oracle sits motionless, her posture unyielding, an enigmatic smile curving her lips—as if amused by something only the stars could understand. When Ming-huà meets her eyes, the smile widens. It is not cruel, but it carries the weight of knowledge too vast to be kind. Ming-huà looks away, unsettled, the image lingering like an afterimage behind her eyelids.

They arrive at the mansion bone-weary, shadows under their eyes deeper than fatigue. Words become obsolete. A few murmured goodnights drift through the air and dissolve.

The next morning, Ming-huà breaks the silence. Her voice is quiet, yet certain.

"I've decided. I'm going back to the island."

Sy starts to object, but Lady Oracle silences him with a single lifted hand. The room falls still, expectant.

"There is a law," she says at last, her voice calm but resonant, as if speaking not just to Ming-huà but to the space between atoms. "A law born from paradox. Quantum Field Theory tells us that nothing—true, perfect nothingness—is a mirage. You can remove every atom, every speck of matter. You can drain all energy, plunge to absolute zero. Still, it stirs. Virtual particles flicker into and out of existence, leaving behind a shimmer, a trace. Even emptiness is haunted by the possibility of something."

Ming-huà blinks. She understands the science, vaguely—but Lady Oracle's words seem to reach deeper than physics. Something in her hump stirs, a faint vibration—the memory of a voice not yet spoken.

"You," Lady Oracle continues, "are that shimmer. That flicker. That paradox."

Ming-huà's breath quickens. A strange heat moves through her chest—not pride, but unease. She does not feel like a flicker. She feels like a fracture.

Lady Oracle's words flow on—a persistent hum beneath her skin, resonating with a truth she isn't ready to name. "Where others are filled with noise and motion, you hold stillness. Not passivity—stillness. A sacred quiet that stretches into realms beyond form. Your father heard the dreams of dogs. You are past that. You carry absence as others carry blood. Through you, the boundaries between what is and what was begin to dissolve."

Ming-huà lowers her gaze, her fingers tightening around the edge of her chair. The memory unfurls: the alley shrouded in shadow, the screams that tore through the night, the terrible silence that followed. The torsos. The severed stumps. She has not wept—not yet—but something within her stirs. Not sorrow. Not fear. Something quieter, more resolute. A recognition. As if some hidden part of her is no longer resisting what she is—but beginning, at last, to accept.

"When you wield your gift," Lady Oracle says, voice now laced with reverence, "you do not harm. You *unmake*. You call forth the stillness beneath all things—the space before birth, the breath after death. What you touch does not die. It returns."

Ming-huà's heart stirs painfully. *Then why does it feel like murder?* she wonders. *Why do their screams still echo in me?* She sees their faces—no, not faces. She cannot remember them. Only the terror. The bloodless blood. The absence that followed.

"Whether you return to your island or not is irrelevant," Lady Oracle continues. "The island is no sanctuary. It is silence without awareness. But you are no longer merely a vessel of silence. You are becoming its conductor. Its wielder."

Ming-huà swallows hard. Something inside her wants to run. But another part—a deeper, ancient stillness—does not move. It listens. It waits.

"You will bear a child," Lady Oracle says now, and Ming-huà flinches. "That child will inherit your gift. But without guidance, without mastery, your child will be lost—adrift in a sea of calamity, a force without a compass. You must stay. You must learn."

Ming-huà's voice trembles inside her. *I never asked for this. I didn't want this. I only wanted to understand the world. Not become its undoing.* But the words stay trapped in her throat. She knows the decision is already being written across her soul.

"The world is unraveling," Lady Oracle says in an iron voice wrapped in velvet. "Humanity spirals toward extinction, dragging the innocent down with it. The forests will go. The oceans. The bees. The whales. Even the sky. Not through malice, but through blindness—through the same failure of vision that led humans to sever themselves from the sacred balance."

Her gaze settles fully on Ming-huà.

"Only those who stand at the threshold—those who dwell in stillness, who listen for the silence beneath the noise—can intervene. You are one of them. Perhaps the last. Or perhaps the first of what must come next. The Superior Ones are not a prophecy. They are an inevitability. But you—your choices—may determine whether they rise as the rightful heirs to a broken humanity . . . or as its replacements."

She lets the words breathe before continuing.

"The choice is yours. But if you turn away, if fear becomes your compass, then you and your child will be devoured. Not by evil—but by ignorance masquerading as order. By a world that has forgotten how to see."

She leans forward, her eyes two moons suspended in gravityless space.

"Learn to wield your stillness—or vanish, as your child will vanish, torn apart by a frightened, primitive world that mistakes the mysterious unknown a curse."

"I'm pregnant," Ming-huà says in a hollow voice. She stands up nervously and fidgets with clearing her dishes.

Lady Oracle cannot suppress her excitement. "Are you sure?"

"I'm sure."

"But that is excellent news!" Lady Oracle exclaims, her face aglow with pleasure.

"No!" blurts Ming-huà. "I'm no longer sure it is good news. What am I bringing into the world?"

"You are one of the first steps; this child will be the next."

"Yes, but they are steps leading toward what?"

"The future."

"And my parents and grandparents?"

"Precursors," says Lady Oracle curtly.

Ming-huà blinks in anger. "Precursors? Is that all? Did the hell they went through qualify them to be nothing more than useful little steps in your grand progression?"

"But, of course, it is not my grand progression. Evolution, chemistry, natural selection, all lead the way. The steps reside in your genes, not your mind."

Ming-huà scoffs. "I repeat, steps toward what?"

Lady Oracle stares deeply into Ming-huà's eyes. "Adaptation. Fitness. Salvation"

"Salvation to you; damnation to me."

"No, salvation to life on earth. Damnation to needless suffering."

"And the corpses and half-men I left behind in the past, or those I will leave behind in the future?"

"As I said, damnation to those who cause needless suffering."

"Lady Oracle, I'm not up to being the salvation or the damnation of anyone or anything. You are looking for a new species, I am looking for peace and tranquility."

"Ming-huà!" Lady Oracle snaps. "I am not looking for a new species, I have found a new species! Do you want to squander this golden chance for humankind to advance? Do you want unnecessary suffering and useless devastation to continue? Do you want *Him* to win, the Vengeful Godhead?"

Ming-huà shakes her head dubiously and paces like a caged animal. "So, we are back to this battle between *Goddess* and *God*? Those are figments of a schizophrenic's mind. Fantasies. They drove my father mad. They drove him to suicide. They are not my responsibility."

Lady Oracle draws herself up and assumes an intimidating air. "Then leave! Go! Flee to your isolated island. Isolate yourself. Grow old and die a lonely old woman whose child will be left without direction because you will not know what direction to give."

"I will have Zookeeper," says Ming-huà feebly.

Lady Oracle laughs heartily. "Go! Take him with you! Leave this world behind, trapped in the suffocating mire humans have made of it, and thanks to you, will continue to make of it until it is no more."

"I cannot change the world."

"Foolish girl! You are the change! Tell the first *Homo sapiens* to evolve in Africa they did not change the world."

"Nothing you can say will stop me from leaving," insists Ming-huà. But her words falter, and everyone in the room feels her uncertainties and anxieties wash over them.

"Go," repeats Lady Oracle. "Run to your island and see what peace you find."

Ming-huà hesitates, and looks at Sy whose face is unspeakably sad, tears running down his cheeks. She turns to Zookeeper who looks on with a grim countenance.

"What should I do?" she asks Zookeeper.

"Do what you think is right."

"But, right for who?" she pleads. "Me? Humanity? You? This child?"

"Yes," replies Zookeeper.

"Zookeeper," she says. "You're the closest of all in this room to the violent world of degenerate humankind. You know their propensities for vile addictions and murderous rages. I owe you the most. I took your arms. I beg you answer me honestly, should I stay?"

He does not waver. "Yes."

Ming-huà reels backward a step as if struck physically. "But . . . I thought . . . why?"

"If there's a chance to change this bullshit world—no, let me be as eloquent as you. If there is a chance to alter the trajectory of our species and create a new age of enlightenment, then I say you should stay and try."

While Ming-huà processes his words, Zookeeper adds in forced levity, "Besides, I ain't no fuckin' hillbilly suited to living in the woods."

Lady Oracle speaks in a low, husky voice. "Correction, Zookeeper. She's not changing the trajectory of your *species;* she's changing the trajectory of your *genus.*"

Zookeeper feels the hairs on his head tingle. "What do you mean '*your* species' and '*your* genus'?"

"A figure of speech."

"Look," says Zookeeper brusquely. "Who the fuck are you? Better yet, what the fuck are you?"

"I am no different than you."

"Bullshit! Tell me, tell us, the truth!"

"The only truth lies in nothingness. All else is deception. Your lost arms are dwelling where there is truth."

"Goddamn it! Speak English! None of your fuckin' riddles!"

Lady Oracle smiles. "Get used to them."

"Forget it, Zookeeper," says Ming-huà. "You'll never get a straight answer. I've heard things they didn't want me to know. My mother had conversations with herself about my father, and I listened. She told me things in moments of weakness. I'm starting to remember. I'm beginning to understand."

"Well, shit, I'm not," says Zookeeper. "What do you understand?"

"I understand, or I'm beginning to understand. You're right. I should stay . . . no, I have to stay."

"Because of what I said?"

"No, because of what she is." Ming-huà points at Lady Oracle. "Her grandmother is Buandelgereen, at least that's the story my mother told me. Now—yes, now—I'm beginning to understand."

"Shit, Ming-huà, you're starting to scare the shit outta me. What *is* she?"

Ming-huà speaks as if she had not heard his words. "Sy also. Both of them. The stories are coming back. I always thought my mother never spoke about the past, but now I realize she did. Strange stories about quests and tunnels and caves and iron doors. Names come up from the depths. Names like Feng shiren. Odd names. Storyteller, Nature, Han Tinh, Mountain Man, Tuyet Mai, and so many others. Yes, she talked sometimes as if in her sleep, and I listened. Can't quite put it together yet, but it's coming back slowly."

"Now you know why it is imperative you stay?" asks Lady Oracle.

"Now I know."

~ *Resurrection and Return* ~

In the months following their return to San Francisco, Ming-huà senses her power deepening. Her ability to interpret the messages her hump draws from the world around her sharpens by the day, and with it comes a rising euphoria—an exhilaration that has nearly erased the shy, innocent girl who once played among flowers with Miss Gladflower. That version of herself now feels a distant shadow.

No longer content to passively receive impressions, Ming-huà begins to actively cultivate her gifts, immersing herself in the study of empathy and extrasensory perception. Like her father once did, she attempts to commune with objects most would consider mute—sidewalks, trees, stones, lampposts—nothing escapes her quiet invitations to speak. And, astonishingly, some do.

Sy and Zookeeper, eager to test her limits, conspire to spring ever more startling surprises upon her, often when she least expects them. They frequently retreat to the nearby mountains, where Lady Oracle oversees her most difficult training. One such task: dissociating a bullet in flight—without warning of when it will be fired. At first, her success is inconsistent, but over time the misses dwindle, the hits multiply. Even when shocked or ambushed, she increasingly channels her power with precision, reducing potential harm while maximizing control. The once-menacing stoshells have become child's play.

These are halcyon days for Ming-huà—days untroubled by the dangers of street life, defined instead by a steady ascent. The training is grueling but often exhilarating, a crucible of growth rather than threat. Guilt lingers, as it always does, but now it lies farther beneath the surface, no longer dictating her every breath.

Then, one afternoon, Sy goes too far. Caught up in the thrill of experimentation, he creeps behind her with a wooden bat, certain—too certain—that it will dissolve in his hands before impact. It does not.

The blow lands hard. Ming-huà crumples to the floor.

Stunned, Sy drops beside her, his face draining of color. "Oh God . . . Ming-huà—are you okay? What have I done? Are you okay?"

But she does not respond and he calls for help.

Lady Oracle rushes into the room and they lay her on the couch.

"Should I call Altan?" asks Sy.

"No! She is only knocked out. I can feel the knot rising on the back of her head. She'll come around. How did it happen?"

When Sy explains, Lady Oracle laughs. "Live and learn. It is an important lesson. Perhaps she felt your presence and your intent, but ignored it assuming you would not carry through. Or worse, she did not pick any of it up."

"You were right the first time," says Ming-huà a bit groggily. "I knew he was there, but ignored the signs. It is entirely my fault. Ouch! It hurts!"

"Never assume, girl!" scolds Lady Oracle. "You could easily have been killed. Remember: simplicity without flourishes! Threatening signals are to be ignored at your peril."

"But I knew it was only Sy."

"She that increaseth knowledge increaseth sorrow."

"That's fuckin' right!" pipes up Zookeeper. "Can't trust anyone, especially in your position. There's no trust, no faith, no honesty in men—all perjured, all forsworn, all naught, all dissemblers."

Ming-huà vows to never again allow Sy, Zookeeper or anyone else to take her by surprise.

~

As all good things must end, one morning Lady Oracle announces the termination of the training period. After making this curt proclamation, she falls silent.

"Well?" asks Ming-huà. "What now?"

"You won't like it."

Ming-huà has visions of being transported to the vilest neighborhoods in America, and is afraid to ask more. Zookeeper, however, is not so restrained.

"Come on!" he cries. "Tell us, goddammit!"

Lady Oracle laughs. "So impatient!"

"Damn right I'm impatient! I want to know what shithole you're gonna to send us to."

Lady Oracle looks at Ming-huà. "And you? Are you also impatient to know what comes next?"

"Somehow I think this is a trap, but yes, I want to know. Tell us."

"Okay, here it is. We wait."

"What? After all this training shit! We wait?"

Lady Oracle nods her head toward Ming-huà. "Look at her. We cannot risk the pregnancy."

"Good," says Ming-huà. "But what about after the baby is born?"

"When that time comes, we'll decide how to proceed. The baby must take first priority. First, let's ensure it's born healthy, then let's take time to observe it."

"Maybe you should rephrase that," says an angry Ming-huà. "I agree the baby must take first priority, but not because we must observe it, rather because we must take time to love and nurture it."

"I agree," pops in Zookeeper.

"And so we will, dear boy. This baby will be surrounded by love—and something else as well."

"What?"

"Curiosity."

"Ah, yes," says Ming-huà sarcastically. "We must be good little scientists, or guides, or whatever, and always observe the little freak to see just how freakish it might turn out to be."

"No," says Lady Oracle. "This baby will be no freak. And trust me, it will receive ample amounts of what you call love."

~

Back in her room, Ming-huà is awash in a quiet euphoria. Her pregnancy is progressing smoothly, the child is safe, and—at least for now—no one intends to thrust her into danger. The space around her is not only secure but soothing, even luxurious. Wrapped in this rare moment of contentment, she lets herself drift.

Then, without warning, a low, thunderous voice tears through the stillness, shaking her from complacency like an earthquake beneath calm waters.

You must flee this place! For your baby's sake—escape before it is too late!

Before she can even process the words, a second voice—feminine, sharp with urgency—cuts through the air.

Hush! Do not listen to this trickster God! He lies to you!

And then—silence. Sudden, absolute. Only faint echoes linger, like the aftertaste of a dream that won't quite fade.

Were it not for those echoes, Ming-huà might have dismissed the voices as tricks of an overstimulated mind. But her hump insists otherwise: it flares with chaotic warning signals, vibrating with a sense of real, present danger. The words have struck something deeper. Now she must ask: whom to believe? The male? The female? Neither?

The warm cocoon of peace she had been luxuriating in curdles into something cold and corrosive. Worse still, she realizes—she has just experienced the ancient war between God and Goddess firsthand, that same divine conflict she once scoffed at as the product of her father's fractured mind.

Once again, the island calls to her—its silence, its stillness, its illusion of sanctuary. But the call is fainter now, no longer a refuge but a temptation to retreat. She forces her thoughts away from the spiral of fear and turns them toward the life growing within her. This child will not be ordinary. It cannot be. Ming-huà senses it already—the latent gravity of a presence not yet born. The world may not be ready, but it will be changed. Whether in gentleness or in fire, the child's arrival will mark a turning. A revelation. Perhaps even a reckoning.

Chapter Seventeen

The Child

Mental Warfare

As the moment of birth draws near, Ming-huà finds herself slipping into a reality she doesn't fully understand. The child within her—once quiet, once waiting—has begun to speak. Not in words, but in thought, vivid and insistent, flooding her mind without warning. The messages come quickly, layered with meanings she cannot fully grasp. They arrive unfinished, urgent, slipping past her just as she tries to hold them.

Behind it all, the voices return. Not soft anymore. Not distant. They roar through her—God and Goddess, no longer contained in the sky or the earth but surging through her nerves, her blood, her breath. When they rise in fury, the child moves with them, its limbs thrashing, its signals sharp and chaotic. There is no separation between what she hears and what she feels. The struggle outside is mirrored within.

She remembers reading that human awareness begins slowly, long after birth. But what lives inside her is not waiting to wake. It is already awake. Already watching. There is no gentleness in its attention. No comfort in its presence. This is not an infant forming piece by piece. This is a mind—fully formed or nearly so—wrapped in a body not yet free.

She places her hand over her belly, trying to make sense of the presence inside. She tries to name it, to claim it. But each time she reaches for it, the sense of strangeness deepens. It is intelligent, yes. But foreign. Entirely other.

"If I am the first of a new kind," she asks aloud, "is this not my kin?"

There is no answer.

Only the quiet hum of thought returning—more forceful now, more complex—and the dull pressure of a body preparing to give way.

And still, it feels like a stranger.

The child's messages are runes without translation, symbols etched in light and silence. Her grandmother once deciphered the tapping language of the Precious Object—but this is no tapping. This is prophecy, encrypted in the syntax of stars.

"What troubles you?" Lady Oracle asks.

They sit together in the anteroom where so many ghosts from the past reside. "Many things."

"Such as?"

Ming-huà speaks quietly, but there is steel beneath her words. "I do not understand this thing you call Goddess. Nor do I grasp the meaning of God. Tell me—truly—are They real? Or am I doomed to the same madness that consumed my father and grandfather?"

Lady Oracle regards her for a long moment. When she speaks, her voice is as calm as still water disturbed only by the whisper of wind. "They are as real as the architecture of your mind allows Them to be. They live in the neural rivers, in the pulses of your hump, in the ancient symmetries encoded within your blood. But listen, Ming-huà: your father and grandfather were not mad. They were gifted—too sensitive for a world that poisons its prophets."

Ming-huà's gaze sharpens. "I don't want riddles. I want truth. Are They *real* or not?"

Lady Oracle doesn't flinch. "The deeper truth has never been yes or no."

A long silence stretches between them. Then:

"Why do you always answer with veils?" Ming-huà snaps. "You speak like a goddess yourself—always circling, never arriving. Why should I bare my heart to someone who wraps every truth in shadow?"

Lady Oracle leans forward—not as oracle now, but as woman. "Because the heart you speak of was never meant to be carried alone."

Ming-huà closes her eyes. Her voice drops. "Then hear this. I have no one else."

Her composure falters; her body trembles. The quiver of her lip betrays the weeping that has not yet begun. But she breathes deeply and gathers herself.

"It's the child. The being growing inside me. I am afraid."

Lady Oracle's features shift—something ancient flickers in her eyes, something that recognizes the fear not as weakness, but as initiation.

"What do you fear?"

"That it is not of my kind. That it is not of *any* kind I know."

"All mothers carry that fear at some point."

"No," Ming-huà says, firmer now. "This is not that. My hump has never lied. It speaks now with the voice of the earth before language—this child is no ordinary life. I expected difference. But this . . . this is a departure."

Lady Oracle's voice is soft. "Yes. We all knew it would be."

"You *still* don't understand." Ming-huà's voice begins to crack. "I was ready for something strange—something shaped in the same mold as me. But this . . . this is *alien*. I am not giving birth—I am merely providing a threshold over which this child will pass."

"You fear what may step through?"

"I fear what may never return."

Ming-huà's voice lowers, reverent and terrified. "We don't know its sex. We chose not to. But it's not the unknown of gender that haunts me—it's the 'it.'

That word is too close to truth. What if this child surpasses us all? What if it sees us as relics? Or worse, as obstacles?"

Lady Oracle is silent for a long time. Then, as if reluctant to break something sacred, she speaks.

"I share your fear. I, too, have felt . . . reverberations. A tremor in the order of things. It is as if something new has reached through time, and placed its mark on this birth."

"You said God and Goddess are metaphors," Ming-huà whispers. "But now you speak as if They act."

"They do," Lady Oracle says. "All true metaphors act."

Ming-huà shakes her head. "You say the child is natural—but this feels like rupture, not continuity."

"Even nature ruptures," Lady Oracle replies. "The stars themselves are born in fire. Evolution is not polite—it leaps, it rends, it reveals. And yes, sometimes it births what cannot yet be named."

Ming-huà stares downward. "This child is not a regression. It is not malformed. It is . . . radiant. And that terrifies me more."

"I understand. You are not just carrying a child. You are hosting a future that does not yet exist."

There is silence between them again. Then Ming-huà speaks more quietly. "The voices are changing. Goddess no longer speaks with compassion. She roars. She curses God. And He returns Her fire with venom. They argue inside me—and the child . . . suffers."

Lady Oracle's expression grows grave. "Yes. The war between Them has entered the womb."

"What if this child eclipses me? I will not be its mother. I will be its burden."

Lady Oracle takes her hand now—gently, deliberately. "You are the bridge. That is not a burden. That is a sacrifice. But not a loveless one."

Ming-huà blinks. "You speak of love?"

Lady Oracle nods. "Yes. Though I do not romanticize. Love is the thread that holds the stars to their paths. It is not weakness. It is structure."

"I never expected you to speak that word with reverence."

"Even your hump is not infallible," she smiles. "Love is not the failing of evolution. It is its deepest secret."

"But what if the child is incapable of love? What if it sees emotion as a contagion? What if love *limits* it?"

"Then teach it love that is not personal. Teach it the kind Goddess holds—love that does not cling, but redeems. *She* loves the world even as *She* prepares to end much of its suffering. That is the paradox of the divine."

Ming-huà leans back, stunned. "Then *She* is real?"

"*She* is the name we give to what calls us upward. That is enough."

The door opens. Zookeeper enters, Bataar behind him.

"Make what clear?" he asks. "Metaphors are supposed to *reveal*, not *hide*."

Lady Oracle turns. "Do you love Ming-huà?"

Zookeeper doesn't hesitate. "More with each passing breath."

"And the child?"

He grins. "I feel great about it. Why?"

"Why?" she presses.

"Because it's mine. Half mine, anyway."

Lady Oracle studies him. "And what if the child doesn't feel what you feel? What if it sees you as lesser?"

He shrugs. "Then good. Means it's an improvement. If it's anything like me, we're in trouble. Hell, if it isn't better than me, I'll be disappointed."

Lady Oracle and Ming-huà exchange a glance—part disapproval, part affection.

Ming-huà turns toward him. "Zookeeper, you have a gift. You sense things others don't. Have you felt anything out of place? Anything that doesn't sit right?"

His expression tightens. "No. Why are you asking?"

Lady Oracle steps in gently. "She's wondering if something perfect might also be terrifying."

Zookeeper laughs. "Perfect? Between the two of us, this child shouldn't even exist. That it does—it's a blessing."

From the doorway, Sy shouts, "Thus spake Zarathustra!" His eyes are bright. His arms lifted as if delivering a verdict the world never asked for.

~ *Dream or Foreshadowing?* ~

Ming-huà lies awake, unable to settle. The room is quiet, but her body isn't. A low tension winds through her—nervous energy without an outlet. Doubts gather at the edge of her thoughts, not loud but constant. When sleep finally comes, it doesn't feel earned. It feels inevitable.

She descends into a half-lit state where nothing holds steady. In that space, the child begins to move. Not softly, not blindly. With force. With purpose. The motion inside her is not erratic. It is deliberate.

She feels it pressing outward, sending impulses through her spine, into her organs, down to her fingers. Thought moves with the body. Not hers. Its. Something alive inside her has begun to search. She feels it examining her, piece by piece. Memory opens under its touch. Things she buried long ago return without warning. Places. Words. The sensation of fear she hadn't allowed herself to name. The child does not ask. It uncovers.

It is not waiting to be born. It already occupies the world. And it knows her better than she knows herself.here.

Suddenly, she is in labor. The body convulses. Pain is no longer hers alone. Tentacles emerge from her, slick and purposeful, gripping her thighs, dragging themselves through the birthing canal as if her body were nothing but a corridor between realms. She screams and wakes—drenched in sweat, soaked in terror. Her chest heaves. No one comes. No sound. Just the terrible stillness of a world poised on the brink of revelation.

And then—light.

Not the gentle kind that comes with morning, but something overwhelming. It strikes the room all at once, sharp, total, unfiltered. Everything is exposed. Shadows vanish. There is nowhere to hide.

Above the bed, suspended in that radiance, the figure appears.

She sits cross-legged on what looks like an enormous white bloom, the surface beneath her glowing in steady rhythm. Her presence is undeniable. Her gaze is steady, deep, unreadable. There is grief in her expression, but not weakness. Her crown flickers with shifting color, not bright, but weighted—each hue carrying its own story. In the center of her forehead, a single stone glows, steady as breath.

Around her neck hangs a necklace—dark, heavy, beautiful. Its elements are impossible to name. Some look scorched. Others look worn smooth by touch. Together, they form something sacred.

One hand rests on her thigh, fingers curled with deliberate stillness. The other is raised, held in a gesture that feels both commanding and forgiving. Nothing moves. Nothing needs to.

Ming-huà cannot form a coherent thought. Her breath shortens. Her body locks. Her mind reaches for language and finds only fragments.

Finally, the words arrive.

"You are not real," she says. The sound of her own voice feels distant, drained of conviction.

Yet here I am.

"Go away! Isn't Your voice enough? You drove my father to madness. Leave me!"

I will, if you truly will it.

"I do!"

Goddess smiles—not cruelly, but with the calm sorrow of one who has seen too much.

Yet still, I am here.

"Do You want to drive me mad too?" Ming-huà whispers, her voice quaking. "Is that why You came?"

You fear the child, but your fear is a veil. There is nothing to fear.

"I am terrified of it. It isn't human. My mind is slipping. Please—let me go."

You are always free to go. But the child will remain. Even after birth, you will not be severed. Your umbilical cord is not of flesh—it is made of what humans mistakenly call soul.

"This child is a monster!" she cries out, trembling.

There is only one monster. And He is not of you, nor of your kind. But He would have you destroy what you carry. And already, you are listening.

"Why? Why would He want that?"

You know. In the marrow of your bones, you know.

"I don't! I swear—I don't know anything! I just want this thing out of me. I want peace!"

Then you must make your choice. If you wish to create a monster, there is one certain path: withdraw your love. That is how monsters are made. Not through birth—but abandonment.

"So be it!" she howls. "I can't survive like this! It's killing me!"

You are killing you.

"I am tired. Tired of being a freak. Tired of being alone. Tired of speaking to squirrels. Tired of being the Other."

Foolish girl! Every human is the Other—to the earth, to the trees, to the animals they claim to love while they extinguish them. Humanity is the great estrangement. You are not alone in your suffering—you are its continuation. Millions have borne it before you. Burned at stakes. Silenced in asylums. Whispering to shadows just to survive. And still, they carried the burden forward. You are that burden's latest vessel. You are the hope—but you cry over your own tears, blind to the fire in which you were forged. You are a Superior One.

"But what is in me is monstrous!"

Because of a dream? A dream sent by Him? Are you so fragile that shadows can shatter you?

"You are the dream! You are the monster!"

Then the room is taken.

Flame bursts outward, red and white, filling every space. But this is not flame in any ordinary sense. It carries thought. It carries judgment. It burns without consuming. It exposes without smoke.

Ming-huà's body cannot hold its shape. Her muscles fail. Her breath stops. There is no ground beneath her, no boundary around her. She is breaking apart, not from heat, but from something deeper.

And in the center of that brightness, the child steps forward.

Naked. Calm. Smiling.

Unaffected.

The fire touches her, surrounds her, passes through her—and she does not react. She stands in it as if it belongs to her. As if it came for her. Ming-huà cannot move. Her voice is gone. Her body is no longer hers. Only the child remains, and the fire holds her without harm.

~

Morning comes.

Ming-huà opens her eyes to silence. Her limbs feel empty. Her skin offers no weight. For a moment, she believes she may no longer be alive. Then the pulse returns—deep inside. Steady. Present. Real.

She gasps. *It's still here.*

Then—movement. A single kick, sharp and certain. It drives the breath from her lungs. She bends forward, clutching her middle. A wave of thought follows, pouring through her spine into her skull. Words arrive, but not in any language she knows. They glisten at the edge of understanding—tender, rhythmic, careful. They press against her as if trying to comfort. Or confess.

She wants to grasp them. Needs to. But they slip through. And what remains is a hollow ache. Not from the pain, but from the failure to receive what was given.

Time drifts.

Later, a knock at the door. Then another.

"Hello?" Sy calls out. "Ming-huà?"

No answer.

He waits, then opens the door slowly.

She is in the corner, crouched low, arms around her knees. Her face is drawn. Her body shudders. Her eyes are wide and distant. The air in the room feels wrong, disturbed. He steps forward, but something stops him.

She is shaking. Not from cold. Not from fear. From something deeper.

Something still happening inside her.

"Ming-huà?" he asks, kneeling beside her, arms around her body.

She shoves him away, her face blank.

"What is it?" he pleads. No response. Her eyes are wide, vacant—gazing not at him but into something far beyond.

He calls for Lady Oracle. Zookeeper arrives first.

"What's wrong with her?" he asks.

"Get her. Now," Sy snaps.

When Zookeeper hesitates, Sy slaps Ming-huà gently. "Ming-huà! Please."

Nothing.

Zookeeper runs. Lady Oracle enters, silent and severe. She orders them out, kneels beside the girl, takes her hand.

And waits.

Hours pass.

Then—a flicker.

The emptiness in Ming-huà's gaze begins to dissolve. Something returns. Not entirely—but enough.

"Ming-huà?" Lady Oracle whispers. "Are you back? You've been scaring us."

No answer. But a flicker remains.

"Ming-huà?"

Still silence.

Just the eyes. Wide. Wondering. As if she sees the world for the first time.

And somewhere far off, the fire still burns.

Chapter Eighteen

Part II: Pythia and Tara

Struggle for Control

~ *Ming-huà Sinks Deeper* ~

Ming-huà has lain motionless in bed for two days, her body tended by the unbroken rhythm of a sacred trio: Lady Oracle and Sy taking turns nursing her like hovering priests, while Zookeeper remains ever near, guarding her with the silent vigilance of a temple sentinel. She is never left alone. Her bodily needs are met with quiet precision, and to their astonishment, she receives every gesture—cleansing, dressing, feeding with eerie passivity. The young hunchback they once knew would have blushed, laughed nervously, or resisted. But now, she accepts it all without a word, without a flicker of discomfort.

It is not apathy. It is *otherness*.

She has not spoken. But they all sense the change. None can explain it, except to point to the fevered shimmer in her eyes—eyes that now burn with a light unmoored from human time. They watch everything with a gaze that feels both ancient and newborn, as if some traveler has taken up residence among them and is still adjusting to the feel of Ming-huà's flesh.

"She looks like a dog seeing cats for the first time," Zookeeper says once, softly. "Like something curious and strange has been let loose inside her, sniffing at the boundaries of her inner world." He shakes his head. "Damn."

When spoken to, she turns toward the voice, not with recognition, but with analytical wonder, as though language itself has become a foreign sound. She listens, but not as a person listens. She listens as the *first listener* might have, when the cosmos cracked open and said: *let there be sound.*

Zookeeper, always the most attuned to subtle shifts, knows that Lady Oracle and Sy are afraid. They do not show it, not outwardly. But fear remains, hanging in the air between them, heavy and unshaken. He senses it in the way they touch her, too gently, as though afraid she might crack. He suspects they feel what he feels: that something in Ming-huà has passed beyond return. With this realization, he silently mourns the loss.

Their fear reminds him of a physician who has glimpsed the worst on the sonogram—the child turned the wrong way, the passage blocked—but dares not speak it aloud for fear the knowledge will kill the mother before the labor begins. Yet Zookeeper is less troubled by the fetus than by the strange and unnerving stillness on Ming-huà's face. It's not the lack of movement. It's the tension beneath the stillness, the elastic pull of something new shaping her expression from beneath. The contours are still hers: the mouth, the cheekbones, the slope of the nose. But the presence behind them is *not*.

He is no longer looking at Ming-huà. He is looking at someone else wearing her face.

And then, on the morning of the third day, she speaks. No preamble. No warming of voice or mind. Just a clear, crisp pronouncement, startling in both tone and authority. It is not her voice, and yet it carries something unmistakably rooted in her marrow.

"We must go out tonight."

The words carry a physical force.

Zookeeper, so stunned he forgets to breathe, can only manage a dazed murmur. "What?"

"Tonight. We must go."

"Why?"

But the vacant gaze returns, falling over her face like a veil. No amount of encouragement by Zookeeper brings her back. He rushes to get Lady Oracle, and when they return, the same peculiar, alert, and inquisitive look stares at them.

"We must go out tonight."

"Why?" asks Lady Oracle.

"We must."

"Ming-huà, we cannot risk your pregnancy. Your due date is too near."

"We will be fine. It must be done."

"Who is speaking?" asks Lady Oracle.

"Who do you think?"

"I don't know."

"Ming-huà, of course. Have you forgotten me so quickly?"

Sy has entered and now speaks. "Excuse me, but you are so different, Ming-huà. We hardly recognize you."

"How can you not recognize a pregnant hunchback?"

Sy is at a loss.

"Now," says Ming-huà. "We have to go out tonight, and I want Sy to accompany us."

"Why?" asks Lady Oracle.

"To be a witness."

"I mean, why do you have to go out tonight?"

"Too many reasons and not enough time."

"Try."

Ming-huà sighs in frustration. "In your terms, to save people."

"I need to know who I'm talking to," insists Lady Oracle.

"Are you not Lady Oracle?" Ming-huà shoots back.

Momentarily confused, she answers, "Yes."

"Are you not the one who put this hunchback through so much in order to stop suffering?"

"Are you not the hunchback?" asks a surprised Lady Oracle.

"Of course, we've established that."

Sy breaks in. "Sorry, but you don't talk like the Ming-huà I know."

"You are Sy, the magical buffoon. Scarecrow, the latest in a distinguished line of jester-guides."

"Yes."

"Then perhaps you know less than your reputation suggests."

"I suppose so. However, question is, who do you intend to save?"

"All of you."

After she utters these startling words, Ming-huà closes her eyes and appears to sleep. The others quietly slip out.

~

Gathered in the anteroom downstairs, Sy, Lady Oracle, and Zookeeper are meeting to sort our the confusion.

"It's not her—it's the fetus," says Lady Oracle.

"That's fuckin' stupid!" says Zookeeper. "No fetus can think, let alone take over someone."

"This one can," says Sy. "How else do you explain it?"

"She's delusional," insists Zookeeper. "Too much strain."

"No, she is not delusional," says Lady Oracle. "But she is in danger."

"Of?" asks Zookeeper.

Lady Oracle shakes her head. "That I do not know."

"So, do we let her go tonight?"

"A late term pregnant woman out on the streets to save an unknown person whose life she imagines is in danger?" says Sy.

"She said it was to save all of us," corrects Zookeeper.

"Whether it's us or someone else, we mustn't let her go."

"Absolutely—we let her go . . . or whoever is controlling her now," says Lady Oracle, to everyone's surprise. "This is neither overactive imagination nor delusion. There's foresight. There's purpose. There's learning going on at an incredibly rapid pace."

But even as these words leave her mouth, Ming-huà enters the room and announces somewhat apologetically, "Sorry, I haven't felt well. I've been dreaming."

"Ming-huà?" says Sy.

"Of course, who else would it be?"

"How do you feel?"

"Strange dream. I dreamed about Miss Gladflower. I dreamed about where I sent her. No, that's not quite right, I dreamed *I* was where I sent her."

Lady Oracle responds cautiously. "You have been . . . gone, for a while."

"Gone?"

"Well, out of it a bit."

"I know . . . sort of. I have felt it. Can't remember much, except something terrified me, and then I'm here."

"Where were you when you were with Miss Gladflower?" asks Lady Oracle.

"That's the strangest part of all."

"Tell us," says Sy.

But once again the transformation occurs, even quicker this time. Its instantaneous arrival takes everyone aback.

"We must go tonight." She stares at Sy. "You will go with me. The other . . . the armless one"—she turns to Zookeeper—"can also come if so inclined. She's attached to the one whose arms are unattached."

"I'll go!" cries Zookeeper.

"I know," says Ming-huà.

Lady Oracle and Sy exchange glances.

Ming-huà notices. "No need to be so worried or to look at each other like that. Now that it's settled, we're going to rest now. Meet us at eleven o'clock here and we will go. The birth date is close—we need rest before tonight."

All stare in wide-eyed wonder at these pronouncements. Sy is startled to see a flickers of the old Ming-huà, like glimpses of movement through thick vegetation. Before anyone can respond, the hunchback is gone, leaving them to gape at one another. Lady Oracle finally breaks the silence.

"We?"

~ *Back on the Street* ~

Rocket had been devoted to curb stomping since early adolescence, treating it not merely as violence, but as ritual, his own perverse sacrament of supremacy. When he first learned the Nazi SS and Gestapo had used the method to maximize suffering, he revered its lineage as though it were sacred, a blood rite forged in cruelty. Ironically, he had once nearly fallen victim to that very method, saved at the last moment by a fellow gang member who pulled his attacker back from the brink of internal decapitation. The near-death experience only deepened his devotion.

Now, any excuse to perform the act is a gift, especially if the victim is Black. He has had a swastika engraved into the soles of his boots, a grotesque signature designed to leave meaning in the broken bodies of his prey. Tonight's target is a middle-aged Black store owner. Rocket believes the man is guilty on two counts: first, of being Black; second, of cursing at him that morning outside the man's shop, while a small crowd of jeering onlookers watched.

In truth, the man had said nothing. Rocket had only caught a look, a glance of quiet disgust, and that had been enough to pass sentence.

The store, a small consignment shop, boasts a vivid neon sign familiar to Rocket as a rendezvous point for hasty drug deals. He knows exactly when the lights go out and when the owner leaves. Now he waits, lurking near the mouth of an alley that feeds into a nearby parking garage, a narrow corridor framed by brick walls and a concrete lip along the base: the perfect altar for his act. He has imagined the scene countless times. The victim forced at gunpoint to kneel, teeth pressed to the curb, neck exposed like a sacrifice. Rocket prefers paralysis over death—too much force and it ends too quickly, too little and the spectacle fails. It is in this balance of precision and brutality that he finds his thrill.

He waits across the street, watching. When the neon light flickers and dies, his breath quickens. The owner emerges: stooped, weary, shoulders hunched against the night, his coat collar pulled high as he shuffles down the sidewalk. Rocket follows, lips parted, fingers twitching with anticipation. That coat will have to go, he thinks. He wants an unobstructed view of the spine, of the crunch of teeth against concrete.

The alley looms just ahead.

His hand finds the pistol grip hidden against his ribs.

He begins to close the distance—but then, footsteps.

Another pedestrian.

With a silent curse, Rocket slows his pace. The timing is ruined. The store owner walks past the alley entrance, unknowing, just as the interloper steps into a shaft of light. Rocket peers forward, annoyed, ready to retreat into shadow, until he sees her.

A woman.

Strangely shaped.

Asian. And, his lip curls, a hunchback, and pregnant.

The sight fills him with a sudden wave of revulsion. He lowers his eyes, avoiding the sight of her asymmetry as she draws near.

But she does not pass.

She stops.

She looks up.

And Rocket, despite himself, looks down at her. What he sees freezes him in place.

Her face is radiant, luminous in a way that unsettles. Not soft, not kind, but piercing, as though beauty itself has turned accusatory. Her eyes lock on his with a gaze that strips him bare. He has known fear before, but this is different. This is judgment.

In that moment, Rocket, the predator, the worshipper of violence, feels something ancient curl coldly in his gut.

He has been seen, revealed, unmasked.

"You don't want to do what you are planning," she says.

Shocked, he automatically assumes his best vicious scowl and says, "Mind you own fuckin' business, bitch!"

"This is my business," she replies.

He grins and spits in her face. "If you know what's good for you bitch, you'll keep walkin' 'till you're out of my sight." He glances at the store owner, who pauses and looks around at him and the woman. "Go on!" he growls at the hunchback. "Get the fuck outta here!"

"No."

Once again, he checks his intended victim who still stands motionless, waiting for something. Good.

Rocket pushes the hunchback away and pulls his gun. "Look, bitch, I'll shoot! If you want to save the brat in your belly, get the fuck out!"

Now the target is slowly walking up to them, hesitantly but steadily. He clearly does not see the gun. The hunchback won't move.

"Is there a problem here?" the man asks from a safe distance.

Rocket makes a split-second decision to abort his mission, but the man sidles a bit closer and says, "Are you in trouble, lady? I know this man and he is not one to fool with. You must come away from him. I'll walk with you."

Infuriated by this impertinence, Rocket rushes up to the man and jabs the barrel of the gun into his stomach. The man yells, but Rocket strikes him across the face and pushes him toward the alley.

"Stop!"

Rocket hears the hunchback, but he ignores her and knocks the man to the ground just inside the alley. Too close to the street, but he no longer cares. He leans over with his gun to the man's head and orders him to bite the curb.

"Stop, or you will regret it!" shouts the hunchback, but Rocket's blood is up, and he savagely kicks the man and orders him to lie on his stomach. When the man does not respond, he kicks again. By now, the man is gasping for breath and issues muffled cries for help. Rocket kicks again, and the store owner's head is now on the curb staring up in terror. Rocket presses the barrel of his gun into the man's forehead and screams at him to turn over and bite the concrete edge. He hears the hunchback screaming warnings, but is far too inflamed to pay any attention. The man turns over, his neck still disappointingly covered by the collar of the coat, but Rocket sees his teeth bared against the concrete. Grinning in satisfaction, he lifts his foot to stomp.

The next thing Rocket knows, he is lying on his back on the sidewalk. Confused, he tries to get up but realizes something is wrong. Terribly wrong. It finally comes to him that he only has one leg. Terrified, he grabs for his gun but discovers his hand is also gone, only a stump of wrist waves helplessly in the night air. His screams reverberate up and down the street. The store owner draws himself to a sitting position and stares in disbelief at his attacker. He looks at the dark figure of the pregnant hunchback, who quickly disappears into the night, then painfully stands and makes his way toward the parking garage, not noticing an armless man passing him on the sidewalk, heading toward the still screaming Rocket.

~

By the time Zookeeper reaches the shrieking man lying on the ground, a few onlookers have gathered. Rocket's eyes bulge in terror and he flails about, shouting, "My leg! My hand!"

Zookeeper is alternately sickened and fascinated. No blood. No sign of violence. Only stumps. Just like him. The barrel of a gun sits on the pavement beside the stricken figure. He catches a glimpse through the swelling crowd of Sy rushing Ming-huà away.

"What happened?" asks an onlooker.

"Don't know," says a newcomer. "Just heard the screams and came to see. Guy has no leg and no hand. Weird. Look at him! Wavin' that stump and screaming like it just happened! No blood. Must be high on some bad shit."

"Yeah, weird. Anyone call the cops?"

"Yeah," says another. "Damn, he's still shouting bloody murder about his hand and leg. It's like it just happened—but there ain't no blood. Weird as shit."

"Yeah."

"No matter what you say, I'll bet there's a wheelchair or crutches laying around here somewhere," claims Zookeeper. He now feels the stares intensify at his own armless figure.

An onlooker edges up and scrutinizes Zookeeper. "Was you involved in this mess?" he asks.

"Naw, just came when I seen the rubberneckers. Still think there's a wheelchair and crutches around somewhere. How else to explain it?"

"Yeah," comes a different voice. "Got to be. Guess you'd know, eh, bud?"

As the words leave his mouth, Zookeeper hears the distant wail of a police siren. Instinctively, he turns and walks quickly back in the direction he came, putting space between them, not out of fear, but out of a need to breathe, to steady his thoughts.

His mind reels. What he has just witnessed is not a hallucination, not coincidence, but evidence—undeniable, dreadful—of Ming-huà's power made manifest. Something has shifted. Something has crossed a threshold.

But a deeper question rises now, cold and urgent: Who commands that power? Certainly, it could not be Ming-huà's gentle soul, could it?

~ *Birth* ~

By the time Zookeeper arrives back at the mansion, Sy and Lady Oracle have seen Ming-huà to bed and are meeting in the anteroom.

"How is she?" he asks.

Lady Oracle shakes her head. "It is odd. Sy told me about the incident. He wisely spirited Ming-huà away before the police arrived on the scene. After she came here, she would not speak or answer any questions. So, I was about to give up asking when she surprised me. She said, 'We must sleep. Now we know. Not sure what happened with the gun, but enough of this until after.' Then she went to bed, and when I checked on her, she was fast asleep."

"Did she say anything on the way here, Sy?" asks Zookeeper.

"Not a word."

"What about the pregnancy? Is she in pain?"

Lady Oracle sighs. "Not that I can tell, but. . . . "

"But?"

"But there is something, something I don't quite understand."

"Now what?" asks Zookeeper.

"Now we wait," says Lady Oracle.

"And hope the police do not show up asking questions," adds Sy.

"Fuckin' A," says Zookeeper. "World don't have an abundance of pregnant hunchbacks to track down."

~

A month passes without further incident.

Zookeeper, restless and increasingly wary, begins frequenting the downtown district near the site of the confrontation. He listens. Watches. Puts his ear to the street like an old tracker following invisible prints. The ground is speaking, and what it's saying disturbs him. First, the police. They're asking questions. Too many, and too pointed. Second, the streets are thick with rumor. Fear breeds invention, and the neighborhood is now aflame with the fantastical: whispers of a wandering demon, a blood-drinking witch, a spectral killer, a zombie prowling for flesh. Superstitious nonsense, yes, but the kind of nonsense that has always carried weight with the frightened and the ignorant. The kind of nonsense that fuels mobs.

The more rational voices have offered theories of a serial killer, one so precise, so sophisticated, that he leaves no blood behind. No bodies. Only fragments. Whatever the rumor, the press has latched on, fanning the flames with breathless speculation and putting the police under mounting pressure to produce results.

Worse still, some threads have begun to tie together.

"They're starting to connect the dots," Zookeeper warns Lady Oracle and Sy one evening, pacing with a nervous energy. "What happened with Rocket. What happened to us at the house. They're linking it. And God help us if they've tied it back to Baltimore. If so, we're in a fuckin' world of hurt."

"Yes," Lady Oracle concedes. "Unfortunately, it was inevitable. But even if they put two and two together, they have nothing solid. What can they charge her with? A hunchback girl who maims and kills from a distance? Without a drop of blood?"

"Maybe," Sy says. "But I don't trust the government to care about logic. If they get wind of what she's capable of—if they believe even half the stories—they'll come for her. They'll want to test her. Contain her. Rip her apart molecule by molecule if they have to."

Lady Oracle chuckles, but the sound is hollow. "You've been watching too many conspiracy thrillers, Sy. Don't be ridiculous." Then, more somberly: "Still, we'll stay low. Make sure the birth happens clean. Then we reassess."

"Best we can do for now," Sy agrees, shrugging.

Zookeeper, lying on his back with a glass of whiskey gripped by his dexterous foot, downs the drink and licks his lips.

"Long as the kid's safe," he says.

The others say nothing. A silence settles over the room, heavy but unspoken. Finally, Lady Oracle rises and announces she's returning to her yang house. Her words are calm, but her mind is not.

~

On the walk home, Lady Oracle lets the night clear her head.

Things, she tells herself, are not yet disastrous. She has arranged for a trusted midwife, someone outside the fold, but reliable. Ming-huà, for all the ominous signals emanating from her womb, remains healthy. No fever. No seizures. No physical anomalies, at least none visible. Still, something gnaws at her, subtle and unrelenting. A shadow behind every plan. A doubt beneath every reassurance.

When she arrives home, she puts on her pajamas and makes a cup of tea. The yang house, usually a comforting refuge, feels colder than usual. Adding a warm robe, she sits, cup in hand, and calls softly into the stillness.

"Goddess?"

Nothing.

She tries again, more forcefully. "Goddess!"

Only silence. Not denial. Not absence. Just that strange void where once there had been presence. She thinks briefly of her grandmother, Buandelgereen, once a source of boundless comfort, now lost to an incoherence imposed by too many years. That, too, weighs heavy.

"Wait and see," she tells herself aloud. "Be patient."

Two weeks later, the waiting ends.

Ming-huà's water breaks. Labor begins. The midwife is summoned.

She still has not spoken since the night of Rocket.

~

Lady Oracle, Sy, and Zookeeper sit waiting in the anteroom, nerves drawn taut beneath a thin veil of stillness. Other than occasional fragments of small talk, they remain mostly silent. Zookeeper sips a beer with his feet. Lady Oracle and Sy nurse mugs of cold tea. All three glance periodically toward the doorway, defendants awaiting an unseen verdict.

The midwife passes by a few times: once en route to the kitchen, once to the bathroom. Her face is unreadable, clenched with a kind of professional solemnity that offers neither comfort nor alarm. She does not speak.

At last, Sy breaks the fragile quiet.

"Zookeeper," he asks, voice low, "you can read people. What's she thinking?"

"Who?"

"The midwife."

Zookeeper frowns. "Hard to say. She's giving off a scrambled signal: determination, confusion . . . and fear, I think. But it's like trying to tune into three radio stations at once."

"Great," mutters Sy.

Zookeeper glances at the closed door. "You think we'll hear the baby cry from here?"

"Depends," Lady Oracle murmurs, eyes fixed on nothing.

The room falls silent again. Minutes stretch into hours. The waiting becomes its own oppressive weight. Then a figure in the doorway appears, riveting everyone's attention. The midwife enters slowly and lowers herself into a chair. Her face is drained of color. Her gaze drifts upward, unblinking, as if the ceiling might offer a rationale for what she's just witnessed. All three stand immediately, instinctively.

"Well?" Lady Oracle asks, her voice firm but restrained.

The question hangs unanswered.

"I'm going up," Zookeeper says, but doesn't move.

The midwife exhales, long and steady, then gestures vaguely toward the chairs. "Sit down."

They obey, unease sharpening into genuine concern. Time passes before she speaks, as if she's gathering not just words, but courage.

Lady Oracle leans forward. "Tell us. Is it bad?"

The midwife hesitates, then begins. "The birth was long but . . . smooth. Ming-huà made no sound. Not even a grunt. It was like watching a corpse give birth."

She pauses, shivers, and gestures for a drink. Sy pours her a glass of wine. She takes a few sips, closes her eyes, then continues. "When the crown appeared, everything stopped. Not the clock, I checked. The second hand was moving. But the *room* . . . it was like time itself hesitated. The silence had weight."

Her voice wavers. "When the baby was clear, I clamped and cut the cord as usual. Then I began the Apgar assessment."

She stops again, drinks.

"Boy or girl?" Zookeeper asks.

"That's when it got strange."

"What do you mean strange?" Zookeeper asks, his voice tight. "Is it a boy or girl?"

"A girl," the midwife replies. "But—"

"But?" Sy presses.

She shivers again. "Let me finish. As I said, Ming-huà never spoke. Still hasn't. As for the baby, she is healthy in appearance. Heartbeat's strong: one hundred beats per minute. But her reactions to stimulus . . . they weren't normal. She didn't flinch. She *studied*. Every test—grip, motion, light response—she met with this . . . eerie calm. Not passivity. *Awareness.* Calculated, deliberate, watching *me* like *I* was the one being evaluated."

"She didn't cry?" Lady Oracle asks.

"Not a sound," the midwife confirms. "She's not deaf, I'm sure of that. She just . . . refused. Or didn't see the point."

"What did she do instead?" Sy asks.

The midwife looks at him slowly. "She stared at me. With the expression of a curious scientist. Like she was waiting to see what I'd do next."

"And the significance of not crying?" Zookeeper asks.

"In most cases, not much," she replies. "But this child . . . the absence of a cry felt intentional. As if crying would have been beneath her."

She shakes her head, lost for words. "It wasn't just cognition. It was presence. This baby *knows* something. Or is *processing* something. And the way she tracks movement, it's not instinct. It's *judgment.*"

"Did Ming-huà bond with her?" Lady Oracle asks.

"No," the midwife says quietly. "She held her, yes. Reflexively. But no emotion. No smile. No softening. And the baby just looked past her. Not hostile. Just uninterested."

There is a silence.

"Does she have a hump?" Zookeeper asks, cautiously.

The midwife straightens, folds her hands, and adopts a clinical tone. "Yes. I examined her spine. There's a curvature, more pronounced than her mother's. But different. Not textbook kyphosis."

She pauses again.

"I'll leave it at that."

Zookeeper exhales. "Oh, God."

Lady Oracle stands abruptly. "Never say that in my presence," she snaps.

"Okay, okay, it's just an expression. Thank *Goddess*, then. How's that? Either way—hump or no hump—two heads or ten, she's still my kid."

Lady Oracle doesn't respond. Instead, she turns to the midwife. "May we see her?"

The woman rises. "My work here is done. I'll be leaving."

"You don't want to say goodbye?" Sy asks gently.

She shakes her head, as if trying to shake something off. "No. I've seen enough."

She sets her glass down carefully, then walks toward the door. "Thank you. No need to show me out. You know where to send payment."

And she's gone.

The three of them look at one another. No words. No quips. No theories.

Together, they ascend the stairs to face the child.

Chapter Nineteen

Not A Human Child?

Authorities Take an Interest

~ First Impressions ~

When the three enter Ming-huà's room, they are struck motionless. The newborn is wide-eyed, watching them with an unsettling intelligence. Ming-huà lies still, her gaze vacant. An electric presence tingles the air, setting nerves on edge. Zookeeper approaches first, bending to kiss the baby. But midway, he freezes. The child is studying his missing arms with unnerving focus. Then, she smiles. It is a deliberate, knowing smile. He straightens abruptly and turns to Ming-huà, whose eyes remain distant.

"Ming-huà, honey, how are you?" Lady Oracle asks gently.

The baby turns her head toward her mother, as if following the question.

"Fine," Ming-huà replies.

"You have a healthy baby girl," Sy adds.

"No," Ming-huà says, her voice flat. "The world has a healthy new . . . inhabitant."

"We talked about names, boys' and girls', but never settled on one," Zookeeper offers. "Any thoughts now?"

To their silent astonishment, the baby follows the conversation intently.

Tears roll down Ming-huà's cheeks. "How about Miss Gladflower?"

Zookeeper frowns. "Come on, Ming-huà. Be serious. What name do you like?"

"It isn't my choice."

"No, it's both our choice."

She lets out a dry laugh. "No. It's neither of ours. It's hers."

She gazes down at the child, who meets her stare in silent affirmation. Zookeeper feels a pulse of something, impossibly forceful, and glances at Sy and Lady Oracle. Both are watching the infant with grim fascination.

"Well, I'm not—" he begins.

"Pythia!" Ming-huà blurts, suddenly loud.

"What?" Zookeeper stares at her, bewildered.

"Her name is Pythia."

"Where did that come from?"

"Where do you think?"

He looks at the baby, then back at her. "Well, okay . . . what does it mean?"

"I don't know," she says, gesturing toward Lady Oracle. "Ask her."

Zookeeper turns to her. "What does it mean?"

But Lady Oracle stands motionless, face drained of color.

He then turns to Sy. "What does it mean?"

Before Sy can speak, Lady Oracle lets out a sudden, raucous laugh, a sound of release, almost joy.

"What?" Zookeeper insists.

She pauses, then stares at Ming-huà with newfound reverence. "This child rises from the rotting corpse of a snake," she says. "Figuratively, of course."

Pythia smiles.

Zookeeper is still lost.

"I don't get it," he says pugnaciously. "Gimme a fuckin' break. What are you fuckin' talking about?"

"Google it," Lady Oracle suggests, then chuckles. "Though apparently, she doesn't need Google."

"Damn straight," says Zookeeper. "Smart kid."

"More than you know," says Lady Oracle.

Turning back to Ming-huà, Zookeeper softens. "How do you feel, babe? Are you tired?"

She nods faintly. "Yes. I think the worst is past. She borrowed my substance, my strength, my soul, if you will, but she's returned it now. I feel it coming back, like a battery recharging. She no longer needs it. But even she will need my milk. Even she."

Zookeeper exhales. "What do we have, Ming-huà?"

She smiles faintly. "To be determined. But whatever she is . . . she's not something the world has ever seen."

"Nor are you," Lady Oracle murmurs. "Nor are you."

"Perhaps. But from now on, we are the helpless babies."

"Indeed," Lady Oracle replies. "Oracle has come to replace Oracle. The more the snake rots, the more powerful she becomes . . . figuratively, of course."

"What's all this snake shit?" Zookeeper asks.

"Pythia will make it all clear, and quickly, if I'm not mistaken. Congratulations, father. Congratulations, mother."

"If the world lets her live," Sy mutters.

"Still obsessed with cinema?" Lady Oracle teases.

"Yes. The longest film ever made: the navel-gazing history of humankind. Very informative."

Lady Oracle nods. "I fear you're right. Caution is the name of the game now."

The next morning, Zookeeper is upstairs with Ming-huà and the child. Sy and Lady Oracle sit in the kitchen, drinking coffee. A loud knocking pounds on the front door. Sy answers to find two men in plain clothes flashing badges.

"Police detectives. May we come in?"

~ *Cloud* ~

"What's your business?" Sy asks evenly.

"Routine check," replies the taller man, flashing a badge. "Does a woman with a hunchback live here?"

"She does. Why?"

"She may have witnessed a serious crime."

"What kind of crime?"

"Violent assault. Happened elsewhere in town. Your name?"

"Sy."

"Sy what?"

"Sy Rung."

"And the woman's name?"

"That's rude," Sy replies coldly. "She just gave birth. She's resting. Can't this wait?"

"She's back from the hospital?"

"She had the baby here."

The tall man lifts a brow. "Here?"

"With a midwife."

"Her name?"

"Ming-huà Powers. Weston, now."

"May we speak to her? Just for a moment."

"No. She's recovering. Maybe later."

At that, Lady Oracle descends the stairs with unhurried grace. "It's alright, Sy. Gentlemen, you won't stay long, will you? She's exhausted."

"We're detectives," the tall one replies. "We'll be brief. Your name?"

"Judith Ganbaatar."

The shorter detective jots it down. She turns and leads them upstairs. Sy watches, uneasy.

At the landing, Zookeeper greets them. "Matthew Weston. Please, make it quick."

The shorter detective's eyes drift to his stumps. He scribbles furiously.

"Sorry about your... condition," says the tall one. "Mind if I ask how it happened?"

"Birth defect," Zookeeper says evenly. "But thanks for your concern."

They step into the bedroom. The child sits propped on pillows, eerily upright, eyes wide and motionless. Her presence alters the room, makes it taut, uncomfortably close. The detectives falter. Years of practiced neutrality peel away beneath her gaze. She is not curious. She is watching. Assessing. Ming-huà lies reclined, head tilted slightly toward the window, face pale but calm. Unbothered. She blinks—once—slowly.

The senior detective clears his throat. "Mrs. Weston, sorry to disturb you. We'll be brief. We believe you may have witnessed a crime."

She nods, not in agreement, but in concession to fatigue. But the child's gaze remains the true center of gravity—undeniable, implacable.

"Yes?" Ming-huà murmurs. A quiet signal to proceed.

The tall detective hesitates, then: "Were you near Twelfth and Halston the night of the assault?"

"Assault?"

"On a man named Bowers. Shopkeeper."

Another soft nod. Barely perceptible.

"Can you tell us what you saw?"

She begins to shake her head. Then lowers it, slowly, as if the question had unearthed something she wanted to keep buried. The room stills. The only sound is the baby's slow breathing, rhythmic and attentive. The shorter detective scribbles, but a change is already underway. It is not physical. Not measurable. But something has shifted. The detectives are being watched, not interrogated, not confronted, but seen through.

"Please," the tall detective tries again. "What did you see?"

"A man being attacked. I left. I was afraid."

"Why were you out?"

"Research."

"Research?"

"I study crime patterns. Data collection."

"Writing a book?"

"Maybe."

As the words continue, their force weakens. The infant's gaze blurs the boundaries of thought. Their sentences lose structure. Phrases trail off. The pen falls still. Silence thickens—not absence, but a quiet fog rolling through their mental fields.

Then the tall one says, softly, "We have what we need."

"Yes, thank you," the short one echoes, almost dreamlike, tucking his notebook away without finishing.

They leave the room with no further questions, no clear resolution, only the strange, lingering sense that something essential had been bypassed, or perhaps absorbed. The air behind them shimmers with what went unspoken.

~

Downstairs, Sy watches them disappear through the front door. "How did you know?" he asks Lady Oracle.

She shrugs. "Isn't it obvious? Pythia's in charge now."

"She's less than a day old."

"That's just paperwork."

Zookeeper joins them quietly. "She's sleeping. What do you mean, 'in charge'?"

Lady Oracle grins. "You know the phrase—'It is what it is.'"

He sighs. "Yeah, well, I've survived worse than childbirth. I know what happens when someone shows their hand too early. There'll be consequences."

"I agree," Lady Oracle says. "We should keep a low profile. But Pythia may have other plans."

Zookeeper mutters, "Jesus. What have we brought into the world?"

"Nothing you didn't already carry," she replies. "Genetics. Instinct. Evolution. We just opened the gate."

"I saw this horror flick once," he says. "Kid turns people into animals. One guy ended up a jack-in-the-box. Is that where we're headed?"

Lady Oracle chuckles. "You and Sy need to watch fewer movies. This is reality now. And it's got real teeth."

"Too fuckin' real. What if I tell her no? Will she take my legs next time? My damn head?"

A soft voice interrupts from the landing. "You don't need to worry," says Ming-huà. She's standing, pale but poised, the baby held gently in her arms. The child calmly gazes out, unblinking.

Zookeeper rushes up to them. "Jesus, you shouldn't be out of bed!"

But Lady Oracle doesn't move. "Why not?" she asks. "Why don't we have to worry?"

Zookeeper yelps. All eyes turn. The child's tiny finger touches his forehead. He goes rigid. Then, withdrawal.

"Holy shit," he gasps.

"You understand?" Ming-huà asks.

Zookeeper nods, dazed. "She doesn't speak. She doesn't have to. Her meaning comes down like a thunderbolt. Jesus Christ! What a goddamn superkid!"

"Please," Ming-huà says gently. "Language. You're a father now."

~ *Safe Refuge* ~

Over the next few weeks, more detectives come. Each leaves with little additional information. Ming-huà answers their questions with a serenity that borders on indifference, and the ever present child sits in her arms or beside her, smiling as if these intrusions amuse her. No words yet from Pythia, only that inscrutable gaze and the occasional raised finger, as though granting or denying consent to the strange demands of the adult world. Oddly, no one questions this anymore. Whatever strange language exists between her and the others has settled into quiet acceptance. Then, one morning, Lady Oracle speaks.

"It's time to go."

Ming-huà nods, unsurprised. The others show no resistance.

Still, Lady Oracle feels the need to explain. "The police grow suspicious. These encounters—men left limbless and bloodless—are too strange to ignore. Word has reached federal law enforcement. They'll be coming. Vague answers won't suffice for long."

At that moment, Pythia lifts a finger, almost ceremonially, as if bestowing her blessing. She remains silent, but the gesture holds weight. The room acknowledges it without discussion.

"Where to?" Zookeeper asks.

"That," Lady Oracle says, "has been a dilemma. Do we flee far, across oceans, or remain here, within the borders of this collapsing dream? Pythia belongs to no single place. She is a citizen of something larger."

"I'd say the safest place possible," Sy offers.

"I agree," Lady Oracle replies. "But the emanations are . . . contradictory. And Goddess—" she pauses "—has gone silent. I've tried everything. No contact."

"Maybe She's no longer needed?" Sy suggests gently.

"No," says Lady Oracle. "She's still vital. But something's interfering. Something happening elsewhere, in a dimension or realm we cannot access. Goddess is a metaphor, yes, but also a tether held by forces we do not fully understand. And for now, that tether is frayed."

She gestures toward Pythia.

Each of them, in turn, tries to reach her—to read her expression, probe her silence, sense her intent. But all they encounter is a veil: thick, shifting, impenetrable. A fog coiled around her mind, not hostile, but resolutely closed.

And yet . . . on occasion, something breaks through. A glint. A pulse. A flash of insight so sudden, so luminous, that each feels, for a fleeting second, they have been chosen to receive it.

Then, just as quickly, it's gone.

~ *Refuge, Training, or Exile* ~

In the nights that follow, Lady Oracle resumes her silent vigil. She reaches for the Goddess through ritual, through dream, through that fragile thread of inner speech that once provided answers. But nothing comes. Not even a shadow of reply. Whatever presence once dwelled beyond the veil has gone speechless, as if the divine metaphor has stepped outside the margins of time, leaving them untethered, left to stumble forward without map or mandate. And none of them say it aloud, but all understand: a misstep now could bring catastrophe. So they wait.

Night after night, they gather—Sy, Zookeeper, Ming-huà, and Lady Oracle—each carrying their own fatigue, their own questions. The room holds their voices in suspension, soft but persistent, as they attempt to coax meaning from the silence surrounding them. They sift through fragments of memory, parse dreams, weigh omens that might be coincidence, might be fate. Every sign becomes a riddle. Every conclusion frays before it settles. What begins as conversation slowly unravels into something closer to ritual: not a pursuit of answers, but a stalling of despair.

At the center sits the child.

Pythia offers no correction, no direction. She listens, or seems to, but gives them nothing. No glance that might be decoded, no shift of breath that might suggest approval or warning. Once they saw her as a guide, an axis around which the future might cohere. Now she has become the question itself. They circle her not as disciples but as witnesses, unsure whether what they're watching is revelation or undoing.

There is no map. No signpost. No voice from the clouds.

Only the quiet presence of something too large to name, too still to grasp.

And still, they return.

They cannot help it. Some part of them believes that truth, even buried, can be exhumed by attention. That clarity can be earned through endurance. But doubt grows. Not just about the child, but about themselves. What if they are the ones who cannot see? What if they are not meant to understand, but only to act, but cannot agree on how?

By the end of each night, the same dilemma remains. Two paths. No promise. No safety.

Each option threatens not only failure, but transformation.

And still, Pythia quietly watches, unreadable, and absorbing everything.

One: cross into the unknown. Leave behind all familiar ground. Train the child in open defiance of whatever forces are coming. Risk everything.

Or two: disappear. Fade into shadow. Hide in some nameless corner, raise Pythia in secrecy, hope invisibility buys them time.

Neither path feels right. Both carry cost. And so again they wait for a sign.

But the world does not wait with them.

One morning, without warning, two unfamiliar men appear at the front door. Detectives have returned.

"Can I help you?" Sy asks calmly.

"We're following up on earlier visits, Mr. Rung," the taller one says. "Some new questions have come up. May we come in?"

Sy steps aside. "Of course. Tea? Coffee?"

They decline.

"There's a man here, Matthew Weston. He has no arms, correct?"

"That's right."

"How did he lose them?"

"I think it's best you ask him yourself."

Zookeeper arrives, casual as ever. "What can I do ya for?"

"How did you lose your arms, Mr. Weston?" one asks, notebook open.

Zookeeper shrugs. "Told you all already. Woke up and—bam—no arms."

"You previously claimed it was a birth defect."

"Yeah, I lied. Didn't want to get involved."

"You were in some sort of fight?"

"Yeah. Couple guys hassled my wife and Judith. I stepped in. Then I woke up with stumps. No clue how."

"In a crack house?"

"Correct."

"Why were the two women there?"

"They were helping people. Community outreach. Found that out later. Took me in, saved my life. That's the story."

"Do you think your wife had anything to do with what happened to you and your . . . business associates?"

Zookeeper laughs. "My wife? Come on. A hunchback girl carving off limbs with no mess? No."

"You don't find it strange that your wife has been present at three different incidents involving . . . unexplained amputations? One even on the East Coast?"

"Coincidence," Zookeeper says flatly. "They work in dangerous places."

"Mr. Weston, people don't just lose limbs, bloodlessly, without cause."

Zookeeper shrugs. "How should I know? All I know is, she's not capable of something like that."

"We'll need you, your wife, Mr. Grafton, and Ms. Ganbaatar to report to this address tomorrow," the detective says, handing Sy a card. "We'd like to clarify a few things."

"Is Judith here now?"

"Out shopping," says Sy.

"No matter. Just make sure everyone shows up tomorrow."

"Are we being charged?" Zookeeper asks.

"No. Not yet. Just some inconsistencies."

"Such as?" Sy presses.

"Such as your wife's name not appearing in any federal database. Same goes for Ms. Ganbaatar."

"Oh, that's easy to explain," says Sy smoothly.

"Tomorrow, Mr. Rung. Mr. Weston."

Zookeeper raises an eyebrow. "And if we don't show?"

"You're all persons of interest in an active investigation. Subpoenas and warrants would follow. But we trust you'll cooperate. After all, you're in the business of helping people."

~

"That's done it," Lady Oracle says, watching their car vanish over a steep San Francisco hill. "We go to the cave."

Zookeeper groans. "Aw hell, that freak-show place? Too many weird vibes. Can't we just go somewhere warm? Hawaii, maybe?"

Sy ignores him. "But have you heard anything? From Goddess? Or the Mentors?"

"No."

"Then what if it's just a cave? No presence, no power, no portals. Just rock. We could be walking her into a trap."

"Use your instinct, Zookeeper," Sy adds. "What do you think they believe, is she a witness or a suspect?"

Zookeeper doesn't hesitate. "A suspect. No question. They're just trying to figure out how she did it."

Sy turns to Lady Oracle. "How about leaving the country?"

"Impossible," she replies. "First, to ease your concerns, Zookeeper, we'll check into a motel near the cave. In the morning, Ming-huà goes in. You stay behind."

"No way! I'm going with her."

"No," she says sharply. "We need to see if the cave still holds power. Maybe the Goddess speaks only to Pythia now. If so, she'll guide them. If not—Ming-huà and the child vanish into the unknown, and we return to San Francisco. Tell the police she left unexpectedly. She knows how to find us, if she needs to."

Sy remains silent. But Zookeeper stiffens.

"I'll go with her. No matter what."

"You will not," Lady Oracle says, voice iron. "You'll wait."

His resistance falters. "But what if they don't come back?"

"That's not our decision," she replies, pointing upward. "It's Hers."

"Zookeeper has a point," Sy says. "What if this is goodbye?"

"Then it is," Lady Oracle answers. "But the change will come regardless. There's no going back for the species. Not now."

~

Two days later, they make the drive. A worn motel, a restless night, and no farewells worth rehearsing. Just a final embrace between Zookeeper and Ming-huà that is necessarily tight, aching, and unfinished. At dawn, they drive. The car moves slowly down the unpaved road toward the cave. Dust rises behind them, a pale ribbon dissolving into morning light. Ming-huà cradles Pythia in the back seat. The infant is still, smiling faintly, eyes shining with an uncanny calm. As if she already knows what lies ahead. Ming-huà, by contrast, looks hollowed. Pale. Sleepless. A woman emptied by something more than childbirth. Up front, Sy drives in silence, hands firm. Lady Oracle stares out the window, lost in futures no longer visible. No one speaks. The dust thickens. The cave nears.

"She looks pleased," Sy says, glancing in the mirror. "Approves of the destination."

Ming-huà strokes the child's arm absently. "She's draining me. Not just my body, my thoughts. It's like she's feeding on me. Recharging. But I feel . . . depleted."

Lady Oracle looks back, alarmed. "You're just tired. That's all. New mothers always are."

"I miss Zookeeper," Ming-huà says, barely above a whisper.

"Don't," Lady Oracle replies. "We have larger concerns now."

Ming-huà doesn't answer. Her gaze is fixed ahead on the dark mouth of the cave, where all paths end.

And begin.

Chapter Twenty

Cave Redux

Boomerang

~ Crisis in the Desert ~

Among the final things Ming-huà remembers is standing near the cave's entrance, Pythia pressed to her chest, while Lady Oracle chanted in a language she couldn't begin to translate, its sounds rough and beautiful, almost too old to be human. The rhythm unsettled her, touched nerves that had nothing to do with language. She remembers someone guiding her toward a side tunnel, but not who. That memory is already gone.

Then, nothing. No sound, no light, no clear line from there to here.

Now she's standing on a rise of sand beneath an open sky. The air tastes of salt and metal. A massive sea crashes below, wild and gray. The cave is gone. Lady Oracle and the others were gone. She clutches Pythia and turns in every direction, but there's no familiar landmark, no path back.

The world has changed, and she is alone.

But Pythia is still with her, resting quietly in her arms. When Ming-huà looks down, the child is smiling, almost laughing, eyes full of delight. As if she's been waiting for this place. As if she recognizes it.

The wind hits hard, almost pushing Ming-huà backward. The waves pound against the dark shoreline, sending up spray that coats her face. Behind her, mountains—no, volcanoes—glow faintly through the haze, releasing plumes of smoke into a sky that looks ready to split. The storm isn't arriving. It's already here.

She bends into the wind and takes a step forward, shielding Pythia with her body. Every movement requires effort. Rain begins to fall, heavy and fast, as if it's been held back too long. Off to her left, beyond the shifting tree line, she spots a narrow gap, barely visible. She doesn't think. She just runs.

The forest closes behind her as she passes through the gap. Then all is silence. The air is still. She finds herself in a clearing. The rain has stopped. The trees stand undisturbed, and in the middle of the space sits a house. Modest, two stories, with a slanted roof and shutters drawn halfway. It looks lived-in, but there are no signs of life. Just stillness.

Pythia doesn't speak, but Ming-huà feels the pull from her, wordless and strong. This place is meant for them. She doesn't know how she knows that. She just does.

Even knowing it isn't real, she lets it happen.

Inside, the warmth feels genuine. The floorboards creak underfoot. The scent of smoke and wood lingers faintly, as if someone has recently stoked the hearth. She climbs the stairs, noting the framed objects on the wall: old photographs, dried herbs, woven cloth. None of it matches, yet none of it feels out of place.

In the small upstairs room, a crib waits. She lays Pythia inside. The baby stares back, calm, alert, awake. Not sleeping. Watching.

Downstairs, Ming-huà finds an old armchair by the window and lowers herself into it. The cushions give beneath her. She lets her breath settle. Her mind pulls in two directions—toward the island she left as a girl, and toward this new island, wild and unclaimed. She doesn't know what time means here. She doesn't even know what "here" is.

Without noticing, she strokes the air beside her. And there, without warning, sits Miss Gladflower in her lap, just as before. Not a memory. Not a dream. The doll looks up, unblinking, patient.

You came back, her expression seems to say. But you're not who you were.

Is this where the pieces of her go, the ones she couldn't carry into adulthood? The parts no one ever asked after?

She tells herself she's still in the cave. That this is part of the hallucination, or some trick of the mind. But her skin disagrees. Her muscles no longer wait for the real world to resume. Something has shifted, and it's already too late to reverse it.

Sleep takes her quickly.

Her dreams are unkind. Her father weeping beside her hospital bed. A soldier with half a face. Her grandmother, locked away, whispering words she wasn't meant to hear. Then come faceless others, wounded and quiet. They don't speak. They just watch. Guilt presses in from the corners.

She wakes with a sharp breath. The light through the window is clear and golden. Pythia stares at her, and without sound, delivers a single word directly into her thoughts:

Beach.

Ming-huà nods slowly. "Let me feed you first, sweetheart."

Beach. It's not a suggestion. It's something deeper. A command that cuts through her.

She dresses in a loose cotton shift, something made to hide the curve of her back and the softness of her belly. Outside, the world is soaked in sunlight. The air carries the scent of crushed leaves and sea salt. She steps forward. The wind rises again.

Everything smells of sea-born memory. And every step tightens something in her chest she doesn't yet have a name for.

Pythia, on the other hand, laughs with abandon.

At the beach, the sand is littered, an unholy offering from the sea. Body parts glisten in the sun, strewn in grotesque procession. And the surf continues to spit more onto the shore, as if purging the refuse of history.

Ming-huà bends, stomach churning. Pythia squeals in delight and writhes to be set free. Once released, she crawls expertly across the carnage, her tiny hands caressing bones and flesh like an inquisitive coroner.

Then she stops. Waits.

Ming-huà draws near, chilled to the core.

From every direction, limbs begin to crawl—yes, crawl—toward a central torso. Head and hands follow. Before her eyes, a figure assembles, stands, and stares.

Lady Oracle.

Her expression holds no comfort. Only judgment.

But Ming-huà is too stunned to speak. Another body is forming farther down the beach. A towering man, hulking, Mongol-featured, wild with archaic power, takes shape. He lifts Pythia as if she were flame itself and speaks to Lady Oracle in a growling dialect that makes Ming-huà's bones vibrate.

She closes her eyes, overtaken by awe.

~ *A New Companion* ~

"This is Altan, your new companion," says Lady Oracle.

The words strike hard, and Ming-huà reels. She blinks, shakes her head—but the ocean, the sand, the storm—all of it has vanished. She is standing once more within the cool hush of the cave entrance, Pythia nestled against her hip. No memory marks the passage back. One moment the sky wept dismembered bodies into the sea, and now nothing but stone walls, shadowed flickerlight, and Sy watching her with silent vigilance.

Then she feels Lady Oracle's stare shift and follows it.

Out from the tunnel's throat strides the man, the colossus from the shore, no illusion now, but bone, sinew, and something else older than time. His face is cut from stone, impervious, unreadable. Yet his eyes are stranger still: each iris cleaved in two, one half a dusky emerald blue, the other a molten gold-brown, as though day and night had decided to share a gaze.

Ming-huà cannot move. She is pinned beneath his presence as though caught in the shadow of a mountain that has decided, without warning, to entomb.

She struggles to gather herself, but her thoughts are scattered—flashing, directionless, gone.

"New companion?" she manages to utter at last.

"Yes," says Lady Oracle. "Do not let his heterochromia bother you. It is from birth." She chuckles. "Your new companion has yin and yang for eyes."

"What does that mean?"

"What?"

"What does new companion mean?"

"It means you are to go with him."

This answer stuns her, and she exclaims, "Why? What about you and Sy? What about Zookeeper?"

"Forget us."

Ming-huà feels faint and lowers herself on a large rock. She stammers, "How can I forget you? How can I forget Zookeeper? He is my husband!"

"He no longer exists."

"I . . . what? . . . what do you mean he no longer exists?"

"To you, from this moment on, the only persons on earth that exist are yourself, Pythia, and Altan."

Ming-huà can barely hold onto a coherent thought. "I want to see Zookeeper," she says vaguely, not knowing even why she says it.

"I told you he no longer exists."

"He's dead? You don't mean he's dead, do you?"

Lady Oracle laughs. "No, of course not. I mean Altan will be taking you and Pythia to many different places."

"You're kidding! Is he some sort of bodyguard?"

"If you want to look at it that way, but he will be much more than a bodyguard. Much more."

Ming-huà sets her jaw and says coldly, "I still want to see Zookeeper, my husband, father of my child."

"Not possible."

"Why not?"

"Because Altan is taking you with him."

"Where?"

"Deeper into the cave."

Ming-huà's eyes widen. "And then?"

"And then you will be in a different place, sort of like the island you just dreamed about."

"Terrible dream," Ming-huà whispers, shuddering. "Did *She* bring it to me? It was really more like a hallucination than a dream."

"Well," says Sy. "Your lineage certainly is chock full of hallucinating . . . relatives."

During this conversation, Altan stands stolidly aloof, his striking features focused almost exclusively on Pythia, and Pythia's on him. They appear to be communicating without speaking, and eventually Ming-huà notices it.

"Excuse me, Mr. Altan," she says abruptly. "What is your background?"

"My background?" His voice is a guttural rumble, Tuvan throat music all its own. Ugly to an untutored ear, but with familiarity, it becomes mesmerizingly beautiful.

"Yes, your background."

"Ahab is Ahab," he says with an ironic smile.

"What an odd thing to say."

Lady Oracle interrupts. "You and Altan will have plenty of time to get to know each other." She looks at Altan. "You need to leave now."

He bows.

As if spurred to action by Lady Oracle's words, Pythia squirms and fusses with surprising force, so much so that Ming-huà sets her on the ground and stands unmoving. "I'm not going anywhere until I know more."

Altan suddenly scoops up Pythia and strides deeper into the cave.

"Wait!" cries Ming-huà.

"Go with him," commands Lady Oracle. She holds out a flashlight.

Ming-huà starts to protest.

"Go with him or you won't see Pythia for a very long time."

Ming-huà lets out a shriek, grabs the flashlight, and rushes after Altan, following Pythia's laughter into the darkness.

When she catches up, he turns to look, his face lit by the beam. Ming-huà stares into the half-blue, half-gold eyes.

"Do not let my yin and yang eyes worry you," he says. "They are only parts of my parts, pieces of my pieces, fragments of my fragments."

"I dreamed you were pieced together bit by bit," she says. "A composite being. Yet, you do not look like some sort of Frankenstein's monster. Dreams are so bizarre."

He bellows with laughter. "Indeed, they are! I am born of a mother, same as you."

"And *her*!" Ming-huà exclaims, nodding toward Pythia now quietly settled in Altan's arms.

"Well, there you are partly right and partly wrong."

"What do you mean? Remember, I was there when she was born. No parts need to have been added after leaving my womb."

"No, you're right, not after."

"What are you trying to say?" asks Ming-huà.

"Careful, you'll trip if you keep talking. We're almost there."

"Where?"

"Another good question—the answer you will soon discover."

"Please tell me now."

"Just the beginning of her education. First Kigali, then Auschwitz."

Ming-huà freezes in her tracks. "No, no, no, no, no. . . . "

"Yes."

"The baby!"

"She will be safe. I am your companion now."

"How do you know she'll be safe?"

Altan smiles broadly. "As you said, it is all just a dream."

"Then what is the point?"

"To see."

"What?"

Altan looks down at the smiling Pythia. "Her response."

"She's just a baby."

"No, she is as old as the hominin species . . . older even."

"You clearly weren't there when I gave birth to Pythia. She was full term. A normal birth. Now—"

Altan begins to hum deep throat tones over her voice as they walk; the deep, guttural sounds reverberating in waves from the cave walls. Immediately, Pythia, still in his arms, begins laughing even more infectiously, evidently basking in the tonal vibrations emanating from Altan's throat.

They take a side tunnel and Ming-huà's flashlight goes dark.

The next moment she squints in the glare of a bright sun.

They stand on a road where hundreds of people are struggling, pleading, screaming.

Black men with machetes. Dozens of them.

The crazed men with machetes are hacking the people screaming for mercy; men, women, and children. Hundreds of them. Hacking them to death.

Ming-huà's hump is overwhelmed with the terror and she drops to her knees, faint, nauseous, trying to scream at Altan to take them out of this terrible place. Chaos clouds her mind and her powers are useless against such mass slaughter. It is as if her hump has short-circuited.

Pythia's laughter turns into wide-eyed fascination. Gradually, her fascination turns to distaste. She lets out a primal screech, clearly terrified . . . or outraged.

Every man swinging a machete is suddenly without arms. Every one of them, arms gone, no blood, machetes scattered on the ground. An eerie silence falls over the horrendous scene as victims and perpetrators look on in disbelief. To Ming-huà, it is like there are a hundred armless black Zookeepers, but she knows she could never pull this off on such a scale. Stoshells, yes. A few people, yes. Not this. She stares at Pythia in astonishment. The stunned silence of the mob lasts only a few moments.

Then the cacophonous wailing commences and carries on without abatement, the armless men running aimlessly around in mad shock as if insanity afflicted all of them simultaneously; the surviving victims ignoring them and screaming for their loved ones who have been chopped to pieces. No one notices the three figures standing at the periphery of this waking nightmare. A hunchback. A giant. A baby.

The three watch. They turn. They walk away.

Back toward Kigali, where horror breeds in real time, undeterred by witness. As they approach the outskirts, the carnage multiplies. New battalions of armless men stagger through blood-soaked streets, howling to a sun that answers nothing. They stumble over the crumpled bodies of the newly dead, over the half-alive who twitch and moan and crawl. Machetes lie scattered like cursed relics—gleaming, blood-slick, and untouched, as if even the wind dares not stir them.

Spectators now gather. Wordless. Wide-eyed. Not one bends to retrieve a blade.

Pythia gazes at the grotesque theater unfolding before her, a stillness anchoring her in the sea of human ruin. Her eyes shimmer with something unfathomable, ancient, inborn, almost divine. A slight smile curves her lips. Not kind. Not cruel. Inevitable.

Ming-huà blinks in disbelief, holding out her arms to take Pythia from Altan who has held her the entire time.

"Not yet," he says. "One more stop."

"This is a dream, right?" asks Ming-huà, her arms still extended.

"Absolutely." Altan quickens his pace, unwilling to surrender Pythia. "Education *is* a dream, to many."

"Where to next?" asks Ming-huà, struggling to catch up. "Not Auschwitz? Please, not Auschwitz! I've seen enough!"

"But *she* hasn't," says Altan nodding toward Pythia.

Ming-huà doubles over in pain.

A blackness renders her blind.

When she opens her eyes, a new horror unfolds before her.

Smoke. Ash. A Great Wailing.

A sign emerges through the gloom.

It is an obscene tattoo carved into the flesh of humanity.

~ *Arbeit Macht Frei* ~

Ming-huà stumbles back, breath catching as her eyes lock onto Pythia, not an infant now, but a girl of ten, standing still and focused, gaze unwavering. The change is total. Time has passed without notice, without sense. Her hands tremble. The ground beneath her feels unsteady. She struggles to hold on to the moment, but it slides away, already lost.

Above them, the chimneys continue to pour smoke into the sky. Ash drifts downward, slow and endless. The cries, thousands of them, maybe more, never stop. Women, children, and infants move forward in silence, faces hollow, limbs weak, bodies carrying themselves as if there is no choice left. The air is thick, difficult to breathe. The sun is hidden behind the haze, its light dulled and distorted, painting the landscape in tones of rust and grief.

Then the line stops.

The guards who had been shouting, striking, pushing, now fall silent. Their rifles drop. Their movements cease. They stand, but not with purpose. Their arms are gone. Sleeves hang empty. Uniforms bunch at the shoulders, crumple at the chest. They remain upright, but there is no life in their posture. Their eyes are open but unfocused, staring into a space no one else can see.

Prisoners begin to notice. One steps forward. Another follows. No one knows what has happened. Voices rise, fragments of speech, cries of warning, questions no one dares to finish. A few reach out, touch the guards as if expecting them to spring back to life. But they don't.

The silence fractures.

From the crowd come low moans, then sobs, then something deeper, a sound scraped from the core of the body, not shaped into words. The sound of survival that never found release. The sound of trauma unspoken until now. It pours out, rough and broken. Some kneel. Some clutch their heads. Others simply stand, mouths open, not in astonishment but in grief, too numbing for reason.

The child, Pythia, says nothing. Her eyes remain fixed ahead, expression unreadable.

Ten-year-old Pythia stands calmly amidst it all. She smiles faintly and nods to the survivors, as if encouraging them to breathe again. Her face glows with quiet triumph.

Altan gives a slow nod of approval, then turns, walking beneath the infamous gate and along the rails that vanish into the distance. Ming-huà follows, dazed and hollow, her steps heavy with the weight of incomprehension. Behind them, the camp begins to dissolve into a nightmare memory.

They journey on, trekking from one theater of brutality to the next. Horrific abuses: slaughter inflicted on humans and non-humans alike. Again and again, the result is the same: mutilated oppressors, stunned victims, and the slow turning of an ancient wheel. Between horrors, a strange interlude: lectures and rituals conducted by otherworldly instructors who remain aloof, detached, and relentless. And then, without warning, the cycle ends.

"Do you see now?"

Ming-huà blinks. She is back in the cave.

Pythia stands at Altan's side, her features mature, composed. Lady Oracle faces them, visibly aged, her voice a low echo in the chamber.

Altan, the silent architect of her journey, says proudly, "Today is her seventeenth birthday, in human terms." The words soften his granite expression. "Few have endured such passage."

"You have guided her well," Lady Oracle replies. "Her formal education is complete. Though sixteen years have passed for her, only a handful have passed here. Even so, the waiting has not been easy."

Ming-huà struggles to form words. "But . . . but . . ."

Lady Oracle lifts a calming hand, her gesture quieting the air—a hush before a storm's retreat. "It will come back to you," she says gently. "All of it. In time, memory returns to those who are ready to bear its weight." She casts a sidelong glance at Pythia, a faint gleam of pride flickering behind the solemnity in her voice. "Pythia has surpassed every trial placed before her. She is no longer bound to this cave. She is ready—to step into the world beyond, and to face those who hunted you both in your absence."

She turns to the girl who is more than a girl. "Isn't that so?"

"Yes. I'm ready," the young woman replies.

But Ming-huà is paralyzed. She stares at her daughter, searching the girl's face for the passage of years she cannot recall, years stolen, smudged out of time. Her eyes flicker with desperation, as though she could distill years of forgotten life into a few seconds of comprehension. But the memories will not come.

The being before her is a stranger, an exquisite young woman, bent with a gentle curve that only enhances her grace. The hump, once feared, radiates a power far beyond anything Ming-huà has ever possessed. That power, once faint and embryonic, now eclipses her own. She feels it pressing down, a sun pouring its oppressive heat against a withered flower.

"Seventeen," she murmurs, awestruck.

A hollow sensation creeps over her. She feels faded, drained, her fragile confidence stripped. She remembers the pride with which she once told Zookeeper that her hump absorbed cruelty like a black hole in silent finality. But now, she understands its limits. Her daughter has faced what she never could. Genocide, rage, mass extinctions, the churning abyss of human evil, Pythia has withstood it.

And Ming-huà has not.

~ *Where the Lost Years?* ~

Ming-huà roams the edges of her consciousness, trying to account for the vanished years of her daughter's youth. What happened? Where was she? Why was she absent?

She recalls only flashes, ephemeral and fragmentary. A laugh. A shadow. A scent. Nothing whole. She suspects Pythia was taken from her, spirited away to some place beyond time, raised far from a mother's gaze until she was no longer a child. When Ming-huà asks questions, they are met with silence or half-truths. Lady Oracle offers vague assurances. Sy and Altan deflect. Trauma-induced amnesia, they say. The memories will come.

But Ming-huà knows what no one will say aloud: the torch has passed. Motherhood, in any meaningful sense, is over. Her purpose has been served, and now she drifts at the margins, irrelevant.

She does not protest.

Not because she accepts it, but because she is too weary to resist.

Still, the regret is a constant ache. The lost chance to raise her daughter, to know her through scraped knees and midnight songs, to witness the first steps, the first words, the first doubts, all of it gone. She is now a relic, A portrait gathering dust in the corridors of her daughter's future.

And the question gnaws: Where was she all those years? The question festers, an old burn which is incurable and unspeakable. She witnessed, yet was blind. Listened, but was deaf.

The memories will not come. And the years, too, remain lost.

With little left to hold on to, Ming-huà turns her thoughts to the island, to that imagined refuge of serenity and familiar voices. She yearns for the company of Zookeeper, the sound of wind in trees, the comfort of talking to creatures that never asked her to be anything more than what she was.

~

Suddenly, the words of Lady Oracle intrude, "... to face those who hunted you both in your absence."

Lady Oracle's words linger in the air. They are troubling, but Ming-huà brushes them aside.

Her eyes remain fixed on her daughter—no longer a child, no longer hers to raise.

The cave feels colder than before, the shadows deepening into silence.

A single question coils through her mind, burning, endless: *When did I lose her?*

Beyond the cave's mouth, she imagines the hunters waiting, faceless, patient.

And for the first time, she fears the greatest danger is not them—but what her daughter has already become.

Chapter Twenty-One

Into The World

Who's Predator,
Who's Prey?

~ First Steps ~

"Hunted." The word escapes Ming-huà's mouth, unformed and involuntary, unraveling the quiet tension that had wrapped itself around her. The moment fractures. Lady Oracle's warning echoes through her mind, not as an instruction, but as a tremor that rises from the core of something far older than her earliest memory. It is not fear born of reasoning. It is recognition. A signal passed down through blood and shadow. A knowledge that lives beneath the surface of thought, waiting to surface when words fail.

Pythia remains motionless.

She does not respond, does not acknowledge the transmission. Her breath is even. Her gaze does not shift. Ming-huà's tentative attempt to reach her, wordless, fragile, and full of restraint, spills outward and brushes against her daughter's mind. There is no resistance, but no invitation either. The contact hovers, unanswered. It is not refused. It is simply left untouched.

Still, Ming-huà sends what she can.

She draws from what remains in her, small threads of warmth, fractured but sincere. A maternal impulse not diminished by powerlessness, but deepened by it. She offers presence. She offers care. What moves between them is not command or demand, but something slower, more vulnerable, persistent. It carries sorrow. Not as reaction, but as condition. It belongs to her, and always has.

Pythia receives this without effort. Without judgment.

She feels the shape of it. The uneven edges. The pain Ming-huà carries not as damage, but as inheritance. It is not power, but something that touches deeper than strength. A grief that listens. A sensitivity that does not turn away. Pythia understands it fully. She understands her mother's ache for justice, her instinct to shield, her helplessness in the face of cruelty too vast to name.

Ming-huà has no illusions about what lives within her child. The distance between them is not emotional—it is elemental. She knows her daughter sees further, feels more, moves within a gravity she herself cannot follow. But that does not stop her from reaching. It never has.

And in that reach, there is love. Worn, quiet, enduring.

Pythia's own blood carries the sediment of centuries. Memory is fused to her marrow, not as recollection but as essence. The anguish of humankind—its fires and famines, its betrayals and elegies—lives within her, encoded not only in history, but in the double helix of destiny. Her inheritance is not merely genetic, but mythic: the collapse of empires that devoured their children, the silence of gods who fed on screams, the wailing of mothers who mourned across ten thousand dawns, and the intimate obscenities whispered in dark alleys—murderer and murdered, rapist and raped.

And so she does not recoil from her mother's ache. She honors it as one might honor the final ember of a fading star.

It is this deep knowing, this archetypal memory, that makes her patient with Ming-huà's fragility. Her mother's power may be faint, diffused through a heart that has always bled too easily, but to Pythia, it is no less sacred. She receives it not as a failing, but as a testament: the quiet, enduring ache of a soul that has never ceased to feel. And she honors it with the stillness of one who has seen civilizations fall, not from malice alone, but from self-inflicted wounds they could not name, let alone heal.

She answers her mother's cry with a pulse of thought, warm and crystalline: *Do not worry. All is as it must be.*

Lady Oracle, barred from the silent communion that passes between mother and daughter, makes a valiant attempt to speak. But language falters where telepathy flows. Words, those stubborn beasts, rear and stumble beneath the weight of too many timelines, too many collapsed possibilities. She exhales in frustration, then flicks her wrist as if to swat away the whole snarled tapestry of meaning.

"Yes, hunted. But, oh, never mind all that now," she says, her voice brusque with weariness and affection. "Time has misbehaved again, as it always does. While eons unraveled in the worlds you wandered, only days have passed beyond these stones. The cave has completed its task. Whatever mystery it was charged to deliver, it has done so. We must leave it behind."

She casts a glance at the cave, at stone striated with opaque memory, and shudders. Something still watches from within the rock, ancient and unfinished.

"Come," she urges softly. "This place has outlived its silence."

Outside, Sy waits, still and alert, behind the wheel of a car that hums like a beast trained not to bite. As they pass through the light-scorched desert, pale and unblinking, Lady Oracle begins her telling. But her tale is fractured. It spills from her, an overturned jar pouring words: radiant, erratic, impossible to gather whole. Ming-huà strains to follow, cupping each handful before it vanishes into the slipstream of waking memory.

What emerges is a riddle more than a record. She, Pythia, and Altan had passed through a labyrinth of time—not linear, but spiral and breathing. A maze shaped by unseen architects, where simulations masqueraded as truth, and truths were cloaked in allegory. Time did not pass so much as convulse: stretching, snapping, healing, folding in on itself. Years were lost, then found. Lessons were seeded in the guise of lived experience. Decades, centuries, perhaps more, were consumed by some mythic engine of instruction, and Altan, ever the cunning navigator, had guided them through.

"But why do I remember nothing?" Ming-huà whispers in a bewildered voice. She feels as if she had awakened from a dream too vast to comprehend. "Why does my mind retain no trace of what you say I've lived?"

Lady Oracle turns to her with a tenderness that feels almost ceremonial. Her gaze carries no answers, only the quiet sorrow of someone who has learned to live alongside mystery.

"Because, dear heart," she says gently, "you were not shaped by the same design. Not entirely."

"What design?"

"We do not know." The reply is naked in its truth, and in that nakedness, oddly soothing.

Before Ming-huà can press further, Lady Oracle shifts the course of the conversation, her tone darkening.

"What matters now is that your absence was noticed. The world did not remain still. Its machinery stirred. Governments lost their balance. Officials whispered. Networks flared with unease. Limbless bodies and unexplained deaths began to surface in places they were never meant to be. Panic moved through the system, not loud at first, but fast, gaining strength behind closed doors. Theories multiplied, not with insight, but desperation. They reached for answers they didn't understand, their logic collapsing under its own weight. And still, they searched."

She pauses, then continues with less emotion but more weight.

"They came. Agencies with names reduced to acronyms. Their faces hidden behind tinted glass and protocol. Even the FBI. All of them chasing a ghost—a girl with a crooked spine and no official past, linked to events that defied explanation. More dangerous than the destruction you left behind was what you carried. Word leaked. They know now. You are pregnant. And that changed everything."

She turns away, her breath uneven.

"They never found you. But if they ever do . . . there will be no restraint. No clemency. You won't be treated as a person. You'll be treated as evidence. Or threat."

By the time they reach the house, Ming-huà still hasn't spoken.

Sy guides the vehicle through a gate of black iron. It closes behind them with finality. The sound is not loud, but it marks the end of something. The driveway curves gently uphill. On either side, open desert waits in silence. The shapes of rocks and low brush slip past the windows, half-seen, half-absorbed into the dark. The road is narrow but unbroken. Nothing interrupts their ascent.

Above them, the sky has lowered itself across the landscape. The night feels close. Unyielding. Still. Not the silence of peace, but of pause, an interval held between whatever just ended and whatever comes next.

Ming-huà watches the house come into view. It does not welcome. It does not threaten. It simply waits. Its architecture speaks in another grammar: angular and curved, deliberate and unfamiliar. The walls are smooth, the windows dark, the roof sloped in a way that resists context. It does not resemble safety, but it does offer boundary.

Sy says nothing as he parks and exits. She follows without question, holding Pythia close. Inside, the temperature shifts. The air is warmer, scented with something faintly resinous. Perhaps sandalwood. Perhaps something older, preserved.

They climb the stairs in silence.

Shadows slip along the walls, drawn to the edges of rooms and recesses, disappearing into spaces that seem carved for their arrival. The house does not creak or settle. It stands in its own logic.

Ming-huà feels the change settle in her chest—not fear, not relief, but recognition. This place was chosen, not by preference, but necessity.

A place not to rest, but to begin again.

At the landing, Ming-huà pauses, caught between ascent and a floating disorientation.

"Tomorrow," she murmurs to Pythia, "we must speak."

"Agreed," Pythia replies aloud, and the sound startles her mother. Her voice, seldom used, reverberates with something ancient: low, sensuous, and not entirely of this Earth.

Once in her room sleep overtakes Ming-huà quickly. No dreams disturb her descent into stillness.

But Pythia does not rest. She waits, poised, a blade unsheathed, shining in the moonlight.

Altan arrives before the first light of dawn and sits down with Pythia in the kitchen. They do not waste words. Seated across from one another at the kitchen table, they settle into quiet rapport, their manner easy, intimate not with romance, but with purpose, like companions who have weathered many lifetimes beneath different names. Their conversation carries the portending of oracles and the gravity of extinction. They speak not merely of survival, but of essence, and of the soul's endurance, of the species yet unnamed. How might a new kind of being, embryonic and radiant with perilous potential, take root beneath the long shadow of a world unraveling? A world still drunk on the myths of conquest and cruelty, still kneeling before the altars of fear and violence?

Pythia is not simply novel. She is an interruption in the lineage of humankind, a luminous fissure in the architecture of what has been. She heals, yes, but she also undoes, reconfigures. Her very being disturbs the scaffolding of *Homo sapiens*, as if evolution itself had accelerated down a different path.

"Your existence," Altan says, "is another step in a quiet apocalypse."

They speak then of the Great Craving—that insatiable human need to both suffer and inflict suffering, as if agony were the currency by which they commune with the Four Idols of illusion. Could this be unlearned? Could a different Idol rise—one nourished not by anguish, but by compassion?

"If extinction is the price," Altan says, "then perhaps the ledger demands it."

Pythia listens, unblinking.

Altan continues. "Your blood is rich with legend. The sagas of your ancestors course through you with the inexorable movement of subterranean magma: John and Meiying, Child of Buddha and Buandelgereen, Michael and Tamara, Ming-huà and the enigmatic Zookeeper. These names are not just memories, they are runes etched into your DNA."

"Yes," says Pythia. "I feel them."

Altan's tenor drops a register. "Take Michael Powers, for instance. Humans labeled him, as they always do, mistaking vision for sickness, truth for pathology. He knew the cost of being Storyteller the soldier in a world that feared what it could not understand. Yet he endures in you, as do they all. Their madness, their vision, their poetry, their suffering—each lives on, alloyed into your being."

From this inheritance, only one command remains: Survive. And seed the future.

"To survive," Altan says, "is to vanish in plain sight. To procreate is another challenge altogether. We know little of how your essence behaves across bloodlines. Past failures and half-successes have taught us that."

"It might dilute," says Pythia.

"Or amplify," Altan concedes.

Then she asks the unaskable: "Could I have stopped the Holocaust?"

Altan breathes deeply. "Perhaps. But how many monsters would you need to silence before they silenced you? One voice cannot unmake a thousand-year scream."

"Then what is the critical mass?"

"No one knows. You will not live to see it."

He leans forward, suddenly light. "First, blend in. Then: reproduce. Even blending in might be too much to ask."

"Don't underestimate me," she says with a sly smile.

"Don't underestimate them," he counters. "To them, difference is danger incarnate. And danger must be hunted."

"Then tell me," she says, "where does one blend in?"

"For a seventeen-year-old human girl? High school. But that would be barbaric. No, you'll take every intelligence test known to man. And then you'll enter university. There, you'll choose a camouflage."

"I want to study everything."

"You have. For our purposes, pick two."

"Which two?"

"Physics. Neuroscience. If you find a mate, let him be worthy."

"Someone like my father would not be worthy."

"Perhaps, but worth is not always housed in intellect. Another mutant, or even an outlier with unconventional gifts, might suffice. Even," he chuckles, "a drug dealer."

Pythia doesn't laugh. "I must also learn piano. It is an offering to Bai Meiying."

Altan nods. "That would be wise."

"And the university?"

"Berkeley."

"Why?"

He smiles. "Close to San Francisco. We'll return to the Yin and Yang apartments. And that grand old Victorian mansion remains in our care."

"And my mother?"

"She prefers her island, where the wind speaks kindly and time forgets its name."

"And my father?"

Altan's eyes narrow. "Zookeeper resists. But he's softening. His fury is cooling. I suspect he'll follow her. He always does."

Pythia tilts her head. "Then he must love her."

"He does."

"And love?" she muses aloud. "Is that something my kind can feel? Or is it a relic of human romance?"

"Another unknown," Altan admits.

She fixes him with her stare. "Why not you, Altan?"

He shifts. "Not possible."

"Why?"

"I am configured differently."

Her smile deepens. "Son of a Goddess? Alien emissary?"

He shrugs. "Configured differently."

"Is that why I cannot read you?"

"Yes."

Altan lifts his hand, gesturing toward the future. "Interbreeding is rare between species. But it has happened. *Homo sapiens* and *Homo Neanderthal* is but one example. It has created many intermediates. It will happen again, only with far more potency."

"Then let's hope they are the *Neanderthals*," she teases, "not us."

Altan grins. "They are. You are the next step, if you tread wisely."

"And you?" she asks. "Am I a *Neanderthal* compared to you?"

He chuckles. "Hardly. I am not of *Homo* at all."

~ *At University* ~

With her admittance to Berkeley, Pythia takes her first steps onto the campus like a goddess veiled in mortal skin. She is nearly seventeen by Earth's reckoning. Classes begin early. Since reentering the fabric of linear time, she has already absorbed the full breadth of human knowledge: every major discipline tasted, swallowed, and stored with instinctual ease. As Altan once predicted, learning comes to her as naturally as breathing. During the long, invisible years of her training, each inhalation drew in the highest principles of physics, chemistry, cosmology, philosophy, history, and myth, anchoring them not just in her intellect, but in her very bones.

Now, by contrast, even the most refined currents of human thought strike her as rudimentary, infant syllables from a species still learning how to ask the right questions. Berkeley, with all its prestige and pedigree, offers only the scaffolding of insight. She soon discerns that much of academia is a hall of mirrors—ideas folding inward, distorted by ego, dulled by repetition, twisted by competition. Even the so-called intelligentsia seem bound to a cycle of endless self-reference, their minds constrained by habit and the invisible permutations of social posturing.

Her peers move past her in slow, habitual rhythms, backpacks slung over shoulders, laptops glowing in their arms, footsteps dull against the pavement. Their eyes flicker with exhaustion. The light in them is dimmed by too many hours under artificial glare, too many nights spent reaching for meaning in test scores, late-night posts, group chats that evaporate by morning. They are bound together not by purpose, but by inertia. Not malice, but drift.

They carry the residue of information rather than its weight, boxy modules memorized, frameworks rehearsed, deadlines survived. The gestures are practiced, the movements nearly synchronized. They are not hostile. But they are not awake either.

And yet, it is not these human routines that catch Pythia's attention. What draws her focus are the living presences tucked between the buildings, the quick burst of birdsong overhead, the low vibration of tree limbs adjusting to the wind, the flickering exchanges of insects moving through grass and soil. These are not distractions. They are patterns. Languages. They move with coordination that needs no rehearsal. Every vibration, every shift in air pressure, every wingbeat holds intention.

She feels their presence not as noise, but as a signal that is constant, layered, and fully awake.

Within that web of signals, something inside her responds. Not intellectually, but in a deeper register. There is no word for it. Only the sense that the natural world is not a backdrop, but an active intelligence, aware, alert, and speaking in ways the human world no longer remembers how to hear.

Her classmates seem distant from this. They breathe, they speak, but they do not seem to listen. Their bodies move forward, but their minds remain sealed, tethered to devices, ambitions, fears. Even the laughter carries a tightness, a need to be heard rather than shared.

Pythia has never felt more apart from them.

And yet, Altan's words remain close: blend in. Hide what you are. Not out of shame, but necessity.

So she follows the instruction. She watches. She adjusts. Her movements mimic theirs. Not perfectly, but close enough. With practice, she has learned which expressions deflect attention, which tones imply normalcy, which pauses suggest thoughtfulness. It is a mask, and she wears it carefully.

In her first lecture, she finds a seat near the center. Around her, the room buzzes: whispers, greetings, half-spoken comments about the professor, the reading, the weekend. There is energy here, but it is frayed. Beneath the surface chatter lie patterns more complex and more guarded. Social rules unfold wordlessly, an economy of glances, shared looks, hierarchies that announce themselves without need of titles. The loudest voices don't always hold power. Influence circulates through posture, reputation, timing.

Every detail carries a message.

Pythia remains quiet. She lets the room wash over her. She hears the laughter, the flirting, the coded self-assessments, all of it calibrated, self-edited. This is not cruelty in its rawest form. But it is control. It is pressure. It is the slow carving away of difference in the name of belonging.

She wonders what this space would become if each person here had access to her abilities. If insight were not rare but common. Would understanding bloom? Would pain lessen? Would insecurity release its grip?

She doubts it.

Stopping genocide is possible. Stopping envy, loneliness, shame—these are harder. They entrench themselves in private spaces. They replicate in silence. She can sense them all around her, clinging to smiles, embedded in jokes, buried beneath ambition.

She sits with the knowledge that she is something else entirely.

Not above them.

Not below.

But something not yet understood.

A beginning, perhaps. Or a fracture. She doesn't know which.

And the experiment continues.

Unexpectedly, a flush of compassion rises in her chest. She sets aside her skepticism. She scans the room: bright young faces, masks barely holding. For the first time, she feels guilt, not for being different, but for seeing so clearly what they cannot.

Perhaps there is more of Ming-huà in me than I believed, she thinks, and the thought unsettles her in ways she cannot fully name.

A youthful professor bounds to the lectern, enthusiasm crackling. But Pythia barely hears him. Her thoughts stretch toward the future: What will her presence mean? If evolution is the silent sculptor, she must become more than a mutation, she must become a guide. Without restraint, her gifts could decimate rather than elevate. Perhaps evolution, at last, is tilting the balance from hawks to doves. In a world balanced on the blade of mutual destruction, peace may become the only viable strategy for survival. But the doves must have sharper claws than the hawks.

Tuning in briefly, she confirms her suspicion: nothing the professor says is unfamiliar. Still, she remains. The ritual of normalcy must be observed. *Blend in.* But her mind flickers and frays under the onslaught of mental static from her classmates. She is astonished by their inward noise—so much of it circling identity, appearance, status, belonging. So many minds devoured by mirrors.

Perhaps advancement is this: the shedding of self-obsession, the move from fragmentation toward coherence. The greatest minds of history rarely gazed inward for too long. Rather, they looked out, beyond, toward the Whole. And the fragmented self? It injures. It bleeds. It infects. It must be healed, or removed.

Weeks pass. She attends each class but listens to none. A pattern emerges: after lectures, she lingers, motionless, while the hall empties around her. She dwells not on course material, but on the fate of her species. Her mind returns often to her mother. Ming-huà's absence aches more sharply now, like a phantom limb. She senses the retreat: the depression, the exhaustion, the fading powers. She understands. Her birth was not without cost. Ming-huà, ever porous to the pain of the world, has exiled herself to an island, not just in geography, but in spirit. Altan once called such beings "intermediates"—souls born on the cusp of two epochs, bearing gifts too heavy for the current world, too fragile for the next. Ming-huà is one. More evolved than most, but not enough to withstand the psychic toll. Or, perhaps, she is risen prematurely.

Now, in her mother's absence, Pythia feels the ache of loneliness, a residue not yet bred out of her kind. She considers it a weakness. And yet, her gaze upon *Homo sapiens*, though sharpened by superiority, remains streaked with compassion.

The cave of genocides taught her a brutal simplicity: to end human suffering, humanity itself may need to end.

But if that end must come, let it be merciful. Let it be gradual. Let it arrive not with fire, but with grace. Still, she knows how delicate her position is, how easily her existence could be extinguished by the sheer inertia of a species that fears what it cannot dominate. If her lineage is to endure, she must act. She must find a mate. She must spread.

Too bad Altan—

"Hello. Do you need help?"

Pythia's deep concentration is broken by a youngish man standing in the aisle and leaning over the back of a seat looking at her sitting in the shadows at the row's end. She is angry at letting herself be surprised, but responds politely.

"No, thank you."

"I just returned to retrieve my notes when I noticed you sitting here."

Now she recognizes the professor whose lecture she just ignored.

"Ah, I see," she says, noncommittal.

"Are you in my class?" he asks.

"Yes."

He chuckles and says, "Quantum mechanics can be the devil of a topic. You would not be the first student bedeviled by its bizarre maths and mind-twisting implications."

"It is quite elementary." The words have escaped before she remembers Altan's admonition to blend in. Such a response is not well-conceived to further that goal. It is obvious he is taken aback.

"Well," he says rather defensively. "It is, after all, only a second-year quantum mechanics course, but nonetheless does baffle many students."

Pythia now weighs her words more carefully, and can come up with nothing better than, "Yes, that is true."

He is clearly interested in this very young-looking student. Always on the alert for a dyed-in-the-wool genius, he continues, "Yet you say it is elementary. I take it you understand everything so far?"

Pythia is somewhat piqued at his persistence (and the implication in his tone that she really does not understand everything) so she says, "Professor Paine, I assure you my understanding is complete."

"Ah, *touché*! Your name is. . . ?"

"Pythia Powers."

His eyes widen. "So, it's you!"

She gives him a quizzical look.

"You are the student who not only has perfect scores, but even goes beyond your answers with explanatory extensions as if I was the student and you the teacher. I often wrote an invitation on the papers to visit me during office hours, but. . . ." he throws up his hands.

"Sorry I create more work for you," says Pythia.

He ignores her comment. "Yet, I get the impression, complete as your work is, that you constrain yourself from going further . . . deeper."

"Perhaps."

Jared Paine stares openly at this young prodigy for long moments as if she were a rare specimen glimpsed through glass, then says, "Will you visit me during office hours tomorrow? There are a number of questions I would like to ask, if you would be so kind."

Pythia is not sure her being so open with this professor is suitable for blending in. "I'll try," she says unconvincingly.

"No, really. You must come. I insist. Shall we say eleven o'clock tomorrow morning in my office?"

Which answer blends better, yes or no, she wonders. The words pop out. "If you insist."

"Excellent!" he cries. "I have a lecture in a few minutes, but I'll see you tomorrow."

As he rushes off, Pythia curses herself for getting into this fix, and vows to play dumb from now on.

~

The next morning, she knocks on the professor's office door. Quickly, she hears, "Come in!" and enters to find him unabashedly leaning forward on his desk in anticipation.

"Welcome, Pythia. Have a seat."

She eyes him critically. Last night in more contemplative moments, she explored the potential of this intelligent male to be a mate. She came to no firm conclusion, but she fully intends to keep open the prospect.

"Thank you."

They look at each other briefly. Jared is suddenly and quite unexpectedly nonplussed. Something about this girl belies her youth. *She is no naïve little undergraduate student anxious to please*, he thinks. There is an agelessness about her that seems to reach through the skin, unsettling him with its weight.

"You said you had questions, I believe?" she asks, startling him out of his musings.

"Yes, yes." Jared's mind seems locked in a sort of haze which confuses him even more as he is used to talking with authority to young students. He tries to focus and, in the meantime, finds himself fiddling with some papers to gain time. In desperation, he grabs at a feeble lifeline and says, "Tell me about yourself. Anything you like."

Pythia silently laughs at his inner turmoil, so clearly conveyed through her hump. She has the mischievous inclination of suddenly dissociating the papers he absently shuffles in his hands, but vows to be good.

"Nothing to tell. Just a typical college student." *Blend in. . . .*

To Jared, the words feel like a costume she slips on, ill-fitting but necessary.

Nevertheless, he has a nucleus on which to build an intelligible conversation. "Based on what I have seen, you are definitely not a typical student. I have been thinking about our conversation yesterday and wondered if you would like to try more advanced material?"

"I don't know."

"What would you say if I give you a graduate level problem to solve right now? Just one."

"Well. . . . " Her voice trails off, both amused and curious, watching the quick churn of his thoughts.

He rummages through some papers and pulls out a sheet. "Here is a problem I just gave to my graduate students. Would you like to try?"

Pythia knows she should follow the script: accept his offer, feign confusion, and plead ignorance once she's glanced at the problem. But something in his demeanor—earnest, unguarded—tells her his intentions are sincere, his curiosity untainted by ego. Still, a flicker of something less noble stirs within her: a quiet, irrepressible desire to impress. It is unbecoming, perhaps even unwise, but she does not resist it.

With a measured sigh, half performance, half indulgence, she extends her hand.

He passes her the notebook. Their eyes meet again, and in that brief contact, something flares between them: an invisible current, sharp and electric. He flinches, blinking in surprise as though a jolt of static had cracked through his nerves—a raw transmission of something vital and unfiltered.

By the time he steadies himself, she is already holding up the completed solution, the equation resolved with effortless precision.

"Do you have one that is more difficult?" she asks, her tone almost playful, though her eyes gleam with challenge.

"You found the solutions already?"

"They are obvious. Here is the answer to the first part of the question about how the scattering amplitude is related to the differential scattering cross-section under the Sommerfeld Radiation Condition equation. And here is the answer to the second part using the Born Approximation."

When he takes the papers from her hand, he feels the same shock and again looks at her wonderingly, then turns his attention to her answers.

While he peruses the solutions, she says, "Rather trivial, don't you think?" She quickly grimaces at this superfluous tag line and rushes to add, "Sorry if that offended." She searches his mind for resentment, but he is genuinely impressed and more than intrigued. *That will do*, she thinks.

Concentrating on her solutions, he keeps murmuring, "Good, good, very good."

Finally, Jared looks up as wide-eyed as a child. "Where did you learn this? I took the liberty of looking at your transcripts and they contain no information on your early schooling."

"Self-taught."

For the first time, he registers clear disbelief. "Impossible!" he blurts. "You must have had a tutor or a mentor."

Pythia reads his conflicting thoughts and detects the first hint of suspicion as well as disbelief. This realization nudges her to adopt a more cautionary position. "Yes, yes, of course I have had tutors. The strength of my knowledge is quite feeble, however. It lacks depth. I'm here to learn from masters like you."

This is Pythia's first candid exchange with a normal human outside her circle. She finds Jared distinctly inferior in some ways, but like a highly intelligent dog, extremely compelling and eminently pettable. She has just given him a first pet. He responds as expected.

"Well," he says. "I am impressed. Very impressed. I believe you are wasting such talents in a second-year quantum mechanics course. The problem is, if it is a problem, that your skills are similarly stellar in all your classes, regardless of subject matter."

"Why is that a problem?" (Pythia already knows, of course, but must force herself to appear unaware of a person's thoughts before they speak.)

"I want to invite you to join my graduate research team. In the beginning, it would be an unpaid position . . . hence, I fear you may already be working with some other professor whose budget is more flexible than mine."

Pythia ponders whether accepting the offer would further the goal of blending in. As for Doctor Paine being a potential mate, she is cognizant of the difficulties involved in professors and students fraternizing. Nevertheless, there should be alternate male options in the form of graduate students.

"I would be honored."

"Good! It is unfortunately too late in the semester to transfer out of my current 'elementary' course, but you will, I hope, be more challenged around my research team. Can you come Thursday after office hours? If so, I will walk you to my lab and introduce you to my graduate students."

With this, Pythia decides to burnish her humility skills. "Certainly. I'm grateful for the opportunity. You know, there are many child prodigies—ten- or eleven-year-olds—already attending universities. I am truly nothing special."

Jared cannot decide whether she is being sincere, or assuming an air of false modesty, but he is convinced the power he feels emanating from her mind is somehow unique. *Time will tell*, he thinks uneasily, though a strange thrill runs beneath his doubt.

"Yes indeed, Professor Paine, time will tell," says Pythia, unable to refrain from this last bit of whimsy.

With this, she smiles and leaves.

~

Outside, the evening air is cool, scented faintly of eucalyptus and asphalt after rain. Students stream past, eyes lowered into their phones, voices tight with chatter. Pythia feels the world close in, ordinary and blind, yet she knows she has already been seen. Not by them, but by those who hunt difference. Altan's warning echoes through her blood: blend in, or be erased. She draws her coat tighter, her smile fading into stillness. Above, the campus bells toll the hour. The sound is measured, human, but to her it tolls like prophecy.

And in that tolling she hears the faint chorus of her lineage: John whispering of roads unwalked, Meiying chanting to the rivers, Michael raging in the tunnels, Tamara grieving in silence, Ming-huà weeping on her island, Zookeeper prowling unseen. Their voices converge, neither blessing nor curse, but a reminder: she is alloyed of them all. A vessel of suffering and vision, of fracture and possibility.

She pauses beneath the archway, students brushing past her like leaves in wind. For a moment she feels the weight of two worlds, the one dissolving, and the one not yet born. The bells fall silent. The hunters wait. The future sharpens. And she walks on, carrying both silence and prophecy into the dark—into the Stillness where all voices gather, and where her own must rise.

Chapter Twenty-Two

Freefall

Pythia Hunts For A Mate

~ Doctor Jared Paine ~

Jared Paine watches the door close behind the remarkable young woman, and his initial impulse is to dismiss her parting words about child prodigies. At first, he had granted her the benefit of the doubt, willing to believe in her sincerity. But upon further reflection, he finds her humility suspect—falsely modest at best, disingenuous at worst. Jared knows prodigies well. He had been one himself, a precocious child whose brilliance in mathematics emerged at the age of four and never waned. No, he thinks, this girl is not like the others. There is something unique about her, something he can't yet name but feels compelled to understand.

The subtle electric jolt he experienced when their hands met to exchange papers still lingers in his memory. It unsettles a self-confidence long fortified by years of guiding even the brightest students. Throughout the interview, he had the strange sensation that his mind was being observed—no, *penetrated*. And her final utterance, an exact articulation of a thought he had not spoken rattled him. A scientist to his bones, Jared scrolls through plausible explanations: perhaps he'd muttered it aloud without realizing; perhaps it was coincidence; perhaps a lucky guess. Any might be true. And yet, each only deepens the sense of mystery surrounding her.

Jared Paine is single, and it has never troubled him. He is not homosexual either; he simply finds the enigmas of the cosmos more captivating than romantic pursuits. Despite his youth and good looks, his self-image is curiously devoid of sexuality. Many women have attempted to draw him from his ascetic orbit of research and reflection, but none have succeeded. His devotion to discovery has always been absolute.

There was no privileged upbringing to explain it. He emerged, phoenix-like, from the damp and joyless ashes of a working-class Midwestern town. His parents, kind but overwhelmed, deferred to his unusual intelligence, retreating into their own tenuous emotional and financial survival. It was thanks to the intervention of a perceptive elementary school teacher and a passionate high school physics instructor that his voracious intellect found the mentorship it required. By twenty, he had already completed his university education.

But I had tutors! he cries inwardly, the phrase echoing with growing agitation as he replays Pythia's words. Yes, she'd mentioned having help along the way, but now he's not so sure. The more he considers their exchange, the more he suspects she was toying with him, throwing him scraps about her supposed limitations. *I don't believe any of that*, he reflects, wounded pride flickering.

~

Later that evening, back in his small, book-lined apartment near Berkeley, Jared sits alone with a glass of wine, still thinking of her. The trace of her presence lingers like the scent of ozone after a summer storm, a disturbance in the steady constellations of his ordered, monastic life. He knows it's irrational. They've met only once. The data are scant. And yet he cannot apply the physicist's golden rule: conclusions drawn from insufficient data are perilous. Still, the thought persists: *Pythia is a puzzle worth investigating*—one that deserves a place among his equations, theorems, and philosophical inquiries.

Even more surprising is the realization that he finds her beautiful, hump and all. But not in any conventional way. Her beauty resists category. It's not the fragile loveliness of youth or the polished glamour of cultivated charm. No, hers is a beauty marked by gravity and wisdom, by something ancient and hard-earned. She seems far older than her years, as if she had survived some vast and terrible trial, something not unlike war, he thinks, or a cataclysm of comparable moral weight. It's not the kind of trauma borne alone, privately, like illness or accident. It is the kind that reshapes nations, cleaves history, and leaves the sufferer forever altered, yet also less alone. Shared trauma, he muses, paradoxically diminishes suffering by revealing one's insignificance in a larger sea of sorrow.

He sips again and smiles wryly. "Bewitched," he murmurs. "Modern quantum physicist undone by medieval witchcraft." The notion amuses him, but the smile fades as his thoughts drift toward deeper questions. What is consciousness? How can mere matter—quarks and leptons—generate thought, emotion, desire? What is the ontological status of love, of hate? Can such forces act on matter? Surely not. And yet why did he feel a *physical* jolt in his mind when their hands touched? It was as real as the reflexive withdrawal of a snail touched by an intruding finger. A reaction of the body. A puzzle.

But the hour grows late. Jared sets aside his wine, shelving these troubling thoughts. Tomorrow brings lectures, papers, research. He must return to the familiar realm of observable phenomena. Still, even as he prepares for sleep, the image of Pythia hovers at the edge of his mind, unresolved, luminous, and quietly insistent.

~

When Jared awakes the following morning, he busies himself with breakfast. No dreams had come to him, and the chilled air brings with it a more balanced, reasoned view of Pythia. Coffee clears his mind, and he chastises himself for the romantic puffery he indulged in the previous evening. *Must have been the wine,* he muses. *She's a very smart student, no more and no less. Let's see how she does with the research team.* With this dismissal, he turns his attention to other matters.

However, as Thursday's office hours approach, Pythia increasingly intrudes into his thoughts, much to his chagrin. Nevertheless, even as he grouses about this irritant, an unmistakable excitement creeps in, and he finds himself unwilling to fight against such unaccustomed arousal. No matter how hard he has tried to bury himself in work, his anticipation has grown. In frustration, he surrenders to the feeling and indulges in choreographing the meeting like an adolescent boy on the eve of his first date. In moments of self-reflection, Jared feels sheepish about his 'foolish romanticism', and mocks himself for giving in to such rubbish. Truth is, Dr. Paine, stuck in his *Homo sapiens* weaknesses, unknowingly aspires to be what Pythia already is. He is a chimpanzee in a rainstorm, dimly aware of the advantages possessed by more technologically advanced humans sitting in dry houses eating bananas.

When Pythia enters his office, that same disorienting sense of being in the presence of someone wholly unique again takes over, and he is once more unprepared for the force she projects onto his otherwise stable mental state. Nevertheless, Jared is determined to maintain a professional demeanor, one that is appropriate for a professor toward his student (especially if the student is of the opposite sex).

"Hello again, Pythia."

"Hello."

"Before I take you to the lab, I wanted to chat a bit more."

"Okay."

Jared takes a deep breath. "Although this is a quantum mechanics course, I wonder what you know about General Relativity?"

Pythia knows where this is going, and she feels comfortable following where he leads, at least for the time being.

"Quite a lot."

"May I ask a difficult question regarding General Relativity?"

"Of course."

Jared settles back in his chair, appearing calm in spite of his nerves. "Why does zero-point energy of the vacuum not cause a large cosmological constant?"

Pythia knows the answer, but is aware this an unsolved problem in physics. Red lights go off in her head, and she knows she must proceed with utmost caution.

"Wow, that is a tough one. As far as I know, it hasn't been solved yet."

Jared nods in agreement, but a niggling doubt suggests she is not being entirely truthful. How he can doubt the words of this young student is beyond his understanding, but the feeling will not go away.

"But you have some ideas?" he prods.

Pythia has read his mind and is aware of his suspicions. On the one hand, she wants to show off her knowledge to this professor and give him further food for thought. She has chosen to play along with these little intellectual games to size up his suitability as a mate. On the other hand, blending in is essential, according to Altan. Safety first, then procreation, then, perhaps, action. Still, she cannot resist leaving him a few more crumbs to ponder.

"I have some ideas, but they are not fully formed."

"May I ask what they are?"

"Give me a chance to put them into a more cogent form and I will be happy to share."

"No problem. I am amazed you have any thoughts at all on the problem. I don't believe you have taken a General Relativity course?" He waits. Her move.

"True."

"You are just interested? Study on your own?"

Now Pythia is becoming perturbed at his persistent probing. *Fine,* she thinks. *You asked for it.* "Yes, Professor Paine, I have researched the subject on my own, and the field equations are not too difficult. As we all know, they have serious limitations. Is there a reason you are asking these questions?"

"Well, my research does involve a great deal of General Relativity, and many of my postdoc research students find it far more difficult than you make it sound."

Pythia shrugs.

"String theory? Any background?"

"Uninteresting. On the wrong track. Some interesting maths, but on the whole, from a physics point of view, a waste of time. No, I'm not very interested in going down that rabbit hole except for historical interest."

Jared is stunned at this sweeping condemnation. "Historical interest! That *is* a mouthful! My string theorist colleagues would be either outraged or amused."

Pythia shrugs again.

"Are you this way in all your subjects?"

"What way?"

"Cocky . . . not that it's necessarily a bad thing in science, if you have the chops to back it up."

"I'm here to learn."

Jared claps his hands. "Well, with that, let's go to the lab and get you acquainted with your lab mates."

As they walk together, Jared finds himself once again unsettled by the depths of her intellect, despite his own attempts at levity. With each passing moment, he becomes more convinced that Pythia Powers is no ordinary student. There is something rare, perhaps unprecedented, in her, an enigmatic quality that elevates her from mere prodigy to something altogether singular. He now regards her not only as a brilliant mind but as a potentially invaluable asset—one to observe with great care and treat with utmost respect, lest she be courted away by another, more perceptive scholar.

Unbeknownst to him, and much to her private amusement, Pythia is reading his thoughts as easily as she might scan a book. She, too, has begun to regard him in a certain light—not as a scientific marvel or evolutionary leap, but as something far more pragmatic: a potential first sexual partner. Jared may not be unique, nor represent the next step in hominin evolution, but he possesses certain qualities—rigor, restraint, intellectual seriousness—that mark him as a suitable candidate. As for any resulting child, she assumes Lady Oracle, Sy, and Altan will manage that eventuality. Motherhood, to Pythia, is merely a logistical concern. If the child is anything like her, it will soon outgrow the need for what she considers the obsolete model of parental care. Her kind will be defined not by personal attachment, but by a profound, non-possessive reverence for all sentient life. Where Homo sapiens are tangled in the knots of individual passion and familial obsession, her vision spans planetary systems and cosmic survival.

Still, in Jared's monastic dedication to knowledge, she sees a hopeful echo, an early glimmer of the better instincts his species might have cultivated, had it not been so enthralled by its own braggadacio and hubris. But while he may envision a future filled with accolades, a professorship, and perhaps a conventional family, Pythia stands on the threshold of a mission far more sweeping: to guide the birth and ascendancy of a new species, one that might, if fortune holds, avert the environmental and moral collapse long foretold by human excess. This is the engine of her so-called passion: a cold, resolute fire, directed not inward, but outward to the preservation of life itself.

Following Jared into the lab, she recalls a writer's analogy that true passion resembles the nature of a seed. It takes root within, finds sustenance there, and bends all tributaries of life toward its quiet but absolute imperative.

Jared introduces her to his research assistants and outlines the experiment currently under investigation. To her, the hypothesis feels pedestrian, an ordinary scratching at the surface of truths she already considers elemental. She casually sifts through the minds of the assistants, hoping to find some unexpected gem of insight, but discovers only fragments of textbook knowledge and the usual entanglements of unspoken rivalries and half-formed romantic attachments. Still, these interpersonal dynamics are not without value. She catalogs them carefully, part of her ongoing effort to mimic human behavior convincingly and deepen her camouflage.

While Pythia adapts to the lab, Jared watches her with growing fascination. There is something uncanny in the way she interacts, fluid, composed, and always just a half-step beyond his grasp. He finds himself drawn to her not just intellectually, but viscerally. Her physicality, once eclipsed by her mind, now strikes him with force: the elegance of her movements, the quiet magnetism of her gaze. Even her hump, which he had once assumed would evoke pity or discomfort, now seems to enhance the unique silhouette of her body. It is an exotic curvature that somehow completes rather than mars her form.

Jared disciplines these impulses sternly. She is still a minor, not yet eighteen, and he reminds himself that indulging such thoughts is deeply inappropriate.

And yet, in moments of quiet reverie, when his ethical instincts soften under the weight of wonder, his mind drifts forward, toward a future in which age will no longer be a boundary, and the strange brilliance of this girl-woman might finally be met with a fuller, more adult intimacy.

~ *Mosquitoes* ~

Months pass. The term ends. Summer arrives. Throughout it all, Pythia has taken great care not to reveal the full extent of her abilities. She has followed the lab manager, Sean Colby, with diligent precision, and is dutifully obedient, unremarkable, and deliberately devoid of initiative. Her strategy has been simple: to quietly perform the menial tasks assigned to her while absorbing invaluable data on human social dynamics and workplace behavior.

What continues to astonish her is the human obsession with the concept of "becoming"—the endless quest to define oneself, to carve out an identity. Jewish students wrestle with inherited trauma and cultural complexity. African American students carry the dual burden of historical prejudice and fierce pride. Transgender students navigate the fluid contours of gender identity. And so it goes, on and on, *ad infinitum*. To Pythia, these differences amount to little more than surface noise, distinctions without substance.

Humans, she thinks, are like dogs whose lives are dictated by the fleas they cannot stop scratching. Non-human animals seem to live without such elaborate constructions of meaning, without the constant need to define, explain, or transcend themselves. But *Homo sapiens*, gripped by the hunger to become something more, lash outward, seeking economic dominance, religious certainty, political control, cultural prestige. In doing so, they leave behind them a trail of destruction, inflicting suffering on the rest of life as a whip in the hands of a cruel overseer in the quest for a more profitable harvest flays the back of a slave.

At times, Pythia considers whether her evolved perspective might, by human standards, appear regressive, even primitive, aligned more closely with the worldview of non-human animals. But she quickly rejects this notion. Her vision is not a retreat but a recalibration. Not a cold indifference, but a broader, more inclusive empathy. Where human caring is tangled in self-interest and tribal loyalties, hers is something wider—less sentimental, but more complete. An evolutionary correction, not a regression. Perhaps even an evolutionary imperative.

Pythia is acutely aware of the unnaturally swift arc of evolution that has produced her kind, and an unrelenting hunger drives her to pierce the veil—to discover at last who, or what, the Mentors truly are.

"What are you thinking?" asks Jared. He and Pythia are walking with a couple of their lab colleagues at the end of a day's work. They have reached a small stream flowing through the campus, and have paused to chat before each takes their own path home.

"Nothing," says Pythia.

Jared waves his hand in front of his face in irritation. "Damn, the mosquitoes are out in force tonight."

"Yeah, I've already been bitten a bunch of times," says Sean Colby.

The others agree, and as gnats and mosquitoes form visible clouds around their heads, they start to break up. Jared is also ready to depart when he notices there are no insects around Pythia's head.

"Mosquito repellent?" he asks.

Distracted by her own thoughts, she does not pick up his question, and responds. "What?"

"I said, did you think ahead and apply mosquito repellent? I notice you seem to be free of the little suckers."

"No, I just blink them away," she says carelessly.

"You mean ignore them?"

"No, just send them . . . elsewhere."

Jared is confused and stares at her. When a mosquito or gnat gets close to her skin, it disappears. He blinks to confirm what he sees is real. It is.

"I don't understand," he says.

Pythia realizes her mistake. "I'm just kidding," she says, finding the need to backtrack. "I really did apply mosquito repellant."

"Ah," replies Jared doubtfully. He peers closer and now sees the insects alighting on her skin. "Seems to be wearing off," he says.

"Yes, they are starting to bother me. Well, I'm off. See you tomorrow!" With this, she walks off at a brisk pace, leaving Jared to grapple with the evidence of his own eyes. *Could be a trick of the light*, he thinks. With no other plausible explanation, he turns his attention to her behavior at the lab. In this case, she is performing far below his expectations. Her passive role would ordinarily be perfectly explainable by her youth and inexperience compared to his postdoc students, but he knows she is not a normal student. Something is holding her back, he concludes. But this leads to a host of other questions, not the least of which is the mystery of what is holding her back. *If only she was older*, he thinks. *Can't take her on a date, but there's always office hours.* Having access to her records, he knows she's turning eighteen in a few weeks. Even so, a thirty-something professor dating an eighteen-year-old girl would raise not a few eyebrows. Jared Paine has no intention of ruining his career, but on the other hand. . . .

~ *Office Hours Again* ~

In order to explore his concerns and satisfy his scruples further, Jared is waiting to meet Pythia for office hours one afternoon late in the semester. To his dismay, the sexual arousal she induces in him is growing more intense. Fantasies of making love with her have intensified, and his determination to block them has weakened. Nevertheless, he has risked calling for a meeting with her alone in order to try and get to the bottom of why she is performing at a mediocre level in the lab. After carefully examining his motives to meet her alone, he persuades himself they are honorable professional concerns rather than personal.

~

The moment Pythia steps into his office, her hump immediately registers the discord tugging at Jared's thoughts. Even before a word is exchanged, she detects a sharp, unmistakable flicker of desire—his vivid, unspoken longing to see her naked. Brief though it is, the intensity of the impulse leaves no doubt. She is not disturbed by it; on the contrary, she files it away with quiet interest. One of the peculiar advantages of being among the first to diverge into a new species is that the morphology of the prior one remains familiar, close enough to stir attraction rather than revulsion. Jared Paine, by any measure, is a handsome man, a strong, well-formed specimen, well-suited for the experience of first-time coupling.

"Hello Pythia, have a seat."

"Thank you."

Jared clears his throat nervously. "I wanted to talk with you a little about the lab."

"Yes?"

"Are you happy there?"

"Yes, why do you ask?"

Jared, now feeling a bit more comfortable, leans back in his chair. "It just seems you are not fully using your substantial talents. Is Sean holding you back?"

"Not at all."

"Is there something else holding you back?"

Though she knows precisely his meaning and the concerns behind it, she feigns ignorance. "Not that I'm aware of. What do you mean?"

"I mean, you seem hesitant to fully engage, make suggestions, come up with new ideas, contribute your own point of view and analyses."

Pythia hesitates, then seems to come to a decision. "The breakthrough you are hoping to make with this research, your hypothesis, is, well, flawed. I can only do what is asked and wait for you and your team to discover the errors."

Jared's face turns red, then white. He remains speechless for a few moments, shocked.

Pythia waits quietly.

"What do you mean?" he sputters feebly.

"Vacuum energy is orders of magnitude weaker than predicted for different reasons than you have hypothesized."

Jared feels faint. "You know?"

"Of course."

In words he barely recognizes are coming from his mouth, Jared asks in stupefaction, "Who are you?"

"As a friend once said, 'Ahab is Ahab'."

Jared rubs his forehead and sits, marshalling his reasoning mind. Nevertheless, his pique gets the better of him. "Pythia, or whatever your real name is, I need you to tell me why we are on the wrong track."

"I will simplify." She balances her notebook on her knees and begins writing equations. After filling a few pages, she hands them to Jared.

Again, he feels an electric shock when he takes hold of them. He scans the papers, narrows his eyes in frustration, and starts again with the utmost concentration. When he reaches the end, he drops the papers on his desk and looks at her in frightened perplexity.

"I don't understand them," he says.

"I know."

"How do you know?"

"Your thoughts are tangled, a mixture of anger and disbelief. I cannot expect you to understand."

He grabs one of the papers and waves it in the air. "But it is gibberish to me! Some terms I don't even recognize as part of physics or math!"

"I am aware."

"What? You can read my thoughts?"

"They are simple enough."

Pythia knows full well she is casting all caution aside. Altan's warning now lingers only as a faint, fading echo. The months of leafy calm above ground have quietly masked a more radical transformation—an unseen surge of roots pushing downward, boring through rock and clay with relentless force. These roots have shattered the hardpan laid down by the deistic overseers, those who still seek to govern through Lady Oracle, Sy, and Altan. In truth, Pythia has awakened to the full extent of her autonomy. She no longer answers to the behavioral edicts of metaphorical Gods, Goddesses, or the host of minor powers that once claimed influence over her. By nature, she leans toward action, not concealment—toward revelation, not restraint.

With this last insult, Jared's face burns red and he flares in rage. "Who the hell do you think you are?"

Pythia remains silent, gazing steadily at him until the brief squall passes.

"Okay," says Jared, forcing himself to be calm. "Do you work for the government? Some sort of secret program? NASA? FBI? CIA? Tell me who you are working for. Or are you. . . . ?"

"Am I what?" Pythia, superior as she is, still is young enough to enjoy the pleasure of cat paws toying with mouse lives.

"I don't know . . . an alien? . . . from the future? . . . Christ! I can't believe I'm even saying these things!"

"I am none of those things," she says evenly.

He loosens a bit. "Well, that's a relief. So tell me, why Berkeley? Why these low-level classes? Why bother with my little lab with its doomed research hypothesis? Why?"

"At first, it was important for me to blend in, but now, I am searching for appropriate mates."

Jared's mouth drops open. He shakes his head and laughs a little crazily. "Well, with statements like that, you're doing one hell of a job not blending in!"

"As it stands now, with you at least, I am less interested in blending in than exploring relationship opportunities. As I indicated, I am looking for mates."

Paine looks duly shocked. "Mates? Plural?"

Pythia is fully aware of the human male's fragile ego, primitive perspective about female sexuality, and obsession with personal property rights. "One as extraordinary as yourself will suffice," she says.

For the time being, she adds in her mind.

~

Jared, for all his brilliance, cannot see what Pythia already knows: their exchange is no mere academic game. It is a prelude, the faint tremor before tectonic plates shift. For him, it is fascination. For her, it is selection. And in her mind, unspoken yet immovable, one thought crystallizes with the clarity of prophecy:

This is how extinction begins—quietly, in an office, between two minds.

Chapter Twenty-Three

Secrets Revealed

Inferior Meets Superior

~ Fallout ~

"Pythia!" Jared cries in horror. "Mates? Really, are you some robot or stereotypical alien, or . . . I don't know what! I hardly know where to begin. First, your knowledge is beyond my understanding, but I know enough to consider you an invaluable asset to science. Second, as for mating, you're only seventeen!"

"Yet, when I first entered your office, you clearly expressed the strong thought that you wanted to see me naked."

Jared's face flushes as red as a beet. "I . . . I . . . that is irrelevant. Is it true that you really can read minds?"

"Yes. For your peace of mind, I will soon be eighteen."

Jared stands and paces nervously. "Pythia, you have to tell me who you are. I need to know. It's incumbent on me to inform people . . . powerful and influential people, what you're capable of."

"Yes, I know that is in your mind, but it will not be possible to let you do that."

"And if I do?"

"I will feign ignorance."

"I . . . I. . . . " Jared splutters. "As far as I know, Pythia, you've escaped from some asylum. For heaven's sake, tell me! You know the government will be interested, Pythia. There is too much here to let pass."

"Professor Paine, I know your thoughts. There is a little larceny in your heart. If I cooperate in your lab, you might forego mentioning my talents, particularly to the government, eh? Am I right?"

Jared is again dumbstruck and has a terrible feeling of impotence before the power of this person. A great, helpless resentment grips his mind.

"Damn you! Who are you?"

"Pythia Powers, hunchback."

He lets out a tremendous sigh. "Regardless of your threats, I will speak out. Science demands it. Now, tell me who you really are and where you're really from."

"Professor Paine, none of what you say will matter to me beyond your consideration of me as a mate, a lover." She holds up a dismissive hand. "After I turn eighteen, of course. Or do you prefer nineteen?"

"Why this interest in a mate? I have to say, your attitude toward the subject is hardly flattering to me, or any male for that matter."

"Yes, *Homo sapiens* males," she says with a touch of contempt, or pity, he isn't quite sure.

Jared tilts his head in an exaggerated manner. "Are you not *Homo sapiens* yourself?"

Pythia stares at him in an odd way. "You are thinking now that I am suffering from delusions of grandeur, perhaps schizophrenic delusions, not unusual in brilliant people. Here, you are catastrophically wrong. My grandfather Michael Powers . . . well, that is a different story for a different time."

"So, at least it is now established you have a grandfather. Since I cannot keep my thoughts secret from you, it is true I have considered the possibility you are suffering from delusions, possibly schizophrenia. Are you?"

"What I am 'suffering from' is very much beyond your understanding right now. Just as you did not recognize many terms in my equations regarding vacuum energy, you would not recognize the terms of my own existence. Suffice to say, I am looking for mates, and I have found you."

"I ask again, do you believe you are not from the species *Homo sapiens*?"

"That is a trick question. One I am not inclined to answer. Now that you at least partially understand me, I will leave. I'm afraid I must also leave your lab. However, I will remain at Berkeley and take classes as usual next semester. I am easily found."

"Blending in?"

Pythia smiles and nods. Without another word, she walks out, and in her wake leaves a mystified, angry, and fearfully conflicted professor who stares at the closed door in a fog of absurd speculations.

~

Jared's vacant gaze dissolves as he jolts upright, rifling through the disarray of papers on his desk. The equations are gone. He's certain he didn't return them. Certain she didn't take them. *Another thread unraveling,* he mutters inwardly. But then an echo surfaces. The mosquitoes. The epiphany jars him into action. He cancels his lectures and barricades himself in the solitude of his apartment, commanding logic to take charge once more. *She's not otherworldly,* he insists. *Just unwell. Delusional.* But these thoughts emerge with a hollow clang—stillborn. Reporting her would go nowhere. She'd evade, mislead. Better to investigate discreetly. Find her roots. Unspool her lineage. Follow the living footprints, not the vanishing ones.

But the buzzing won't stop. Those damn phantom mosquitoes, ghostly, relentless, needle into his resolve. He grits his teeth and distills his purpose into a simple mantra: *Find the parents. Speak to them. Follow the scent.* He toys with the idea of a leave, but summer's break is near; time may yet bend to his obsession.

The next day, with practiced precision, Jared extracts her student records. He dials Ming-huà Powers. Dead line. He tries Matthew Weston. Dead again. Her name—Pythia Powers—tilts towards the maternal. Curious. Emails disintegrate. Addresses dissolve. Ghost data. Still undeterred, he plunges into the digital abyss: public records, social webs, asylum logs, gun permits, birth certificates, grave registries. All trails wither. No trace, no scent. As if she were conjured from fiction. Or erased.

Yet with each void uncovered, Jared's conviction grows stronger. She must belong to something real—hidden, yes, but real. An experiment? A sleeper agent? CIA? An exiled daughter of tragedy? He discards the alien hypothesis—it reeks of madness. But a deeper madness begins to whisper. A design behind the data loss. A pattern in the vanishing. He's ruled out nothing, and yet, proven nothing. Still, the compulsion grips him: a sacred hunger for the truth. The kind that ruins sleep and rewrites careers. The equations haunt him. The mosquitoes greedily drink at thought itself.

He might've spiraled forever into conjecture, had it not been for the summons. Late morning came a call. Severe administrative tone. He arrives, a heartbeat too fast, and is met by two men in tailored civilian clothes. FBI. The door clicks shut. One presses *record.* The other says, "Do you mind?" A line is drawn. He is now part of something larger.

"No."

"Have a seat, please."

"Thank you."

"Sorry for the intrusion," says the one who is evidently senior. "We have been asking a number of your colleagues some questions pertaining to a student of yours, and now we would like to ask you."

"Yes?"

"Her name, as far as we can ascertain, is Pythia Powers. Berkeley has kindly provided us with her records."

"Yes?"

"Her mother, Ming-huà Powers, was a witness many years ago to a rather odd incident. Take a look."

The agent hands Jared a binder. He opens it to find numerous old San Francisco newspaper articles about victims inexplicably losing their arms at a presumed crime scene. He scans the clippings and looks up.

The agent hands him a second binder, this time with articles from Baltimore about a similar incident where people lost more than just their arms. In both instances, the bloodless nature of the mutilations could not be explained.

"Are you sensitive to graphic pictures, Professor Paine?"

"Not particularly."

A third binder is handed him, this with official police photographs. Multiple men are shown in an alley with missing body parts, including heads. There is no blood. Jared murmurs, "Oh, my *God*, these are awful. What happened to them?"

Shaking his head in horror, Jared returns the binders and waits. The agent ignores Jared's question and continues in a clipped, professional manner.

"We have recently received new evidence so the case has been reopened. Since your student's mother was a witness to both the San Francisco and Baltimore incidents, we wish to speak with her. Unfortunately, she has disappeared, so we want to talk with her daughter and hopefully find her mother's whereabouts."

"Yes, I can see that," says Jared, reddening. "Why not just ask the daughter, Pythia Powers? What do you want of me?"

"Before approaching Ms. Powers, we have asked her professors to inform us if any of you have noticed peculiarities or areas of concern regarding the girl."

"I see."

"Have you?"

Jared feels faint. He never anticipated this eventuality. His heart fluttering in an agony of indecision, he stalls.

"Is she involved in some crime?"

"No, not that we know of."

"Her mother?"

The two men glance at each other. The one who has not yet spoken now looks at Jared and says, "A witness only, as far as we know."

"Then I'm not sure why you're asking me these questions."

"They are harmless enough," says the same man. "We're just trying to find her mother."

"But why ask about peculiarities?"

"Professor Paine, if you are unwilling to answer our questions, please tell us now."

Jared pales. "I am willing, I am willing. Well, to answer your question, she is a very, very smart girl. That is the only peculiarity I have noticed." Jared assumes his best poker face, but inside his stomach is churning. *I just lied to the FBI*, he thinks.

"Has she ever mentioned her mother to you?"

"No."

"Have you met her during your office hours?"

"A few times."

"Anything she said or did that strike you as different?"

"How do you mean?"

The first agent says rather sharply, "I am sure you understand the word different, professor. Anything out of the ordinary, other than her brains, that you noticed?"

"No."

"Did you ever notice anything missing at the end of your meetings?"

"Missing, like she stole something?"

"No, like it was there and then it was gone."

Worse and worse, frets Jared. He hesitates, then speaks with as much confidence as he can muster. "No."

Again, the two agents exchange glances, which makes him even more nervous. Jared now feels certain they know he's lying. A strong urge to backtrack and tell the truth almost overcomes him, but he is in too deep. Even if he corrects the record, how are they now to believe what he has seen and suspects? They would think him either a liar or crazy.

"Professor Paine, are you sure you noticed nothing at all unusual other than her academic skills? Anything at all?"

"Absolutely not." When will they stop? After answering each one with a lie, Jared feels increasingly trapped, panicky, and angry. He feels compelled to elaborate. "I mean, we only talked about her classes, assignments, working in the lab, that sort of thing."

"We know she has been working in your lab."

"No longer."

"Why not?"

"I don't know. Summer break. She had other projects and interests. It happens all the time with lab assistants."

"She is a bit young to be working in your lab with graduate students and post-docs, isn't she?"

Jared is afraid he will soon fall apart, but continues with what he prays is a steady voice. "Yes, indeed. But, as I said, she is an extraordinary student. Very advanced."

"Anything else?"

"No." He worries he spoke the word too quickly.

Both agents rise. "Thank you, Professor Paine. Here are our cards. If you think of anything, please call. Call anytime, day or night."

"Yes, okay. I can go?"

They both nod and gesture toward the door.

Jared walks very carefully out of the room, not wanting to appear in a hurry. His mind is whirling with a host of questions and suppositions. His nerves are jittery and he goes over the interview many times, cursing at himself for lying. *Why didn't I just tell the truth?* he keeps asking. No answer comes. Now, he wants to get as far away from Pythia Powers as possible. Stop his search, stop talking with her, stop any and all communication. *I'm in enough hot water as it is*, he thinks resentfully.

~ *Enter Pythia* ~

Jared strolls briskly toward his car, his laptop case swinging rhythmically at his side. His thoughts dart down a thousand mental alleyways, none leading anywhere except back to the central dilemma: he is torn. On one side lies the fear of entanglement, especially in murky criminal investigations that could soil his reputation. On the other, a mounting exhilaration—scientific, almost ecstatic—that he has stumbled upon something, someone, utterly singular. Pythia.

He begins to question the foundation of his own panic, the swiftness with which he chose to distance himself. After all, he hasn't broken any laws. If the FBI's interest is focused on Pythia's mother, merely as a witness, then why this instinct to run? And should things become precarious, academic confidentiality might provide a shield.

But Pythia herself remains an enigma, unsolved and unyielding. The driving questions torment him. *Who is she? What is she? Where did she come from?* Should he reach out to her later, after the dust has settled and the agents have moved on? What would he say?

If he plays it right, if she cooperates, perhaps there's a Nobel in the future. *But then, this business about being her "mate" . . . absurd. And yet . . . she is attractive. And the mosquitoes! The equations!*

Lost in this storm of contradictions, Jared fails to notice someone walking in parallel, just off to his side. The figure draws closer. Shoulder brushes against shoulder, jarring him from his thoughts. He halts abruptly and turns with irritation to confront the stranger, only to find himself staring into the calm, amused face of Pythia.

Drawing a sharp breath, he is momentarily struck dumb. Before he can speak, she laughs—a light, knowing sound, with a hint of patronizing superiority.

"Don't be alarmed," she says cheerfully. "You did the right thing. I'll speak with them and put to rest any concerns about your . . . involvement."

"Damn it, Pythia!" Jared hisses. "I could lose my job, or worse, if the FBI decides to make an example of me."

"If that's how you feel, why didn't you simply tell them the truth?"

By now, Jared has long abandoned disbelief in her clairvoyance. Of course she knows what he's thinking.

"You already know the answer to that," he snaps. "Though God knows I don't. That's a damn good question, actually. *What* is the truth, Pythia? You've never told me. Not once. And here I am, risking everything for someone who won't even give me honesty in return. Why am I doing this? Why am I sticking my neck out for a person who keeps me in the dark?"

His voice rises, unfiltered, raw. "It's ridiculous. Just plain stupid. I've put myself in harm's way for you. The least you can do—the very least—is tell me the truth."

Pythia remains unperturbed, and says, "You humans—I mean we humans—are perpetually in search of truth, which in fact is as pliable as potter's clay."

"Christ! No armchair philosophy now, Pythia." He looks around anxiously. "We're probably being followed by the FBI as we speak."

"In point of fact we are, so let's lead them to somewhere more comfortable. I know a nice little restaurant which serves excellent tea and we can talk."

"Christ!" Jared mutters again, but reluctantly follows, one hand planted firmly in his trouser pocket to hide his nervousness and convey nonchalance, the other gripping the laptop handle with white-knuckle force.

Once seated and tea served, Pythia proceeds in what Jared considers an infuriatingly calm voice.

"Professor Paine, I understand you have been shaken by your experience, but your unwillingness to give information will serve you well in future."

"Oh, really? How nice. What good does that do me now?"

Pythia detects in his thoughts a troubling flicker of weakness, a kernel of fear that unsettles her more than she expects. For a moment, she is taken aback. But she quickly tempers her judgment, reminding herself that he is far removed from the safe, insulated world of academia. She offers him the benefit of the doubt.

With a trace of wry sarcasm, she asks, "Is your fear of external consequences outweighing your scientific curiosity? If so, Galileo would be sorely disappointed."

Jared, clearly unsettled, knows there's no point in pretending. "Why ask a question when you already know the answer?" he replies. "Of course I'm afraid. And as for curiosity, how far can it take me when you've given me so little to work with? If I lose my job over this, I won't be in any position to pursue science at all."

Her eyes drill into his soul. "I am your science," she says.

Again, he is taken off guard. "What do you mean?"

"I mean there is much more to me that you can possibly imagine."

"Oh, don't worry on that score, I have been imagining you and your . . . uniqueness, for a very long time."

"Professor, you haven't scratched the surface."

"Tell me."

"No. At least, not yet. There are things that must first be settled."

"Such as?"

"I know you will instinctively recoil when you hear, so let us leave it for the time being. I must think further. It is possible I have made a mistake. A very grave error, which I do not want to compound."

"Goddamn it, Pythia!" he cries, then catches himself and exercises damage control. "Didn't know you made mistakes."

"A major mistake in adaptation can end this experiment in evolution."

"You talk in riddles."

"That propensity is apparently in my genes."

"No more riddles. Tell me who you are. Tell me everything. If not, I swear I'll go to the FBI."

"Yes, yes, I see now. This was a mistake," Pythia says quietly. "Professor Paine, if you feel compelled to go to the FBI, then do so. There's nothing sinister at play. No grand criminal conspiracy. They're simply searching for my mother, who happened to witness a series of terrible events. I'll gladly tell them where she can be found."

She pauses, then adds with cool finality, "It's *you* who disappoints me. However skilled I may be at reading thoughts, reading *character* is a far more elusive art."

Jared turns away, his gaze drifting into the middle distance. A strange mix of guilt and shame coils in his chest, unearned yet undeniable. But just as he's beginning to wrestle with this discomfort, his eyes catch two familiar figures entering the restaurant. And in an instant, guilt gives way to something sharper.

Panic.

"It's them!" he whispers to Pythia.

"Yes, I know. They followed us here and have been waiting patiently outside. I don't need to read their minds to know they are tired of waiting. Invite them to join us."

"What?"

"Invite them!"

Stunned by the power of her command, he hails the two agents. As they approach, Jared gestures toward two empty chairs. "Have a seat," he says as nonchalantly as he can.

"Hello again," says the older agent smiling. "Long time no see."

"Yes, I just unexpectedly ran into Pythia and we opted to have tea."

"I see that."

Jared introduces them to Pythia.

She smiles sweetly. "Professor Paine tells me you are searching for my mother. Is that correct?"

"Indeed, it is."

"Well, that is simple enough. She is living with my father on an island off the coast of Washington State. What do you want of her?"

"She witnessed some nasty business years ago. Actually, she witnessed two rather violent incidents. People were killed. New evidence has recently emerged causing us to reopen the case."

"New evidence?" In asking this question, Pythia probes their minds to learn about this new evidence. Once she finds out what she is seeking, her interest in these men melts away.

"Yes, but we cannot divulge that information," says the younger agent. "Do you know anything about the incidents she witnessed? Did she talk about them to you?"

"There were more than one?"

"Yes. As I just said, there were two, each a continent apart."

"And a third as well," injects the senior partner.

"No, mother never told me. However, I do know she will want to cooperate with the FBI. Do you have paper? If so, I will write her address and telephone number."

The younger agent hands her a dog-eared notebook. "You can write it in this."

Meanwhile, the older agent asks, "Have you ever noticed anything unusual about your mother?"

"Unusual?"

"Yeah."

"Like what?"

"We were hoping you could tell us."

"I mean, what do you mean by unusual?"

"Oh, anything. Unusual abilities. Unusual powers, that sort of thing."

Pythia laughs. "Not at all. Only the power to make me feel awful when I was naughty."

"Miss Powers, let me be honest. We have reason to believe your mother saw something that we have not yet been able to explain."

"Oh?"

"Would you mind looking at some crime scene photos for us?"

"Here?"

"Well, we can go to our offices if you wish."

"No, here is good. Much more relaxing, don't you think?"

"Are you at all squeamish, Miss Powers?" asks the older agent sharply. "The pictures are quite graphic."

"I don't think so."

The younger agent gives her the binders. As Pythia leafs through the pages, the older agent says, "This is what your mother witnessed. What we do not understand is why there is no blood, no signs of violence. The survivors swear they had all of their limbs before the incidents. Either they are lying, or there is something very odd going on here."

"And you think my mother saw what caused this?"

"Well, yes, that is our hope."

"But didn't you already interview her?"

"Yes."

"And what did she say?"

"She knew nothing about how it happened."

"Do you think her story will have changed now?"

"As I said, new evidence has emerged. Maybe her memory will be jogged."

"This is terrible," Pythia says returning the binders. "I hope she is able to help solve the mystery."

"So do we. Here are our cards, Miss Powers. If you think of anything, please call us."

"Of course."

"Thank you. We may be in touch with both of you in the future."

They nod to Jared and leave.

~ *Reverberation* ~

When the agents are gone, Jared dares a sigh of relief. But Pythia is already rising from her chair, her eyes distant.

"Do you know what they really want?" she asks softly.

Jared shakes his head.

"They don't care about my mother. They want to understand the fracture that has already begun in their species. They sense it without knowing. They feel the wound, but not the knife."

She places a coin on the table, spins it once. It wobbles, then steadies, balanced impossibly on its edge.

"That is humanity, Professor. Spinning. Waiting. About to fall."

The coin tips, clatters, and lies still.

Chapter Twenty-Four

A Suitable Mate?

Sinking Deeper

Jared stares in perplexity at the coin, then turns on her with seething disbelief.

"You lied again."

Pythia tilts her head slightly, calm as glass. "How so?"

"You played dumb the entire time. What's your game?"

"I gave them what they requested. Did I not?"

"Don't twist it. That act of yours—all that pretend innocence—what the hell was that?"

A shadow flickers across her brow. "There are too many ears in this place. Too many eyes. Let's leave. I'll tell you what I can."

"No. You go your way, I go mine. I'm done. I'm a physicist, not some paranoid truth-chaser with a red string map of conspiracy theories in his garage."

He throws a few bills on the table and steps outside, where she waits beneath a canopy of passing faces. The street is loud, indifferent. He joins her one final time.

"Listen," he says. "I'm going home. Tomorrow I return to work. I meant what I said—I can't get more involved. I don't even understand what this is anymore."

She doesn't blink.

"Foolish man," she jeers. "You're not helping me. I am helping *you*. I'm offering you what no scientist has ever been given . . . a portal. And you recoil like a child. Your thoughts reek of fear. Is your mind so brittle?"

"Maybe," Jared mutters. "But I refuse to get pulled deeper into a vortex I can't define. Especially not with the FBI circling overhead."

A pause. Then, with unnerving calm: "Perhaps you'll understand *this*. Look at your laptop."

He glances down instinctively and gasps. Nothing.

His arm hangs in stunned suspension, fingers still curled around absence. The laptop is simply *gone,* as though it never existed. Around him, pedestrians mutter and jostle past, unaware of the metaphysical sleight of hand just performed.

He stands statue-like, eyes hollow, brain awash in a hurricane of half-formed thoughts.

Pythia is already walking away.

He starts to call after her, then stops and turns in the opposite direction.

That night, sleep eludes him. His mind runs in disjointed loops, clawing at puzzles he cannot grip. By morning, clarity still does not arrive, but resignation does. Over coffee, in the tender hush before sunrise, a shift begins. Time and space have dulled the sting of government intervention, and in their place, a deeper reckoning unfolds. She may be reckless. She may be a liar. But she is not ordinary. No rational force could have explained the mosquito vanishings. The equations. And now, the disappearing laptop.

The absurdity of it all only sharpens his hunger. Who is she? What is she? What ancient, alien logic runs through her blood?

Worst of all, he drifts in bewilderment, haunted by a single question: what does it mean that she has chosen me?

He swirls his coffee in silence. His career, he tells himself, has been enviable. Methodical. Esteemed. But sterile. *If she's right about my research. . . .* —he can't even finish the thought. *She is right.* Every atom in his body agrees. That leaves only one choice.

To walk away would be to spit in the face of wonder. To amputate the limb that reaches toward fire. Like Galileo, he will murmur defiances under his breath.

But then there is the matter of mating. That word plagues him—an endless echo. *Mate?* She's beautiful—yes. Mesmerizing. But how does one share a bed, let alone a life, with someone who can read every unspoken thought? Who sees into you as effortlessly as through glass? It is unbearable. It is intoxicating.

The day unspools in strange rhythms. His bold decision takes root and falters. Springs back. Withers again. He circles it like a predator stalking its own uncertainties. But the current has already shifted. And in the deep places of his mind, something stirs. A door creaks open. And this time, he does not slam it shut.

~

One late afternoon, Doctor Jared Paine stands in front of Pythia Powers' apartment, hesitating momentarily before he takes the plunge and lifts his hand to knock. Just as his knuckles are about to strike the door, it opens and Pythia stares at him in all her glory. She looks gorgeous, clothed in a long, understated dress, eyes lustrous with an air of amusement creasing the corners.

"Hello Professor Paine," she says brightly, without any hint of surprise.

"You have been expecting me, I suppose," he says a bit morosely, his hand still raised in preparation to knock.

"Of course. I once questioned your character, but your presence here is quite reassuring. Come in."

A sudden desire to see her naked again pops into his consciousness, and he quickly tries to suppress it before she notices. Too late.

"If all goes well," she says as she leads him to a small living room. "You will see me naked soon enough."

"This is impossible," he bellows. "Reading minds is like a form of rape."

"You're the one who wants me naked, but I will desist from verbal observations of your thoughts. Although, I have to admit, I cannot resist one more comment; you are fascinated to know what my hump looks like unclothed."

Jared reddens even more, but holds his tongue.

"Wine?" she asks.

"Yes, that would be nice."

"Red or white?"

Jared laughs. "You already know."

"Red it is."

He accepts the wine and takes a rather long swig. "I guess you also know why I'm here?"

Pythia looks at him sympathetically and says, "Professor Paine, although I can read minds, more often than not only a few thoughts rise to clarity above the low-level gabbling which is non-stop and basically undecipherable to me. From now on, just speak what you have to say and there should be no confusion. As I said, no more verbalization of your mental cognitions on my part. Please recall what I also said; words are transparent, but character is opaque. Now, let's start over. Why are you here?"

Jared flashes a mischievous smile. "To get my laptop back."

"Unfortunately, that is impossible."

"One way street, eh?"

"Correct."

"Did you really make it disappear, or are you a master hypnotist? Tell the truth or I'll be well on my way to Bedlam."

"I really made it disappear, at least in the current dimensions we occupy."

Jared's eyes widen. "Your mother! Those poor men! Can it be?"

"It can and is. Those 'poor' men, by the way, were rapists and murderers."

"Yes, perhaps, but you can't just go around killing people and removing their limbs."

Pythia remains silent.

"How is it done? I mean, tell me the physics of it."

"Even I do not fully understand. For seventeen years, I was taught knowledge far beyond humans, yet that was never explained to my satisfaction. Some concepts are beyond even me."

"Beyond humans? Are you not human?"

Pythia shrugs. "Depends on your definition of human."

"Okay, I'll be more precise. Are you a member of species *Homo sapiens*?"

"If I tell you, I fear you will feel insulted."

Jared swallows nervously. "Just tell me. I am a scientist after all."

"No, I am not of your species . . . or perhaps better to say, not entirely of your species. But we can still interbreed."

"Great, like a donkey and horse producing a sterile mule?"

"At this stage of the evolutionary process, reproduction with a member of *Homo sapiens* is possible. And the offspring would not be sterile."

"How nice and romantic! Look, Pythia, my interest in you is purely scientific."

"That is why you want to see me naked? Careful, I can read minds, professor. Your statement is not entirely accurate."

"Christ! This is impossible! Can we get back to science? I want to understand what you understand. I want to learn how your powers work. You are research enough for a hundred physicists for a hundred years."

For the first time, Pythia looks at him with sadness in her eyes. "Professor Paine, you cannot understand what I understand, not even in a hundred years. I am not your research subject, you are mine."

"Why is that?" huffs Jared. "Are you so advanced that a Ph.D in physics will never understand?"

"Correct."

"But, that's absurd!"

Pythia is tempted to use the *Homo neanderthal-Homo sapiens* analogy, but thinks better of it. "Be that as it may, it is so."

"In other words, I can be no help to you as a scientist; only as a lying co-conspirator with the FBI?"

"Not entirely true."

"Don't tell me; it's the whole mating thing again."

Pythia abruptly stands and holds out a heavy marble bookend. "Here, take this and stand on the other side of the room."

"Why?"

"Please, just do it."

Jared moves to the far wall and waits, weighing the heft of the bookend, wondering what this alien hunchback is up to now. While waiting, he feels an increasingly exhilarating excitement complemented by a new appreciation of her beauty. This appreciation is not born of any ordinary sexual attraction, but of some undiscovered sensation—something akin to physically perceiving other dimensions. The impression is bone-chilling yet breathtaking: an awareness of complete alienation from earthly reality.

"Throw it," she says.

"What?"

"Throw it at me!"

He tosses it underhand to her.

She catches it and tosses it back. "No, no! Throw it at my head as hard as you can! Try and hit me. Try and hurt me."

Jared hesitates.

"Do it!" she commands.

"No," he objects. "If I hit you, it could be fatal. Don't be ridiculous!"

"I told you to do it! You are the presumed scientist. Here is your experiment. Are you that weak?"

"I don't want to hurt you! I have a strong arm. Used to be a pitcher in high school."

"I understand. Now, throw it as hard as you can. Now!"

Jared throws the object at a much-slower speed than he is capable of.

Pythia disgustedly catches it in one hand and tosses it back. "For the last time, as hard as you can!"

Jared reaches back and flings it as hard as he can at her body, trying to avoid her head. It disappears in mid-flight.

Before he has time to close his astonished mouth, she tosses him the matching bookend. "Again! Harder! At my head!"

His competitive juices primed, he winds up and throws all his weight into the pitch using her head as a target.

Again, it vanishes.

"I don't believe it," mutters a shocked Jared. "I can't believe it! Hypnosis, or some parlor trick! Has to be."

"No, Professor Paine, no parlor trick. In reading your mind, I can tell you are struggling to make sense of the nonsensical. Nevertheless, it is true. What you just saw is real."

"Where did they go?"

Pythia spreads her arms. "Atoms and molecules disbursed into the environment. The entity that constitutes what you call a bookend—the whole that is greater than the sum of its parts—is elsewhere. For all intents and purposes, gone, but for its constituent particles. One might say, the parts are greater than the sum of its whole. This, at any rate, is the simplest answer. Other dimensions are involved, but I prefer not to go there."

"Like the mosquitoes? Like the equations? Like my laptop? Like those men in the photographs? Right?"

"Yes."

"Pythia, you need to tell me everything, from the beginning, so I can understand all this."

"You will not understand. I want you as a mate, not a disciple."

"Don't think of me as a disciple, think of me as a student. Role reversal!"

Pythia laughs. "Charming. Professors should not sleep with their students. Especially young students, like you."

"Pythia, I'm older than you, by a lot."

This time, it is Pythia that appears confused. "I'm not sure about that. Remember I mentioned being taught for sixteen years?"

"Yes."

"Well, I don't think they were the kind of years that pass here."

"Here?"

"You see, impossible to explain and impossible for you to understand. Let me ask you this: you are a physicist, correct?"

"Correct."

"And modern string theory posits multiple dimensions, correct?"

"Correct."

"Now, here is the crucial point: can you visualize (or even really comprehend) a fifth or sixth or tenth dimension, let alone a hundredth?"

"The maths—"

"No! Not the maths. Can you visualize it? Comprehend it beyond the equations?"

"Well, no."

"And even the equations are unknown to you."

"Well, there are those who—"

"No. I guarantee you and your colleagues do not know, and in fact are gerbils racing on the wrong wheel. You are a prisoner of the four dimensions your brains evolved to experience. No amount of abstract knowledge or imagination will ever truly free you from this four-dimensional incarceration no matter how hard you try. Now do you see what I mean? You cannot visualize multiple dimensions, you cannot comprehend multiple dimensions, and you do not even have the maths correct."

"And you can. . . . "

"Yes, I can visualize some multiple dimensions, I can comprehend them, I can enter them, I can experience them, and I know the underlying maths. In your frame of reference I am now eighteen."

"But you just said you're not sure."

"Yes, but that uncertainty is the great grey area of my life. I believe those seventeen years were much much longer, and they passed in some space unconnected to the here and now on earth. However, I simply do not know for sure; perhaps a hundred years, a thousand or more, perhaps less."

"Then who taught you?"

"That is as far as we can go, Jared."

"First time you called me that. Now I feel extremely young compared to you. You really want a thirty-something *Homo sapiens* male to mate with a potentially ancient female of unknown origin? A female of a different species?"

Pythia assumes a sly smile. "I understand many males prefer exotic relationships, exotic sex. And you?"

"Damn it, you ask that question to get me thinking and probe my mind. I can feel you rummaging around. Get out!"

"Okay, I am out, but I saw enough to know you are definitely a fertile *Homo sapiens* male, one who has abstained from sex for far too long."

"Regardless of what you say, I am still a scientist. Simply being a stud service for you is unacceptable. What do I get out of this mating business?"

"Oh, Jared, you get to father a new species. Your genes are serviceable and will act as a substrate for mine."

"That will go down as the most bizarre pick-up line in history."

"Think of what worlds will open before you!"

"As an inferior slave?"

"No, that is not in the consciousness of our kind. You are thinking like a monkey. Inferiority is a *Homo sapiens* concept. You will be by my side if you make the decision to go forward."

"Go forward? How do you mean?"

"I mean, you will be my interpreter of the intellectual intricacies and eccentricities of your species, just as Zookeeper was my mother's interpreter of the psychopaths and sociopaths. There are many places to go, many injustices to prevent, and much suffering to be addressed."

Jared is too overwhelmed to take it all in, so he says simply, "I can't understand why I am chosen for this."

"One important caveat you must remember and accept."

"What is that?"

"While you will be the first mate, there will of necessity be others."

Jared nods. "I'm not so stupid that I didn't figure that out. If I agree, what next? Hop in bed?"

"One asset possessed by *Homo sapiens* is their endless penchant for expressing humor at precise moments. No. Next step is to meet those who have guided me."

"Introduction to the parents for approval?"

"Something like that. Be here next Tuesday at ten and we will leave for San Francisco."

"I don't . . . okay, I'll be here."

"Meanwhile," says Pythia with a wry smile. "I have to find a couple of new bookends."

~ *A Meeting* ~

The echoes of their final exchange trail Jared, whispers he cannot shake. For several days, he retreats into the dim solitude of his apartment, each hour peeling away layers of identity he once believed immutable. What had happened between them—what *was* still happening—refuses to resolve itself into any stable narrative. No language, no model, no hypothesis suffices. Instead, he enters a strange and silent storm, a reckoning with self. Emotions rise that feel wholly alien, not just in content but in structure. They do not resemble human feelings so much as *precursors* to them; something older, or from elsewhere. In their wake comes a quiet undoing: of the man he had performed, the roles he had embodied. A dissolution of the benevolent tyrannies that had governed him with velvet-gloved hands—career, reputation, intellectual vanity, and the petty insulations of a life confined to academic prestige.

Now, in the light, or shadow, of Pythia's superiority, both cerebral and spatial, those old moorings dissolve. The force that once held him to Earth's conceptual gravity no longer applies. He floats, untethered. And the feeling is not terror, but *freedom*.

He does not deny her power. Nor the breathtaking, categorical difference of her being. He concedes her brilliance, her dominion over matter, her command of dimensions he cannot even visualize. But he does not, *will not,* concede her judgment. She believes he cannot understand. That comprehension lies eternally out of reach for *Homo sapiens.* But Jared Paine refuses the fate of a passive satellite orbiting her star. Given enough time, he insists to himself, given enough proximity, he *will* find the thread. His intelligence, if wielded like the blade he believes it can be—disciplined, honed, and relentless—*will* carve a path into what she calls the impossible.

Let her underestimate him. She will do so at her own peril.

He knows, of course, that she intends to use him, to propagate, to seed whatever hybrid future her kind has charted. But he, too, will use *her.* He will draw back the veil of reality itself, pierce the seams she so effortlessly traverses, and translate the untranslatable. This pact, however unequal, will not leave him unchanged. And yet . . . in the hush between thoughts, he feels her presence flicker. Watching. Listening. He knows that even these inner declarations are not private. She sees them all. He will deal with that when he must.

Despite the disorientation spinning through his thoughts, a current of exhilaration rises within him. It is unfamiliar—not the thrill of discovery in a laboratory or the satisfaction of proving a theory, but something more immediate, more physical. The sensation moves through him without permission, loosening the ties to the life he has known. A boundary has shifted. On the far side of it, something stirs which is raw, unformed, and waiting to be named.

He begins to imagine a different future.

Not one written in drafts or footnotes, not one confined to lecture halls or academic panels. He sees himself with her, not just beside her, but bound to whatever purpose she carries. He envisions the surrender of routine, the quiet withdrawal from systems and structures that once gave his life meaning. The idea does not frighten him. It quickens him.

Marriage crosses his mind, not in the ceremonial sense, but as a joining. A vow, unwritten, that he would follow her wherever the path leads, no matter how unclear. Her quest is not his, but he feels its pull all the same. He sees himself moving through her world, even if he does not understand it. He does not need to understand it. He only needs to be there.

And with this opening, thought pours in.

Possibilities multiply. Scenarios branch in every direction. His mind races ahead, unspooling variations, interpretations, consequences. He knows most of them are unlikely. He knows he is projecting onto a moment that has not yet settled. But the energy cannot be contained. It builds with every breath, and with it, a quiet conviction forms:

Something is beginning.

And he wants to meet it, not as a witness, but as part of it.

Could she disintegrate a bullet before it strikes? What if someone fires from behind, across a great distance? Would she sense it? Would she vanish? How could any nation contain her? Arrest her? Censor her? Would they try?

Even more chilling questions rise. *How would the world receive her? Could* Homo sapiens *even tolerate her existence, let alone her reproduction?* What if she *multiplies? What if her kind, slowly and methodically, replaces humanity?*

And there, at the center of it all, sits the questions he dare not stare at directly: Does he help her? Does he assist in the eclipse of his own species?

That scenario too, he locks away—for now. It is a fire too bright to look at. A truth too large for the present moment. Let the future pry it open, if it must. For now, he surrenders to the current. Not because he is weak. But because he senses the tide carries him not away from himself, but *toward* the man he was never allowed to become.

~

"So, you are Professor Paine," says Lady Oracle, extending her hand with stately composure. She stands in the foyer of the old Victorian house in San Francisco, flanked by Sy and Altan—three figures who seem drawn from vastly different archetypes, now incongruously sharing a single stage.

Jared clasps her hand. Her grip is both firm and distant, like shaking hands with a prophecy.

As introductions unfold, Jared finds himself disoriented. Lady Oracle appears as though carved from some ancient monument: her figure tall, her spirit ageless, and her presence formidable. Sy, in contrast, flits with kinetic charm, a jester who conceals daggers in his laughter. Altan is stillness personified, his expression inscrutable, his posture granite, his eyes hypnotic.

Soon they gather in a grand, sunlit parlor. Late morning light spills through tall bay windows, casting elongated shadows that move as if thinking.

Lady Oracle pours coffee and hands Jared a cup. Her tone is casual but her gaze is clinical.

"You're aware of Pythia's powers?"

"Yes."

"And that doesn't concern you?"

"Concern me how?"

"Your safety. Your sanity. Your reputation. Your sense of self. Your sense of worth. Your career. Your species. I could go on, but I imagine you take my meaning."

Jared sips. "Yes. I'm concerned about all of it. But before we go further . . . what exactly is your relationship to her?"

He glances at Sy and Altan, then returns his gaze to Lady Oracle.

"Consider us her guardians," she replies.

"Do you share her powers?"

"No."

"So you're . . . normal? Human?"

"For your purposes," she says.

"My purposes?"

She doesn't answer. Instead, she offers a plate of almond cookies. Jared waves them away, distracted.

The silence settles mistlike. Finally, he breaks it.

"I honestly don't know what I am to any of this, aside from, apparently, a donor. So . . . what exactly is my role?"

Sy's eyes light up. "You, my good sir, are to be her translator. Her emissary. Her interface with the clunky, contradictory, ever-baffled world of humanity, particularly its so-called intellectual side." He twirls flamboyantly. "You may lack my theatrical flair, but your mind is sharp. That will serve her well."

Jared scoffs. "So, I'm a clever dog with a clipboard?"

"No," says Altan. His voice is low, tectonic. "You are to be her husband. The father of what comes next."

Sy pirouettes. "Like Peleus and Thetis!"

Jared raises an eyebrow.

"Thetis was a sea goddess," Sy explains, still spinning. "A nereid—beautiful, immortal. Peleus was a mortal king. Together they birthed Achilles, divine in all but his heel. Pythia is Thetis. You are Peleus."

Jared chuckles. "Then I'm royalty now?"

"No," Sy grins. "But you might one day be the King of Science."

Despite his sarcasm, Jared feels something building within him. A kinetic thrill, coiled and ready to surge. He suppresses it with the practiced stoicism of a man trained to doubt anything that excites too easily.

Pythia, silent until now, tilts her head. Her hump pulses gently beneath her dress.

"He knows," she says. "He's just looking for vocabulary to match the intensity. It's what I like about him."

A hush settles. Jared notices it, then misreads it, until Pythia speaks again. "No, Jared. They aren't subservient to me. In what comes next, hierarchy must die. The personal must be tempered, or we risk unraveling the weave entirely. Equality isn't a slogan—it's a law of balance."

Lady Oracle nods. "Exactly. From John and Meiying, to Michael and Tamara, down to Ming-huà and Zookeeper—the trajectory was marked by the one you call Goddess. Her aim is simple: reduce suffering, preserve the future."

"This Goddess," Jared asks, "who is she, really?"

Altan answers without hesitation. "She is the rock beneath your feet, the breath in your lungs, the blood in your veins."

Jared frowns. "Sounds like metaphor. Goddess is an ancient term. Doesn't it feel . . . outdated?"

"Archetypes never age," says Lady Oracle. "They live where science cannot reach. Pythia's great-grandmother, Child of Buddha, learned to interpret the Oracle through sound alone, by listening to the Precious Object."

"This is all foreign to me," Jared admits. "These names, these stories. It's a web I haven't yet mapped. But I can still walk the line forward. What happens next?"

Lady Oracle smiles faintly. "Business, with pleasure. A trip. A sort of honeymoon, absent the wedding rituals your species adores . . . and sometimes regrets."

"No wedding?"

"Too conspicuous," she replies. "Paper trails invite governments."

"Where are we going?"

"Before that, there's one last introduction. You must meet her parents."

Jared nods slowly. "Off the coast of Washington, right? The island."

"Correct," says Pythia, handing him the almond cookies once more.

"Take one," she says with a smile. "It's good."

~ *Another Meeting* ~

Weeks later, on a forested path sloping gently toward a seaside cabin, Ming-huà and Zookeeper stand at the window, watching.

"There she is," Ming-huà murmurs. "Just look at her. Always driving squirrels mad."

A nearby squirrel chatters wildly at the approaching figures. Ming-huà smiles.

"Like mother, like daughter."

Zookeeper squints. "Jesus. She's nearly as beautiful as you are."

"The professor's not bad either," she replies. "Smart, I hear."

"Smart for a *Homo sapien* like me?" Zookeeper grumbles. "At least the fucker has arms."

Ming-huà ignores the jab. "He'll have questions. Pythia says she's saved the harder answers for us. It's story time."

"Great. Bet he doesn't even smoke weed. As the Bard put it, 'Nature betrays itself to harder bosoms.'"

"Zookeeper, he's a physicist. Not a literature major."

"Yeah, yeah."

When they open the door, Jared can't help glancing at Zookeeper's armless frame. Inside, seated with lemonade, he watches in astonishment as Zookeeper deftly lifts his glass with his feet.

"Before we get too comfortable," Ming-huà says, "does Professor Paine know how my husband lost his arms?"

"He does," Pythia answers.

Jared leans forward. "Please, just call me Jared."

"Does Jared know why he's called Zookeeper?"

"That too," Pythia replies.

"Good," Ming-huà nods. "Then let's begin."

Jared hesitates. "I suppose I do have more questions for you than you for me."

Pythia cuts in. "Mother, I want to hear about the FBI. How did it go?"

Ming-huà sighs. "They left with more confusion than answers. I remain a person of interest, naturally."

Jared says nothing, but Pythia fills the silence.

"He knows what happened. He knows why. Maybe it's time you told him yourself."

Ming-huà nods and begins. Her voice is calm but carries weight, truths wrapped in risk. She recounts the events in full, exposing the threads of her choices and the consequences they wrought.

When she finishes, she looks toward her husband with tenderness and sorrow.

"You see, Jared . . . such power, used unwisely, becomes cruelty. Even righteousness must be wielded gently. Or else, we become the very thing we meant to stop."

"Unintended consequences," Jared murmurs.

"Precisely."

He turns to Zookeeper.

"How do you live with someone like her?"

Zookeeper grins.

"Easy. I don't lie. Can't hide what isn't hidden. Most people think that's a burden. Truth is, it's freedom. All I had to lose were my arms. I got peace in return. Try finding that deal on the street."

~ *A Walk* ~

That night, Jared walks home under a sky streaked with fading crimson. His mind thrums with an electricity unlike anything he has ever known. Every step feels stolen from two worlds: one still bound to lecture halls, equations, and polite academic applause; the other pulled toward a terrifying, luminous threshold where reason falters and the unimaginable beckons.

He pauses on a bridge, watching the river coil beneath him in black, slow waves. The world he thought immutable now shudders with possibility. The mosquitoes. The equations. The vanished laptop. The bookends. And above all—her.

A breeze carries the scent of eucalyptus, sharp and clean, like air rinsed in some higher dimension. Jared grips the railing, pulse quickening.

She has chosen me.

The words ring like a verdict, both crushing and exalting. What does it mean to be chosen by someone, or something, that might not even belong to his species? It is as though history—or even fate itself—has tapped him on the shoulder, whispering: Step forward. Your era ends. Another begins.

He pictures himself not as a passive witness but as a necessary hinge, a bridge between species, between ages. His fear has not vanished, but it has been re-forged into resolve. He will meet her parents. He will step into whatever labyrinth they open. And if that means the death of the old Jared Paine, the sterile, respectable professor, then so be it.

The river slides on beneath the bridge, silent and endless. He watches its surface until he sees not water, but a mirror. And in its reflection, he no longer knows if he is staring at himself—or at the future staring back.

~

He hears Ming-huà's voice again, carrying the words of Zhuang Zi like a small ripple on the current: *"Only still water can reflect stillness. Running water cannot mirror a face. Only that which is still can still the stillness of others."*

Yet even a ripple, he wonders, may widen into perilous waves.

The thought settles inside him, vast and troubling.

If she has chosen him, then perhaps he too must learn to still his own turbulence, to become a mirror for what is coming.

Chapter Twenty-Five

Preparation

Fever Dreams

~ *A Vision Before Sex* ~

Pythia and Jared have stayed in Ming-huà's cramped guest room for two days, with plans to remain another week. Though neither names it aloud, this is their honeymoon. To both, it is a hush between storms, a window in which conception might occur untouched by interruption. That first night is scorched into Jared's memory, not as a singular emotion but a collision of opposites: ecstasy braided with horror, love interlaced with fear, lust poisoned by revulsion. He would never be the same.

When they entered the room, Pythia undressed with a calm as clinical as it was unsettling, as though disrobing for a ritual bath long overdue. Jared sat rigid at the bed's edge, heart hammering, breath shallow, sweat blooming beneath his arms. She stood before him, naked and unashamed, her body fully offered—not seductively, but ceremonially—as if daring him to look, daring him to understand. He studied her with trembling intensity, fighting a swell of impulses he dared not name. His flesh responded too quickly, his mind unraveling. Worst of all was the dark current that rose from somewhere beneath his civilized skin—a sick and ancient urge to violate what he could not possess. He did not act on it, but its presence shamed him.

Her hump haunted everything. Even as she stood in radiant frontal beauty, he knew the true revelation was yet to come. She was toying with him, inviting him to wait, to ache, to watch as she slowly turned.

And then, she did.

~

At first, Jared saw only the curvature, a line so precise it arrested his attention before he could name what it was. The hump emerged seamlessly from her back, a formation that defied expectation. It shimmered under skin the color of creamed coffee, the surface drawn taut over something that felt neither entirely human nor inert. There was a pulse beneath it, subtle but insistent, as though the form carried its own rhythm, independent of the body to which it belonged. Yet despite that quiet motion, there was a stillness in it. Not deadness, but permanence. It offered nothing to the eye and yet demanded everything.

Jared felt caught between contradictions. The form radiated heat, yet carried the sheen of something untouched by time. It drew his gaze the way ancient structures do, not with decoration, but with gravity. He had never seen anything like it. The impression was not purely physical. It reached into something deeper, a place below thought.

And then it changed.

From beneath the surface, subtle shifts began to occur. Lines of red emerged, almost imperceptibly at first. Thin, fine, precise. They began to move, slowly at first, then with increasing confidence, drawing paths across her back in patterns that defied randomness. The lines did not stay fixed. They twisted and reformed, curling in and out of one another. They pulsed, but not with pain or illness. With purpose.

Jared leaned closer, barely aware of his movement. His breath slowed. The distance between his face and her skin closed until the warmth of her body touched the air around his lips. The surface shimmered beneath a growing film of sweat, refracting the light, distorting the forms now dancing across her back. He did not fully understand what he was seeing. Yet it did not feel foreign.

Figures began to take shape.

Not static images, but impressions: bodies in motion, hands reaching, faces shifting between sorrow and command. Shapes emerged and receded. He was not reading a story. He was being drawn into one. Time slipped. Meaning hovered just beyond comprehension, but the feeling was unmistakable: he was witnessing something alive.

The channels deepened, spreading outward in layers, forming a network across her back. And within that network, movement continued. Not as metaphor. Not as illusion. But as life.

He saw villages rise along those shimmering streams. Dwellings. People. Children running, fires burning, wind in trees too small to name. The deeper he looked, the more the landscape revealed: not a symbol of a world, but a world itself. A miracle rendered in miniature on the slope of her flesh. And it moved. It *lived*.

Time no longer held. He forgot his breath. His questions hung weightless in the thickening air. Whatever governed his eyes now was no longer his own—some ancient deity had borrowed his gaze, lifted the veil, and shown him not a body, but a cosmos. Not a woman, but a genesis.

And still she stood, silent, unmoved, as the story beneath her skin unfolded without end.

Time seemed suspended, his questions frozen as scenes shifted and re-shaped themselves across the landscape of her flesh. . . .

~

Spread before him, etched in living contours across Pythia's back, were two villages, both unmistakably Asian, yet unmoored from any known country or era. They pulsed with ceremonial joy, the air thick with incense, laughter, and rice wine. Jared saw, not as a voyeur, but as one who belonged, as if he had once lived within this scene and would live there again.

In one village, a wedding unfolded with intricate purpose. It was more than celebration, it carried a clarity that bypassed thought and settled deep within Jared's awareness. What happened before him did not feel observed so much as absorbed. He did not remember the events. He recognized them, as if they had always been waiting to rise into view.

The match had been arranged by a discreet go-between. Elders, faces lined by time and custom, nodded in slow agreement. A fortune teller had been summoned to consult the signs, to balance the needs of the living with the demands of those who no longer spoke aloud. Dates were drawn from the lunar cycle with careful deliberation. And then, everything began.

Jared watched as the bride moved from doorway to doorway, offering candied fruit, porcelain cups of tea, and almond pastries so fine they looked breakable in the hand. Her smile was hidden, but her presence was sure. Her steps followed an inherited rhythm. The groom, formal and subdued, extended his offerings—gold earrings set in crimson velvet, a folded scarf of embroidered silk, rings polished to a perfect gleam. None of it felt performative. Every gesture held weight.

At the altar to the ancestors, candles stood lit in unwavering rows. Smoke curled toward the ceiling in slow ascent. Around the village, fronds, branches, and wild blooms filled thresholds and ledges until every dwelling seemed reshaped by color and scent. There was no division between space and ceremony. Everything participated.

Then the procession began.

It moved through the village with deliberate pacing. Jared saw bodies weaving in coordinated motion—bride, groom, family, and guests all flowing toward a shared center. Music accompanied them: soft strings, low rhythms, tones that hovered more than advanced. He strained to see the faces. They were close, yet indeterminate—blurred at the edges, as though the moment refused to commit to permanence.

The older women walked with quiet dignity, hands folded, eyes forward. Young girls in long, flowing garments moved in patterns both playful and restrained. A few men, flushed and animated, danced with unsteady energy, their voices raised more in joy than in excess. At the groom's home, the entrance had been transformed—walls removed, a canopy erected, space opened to hold what could not be contained indoors. Red banners stretched from post to post, each one bearing words of blessing. Behind the house, the work of feeding continued in constant motion—women stirring, lifting, slicing, boiling. Their movements formed a kind of liturgy all their own, not bound to any temple but no less sacred.

Jared's attention fixed on the man leading the procession. His frame was slight, but he moved with ease, one hand raised in greeting, the other clutching a flask he passed between grins. He carried the posture of someone who knew too much but refused to be burdened by it. This was the matchmaker. His smile suggested every secret had already been told, and none of them mattered anymore.

Nearby, one of the groom's friends tossed a parasol into the air, caught it with practiced ease, and let out a whoop of approval. The moment struck Jared in the chest—not for its novelty, but for its familiarity. Something about it echoed a memory not yet lived. In the movement of the crowd, in the firelight, in the rhythm of preparation, he sensed the outline of his own wedding taking form. Pythia's presence rose behind the vision, indistinct but certain, waiting for the right moment to emerge.

Then, the flow broke.

Near the center of the square, raised voices erupted. Two men faced off, the cause of their quarrel immediately clear—a dispute over ownership of a prized water buffalo. The guests fell back, creating a clearing edged in caution. Before the tension could solidify, a third figure stepped between them. Jared blinked, startled not by the man's intervention but by his face. The posture, the smile, the slanted eyebrows filled with mischief.

Sy . . . aka Scarecrow.

Effortless, poised, just amused enough to disarm both parties.

Even here. Even now.

Jared nearly laughed aloud, but the sound caught in his throat. The moment didn't need explanation. It confirmed what he already knew: whatever this was—a dream, a memory, a vision—he was meant to be in it.

One man protested that the other had struck him across the face, leaving him disfigured. Sy, with a theatrical pause, suggested that the accused be allowed to strike the other cheek—for balance, of course. The crowd burst into laughter. Even the wronged man chuckled. Harmony restored, Sy vanished into his study, its walls lined with books both sacred and profane. *Buddhist sutras, Confucian codes, Daoist paradoxes . . . and a discreet shelf of illustrated erotic classics.* Yes, Jared thought. *That's Sy.*

But the scene shifted again—too fast, too fluid.

Jared closed his eyes to steady the rising nausea. When he opened them, the wedding had long since passed. In the sun-drenched fields outside the village, a husband and wife bent over rows of rice, their hands mud-slick, their laughter unbroken. Two older children worked alongside them, while their grandmother cared for infants inside a hut of reed and earth. A toddler giggled while rolling an enormous jackfruit. A baby slept without care. These were not symbols; they were lives. Despite their poverty, the couple worked with a rhythm that spoke of joy, of knowing something deeper than hunger. Jared sensed, without knowing how, that they were literate, that they would one day prosper, that this scene was not their beginning nor their end. Then, the husband pointed upward, grinning. Both he and his wife looked directly at Jared—*through* him—as if he were the very sun warming their backs. Their gaze pierced the veil of vision, and Jared staggered backward.

It was them. *The bride and groom.* Transfigured through time. Farmers, lovers, prophets. He had witnessed not just a wedding, but a lifetime.

Another blur. The world spun. He shut his eyes again, dizzy.

Now the woman was old, seated on the front porch of a stately wooden house with tile roofing. Other women surrounded her, laughing, gossiping, sipping tea, nibbling cookies with the same ease as centuries passing. Children played beneath a great banyan tree, but the old woman gently scolded her daughter to shoo them away—*let the ancestors have their shade.* Jared felt the echo of sorrow in her smile. Her husband, *that grinning farmer, that joyful groom,* had long since died of illness. The sadness of his absence hovered at the edge of the day, never gone, never dominant.

Still, the village was alive with celebration, wrapped in the fragrance of continuity. Almond cookies. Tea. Laughter. Spirits overhead. Feet on soil.

The wheel of life had turned, but had never truly moved.

~

And then again, the wheeling.

But this time it was not a turn, it was a *plummet.* Jared felt his stomach drop through the floor of time, his whole being tilting into a vertigo beyond physics. His instincts screamed not to open his eyes. Something unspeakable awaited. But he opened them anyway.

A second village had emerged across the vast curvature of Pythia's back, its contours twisted, darker, poorer, frayed at the edges of form. The air around it quivered with disturbance. Spirits haunted the space, not as visitors but as prisoners. Something here had gone deeply wrong. The fields were skeletal, their paddies hollowed by neglect, helpless against the slow, encroaching seizure by forest and root. The groves stood like massacred sentinels, their trees dry as bone. The few fruits that clung to life pulsed with swarming ant armies—bloated, staggering, writhing like drunk dancers at a wedding soured by death.

In the square, armed men loitered beneath the rusted helix of a machine long at rest, rifles slung across shoulders, sunlight flashing off their barrels in blinding intervals. No sheltering banyan tree stood here. No ancestral shade. The villagers had retreated into the heat-stifled interiors of shuttered homes, filthy ditches, and collapsing tunnels. The oppressive weight of fear overpowered the air. Suspicion had torn apart kinship. Families had fractured into factions, and factions into fragments. Trust had decayed to ash. Parents no longer believed in their own children. The young had scattered, some to war, some to hunger, some to the seductive glow of urban neon. Most were dead.

Boys had become men. Men had become corpses, or killers. Some lay supine, slack-jawed beneath the indifferent sky. Others stood above them, grinning with teeth too white, challenging gods who no longer answered. Girls had become women. Women had become victims, or merchants of flesh. Some lay back with legs parted, accepting the intrusion of lust and hatred shaped like men. Others stood above them, counting oily currency with greed-palsied hands. The old men, the once-respected patriarchs, now fed on their lineage like cannibals, gorging on the despair of their children, chewing the flayed skins of their grandchildren. Pride had died long ago. The old women rocked and keened, unheard, unheeded—forgotten relics in a culture of forgetting.

In the square, the war council had begun.

Leaders crouched low, drawing strategies in the sand with bamboo sticks. Their faces were warped with fury, their voices cracked and urgent. They plotted an assault on a stone fortress outside the village, a structure visible only as a silhouette of menace in Jared's periphery. Ragged soldiers clustered around the drawings, listening with feral eyes. Among them were women—broad-hipped, breastplate-strapped, armed to the teeth. One pair stood out: a man clutching the hand of a squatting woman, both bearing rifles. The man whispered something and pointed upward.

Then they both looked up, directly into Jared's eyes.

Time seized.

He knew them. The same couple. *The bride and groom*. No longer vibrant. Now ravaged by fear, famine, and the relentless abrasion of betrayal. Their eyes, once luminous, were dark caves of worry. They had left their mother in the tunnels. Their children were hidden in a hundred nooks and crannies, half-starved. Their laughter, brittle and aching, did not lift the curve of their backs or the burden of knowing too much and understanding too little. The connection between them had not died, but it had been warped by the weight of survival.

Then the vision turned violent.

A churning of fog, of rain, of red mist. Thunder rumbled through the earth, or was it within the vast landscape of Pythia's back? Jared couldn't tell. The sky tore open. A battle exploded. He saw men and women carrying bodies through jungle bramble, blood soaking into every thread of cloth, the moans of the wounded a perverse requiem. Hatred howled between the trees. Fear galloped beside the living. Even the non-human creatures—the monkeys, the tigers, the dogs, the rats—cowered in silence, sensing the end of something ancient.

And then, *She* came.

A young woman. A hunchback. Barefoot, calm, walking through the carnage like an angel of reversal. *Her* eyes were unblinking. *Her* presence unearthly.

And all began to undo.

Blood vanished. Wounds sealed. Rifles disassembled into raw materials. As if the world itself were being played backward, the battlefield emptied. The dead returned to life. The wounded returned to their homes. A great un-suffering moved across the land. Laughter returned, and human voices lifted in song, entwining with the melodies of birds.

And then the stories ended.

The pulsing red veins that had inscribed all this—village, wedding, war, despair, resurrection—began to recede. The ochre marble beneath glistened once more in its cold, implacable serenity. The creamy skin shone smooth and clean. The theater of time dissolved.

~ *Aftermath* ~

The image of Sy, grinning between two furious men, hovered in Jared's mind long after the vision began to dissolve. The music faded. The colors bled into shadow. One by one, the faces vanished, replaced by the dim awareness of his own breath, his own hands, the familiar texture of air against skin.

He stood alone again, but not unchanged.

The wedding's warmth had not left him. It lingered, not in his eyes or ears, but somewhere deeper—beneath language, beneath thought. The experience had imprinted itself into his body, not as recollection, but as substance. His chest ached, not from sorrow, not from joy, but from the pressure of something unspoken pressing inward, as though meaning itself had taken up residence just beneath the sternum.

He did not feel nostalgia. He did not feel longing. What settled inside him was older, quieter. It was an awareness that had no clear origin, but made itself known in breath and skin. Recognition moved through him without needing justification. It was not attached to reason or to memory. It simply was.

He closed his eyes in an attempt to hold the images, but they drifted beyond reach. Not lost, only dispersed. They had entered him, fragment by fragment, taking root below the level of conscious thought. The matchmaker's grin, half-mocking and half-divine. The procession of girls in silk, their movements like whispers of another time. Pythia's face, never fully revealed, yet unmistakably present, felt rather than seen, expected long before she ever arrived.

He had not been a guest at the wedding. He had not been an observer. He had been placed within it, as if summoned not to witness, but to remember. And with that memory came something else.

Not comfort.

Not hope.

A quiet, pervasive unease.

The ceremony had been complete. It had unfolded without flaw, without resistance. But it had also been ancient, as though repeating a sequence already etched into time. Nothing in it had been new. Only his presence was new.

And that raised a deeper question: *Whose prophecy is this?*

The air around him felt thinner now. The body he returned to felt heavier, more bounded by time. He inhaled slowly, then opened his eyes. The room was unchanged. No garlands. No drums. No Sy.

And yet, something in him remained anchored to that other place.

A union had been witnessed.

A joining had been written, if not yet lived.

And part of him, whether ready or not, had agreed.

Pythia turned to face him.

Jared staggered backward, lowering himself to the bed like a man who had returned from drowning. He could not stop staring at her. His voice was barely breath.

"What did I just see?"

Pythia's eyes were steady, ancient.

"You saw one slice of space and time that my ancestors, your ancestors, and all the ancestors of humankind have endured. I am full of billions of such stories. You must prepare yourself. They will not stay hidden. They are rising—unrepressed tales, unfolding from the deep marrow of my hump, written in filaments that never rest.

"I feel them even now, moving like ant-threads through the soil of memory, forming and reforming. So many stories. Human. Non-human. All in flux. All waiting to be seen by those who will see."

~ *Sex* ~

Looking back on that night, Jared remembers two emotions—twin moons rising—utter terror, and a joy so radiant it nearly blinded him.

Pythia had never seemed more foreign, more *other*. Not alien in the sense of distant stars or little green men, but alien the way a jellyfish is—translucent, unknowable, shaped by fluid laws beyond vertebrate comprehension. The very act of touching her, of entering her world through the threshold of sex, had filled him with a primal urge to flee. He had never before associated arousal with such profound dread. The thought crossed his mind like a sliver of ice: *Am I about to have sex with a deity? Or a nightmare?*

The image that struck him was not human, it was some tentacled, morphing being from a sea before time. It wasn't erotic. It was sublime. And it terrified him. But Pythia, who needed no language to understand the storm inside him, responded with grace. She sat beside him, warm and grounding, and took his trembling hand.

"You've seen what no other human has," she said softly, her voice the echo of oceans and stars. "I know you're afraid. But remember, our DNA is compatible. Our mating can create life—strong, healthy children."

Jared grimaced. "Please . . . stop saying *mate*, Pythia."

"What word should I use?"

"*Love.* Or even just *have sex*. *Mate* makes me feel like I'm in a zoology lab."

She tilted her head, studying him. "It's difficult for me to adjust to these nuances. But I'll try. Even so . . . I can't change what I am."

"You *are* an alien to me, Pythia."

"I am not," she said quietly. "But I understand why you'd think so."

There was a pause, filled with something unnameable.

Then she said: "Jared. Undress for me."

"I . . . I don't know if I can."

"Please. I want to show you something."

Her voice did not invite. It consecrated. Each word carried a weight that made refusal impossible. It was not seduction he heard, but reverence, an invocation spoken across the boundary between flesh and meaning.

With a quiet mix of hesitation and desire, he complied. One by one, his clothes were removed, not discarded, but relinquished. Each garment left him more exposed, less defined, until he stood bare before her, unsure whether he had been stripped or revealed. Her eyes never wavered. They held him still, not with force, but with recognition. She was not watching his body. She was reading what lived beneath it.

Naked now, his muscles tight, breath uneven, Jared felt arousal rise, not as appetite, but as release. He no longer knew whether he was preparing for something to begin or something to end. He felt himself disassembled into sensation, each part aware of itself in a way it had never been before.

Pythia moved to her knees.

The light met her skin without sound. She extended her hand, wrapping her fingers around him in a gesture that was both intimate and impersonal—an act performed not for effect but for alignment. Her movements were precise, controlled, free of tension. Jared's body responded instantly. A shiver ran through him, and the outer world retreated.

She took him into her mouth slowly.

The motion was unhurried, steady. She seemed guided by something internal, a rhythm he could not hear but could feel in the way her body moved in sync with his. His awareness narrowed to sensation. Every nerve sharpened. Thought became disorganized. There was no distance between touch and meaning. Identity itself began to dissolve, familiar boundaries crumbling beneath the weight of feeling.

Just before the breaking point, she withdrew.

Without speaking, she lay back on the bed and opened herself to him, not with demand, not with urgency, but with full permission. He moved to her, guided less by will than by necessity, and entered her.

What met him was not just warmth, not just depth. It was presence, total and immediate. She did not receive him passively. She absorbed him, met him, held him with a stillness that magnified everything. The connection was not confined to skin or rhythm. It lived deeper, in the space where memory and inheritance reside.

Something in him broke.

Not in pain. Not in fear. But in recognition. A barrier long held against sorrow and longing gave way. What spilled out was not despair, but the truth of his need. It engulfed, unfiltered and unguarded.

He did not resist.

There was no reason to.

His release came not as ecstasy alone, but as collapse, a storm breaking through the final barricade of a self built to endure. That wall would never rise again. And in the exposed chamber of his being, raw and defenseless, the old griefs would gather, unguarded and unready, for the long march of sorrow yet to come.

They made love again, and yet again, each time more freely, more tenderly, until they became less man and woman and more two forces of nature in temporary alignment. When dawn finally crept in through the window, Jared lay beside her in a holy exhaustion. He had never known a deeper sense of being.

He had crossed some mythic border and come through not untouched, but reconfigured.

~

In the days that followed, their lovemaking became an act of communion. They spoke afterward in quiet tones, exploring what had passed between them, inventing a language of mutual unfolding. Their intimacy deepened, not with possession, but with awe.

Yet time, indifferent to rapture, continued its crawl. Their days in the little house grew short. The nearer their departure loomed, the more urgent their lovemaking became. It was frantic, tender, both desperate not to forget the shape of each other. Jared noticed one thing: Pythia never again turned her naked back to him. She would not reveal her hump a second time.

That vision, the living stories beneath her skin, the ancestral archive in motion, was a singular gift, and a dangerous one. Once was enough. Perhaps too much.

She had shown him what no human had ever seen. And now she withheld it, not out of shame, but reverence.

Some stories are not meant for repeated viewing. Some are reserved for those who will follow her path, not as partners, but as kin.

~ *The Ripple Grows* ~

Jared told himself once was enough. Yet the truth gnawed at him: hunger always returns. To see again, to know again—not only the power of her flesh, but the terrifying radiance of her superiority. And one day, he feared it would consume him.

Chapter Twenty-Six

To Work

Urban Horror

~ Alarming News ~

On the morning of their departure, the air holds weight, dense with meanings that remain unspoken. Yet Pythia and Jared move with quiet steadiness. There is no rush in their gestures, no panic in their eyes. The suitcases are zipped and waiting by the door.

The essentials have been checked and rechecked.

They have reached the threshold of departure, and both seem ready to cross.

The final cups of coffee sit cooling in their hands, the aroma still drifting upward. No one drinks much.

The conversation is sparse, measured in glances and half-finished thoughts. Across the table, Ming-huà and Zookeeper are present but distant, each carrying their own reluctance in silence.

The room is subdued. Not heavy, but suspended—held in that narrow space before goodbye, where everything feels more vivid, more fragile, and more awkward.

Time seems unwilling to move forward, but the moment won't last. They all know it. And still, they stay a little longer, breathing in the quiet, holding back whatever needs to be said for another time.

Finally:

"Give our best to Sy, Altan, and Lady Oracle," Ming-huà says.

The words have barely left her lips when Pythia rises from her seat, gaze already shifting toward the front door.

"Come in," she calls, voice serene.

Jared, though hearing no knock, no shuffle of approaching feet, doesn't question it. By now, he's learned not to resist the strange synchronicities of her mind.

A few heartbeats later, Sy materializes, his silhouette framed in the open doorway. He removes his floppy hat with exaggerated flair and sweeps a grand bow, as if stepping onto a stage. "Behold, the curtain rises—whether for comedy or tragedy, we shall see."

"Scarecrow!" exclaims Ming-huà. "So good to see you!"

Zookeeper grins. "Yeah, likewise. So, still playing the jester, or finally ready to offer your skull to Hamlet for a proper moan about life and death?"

Sy cackles. "My skull is still encased in all that juicy gray matter. It sloshes around like seawater most days, but I've yet to puke into the wind. That must count for something."

Then, as abruptly as he arrived, he halts and turns to Ming-huà with uncharacteristic gravity. "Well then. You ready?"

Pythia tilts her head. "Your presence was not anticipated. Not even by me."

"Always expect the unexpected, darling," Sy replies, tapping his nose. "I've come to chaperone you and your beloved back to San Francisco."

"Why?" asks Jared, his tone clipped, a defensive edge masking the old unease of being the outsider.

"So I can brief you. Vacation's over." His grin flashes, sharp as a blade. "You won't be staying in San Francisco long. Not even long enough for a fly to dodge the swatter."

"Where to, then?" Pythia asks, her voice light but her posture keen.

"Long story," says Sy, with a glance at Jared. "We'll get into it on the road. You too, youngster."

Jared says nothing. The old sensation returns of being a peripheral figure in someone else's myth.

"Well," Sy continues, "if you must press me—where to from San Francisco?" He spreads his arms in mock sincerity. "I don't know."

Ming-huà chuckles. "Lady Oracle keeping you in the dark again, Scarecrow?"

He pulls a tragic face. "Yes."

Sy clutches his chest in mock agony. "Yes, the jester carries the tidings no king can bear. Tough being just a fuckin' messenger . . . but remember, even fools deliver fate."

Sy eyes Pythia with mischief. "Speaking of sucking, I assume you enjoyed your little vacation?" He winked, then lowered his voice. "Enjoy it well, Jared. Honeymoons are brief. History has sharper teeth."

Jared flushes red, but Pythia only laughs. "Indeed. Sorry it's over. I'm eager to begin."

"Begin?" Jared echoes, still blushing. "Begin what?"

"Work," Sy answers, smoothly. "She expects great things from Pythia."

Zookeeper glances sideways at Ming-huà, looking for a flicker of resentment.

But Ming-huà merely smiles and shakes her head. "Don't worry, sweet one. I'm happy to be put out to pasture. Especially here. Pythia has the mind for it. I was always just a stepping stone, and gladly so."

Pythia steps forward and kisses her mother's cheek. "You are much more than that. Both of you. Without you, there would be void. No path. No hope."

"Well said!" cries Sy. "And with that, we go. Otherwise, we'll miss the boat."

~ *Return* ~

The drive back toward San Francisco winds through a haze of shifting sunlight and silence. Sy, true to form, refuses to be useful. He tells jokes. Rambles about trivialities. Anything but what matters. Then, out of nowhere, he mutters: "When the rooster crows at midnight, don't follow the feathers."

Jared rolls his eyes, but Pythia's gaze sharpens.

"I thought you were going to brief us," Pythia finally says, her voice sharp beneath its calm. "You really have no idea?"

"None," he replies.

But she hears something in his voice—regret, perhaps. Or sorrow. Or the quiet ache of uncertainty. She glances at Jared. He is staring dreamily out the window, blissfully unaware of what awaits them.

And at that moment, she wonders: do I love him, by the human definition of love?

The answer is clear. No.

She feels no possessiveness, no hunger, no delusion of fusion. Jared is not a singular beloved, but a small part of a vast and troubled whole. She sees in him not a man, but a species. One for whom she feels deep empathy. And deeper sorrow.

She remembers that first night—how she had tried, for his sake, to understand human desire. Had even experimented with lipstick, mascara, paint-on femininity. The whole masquerade. But in the mirror, it felt obscene. Like a wolf trying to purr. She had washed it off with a kind of spiritual nausea.

Yet the outcome had been . . . satisfactory. She is, even now, monitoring her body for signs of conception.

From the driver's seat, Sy glances at her in the rear-view mirror. Something unreadable flickers in his expression before he quickly looks away. The gesture unnerves her. Something unsaid. Something waiting.

The San Francisco skyline unfurls in the distance—a memory rising from fog.

Her limbs tense—not in fear, but readiness. Her mind sharpens. She is a coil of potential, a predator waiting for the gate to lift.

And when they are finally ushered into the front parlor of the Victorian house, Lady Oracle's words are exactly what she expects. What she has longed for.

"Are you ready," Lady Oracle asks, eyes luminous, "to be released from all artificial restraints?"

"More than ready."

"Yes," says Lady Oracle looking askance at Jared. "You have already flaunted your independence."

"To good purpose," says Pythia.

"We shall see."

Jared squirms.

Altan, stoic and stony-faced as always, notices his discomfort and comes to Jared's defense. "Jared will be the father. Although not possessed of Pythia's powers, he is a good man, intelligent, and will, I believe, be a loyal and devoted friend. There will come a time when he will be tested." At this statement, Altan looks at Jared and says sternly, "You will be torn by loyalties that may present unspeakable choices to a human being. Let science and reason guide you, as they have done up to now."

Jared replies firmly. "As I have always tried to do. If I had not adhered my entire life to the two touchstones you mentioned, I dare say I would not be here now."

Sy jumps up and twirls. "Well said! The dog may bark, but the moon remembers." He collapses into laughter, leaving Jared bewildered.

Lady Oracle is unmoved. "We shall see."

Even as these words are leaving her mouth, Pythia is gazing proudly at Jared as if her favorite dog just won the Grand National. At least, this is how Jared himself interprets her look, and as evidence of his evolving view of himself and his place in the world, he is not dissatisfied with Pythia's attitude. Sometimes, it still shocks him to realize how far he has come in depending upon Pythia's good graces and craving her reinforcing pats. He has stopped flailing in the great sea of her being. Now he floats, waiting to be called forth by the mesmerizing feel of her gentle waves lapping against his body.

Lady Oracle looks around regally and says, "I know you are ready for this task. In any case, you will be traveling abroad, but will still be close. Staying in this country is out of the question due to the questions that would be raised. At the place you are going, you will be exercising your powers in an environment not unlike what *Homo sapiens* ancestors dealt with—Nature red in tooth and claw, to paraphrase Mr. Tennyson."

"I understand."

"Neither we, nor you, really understand the extent of your powers. Your mother was tested, and she displayed, in a limited way, what these powers can do. But, in Ming-huà's case, the result of her actions devastated her gentle nature and almost destroyed her physically. You are different, but the extent of that difference is a major unknown. You are familiar with human trafficking, I presume?"

"Of course."

"If you agree, we would like to send you to Tijuana, Mexico, a notorious center for human trafficking and one of the most dangerous cities on the planet. You will know what to do once you get there. Jared can go with you if he is willing, but in any case, Altan will also be there watching over the. . . . "

Lady Oracle lapses into silence.

"Experiment!" exclaims Jared in disgust.

"No, I think 'test run' is a better description," replies Lady Oracle placidly.

"It's out of the question," says Jared. "It's far too dangerous. I mean, for *God*'s sake, she might already be pregnant! Did you think of that?"

Before Lady Oracle can respond, Pythia says, "No, it is fine, Jared, but thank you for your concern. It will not be dangerous for me."

"How do you know that? Is this how you intend to start a new species? By killing off one of its first individuals? And perhaps an unborn child to boot?"

Lady Oracle continues calmly, "*Her* goals are twofold: reduce suffering and elevate genus *Homo* to a new level."

"*Her*?" asks Jared.

"Who others before you have called *Goddess*."

"Yes, I've heard the name. A term of convenience, I presume?"

"In a manner of speaking. Purely metaphorical."

"Who, or what, is this *Goddess*?" demands Jared.

"That is beyond your purview."

Pythia looks sympathetically at Jared and tries to take the sting out of Lady Oracle's admonishment. "My great-grandparents, my grandparents, my mother, have all dealt with this entity before. As Lady Oracle said, the term is only metaphorical. I will give you the details later."

"Pythia," says Lady Oracle. "You know what you have to do. Can your powers carry you through the furnace of natural selection at its most extreme?"

"I am confident," says Pythia.

"I'm not," objects Jared. He is struggling with the more selfish notion of living in the most crime-ridden sections of Tijuana. "Remember, I don't have your powers."

Altan nods agreement. "True. Best you stay here."

Instantly, Jared feels guilty, and tries to backtrack. "Well, I didn't mean I wouldn't go, just that it will be difficult."

"I agree with Altan, I think you should stay here," says Pythia. "If you stay here, I won't have to worry about you."

"Your decision, Jared," says Lady Oracle. "But you don't have much time to decide. Pythia and Altan leave day after tomorrow."

He does not hesitate, but bursts out defiantly, "Then, in that case, I'm going. No arguments!"

Jared feels a bit foolish after this outburst, but he takes comfort in the lack of pushback by anyone in the room. Perhaps, just perhaps, he will have more influence than they currently give him credit for. After all, a physicist must surely be more useful for survival purposes than an uneducated layman.

To his dismay, Pythia says in a scolding tone, "Such thoughts are quite foolish, Jared. You should know better."

~ *Arrival in Mexico* ~

Lady Oracle had selected their destination with deliberate precision—a choice equal parts strategy and symbol. Pythia and Jared would be checking in to a motel called Vargas, a derelict stain in the infamous red-light district of Tijuana—Zona Norte, known locally and globally as the Hong Kong district. A place where even nightmares feel redundant. Altan would operate as an independent shadow, never far, never seen, always near enough to intervene should things go awry. During her preparations, Lady Oracle had considered several international destinations. All were grim contenders. But Tijuana ranked near the top of the global index for violent crime, and Zona Norte stood as its darkest artery. Human trafficking here was not just endemic, it was engineered. More profitable than the drug trade, more efficient than arms smuggling. Six-year-old girls to teenagers, sold again and again in a single day.

A crack rock can only be used once. A body can be used endlessly.

Lady Oracle had spoken with bitter clarity before their departure.

"There is more slavery now than at any point in human history," she said, her tone a chilling frost on glass. "The suffering endured by millions of girls—girls discarded before they even reach adulthood—is suffering at its most distilled. Most never escape. Not after years. Not after lifetimes. They are used, broken, polluted daily, sometimes hourly, by the insatiable appetites of predators. Men. Women. Entire systems. And of those countless victims, less than one percent are ever saved. The rest? Hollowed out. Mindless. The walking dead."

She turned her gaze to Jared. "Now imagine, if you will, that such girls had Pythia's powers. Imagine if every one of them did."

Jared had recoiled. "A bloodbath," he said. "It would be chaos. The world would burn."

"Perhaps," Lady Oracle murmured. "Or perhaps . . . a world finally forced to behave. Peace, not by consent, but by mutually assured destruction."

Her eyes slid to Pythia. "Especially if such power were paired with heightened intelligence. And an empathy beyond what humans have ever known."

~

Once in Tijuana, Pythia and Jared check-in to the Motel Vargas and peruse the sparse, dirty, bleak room; he with dismay, she with satisfaction.

"Perfect," says Pythia.

"For what, a cockroach?"

"Jared, it provides some degree of anonymity. There is a large Asian population here in Tijuana. I have Asian blood, my skin is dark, and hopefully, I will—"

"Blend in," interjects Jared morosely. "I've heard it before."

"I will be fine."

"Until you're kidnapped and raped."

"Jared, you know I will not allow myself to be raped. You must not underestimate my powers, nor should you underestimate my intelligence. You have done so in the past and been burned."

"Maybe, but you do not possess this kind of intelligence; the streetwise kind, the kind you need to survive out there."

Pythia snorts dismissively. "Why do you think my father was chosen to mate with mother? Zookeeper's raw survival-savvy blood runs in me."

"Yeah, and look what happened to him."

"Yes, but not by the actions of his vicious comrades, but by mother herself."

Jared assumes his sarcastic face. "Are you planning to remove a lot of arms? Legs? Heads?"

Pythia's expression hardens. "If necessary to free these girls from the hell they are in. Unfortunately, I have to do this undetected. My hump will mark me as unusual, which although something I can use to my advantage, is also something that will stand out to witnesses, and worse, to the police."

"Aren't they all corrupt? I've heard they are in the pockets of the cartels."

"Not all. And another consideration is that Tijuana is right on the border with the U.S., so word will spread north, if I am not careful."

"Bottom line is that I am to sit around this disgusting room and wait? I'll be sick with worry."

"I'll be in touch, Altan will be in touch, and if I become incommunicado, that means I am succeeding."

"Or dead."

Pythia shakes her head. "You're incorrigible. Enjoy the sights. Catch up on the latest in physics. Be a tourist."

"You're the latest in physics and I can't even catch up with you! And as for being a tourist, this isn't exactly Paris."

"Jared, I can't deal with this now. Do your best. Remember, you had the chance to stay in San Francisco."

"True, I'm here because I've actually fallen in love with you, even though that particular concept is not in your vocabulary—or rather, in your genes. Anyway, you're right. Let's take a taxi to a nicer part of town and have a good dinner."

"Yes, okay. A last supper, if you will. Tomorrow, Jared, I'm on the street and we may not see each other for some time."

~ *On the Street* ~

By morning, Pythia has transformed herself into something plain. She dresses in worn, shapeless clothing—the kind worn by those who have long since stopped being noticed. Her goal is simple: appear lost, appear desperate. Appear disposable. She chooses "María" as her name, the most common and forgettable of names. No rings. No makeup. Just a pair of earrings, which she loathes the moment she clasps them on. She hates costumes. She hates pretending. But she knows what must be done.

The absence of Spanish in her linguistic arsenal is a liability, but not a fatal one. Tijuana speaks many languages, chief among them, the language of predation. And predators, almost universally, understand English. Still, she rehearses her cover story. Polishes its edges. Projects it from her hump in soft, helpless frequencies. She is not merely performing a role; she is shaping a myth of vulnerability. A dark flicker of amusement crosses her mind: how might a Homo sapiens woman act to fit into Neanderthal society? The rules would be the same: dull the intellect, stifle the voice, avoid eye contact, yield to physicality, radiate fear. Above all, do not appear intelligent. It is hardest, she knows, to erase the light from one's eyes. But she does it.

At dusk, draped in anonymity and certainty, she steps out of Motel Vargas. Behind her, the door shuts with a sharp finality, and Jared, riddled with helpless dread, feels the full weight of that gut-wrenching sound.

~

The first two nights reveal almost nothing. Only faint vibrations drift through the margins, subtle pulses in the air that hint at a presence. Someone is tracking her, but from a distance too great to define. The shape is still forming. The intention is not yet clear.

Tijuana moves as it always has, caught in its endless cycle of survival and performance. The streets heave with noise and hunger. Crowds pour along the boulevards, restless and indifferent. Vendors line the curbs with tables of useless items, calling out to passersby with practiced desperation. Children with hollow eyes peddle gum to strangers who pretend not to hear. Musicians fill the air with songs that no one really listens to. Tourists smile nervously, uncertain whether they are spectators or targets.

The taco stands flare with smoke and oil. The food is fast, the heat overwhelming.

Men gather in loud, uneven clusters—some boasting, others watching. Laughter spills out in bursts too sharp to be careless. Beneath it all, a low current of menace hums.

There are predators here, but for now, they are content to wait.

And the one she feels behind her, the true danger, still does not reveal himself.

He stays just beyond reach. Her hump registers him not as a figure, but as a frequency: low, distorted, almost melodic in its cruelty. He drifts through the city's undercurrent like a presence half-formed, yet unmistakably real. He is close. He is deliberate. And he does not make mistakes.

She senses him hovering in the corners of her awareness. He is never bold enough to approach, never foolish enough to flee. A pressure against the edge of her perception, steady and relentless.

He is not confused. He is studying her.

Once, she spots Altan.

He appears without warning, seated calmly in a folding chair while a boy shines his shoes. The gesture is ordinary, almost crude in its disguise, yet irrelevant. The force of him is intact. He radiates an authority that needs no display—utterly self-contained, wholly unreadable, profoundly intimidating. His eyes drift past her without pause. If he sees her, he does not grant recognition. He is not here to intervene. He is here to remind her: presence itself can be power. And to her, that power is comforting.

She knows it is not him she must fear.

The other one is closer. The one who does not look. The one who listens. His presence never wavers. His intent is sharp, silent, and watching.

Let him.

Each night, she follows the same pattern. She steps into roles with effortless control: the frightened newcomer, the desperate sister, the young woman willing to do almost anything for a few dollars. She lets her voice tremble at just the right moments. She lowers her eyes. She asks questions designed to travel. How does one meet a coyote? Where do the jobs pay in cash? Who might be kind to a woman in need?

Every word is planted.

She does not chase him. She waits for him to collect what she leaves behind.

He believes he is watching her.

But she is watching him.

The only complication is losing him before she returns to the motel. He must not follow. Not yet. Only when she's certain she's not being tailed does she reappear at the door, stepping back into the sour fluorescent dimness of the motel and into Jared's tightly coiled relief.

~ *Contact* ~

The third evening unfolds like the last, but this time the air vibrates with subtle change.

Pythia wears the same drab disguise. Walks the same circuit. Adopts the same posture of resigned confusion.

She passes Altan again, this time hunched at a taco stand, devouring his meal with practiced indifference. They do not acknowledge one another. Not even a flick of the eyes.

Some of the locals recognize her now. Familiarity softens their suspicion. A few prostitutes even nod in her direction, bored queens of the asphalt jungle leaning against crumbling walls, skirts barely concealing their sexual theater. One of them, thick-limbed and glassy-eyed, regards Pythia with a clouded expression. Pythia probes gently. The woman's thoughts arrive in broken fragments: pity for the hump, curiosity, admiration, and finally, fear. Fear that this strange beauty might be a rival. A novelty. A threat.

And then, he returns.

The signal hits like a shiver beneath the skin. Her hump pulses. He is close. Closer than ever. She scans the street. Lights shimmer. Shadows blur. But again—nothing. He is here, but unseen. Watching from behind one of a thousand faceless masks. Her body knows before her mind does. She veers instinctively away from the light, toward the alleyways where predators stalk their offerings. She walks as her mother once did: soft steps, lowered eyes, luring a hunter into range.

At the edge of a darkened alley, she pauses.

And he comes.

A silhouette moves beneath a jaundiced streetlight. It is massive and lumbering. But it is not a man. It is a woman. Big hair, large breasts, wide hips squeezed into fishnet and lace. Her makeup is thick enough to qualify as armor. Everything about her screams excess and distortion. For a moment, Pythia feels a flicker of disappointment. This grotesque parody was not what she expected. But she adjusts. Every predator wears a mask. She tunes her hump sharply toward the woman. The feedback is immediate, and jarring. Her senses scramble. The signal is a cacophony, layered, confused. Her receptors flood with noise.

And then comes the voice.

"*Hola, cariño,*" the woman purrs. "*¿Necesitas ayuda?*"

"I don't speak Spanish. I'm Chinese. My father brought me here, but went back to China."

"Why didn't he take you, *cariño*?" asks the woman in almost perfect English.

"We fought. I'm alone."

"Where are you from?"

"Michoacan. My father had a store."

"Oh, *cariño*, you do need help. *Pobre bebé!*"

Pythia feigns nervousness and cringes back. "No, not really."

"Oh, *cariño*, I think you do. Are you lost?"

"I'm trying to find work."

"Here? In Zona Norte? Near a dark alley? *Cariño*, you must truly be lost in the head, or have suicide on the mind. You can be attacked here. Murdered. Raped." The woman leans forward for a closer look. "Are you *loco*?"

"No."

"*¿Cómo te llamas?*"

"What?"

"Your name, *cariño*. What is your name?"

"María."

"Ah! Not very Chinese, is it?"

"My real name is Meiying," Pythia replies, allowing herself the flicker of a private smile.

"Well then, María or Meiying or whoever you are—come with me," the woman coaxes, her voice honeyed with false promise. "I'll take you to a safe place. A shelter for girls."

Pythia tilts her head. "Where?"

"A church-run place. A priest. A good man. You'll be safe. Might even find work."

But even as the words pour out, something is wrong. Pythia feels it not in the sound, but in the air around the speaker—an invisible dissonance, an off-note in an otherwise perfect performance. She cannot place it. The incongruity floats just beyond comprehension, teasing her attention, resisting identification.

Then, it strikes. Not gently. Not subtly. It crashes into her with the force of a slap.

This is no woman. This is a man.

She releases a quiet, involuntary gasp.

"What's wrong, *cariño*?" the woman asks, eyes narrowing.

Pythia makes a snap decision. No performance now. Just the truth, a stone dropped into still water.

"You're a man."

The voice drops. It loses all pretense, uncoiling into a low, wolfish growl. "Well. Smarter than you look."

The wig comes off with a practiced flourish. Beneath it, a broad, satisfied grin spreads across a masculine face.

"Actually, I'm with the *policía*. Undercover. Here to help girls like you."

A lie, of course. Obvious, clumsy. But now, the roles have reversed. Pythia is no longer prey. She is the net tightening.

"Oh thank you, sir," she says softly, infusing her voice with feigned tremor. "I'm so scared. I don't know where to go. Please . . . help me."

He nods with faux reassurance. "Just come with me to my car. We'll go to the station. You'll get food. Counseling. Everything will be okay. Come on, María. We'll get you fixed up."

She lowers her eyes, steps closer, follows him meekly.

Inside, she is still as stone.

The trap is closing. The iron door is about to clang shut. And this time, she is the one holding the keys.

A single flick of her will, and the hunter will learn soon enough what it means to be prey.

Chapter Twenty-Seven

Into the Snake Pit

First Blood

As they approach the parked vehicle, Pythia sees it for what it is: a white cargo van, old and unmarked, with no windows in the back. A second man stands beside the driver's door, smoking and nodding to the beat of some inane pop song blaring from the radio. Her hump begins to surge, sensing their hostility not as words or gestures but as a frequency, hot, serrated, and crackling with tension. Then, layered beneath that, another signal emerges: faint moans, muffled sobbing. Many voices. Inside the van. The sound is inaudible to the men. But not to her.

She does not react.

Instead, she follows in silence, her posture meek, her face drawn into the mask of helplessness she has rehearsed so well. When they reach the rear of the van, her stalker throws open the back doors. The stench of despair spills out first, followed by the unmistakable chorus of crying girls. The moaning is no longer hidden. It pierces the night.

Pythia recoils instinctively. "What are you doing? Aren't we going to the police station?"

The man laughs, a dry, vicious bark. "Don't worry. Just some *putas* on their way to jail. Get in!"

She stumbles back. Tries to run. Just enough to make it look real. He grabs her roughly and hurls her into the van. She lands hard, knees scraping the metal floor. Behind her, the doors slam. The lock snaps shut with a brutal finality. The dim interior stinks of sweat and tears. Benches line the walls, each crowded with the hunched forms of girls, some as young as six, others near adulthood. All trembling. All silent save for the soft sounds of weeping. No one speaks. There is no need. Still crouched on the floor, Pythia pulls a small flashlight from beneath her shirt. She clicks it on for just long enough to scan the faces. Wide eyes. Tear-streaked cheeks. Arms wrapped around knees or siblings. Bodies pressed together in mute solidarity, in horror. She switches the light off. Then sits cross-legged in the dark, arms hugging her knees, radiating stillness.

She will wait. She will not act. Not yet.

Her purpose now is containment. Delay. The longer she maintains the guise of helplessness, the more intelligence she gathers—the more lives she can preserve, the more predators she can neutralize. A few of the girls glance toward her. They don't seem alarmed by her hunchback. What disturbs them is her calm. Her unnatural quiet. In a place like this, stillness is not a virtue. It's madness. Or ignorance. One face stays with her, a girl of ten, whispering comfort into the ear of a sobbing younger sister. Arms wrapped protectively around the child.

Pythia's blood rises. Her body tenses.

She could end this now. Obliterate the two men. Tear the doors from their hinges. Walk the girls out into the night and be a shining saint.

But the belly of the beast awaits. There is more to see. More to do.

From the darkness, a girl's voice rises.

"*¿De dónde eres, hermana?*"

Pythia turns her head toward the voice. "*No hablo español.*"

"English?"

"Yes."

"I thought so. You look different."

"Part Chinese."

"Ah. Makes sense." The girl's tone carries grudging respect. "Rogelio finally got me. Looks like he got you too. How'd he do it?"

"The usual," Pythia replies.

"Not me. Not the usual. I don't fall for that bullshit. He waited until I dropped my guard. Put a knife to my throat. Bastard."

"Who is he?"

"*El Diablo*," the girl spits. "Works for one of the cartels. A fucking animal. Been wanting to rape me for months. Guess he'll get his chance now."

"*Y un centenar de hombres más también,*" another voice mutters in the dark.

"Yeah. A hundred others. Let them try. I'll fight."

"What's your name?" Pythia asks.

"Luciana. Yours?"

"María."

A brief pause, then Luciana stifles a sob.

"Don't worry, Luciana," Pythia says gently. "I'll fight with you."

~

The van lurches to a stop after only a short drive. One by one, the girls and women are herded out into the night.

Before them rises a hulking industrial structure, its silhouette jagged against the distant haze of city lights. It looks abandoned, faceless, windowless, a graveyard of concrete and rust. But it breathes. Men line the walkway to its entrance, rifles slung over their shoulders, eyes hollow with the indifference of the damned. The girls are driven forward up the steps and into the maw of the building. Inside, they are separated, some taken down corridors, others ushered up stairwells into dim, empty rooms. The only furnishings are stained mattresses scattered across cold concrete floors. Pythia loses sight of Luciana. She is taken higher, to a room near the top of the building. When the door opens, she finds three girls already there, standing, shivering, their bare feet on dirty cement. Their nightdresses are little more than rags. Two look around fifteen. One could be twelve.

An armed man gestures for her to enter, then steps in behind and grunts toward a battered cardboard box in the corner.

"*Ropa*," he says, pointing. Clothes.

Pythia hesitates. He scowls. She strips down to her underwear, folding her clothes and placing them in the box. Then, covering herself with crossed arms, she stands still as the man stares, eyes crawling over her body like slugs.

He grins and tosses her a thin, soiled nightgown. "*Jorobada! Ganar mucho dinero!*" he brays, mimicking a jackal. "*Aiee! Quiero follarla!*"

"I don't understand," she says flatly.

He tilts his head, mocking. "*No hablas español, jorobada?*"

"No," she replies—then adds, too quietly for the others to hear, "Are you fond of your body parts, señor?"

"*¿Qué?*"

From across the room, the oldest girl speaks in a deadpan voice. "*Dijo que eres bien parecido. Supongo que las chicas te quieren.*"

The man narrows his eyes, suspicious. But she keeps her face blank, indifferent. He steps closer to Pythia, breath hot with the stink of sweat and rotting fish. She forces herself not to recoil. Her mind begins to inventory his punishments. But her body remains still, her expression frightened. A perfect performance. He laughs again and gives her one last leering look before slamming the door behind him. The lock clicks.

Silence.

Pythia turns to the older girl. "Do you speak English?"

"Yes."

"What did you say to him?"

"I told him you said he was handsome. That all the girls must want him."

Pythia allows a brief laugh to escape. "Why?"

"That man, Mateo, is one of the cruelest. If he thinks you're mocking him, he'll make you pay. That was my way of buying you a little time."

"Thank you. What's your name?"

"Elena. Yours?"

"Maria."

"Where are you from?"

"That's . . . a long story. My father's Chinese. We lived in Michoacán before he left me and returned to China."

"So you're stuck here?"

"Yes."

Elena nods grimly. "Well, you're really stuck now, sister. We're slaves. And every hour is hell."

"That's why you lied to him?"

"I lied because I've seen what happens when you don't. He'd stick a broken bottle inside you and twist. He's done worse."

"Thanks for the warning. What happens next?"

"Sleep. In the morning, rice and beans. Then the customers come."

"And if I refuse?"

Elena's voice goes flat. "Then I can't help you."

Pythia shifts her tone. "How long have you been here?"

At that, Elena begins to tremble. The words come brittle, fast, as if torn from her.

"Years. I don't count anymore. I let them take me instead of my sister. I pushed her away, told her to run. I took her place. And thank God, she got away. But me .. . I've been here ever since. And now I'm hollow. Something broke—down there, and in here." She taps her chest, then her head. "After a thousand fucks, and a thousand more, I'll die, or be killed, or kill myself. Doesn't matter. *Mi hermana está a salvo.* My sister is safe."

She looks at Pythia, eyes hollow. "Soon, you'll understand, Maria. Men are spiders. We are flies."

Pythia watches her carefully. "You sound sad, but also smart. Why haven't you escaped?"

"I tried. Many times. But they always find me. Or the police return me. Every time, the beatings get worse. The rapes get worse. After a while . . . I gave up. There's nothing left."

"The police?"

"Pigs," Elena spits. Then, collecting herself, she grunts, "Sleep. You'll need it to survive."

"One more question. How did you learn to speak such good English?"

"I used to study. Wanted to be a teacher. Help my people. That was before."

Pythia's voice is soft. "You will help them. I promise."

"No," Elena murmurs. "You'll see. Now sleep."

~ *Contemplating Chess* ~

Pythia does not sleep. She lies motionless in the corner, her breath slow, her body obedient—but within, her mind contracts, drawn to a single point, refined by silence, honed on the whetstone of superior genes. The darkness becomes a chessboard. The enemy's pieces are crude but well-positioned: pawns with guns, bishops with knives, kings wearing the crowns of sadism. She knows the first rule: protect the Queen. Herself.

No man will enter her body.

This rule narrows her options but defines the board. To violate it, even in pretense, would be like a human forced to mate with walruses, she thinks with clinical revulsion: obscene not merely in the physical sense, but in the genetic, the spiritual. These men are not simply evil, they are polluted matter, warped flesh, aberrant echoes of a species long past deserving continuation. So she calculates.

Every move she might make comes with its counter. Each advantage has a price. Sacrifices may be required, but not the Queen. Never the Queen.

Briefly, her mind flickers to Jared. Could she be pregnant already? Her period is late, but not conclusively so. If she is pregnant, then further violations won't end in biological catastrophe, but the disgust remains. And what would be gained by playing along? Time. But time for what?

Time to locate the apex. The head of the cartel. If she can reach him—see him, speak to him—the thoughts will betray the rest. Names cannot remain hidden in the presence of her gift. From there, it's a matter of climbing: head by head, room by room. All the way to checkmate.

But how to ascend without being used? How to ask without appearing to know? How to harvest meaning from minds that think in Spanish? These would be real problems for others. Not for her. She's already solved them. The question now is refinement. How precise can she be? Can she sever with elegance? Can she remove a fragment of anatomy, surgically, without triggering alarm? Or will she mar the flesh too broadly, drawing suspicion, compromising her hand? It will be a test of finesse under fire. A trial not just of her will, but of her artistry.

By the time the sun begins to rise and dust motes drift across the concrete like ash from some invisible fire, she is prepared, not for one single plan, but for dozens. Variations on a theme of rescue and retribution. Each contingent. Each alive. Her opening move: Rogelio.

Pawn? Knight? Hard to say. But clearly advanced, respected by the others, feared by some. A minor noble in this filthy court of cruelty. Today, she begins with him.

And by nightfall, if fortune allows, he will no longer exist.

~ *The First Day* ~

The first day of her captivity turns out to be a disappointment. After eating their meager breakfast of rice and beans, Mateo appears with three men. Pythia uses her telepathic powers to determine two of the men are wealthier Americans, and one is Mexican, middle-class by the look of his clothes. Mateo is disgustingly obsequious toward the men, but glares at the girls with an unmistakable message to cooperate or else. Already the twelve-year-old, whose name is Margarita but called *mija* by the girls, is crying and whimpering, while the others try to console her. Mateo scowls at their behavior and orders them to line up in front of the customers, and snarls, "*Tira!*"

"Take off your clothes, Maria," says Elena under her breath. Mateo hears, but allows her to interpret.

Standing naked, the girls whimper as the men inspect their bodies, turning them this way and that, probing the most private places.

When Pythia is ordered to turn around and face backward by one of the men, an American, he takes one look at her hump, steps back and shakes his head. "No, no. No good! Ugly!"

Mateo shows his teeth. "No, *amigo*, pretty. Very pretty *jorobada!*"

"No!" exclaims the man, then says in bad Spanish, "*Muy malo!*"

"Want another?" asks Mateo in bad English.

"*Si,*" says the man, turning to the twelve-year-old. "This one. *Muy bonita!*"

Mateo pulls Margarita forward and hands her to him, saying, "*Si, la hijita es muy bonita!*" She cries out, but there is no one to help. The American pulls her out of the room, saying, "Quit your crying little girl," he says vexingly. "I'll make you feel better." He winks at the other American and adds, "And she'll make me feel better, eh, Bud?" Pythia is frozen, agonized that she has to stick to her plan or else lose everything.

Mateo now turns to the Mexican, still undecided. He gestures toward Pythia. "*Ella es la major follodora!*"

Elena, on her way out with the other American who chose her, says over her shoulder, "Maria, you see? You see? Mateo told the man you are the best fucker."

"Shut-up, bitch!" says the American, jerking her elbow. "I have a little surprise waiting for smart ass wetbacks like you."

But Mateo's efforts are to no avail. The Mexican choses Juana, the other girl, and Pythia is left standing alone, naked, inwardly shaking with rage but outwardly meek and trembling, using all her energy to keep from erasing these men from the face of the earth. Mateo returns alone, fuming. He slaps Pythia hard across the face, but she has read his mind and avoids the worst of the impact. She pretends to fall down in pain and fear, which clearly give him pleasure.

"*Estúpita! Estúpita jorobada!*" He spits on her and stomps out.

This procedure occurred three more times that day, with the three girls always being chosen over Pythia. Late that night, when all are in the room, Pythia is struck at how subdued and broken they are. Eyes glazed, no affect, weary hopelessness and pain. Elena finally looks at Pythia.

"You're so lucky! I wish I had a hump! That bastard American liked to hurt me."

"Your luck will change soon, Elena. Trust me. Stay strong. Tell the others."

The second day is very different.

~ *The Second Day—An Error* ~

The morning routine is the same, but now only two men arrive: an American and a German.

The American chooses Elena.

The German sees Pythia's hump and stops dead. His mind erupts with vile imagery. Pythia recoils inwardly from the deluge of twisted fantasies. This one delights in filth. The more obscene, the more thrilling.

She turns, allowing him to see her back.

His thoughts become a fever of violence and lust.

"This one," he says, breathless. "This one, definitely!"

Mateo grins with that same oily joy. "*Muy bien, señor. Muy bien!*"

Pythia lowers her eyes and follows him meekly. Mateo exhales in relief.

They enter a squalid room, windowless and stinking, walls cracked like old wounds. A stained mattress lies on the floor.

The man reaches to kiss her. She steps back and turns around, letting him fondle her hump. His excitement is palpable.

Turning back to face him, she barks, "Strip."

As he begins undressing, she strikes—silently, surgically. His hands tremble. He claws at his private parts.

"*Irgendwas stimmt nicht!*" he howls.

Half-naked, he stumbles from the room in panic.

Down the hallway, a scream.

She smiles.

If she was precise, he will now piss blood. She severed his urethra from prostate to tip—no more erections, no more rape. Urination will require an incision and a drainage bag. Permanently.

She listens to the noise his condition creates, a devil's mix of concern, confusion, and alarm. Eventually, they send him away. No one can explain what happened.

She is not punished.

That night, she wrestles with herself. Was it strategy? Or revenge? If revenge, the guilt stings. If strategy, she feels clean.

~ *The Third Day—A Correction* ~

On the third morning, as the girls pick listlessly at their breakfast, Elena leans toward Pythia and whispers, "One of the girls who saw the German last night swears he only had half a penis."

Pythia, though outwardly unmoved, nods slightly. She's confident she had only meant to remove his urethra, an internal redirection, a disabling, not a dismemberment. But perhaps she'd gone too far. A slight miscalculation. It doesn't trouble her yet, but it warns her: refinement is essential. Future interventions must be limited to invisible damage, internal alterations that do not rouse suspicion. Still, she knows she must accelerate her plan. This cannot go on indefinitely. One slip and the illusion collapses. She must get past Mateo. She must reach Rogelio.

But fate offers no respite.

Soon after breakfast, Mateo appears with three new men. Pythia stands naked once again, the ritual now familiar, revolting. Mateo looks drawn, sullen and distracted, no doubt still reeling from the previous evening. To Pythia's quiet relief, none of the men select Margarita. But then one of them, the ugliest—a bloated American reeking of marijuana and stale beer—eyes her with lewd interest.

When he sees her hump, he grins. "I like ugly," he slurs. "But this one? Ugly-pretty. Never had one of them before. You like to fuck, honey?"

The stench of him is almost unbearable. Pythia turns to Elena. "Translate, please. Clearly. I want Mateo to understand every word."

Then, facing Mateo with perfect stillness, she says, "I will not fuck this bastard. Go tell Rogelio I want to speak to him. And tell him I know what happened to the German last night."

When Elena finishes relaying the message, Mateo explodes. Without warning, he punches Pythia hard in the stomach. The breath leaves her lungs as she collapses, then he kicks her twice in the ribs, screaming, *"¡La maldita perra! ¡La jodida jorobada!"*

Turning to the American, he says, all deference again, "You want another girl? I get you better girl. *Mucho mejor.*"

But the American is already licking his lips. "No. I want this one. Ugly-pretty and feisty. I like 'em feisty."

Mateo hesitates. "No, *señor*, I can—"

"I'll pay double."

Greed stabs through Mateo's rage, sharp rays of sunlight through fog. "Okay, *señor*. I bring her to you."

But the man grabs Pythia and hoists her off her feet. "Hell no! I'll carry the bitch myself. Show me the way!"

Pythia lets herself go limp in his arms, all her energy focused on calculation. *Now I've done it,* she thinks. *Think. Think harder.*

He carries her into a foul-smelling room and drops her on a stained mattress. As he strips off his clothes, his bulk jiggles obscenely. His body is plastered with grotesque tattoos. His penis is lost somewhere beneath folds of flesh.

Pythia watches impassively. Her plan is ready.

When he growls, "Put your mouth on my cock," she responds in a flat voice, "What cock?"

He blinks, confused. Then he reaches down, parts his belly, and stares. His eyes widen in horror.

"What the fuck?" he gasps.

Fear overtakes him. Panic follows.

He bolts from the room, pants barely up, howling, "I'll be back! Something's wrong! Oh shit—oh God—something's wrong!"

Pythia lies back and listens. A scream rises from the bathroom. It echoes with a sharp, agonizing finality. She smiles. This time, she had been precise. No external mutilation. Just a clean internal severance: total penectomy, the urethra rerouted to the perineum. Urine will still flow, but differently. No penis. No erection. No future rape.

Shouts swell in the hallway, confused and frantic. Mateo bursts in and hauls her back to the room. He says nothing. But his sweat, his twitching, the way his lips curl with hatred, all speak to his frenzied rage.

At the threshold, Pythia stops. The American is still sobbing somewhere out of sight, and cartel thugs mill about in impotent confusion. She turns to Mateo, calm as death.

"Tell Rogelio," she says coldly, "or whoever your boss is, I want to see him."

Mateo raises a trembling hand, but she lifts her own in warning.

"You touch me," she says, "and what happened to them happens to you. Get me your boss. Now."

His eyes roil with hatred, but beneath it, fear pulses in waves. He lowers his arm and walks her silently to the room, locking the door behind her. She sits. Waits. No one comes. The other girls do not return. She is not fed. Darkness falls, both literal and strategic. But Pythia remains patient. If necessary, she can vanish at any time. Yet something strange is unfolding, and her curiosity is piqued. She lies awake pondering the pattern, and finally, sometime before dawn, she falls asleep.

A dream claims her.

She stands alone on a jagged precipice, high above a vast plain teeming with people. The crowd is a blur, and they are screaming. The words are unclear, they rise either to worship her or to tear her down. She raises her arm in acknowledgment. That's when the stones begin to fly. Rocks pelt her body. Blood pours. She wonders how they hurl them so far, so high—*so much fury*. She tries to dissolve them with her mind, but they multiply instead. They shred her flesh until nothing remains.

When she wakes, the second day of isolation has begun. By afternoon, hunger gnaws at her. A change in strategy may be needed. Just then, a man she's never seen enters, holding a tray.

"Eat," he says.

"You speak English?"

"Yes."

"Where is Mateo?"

The man is unreadable. She probes his mind and finds only murk, no thoughts of his own, just a fog of obedience and the residue of implanted commands.

"Don't know," he mumbles. "Eat."

He locks the door behind him.

~ *Altan* ~

After the food is gone, another man enters. His English is better.

"A man has asked for you," he says. "Word's out on the street. Some men like *demonio* bitches. This one paid well. Rogelio says if you fuck him and all goes well, he'll speak with you. But if you refuse, or if something happens to the man, you die. No delay."

"I want to see Rogelio first."

"Shut up. Get naked. Wait." He leaves.

Now Pythia feels it—*the trap.*

Refuse, and her plan collapses. Act, and it may provoke suspicion or chaos. Freeing the girls now would mean a bloodbath. Fleeing would mean abandoning them. The head of the beast remains elusive.

She's still deciding when Mateo returns, eyes burning, hate trembling in his jaw. He steps aside, and another man enters. Tall, dark.

It is Altan.

Pythia does not move. She says nothing.

Mateo speaks: "*Aquí está ella, amigo. Inspecciona su cuerpo.*"

"*No hay necesidad,*" Altan replies smoothly. Then in English, "No need to inspect her."

"*Bien. Ven conmigo.*"

Altan shakes his head. "No. This room is fine."

"But, señor—"

"Leave. *Déjanos en paz.*"

Mateo obeys.

When the door closes, Altan looks at her. "How are you?"

"I'm fine."

His gold-and-blue eyes fix her in perfect stillness.

"Tell me everything."

She does.

When she's done, he nods. "Good. I'll say you serviced me well. Rogelio's clever, brutal, but not the head."

"The neck?" she says dryly.

"Yes. But severing the neck might buy you time."

"I have a plan. To get to the head, I will go through the neck."

"Good. I'll leave soon. Oh, Jared sends his love."

She rolls her eyes. "*Homo sapiens* males. So unstable. His love should be for all of them."

"Humans?"

"Yes. These girls. These sad little creatures we'll have to free . . . gently, when the time is right."

"If the time comes," Altan says softly. "Are you pregnant?"

"Yes, but you already knew."

Altan inclines his head, the faintest echo of a bow. His eyes, gold shot through with blue, hold hers with unflinching certainty.

"Then the clock has already started," he murmurs. "Every move you make now belongs not only to you, but to the one inside you. Remember that. The world will not wait. Neither will the hunters."

Pythia closes her eyes. For a heartbeat, she imagines the child stirring—whisper of promise, whisper of warning. She cannot tell which.

Outside the door, the hive of men stirs. Inside, the future has already begun.

Chapter Twenty-Eight

Off The Rails

Stubborn Alphas

~ Prelude to Disaster ~

After hearing Pythia's announcement, Altan settles cross-legged on the floor, stoicism etched across his face. He says nothing. Waits. Listens to something deeper than sound. Pythia studies him in silence.

With humans, she moves easily, even when flooded by their chaotic, emotion-saturated thoughts. But Altan, like Sy and Lady Oracle, belongs to another order entirely. Each conclusion only deepens the mystery.

First, there has never been doubt, not in her mother's mind nor her own, that they descend from a superior lineage.

Second, she cannot read them. Every attempt to penetrate their minds returns the same result: a thick, featureless fog, like a cosmic background hum, the residue of the universe's birthing pangs.

Third, and perhaps most troubling, she is certain they are immune to her powers. Even the most potent one, what Sy calls "object reconfiguration." She has rarely tested this, but instinct tells her it would fail. Worse, she is equally certain they possess abilities far beyond her own, on scales she cannot yet imagine.

Whenever she tries to classify them—gods, post-beings, mythic projections—she's met with mild disdain. Childish terms, they insist. Yet here she stands: naked before Altan, in the heart of a brutal cartel compound, surrounded by threats and consequences, and he gazes at her as if contemplating the tide. Not the grains of sand caught in its pull, but the tide itself. Aware of the whole, indifferent to the particular.

She wonders: what secret force moves behind his silence? What do they carry inside, the three of them, that renders her, the first of her kind, still so naive?

"Altan," she says finally, breaking the meditation. "What do you truly think of *Homo sapiens*?"

"Cobbled intermediates," he replies, eyes still closed. "Blinded by the glare of nascent intelligence. Unfinished."

"And me?"

"A step."

"And you?"

A faint smile. "Another step."

"Is there an end to the steps?"

"Yes and no. Extinction or adaptation."

"Some humans are trying," she says. "Multiculturalism. Environmentalism. Attempts to adapt."

Altan inclines his head in a gesture almost tender. "Some reach for multiculturalism. But even those rare few can't extend the concept beyond their species. They won't grant equal culture to elephants, ants, sparrows, sequoias, lobsters. They consume them instead. Devour everything in service of an unrelenting, gluttonous dream. As for environmentalists—they're a tragic chorus, too late, too faint, trying to shout over a theater filled with screaming fools."

"But there are some," she insists. "A few."

"Yes," he says. "Those who leave handprints on cave walls. Who hint at a creative path their genus might take. But such ones—the navel-gazers, hand-wringers, and hand-claspers—are like canaries in poisoned air. When they die, no one notices. Or worse—" he leans forward slightly "—they become the meal. Their fears, their visions, their prophecies of collapse are twisted into gold by more primitive forces, devoured by those who would accelerate the extinction of all that breathes. This," he says, "is where you come in."

She is quiet for a beat. Then: "The knowledge given to me those seventeen years. Was it all of your knowledge?"

"Not possible."

"You sound like me talking to Jared."

He shrugs lightly. "It is time for me to go. Now that you are pregnant, you must be especially cautious."

"I can't be killed."

"Perhaps not. But I meant something else. Be careful not to draw too much attention."

"Then why place me here?"

"There are powers beyond me. She is tired. Tired of countering His addiction to First Principles. She wants you tested sooner."

"Why?"

"If you and your child delay too long, Her other joys on this planet will vanish. Even She is capable of impatience."

"But She's just a metaphor, isn't She?"

"Yes. But what waits behind the metaphor is not yours to know. Not yet."

"And if She's a metaphor," Pythia persists, "isn't She supposed to be timeless?"

"There is no such thing," he replies. "Metaphors wear out."

Then, abruptly, Altan stands. "Goodbye."

He nods once, with a conspiratorial wink, and leaves.

Pythia dresses quickly, slipping on her nightgown. And waits.

~

By mid-afternoon, Pythia has received no visitors. Just as she begins to wonder, the door opens and Mateo shoves in her three roommates, each looking haggard and defeated. Only Elena's eyes briefly light up at the sight of Pythia, but little Margarita, evidently in pain, hobbles to her mattress and rests in the arms of Juana, who herself stares into space with a hollow expression. Mateo, a satisfied smirk on his face, turns to leave.

"Where is Rogelio!" demands Pythia.

Mateo guffaws. "Who? Never heard of him, *jorobada*."

"I did my part of the bargain!" exclaims Pythia. "Where is he?"

"*Yo no hablo inglés*," replies Mateo, who abruptly leaves and locks the door behind.

Pythia is left fuming, her patience at an end. She sees Elena looking at her expectantly, and hears twelve-year-old Margarita moaning in Juana's arms. She recalls Altan's cautionary advice, but the volatile mix of genes still carrying the roots of human emotion—anger at injustice, hunger for revenge—now surges in full force. *You are right, Altan, even a Goddess can be driven beyond endurance!*

An hour later, Mateo returns, accompanied by four brutal-looking men, and orders only Pythia to disrobe. Still furious, she forces herself to bide her time and strips, hoping the men will be disgusted by her hump and leave. This time, Mateo steps back and lets the men speak for themselves. Pythia has read their minds and now knows they are all cartel thugs. The spokesman, a tall, heavily bearded Mexican with multiple piercings and covered in tattoos, speaks for all of them.

"So, you are the famous hunchback *demonio*. We are all going to fuck you. This will help soften you up so you are good to our paying customers. After this, bitch, you will be nice to them, or we will return and fuck you to death." He grabs her arm and pulls her into the hallway.

"Do not fight us, bitch! Do exactly what we command."

Mateo trails after the four men with a gleeful sneer. They take her into the "fucking" room. She sees the same soiled mattress, still wet with multiple stains. Same cracked walls, but seemingly more so. The same cracked walls gaping wider, the same chipped red paint peeling further to reveal the ugly concrete beneath.

But not the same Pythia.

She twirls around, assumes a wild, crazed expression, and starts chanting loudly in gibberish. The men pause and look at each other uncertainly, taken off guard by this sorceresses' mad incantations. She dances before them as if possessed. The leader boldly steps forward to twist her arm.

"*Esta la maldita perra está actuando!* This fucking bitch is acting, *amigos!* Hold her down! *Sostenia abajo!*"

As soon as his fingers grip her arm, Pythia howls like a wolf. Instantly his hand, up to the wrist, disappears. He freezes in horror, raising a stump in front of his stricken face. No blood, no pain, no hand.

His companions are also struck dumb. An eerie silence momentarily pervades the room. Then, all hell breaks loose. The handless man screams and runs out the door, the others following, shouting obscenities and yelling threats. Pythia picks up bits and pieces of their rants. They will return with guns! They will kill this fucking bitch! This *demonio*!

Pythia knows she must leave before this debacle gets worse. How to free the captive girls, possibly dozens in multiple rooms, with cartel men surely arriving in droves? Faced with this dilemma, she starts to act when Rogelio suddenly appears in the doorway. He calmly walks in, boldly, arrogantly, and supremely confident of his position and ability to turn the situation to his favor. Pythia immediately notices he carries no weapon.

"*Cariño*," he purrs. "I am impressed. Your magic is powerful. Is it mass hypnosis?"

She is surprised at his sophistication.

"Yes," she lies.

"Then I can kill you now, with my bare hands, if all you have is hypnosis. I cannot be hypnotized—too dangerous. Foolish, superstitious *peons* can, but not me. So, I will now break your neck, unless you prove to me your magic is real and not a trick."

Pythia remembers her mother told her once, "A definitive answer will never come. With power comes burden. With burden comes doubt. With doubt comes wisdom."

Rogelio moves toward her, a confident grin still lining his cruel face.

"Stop!" exclaims Pythia. "Look at your ring."

He stops and holds up his hands, displaying multiple rings. "Which one, *cariño*?"

As he speaks, they all vanish. The color drains from his face and for the first time his eyes reflect fear.

"All of them, as you see," says Pythia.

Rogelio blusters. "What kind of bullshit is this? More tricks?" His eyes narrow to slits as he assumes his most intimidating face. "Put them back!"

"No can do. Once gone, always gone."

"Put them back or I kill you now."

"Take one step toward me and you lose your fingers. Take another step after that and you lose your penis and scrotum. After that. . . . "

Rogelio stares in disbelief, then Pythia watches in fascination as his expression melts into a broad smile. She reads his thoughts and waits for the inevitable.

"Ha, ha! *Cariño*, your tricks are very good! Work with us! We can make you very rich. I can put you in charge of this operation, then you can treat the girls good, eh? One word from me and you're in with some of the richest, most powerful men in Mexico. One word, and you're rich."

Pythia remains stone-faced. "First, you will release the girls here."

"Release them?"

"Yes."

Rogelio's face is flushed with wrath and he takes a step forward.

"Stop!" cries Pythia. "Look at your hands!"

Stunned by her command, he raises both hands and sees the ring fingers missing.

He lets out a stifled scream and sputters, "How can this be?"

"It is."

"You will die for this! I promise you! You're dead, bitch!"

He pauses to calculate the effect of his words, but there is no effect; Pythia remains pitilessly unmoved.

"No, no! I didn't mean it! Oh, *God*! Put them back! Please!"

"If you are not anxious to lose more body parts, release the girls."

"I can't!" he wails.

"Why?"

"They'll kill me!"

"Who?"

"All of them. My bosses!"

"Write down the names of your bosses and give me the list. That is the only reason I removed just your ring fingers—so you can still write."

"You don't understand. If I do, I'm dead."

"Well, you can rest easy, I have already read your mind and now know who they are."

"You can read minds?"

"Of course."

Rogelio again assumes a calculating demeanor. "What am I thinking right now?"

"You are afraid of me, but also admire me. You want to fuck me and make me your silent partner so you, not me, of course, can rule an empire. Your thoughts are a bit chaotic, but that is the gist."

Rogelio sags back into speechless incredulity.

"Now, release the girls and give them each ten thousand *pesos* so they can escape this hellhole."

"What? Ten thousand *pesos*?" Now his eyes are pleading. "No! I can't! My own men will not allow it! They have guns!"

"Tell them there is to be a raid by the *Federales* and DEA that will be worse than Tlaxcala. Tell them anything, but make it happen!"

"Yes, yes, maybe. Oh, *God*! What are you?"

"A next step."

"¿*Que*?"

"Just do it. Give them, and me, back our clothes, plus ten thousand pesos for each of them, and you will be rid of me. If you don't, I will remove you piece by piece until only your head and torso remain. No arms, no legs, no penis, but you will still live. My offer is generous, for I would happily reduce you to an utterly helpless lump of flesh."

"Okay, but then you replace my fingers."

"You have no bargaining power, Rogelio. Besides, I cannot. As I said, once gone, always gone."

"Oh, *God!*" he simpers.

"By the way," says Pythia as he starts to back out of the room submissively. "I can read your mind, remember? Much of your crying and whining is faked. I know you intend to have your men shoot me from concealed locations. Any man with a weapon will vanish forever, and you will be left to account for their disappearances to your bosses. Also, I hardly think you will be foolish enough to report this to the *policia*. Who would believe such a fantastic story, particularly by a leader of an illegal sex trafficking cartel? Go and make the arrangements."

Rogelio listens to this speech with the gaping air of a village idiot. His brain cannot cope with the avalanche of *demonia* miracles he has witnessed, and his feet seem glued to the floor.

"Go, or I will start removing parts of you now."

Rogelio quickly leaves, his mind desiccated, curled like a dead spider.

~ *Denouement* ~

For Pythia, this momentary triumph tastes bitter. A fleeting victory disguised as something far more permanent: defeat. Yes, she has liberated the enslaved girls, humbled the men who brutalized them—but at what cost? Foremost in her mind is doubt. Doubt that it worked. Doubt that it will hold. She has made threats she may not be able to enforce. A shooter from afar with a high-powered rifle might still succeed. Her skin is not invincible. Worse, she is still blind to the true limits of her powers, a flaw she must correct. No simulation from her sixteen-year tutorial had prepared her for this kind of chaos. This, here, was real. Yet, within weeks, she knows, the cartel will rebuild. Perhaps even some of the girls she freed will return, dragged back by poverty or coerced by threat. What has truly changed? Still, the path has been set, and she must walk it.

She returns to the room where her roommates huddle, trembling.

"We heard shouting, María!" Elena cries. "The men—horrible things they're saying—what's happening?"

"If all goes well—" Pythia begins.

Just then, a box is tossed into the room. It lands with a thud. Their clothes. The man who delivered it flees down the hall, too frightened to linger. As she dresses, Pythia scans the building, her mind sweeping outward, combing through layers of thought. Nearby minds scream in confusion and fear, but the farther she reaches, the murkier it gets. She casts a wide psychic command: *All weapons, vanish.* Her power stretches out, indiscriminate, as far as her reach allows. There is no confirmation. No signal. No proof of success. Only silence.

And risk. She will walk these halls exposed to whatever slipped through. Soon the girls are gathered, buzzing with anticipation, trembling with fear. Elena stands beside her. Luciana runs to them, breathless.

"María, what is happening? Rumors are flying!"

Pythia embraces her. "If all goes well, Luciana, you'll soon be free. But first, we have to get out of this building."

She leads them through the corridor, a gauntlet of hardened men. But to her great relief, none are armed.

Rogelio waits at the exit beside a box of cash. When their eyes meet, he nods grudgingly.

Pythia gestures to the girls. "Take the money. Leave now. Find your families. If you have none, go with those who do."

Elena translates. Cries of joy erupt. They rush forward. Pythia lingers at the rear, watching. When all but two have gone, she turns to them.

"Go, Elena. Luciana. Hurry."

"We will wait for you outside, María."

"No. I have business with Rogelio. It may go badly. Leave now—before it's too late."

Reluctantly, they obey. Rogelio watches them pass, then laughs.

"I have magic too, *cariño*."

Then, two gunshots.

A scream.

A third shot.

Pythia's mind flares. Primal outrage floods her. She whirls on Rogelio, rage incarnate.

"Your friends are dead," he sneers. "Do your worst. I'm dead either way. My own men will kill me. Go join those two whores in hell!"

Pythia raises her hand, prepared to make good on every threat—to unmake him piece by piece—but before she can act, Altan enters through the door. Cartel guards move to stop him, but a single look from Pythia sends them fleeing.

Altan walks calmly toward Rogelio.

"It is your shooter who is dead," he says. "Or rather, gone. Where your fingers and your rings went. The two girls are alive."

Rogelio lets out a strangled sound. Curses bubble from his lips, then dissolve into inarticulate rage. Pythia steps forward and, without ceremony, removes his arms, legs, and genitals. His screams echo off the walls. The cartel men scatter. As she and Altan walk into the distance, Rogelio's cries grow faint. At last, she turns to Altan.

"I suspected you had powers like mine," she says. "But I didn't think you'd intervene."

"I didn't," Altan replies. "The rifle misfired because your command—weak though it was—reached the gun. Some part of it disappeared or altered. It made noise, but no bullets struck. The scream was from the shooter . . . just before he ceased to exist."

"So you *did* intervene."

"No. You did. The instant you heard the shots, your mind responded. Instinctively, you willed the threat gone. I merely delivered the bad news to Rogelio."

Pythia is quiet.

"Now what?" she asks.

"Now, you disappear, from this country, at least. We've learned much. Real-world data. Limits. Expressions of genetic force. But one question remains."

"What question?"

"What will your child be?"

He gives her a small smile.

"Jared, by the way, will be a very happy human to see you again."

Pythia blinks. "*Homo sapiens* males," she murmurs.

~ *A Postscript* ~

When she returns to the waiting arms of Jared at Motel Vargas, Pythia tells him as much as she deems necessary. Much is left unsaid—details he would crave. But her resentment lingers. A shadow of fury toward all men, not just the cruel ones. It will take time to recalibrate, to let herself receive Jared again, to accept him as the kind of male who thinks before touching, who listens, who sees.

Altan stays close, preparing to leave.

"There is still the question of who leads the cartel," Pythia says. "We haven't finished."

"No, Pythia," Altan replies. "You've risked enough, not just your body, but your nature. The cartel men will talk. Stories will spread. But no one will believe them. Not the *policía*, not the government, not even their enemies. No one wants tales of magic and madness from a trafficker's mouth. Rogelio is likely dead already, killed by his own."

She doesn't respond. Her eyes narrow.

"If you go after the leaders," Altan continues, "you'll reveal too much. You're still vulnerable, Pythia. You don't see it yet, but we do. This event has given us something rare: a glimpse of the boundary of your reach. You are not limitless. And if your powers become known, even *rumored*, you become a threat. Not just to the cartels, but to governments. Institutions. The species itself. And humanity—primitive as ever—does not suffer threats quietly."

"You're warning me."

"No. I'm stating a fact. Your kind, like the earliest *Homo sapiens*, must survive in the shadows. That is how your ancestors endured the other hominins and a host of apex predators. And that is how you must endure now."

Chapter Twenty-Nine

No Escape

End of the Beginning

Upon their return to San Francisco, Pythia and Jared spend a few quiet days in the old Victorian house before parting ways. The decision is mutual: Jared will return to his post at Berkeley, while Pythia remains hidden with her mother until the child is born.

A hospital birth is out of the question as no one knows what the child will be. Will it resemble a human infant? Inherit Pythia's singular morphology? Or become something else entirely, perhaps a leap beyond both Ming-huà and Pythia, toward a being not yet imagined?

Within the spiral folds lie countless unexpressed genes, some engineered, some mutant, all lurking in silence. Lady Oracle insists the child's genetic unfolding must proceed naturally, untouched by clinical interference.

"What do you mean by 'undue manipulation'?" Jared asks.

"Ming-huà and Pythia are products of saltation," replies Lady Oracle.

"I'm a physicist, not a geneticist. What's saltation?"

Sy adopts a rare seriousness. "A sudden, large-scale mutation, a single-step leap that leads to speciation."

"I thought massive mutations were fatal. Isn't saltation one of those pseudo-scientific arguments used by Creationists?"

"They do invoke it," Sy concedes, "but like most of their claims, they've twisted it beyond recognition. Saltation often leads to failure, but not always. And when it succeeds, the result is radically new. Ming-huà and Pythia are almost certainly the result of polyploidy—triploid, tetraploid, maybe even hexaploid chromosomes. In mammals, it usually ends in miscarriage or deformity, but in rare cases it can stabilize. It's well-documented in plants, and even in some animals. This kind of chromosomal multiplication can drive sympatric evolution, which Pythia's pregnancy now suggests. Her genome likely carries vast unexpressed regions, dormant regulatory sequences waiting for activation, scripts written but unread. In her descendants, they may surface. Where it leads, no one can say."

"Sympatric evolution?" Jared repeats.

"A new species emerging from an existing one without geographic separation," Sy explains. "Same terrain. Different destinies."

"But wouldn't something like this show up in their medical records? Surely the journals—"

"Ah!" Sy interjects. "That's the beauty of it. There are no medical records."

"None?"

"None. Both births were overseen by handpicked midwives. No paperwork. No digital trace."

"Deliberate?"

"Perhaps," says Lady Oracle. "That's what I meant by 'undue manipulation.'"

Pythia strokes her stomach. "So you see, Jared, no one knew what I would become. And no one knows what this child will be. The saltation continues."

"And this Goddess everyone keeps referring to?" Jared presses.

"That subject is closed," Lady Oracle snaps.

Jared flinches, then rallies, his scientist's pride urging him to resist. "Can't we at least run some tests? This could be invaluable to medical science."

Lady Oracle's eyes flash. "Jared. Don't even think it. Do you understand the implications?"

"Yes," he sighs. "You're right. But I want to be there when the baby comes. I'm the father."

"And you will be," she replies. "But for now, especially after Mexico, Pythia must remain hidden. She needs peace, safety, privacy. You, on the other hand, must continue your work at Berkeley. As if nothing has changed."

"I wonder . . . " Pythia murmurs.

"What is it?" asks Sy.

"I wonder how long this gestation will last."

"Indeed," says Lady Oracle. "We all do."

Jared's brow furrows. "Saltation and polyploidy may explain rapid shifts in plants or amphibians, but even then, they're still bound by the laws of physics. Mind reading, telepathy, clairvoyance, psychokinesis—these aren't biologically feasible. They violate fundamental physical laws."

"The *known* laws of physics," Pythia corrects him. "The equations I wrote and destroyed, those began to account for the unknown by describing a unified field incorporating neuroquantum resonance . That's why your String Theory fails. It hints in the right direction but can't bridge the conceptual gap. Right now, human understanding is equivalent to chimpanzees stripping branches to catch termites. A space shuttle is outside their grasp. No matter how clever the chimp."

"Gee, thanks. Or should I just grunt?"

"Same difference," Pythia says, her voice frost-edged.

The comment lands hard. Jared absorbs the blow, filing it among a growing list of quiet resentments. Despite their sweeping claims, something about their biological account doesn't sit right with him. His native brilliance whispers that a key piece is missing. He resolves to consult a trusted colleague in genetics. As Pythia's mind brushes his own, he blocks her out, instead flashing an unmistakable image for her to read: *Something is rotten in the state of Denmark*. Never has he felt so deeply human, and so far from her.

But Pythia, too, is grappling with doubt. Her residual human genes have expressed themselves as guilt. She has spoken of it to no one, but when she dismantled Rogelio, a scream of psychic anguish tore through her—his final, desperate thought had been of his mother. A woman he had loved. A woman who would be devastated, emotionally and financially, by his death. That flicker of humanity, so tender, so private, penetrated her defenses. She has long known conscience is essential to the wise use of power. But tribalistic pity, personal sentiment? These must not be allowed to sway her.

Jared's turmoil also clings to her mind, unresolved. She cannot assuage his unease, perhaps because she shares it. Even Sy, Altan, and Lady Oracle seem wrapped in fog, as if withholding truths from her. And over everything, like mist over a battlefield, hovers the excruciating pressure of legacy: this child must not merely survive, but carry forward the next phase of evolution. She does not share her mother's introversion or her fragile conscience, but she is not immune to the weight of new capacities. Like the first humans, she stands at the cave wall, tracing her hand in ochre. But unlike them, she already knows how to bring down the beast and skin it for warmth against the cold.

~ *The Island Again* ~

The anxieties that once clung to Pythia dissolve as she returns to the island with her mother and Zookeeper. The quiet of the forest, the rhythm of the sea—these natural cadences restore her. With distance from Lady Oracle, Sy, and Altan, she feels lighter, freer. The focus now is the child growing inside her.

Back in Berkeley, Jared resumes the routines of academic life, though they feel artificial, an elaborate pantomime. Lectures, office hours, research meetings, all tinged with the surreal. His time with Pythia feels like a dream still leaking into reality. He texts her often, and though they speak little of it, the silence between them holds both comfort and buried tension.

He has begun reviewing scientific papers on polyploidy and saltation but hasn't dared ask his genetics colleague the questions pressing in his mind. How does one pose the possibility of another species without sounding mad?

~

Unburdened by Jared's brittle ego and neurotic caution, Pythia turns inward, charting the edges of her power. Mexico taught her she is still early in her evolution, still flint and spear when she must leap toward quantum tools. Zookeeper is eager to help. Though he loves his life on the island, echoes of his past life—the thrill, the danger—still call to him. Pythia's experiments offer a kind of return.

Most days they walk the woods. Sometimes Ming-huà joins. They test her range, how far she can sense, what minds she can read, and whether she can filter thought the way one might tune static from a signal. She likens herself to an octopus, able to change psychic texture and hue, vanishing from detection or launching misdirection. But still she fears the long-range rifle, the unseen assassin. Could she stop a bullet in flight? Ten bullets? A thousand? Could she survive coordinated violence? Beyond defense, she begins to test the limits of destruction. Objects vanish at her command, not one by one, but *en masse*. She is no longer bound by the slow crawl of evolution. She does not have centuries to learn; the world is already burning. And what of the child? Will it carry the line forward? Or become a monstrosity born not of bestial rage, but of hyper-intelligence unmoored from conscience?

She thinks of monsters. Not vampires. Not dragons. But those birthed in neurons: greed-struck, god-drunk, salivating behind machinery.

Zookeeper, ever irreverent, breaks her reverie with a new test. This time, not to read thoughts but to send them. He distances himself over a mile, whiskey bottle hidden, and poses a silent list of questions, syncing his watch with hers.

What am I thinking?

What am I doing?

How do I feel?

Now make my feeling your own.

Now reverse it. Make me feel as you feel. Make me sober.

She nails the first four. She senses the whiskey, the act of drinking, the spreading intoxication. She becomes drunk by proxy. But she fails the last task. He remains drunk. Her empathic reach cannot reverse his altered state.

For Zookeeper, it's exhilarating, a parlor trick for wiping out the "fuckin' idiots" of the world. For Pythia, it's something else: a revelation of vulnerability. The power to absorb others' physical states threatens her emotional autonomy. The deeper her gift goes, the less she belongs to herself.

She warns him. "Father Zookeeper, I know you love Shakespeare. But if I destroy those I deem evil, I deny them any chance for redemption. Their evil then lives on unchallenged, while the good they might have done is buried with their bones."

He grins. "True. But also remember: 'Come not between the Dragon and her wrath.' You, daughter, are that Dragon. Burn the bastards down. Salt the ashes. Let Phoenixes rise."

"You're poetic today."

"You're my muse. Just don't forget, your kind took my arms."

"Mother let light into your soul through those wounds."

His grin fades. "I heard you nearly became ash in Mexico. I can't lose you. Or the baby. If they think you're a threat, and they will, they'll try to kill you. It's the law of power. Stay ahead of it."

"I hope it doesn't come to that," she says. "You survived the streets not by fury, but restraint. It's not evil that drives the human race, it's blindness. They do not know how to wield power without destroying what they touch. Their good dies with them. Their evil endures, refined by each new invention."

He lowers his voice.

"I'm worried about your mother. The FBI keeps calling and she refuses to respond. There's new evidence, remember? Listen to me: it's governments you must learn to fear, or at the very least, to respect their power. Not these flimsy cartels. They're all Humpty Dumpties once pushed from the wall."

"Yes," Pythia says, alert now.

"She left traces. So did you. And me? I'm still a walking mystery—no explanation for how I lost these arms. We're vulnerable."

"She knows what she's doing."

"She's fragile. Haunted. She carries guilt for me, and for the others. Her only mission now is you."

"I understand. But remember, we don't attach only to kin. Our sense of family extends to all DNA. To the particles that make us. We are stitched from the cosmos."

"Yeah, yeah," he mutters. "Still, I'd like to think Ming-huà feels closer to me than a ringworm."

Pythia doesn't answer. The question is small, but not without poignancy. Many humans have done more harm than any parasite. The real question isn't sentiment, but legacy: will *Homo sapiens* destroy the planet before a more empathetic species can emerge?

"Pythia!" he calls. "Do you think Ming-huà loves me more than a ringworm?"

She smiles faintly. "Of course. Don't be absurd."

"And you?"

"You're my father."

"Jesus fuckin' Christ. Why doesn't that comfort me?"

"Be comforted. If we survive, you'll be revered."

"Great. Let's go. I gotta shit."

"Father Zookeeper, your blunt language is always a jolt." She points to an old Douglas fir. "So you feel a deep kinship with that tree?"

"Hell no. But I do with whiskey. Let's go."

~ *A Bad Day* ~

A few days later, in the golden hush of afternoon, Ming-huà and Pythia sit in the kitchen, idly chatting about the child's future. Then, without warning, they both stiffen. Their eyes lock. The silence deepens.

"I'll get it," says Pythia softly.

She moves to the door, waiting. A knock comes—tentative but official. She glances back once at her mother, then opens it.

Standing on the porch are the two FBI agents who had questioned her at Berkeley—Agents Saunders and Dunlap—flanking a gaunt woman with sunken eyes and twitching fingers. Her skin is prematurely weathered, her aura one of exhaustion and rot. Pythia reads her mind in an instant and feels her stomach twist.

"Good afternoon, Ms. Powers," says Saunders. "Agent Saunders. We've met."

"Yes," says Pythia. "I remember."

Dunlap nods. "Agent Dunlap, ma'am. Good to see you again."

Pythia keeps the door open but does not step aside. Her gaze flicks to the woman, who scratches violently at her arm. *This one is a ravaged husk,* thinks Pythia. *Drugs have hollowed her out.*

"This is Jasmine Walker," Saunders says. "Is your mother home?"

Ming-huà appears behind her. "Yes. Can I help you?"

"May we come in and ask a few questions?"

"Of course."

Inside, Dunlap asks, "Is your husband home?"

"No. He's gone to the mainland."

They occupy the living room with the quiet intensity of those who are not merely waiting but measuring. Every breath, every glance, carries weight, honed by training and purpose.

"Mrs. Powers," Saunders says evenly, "do you recognize Ms. Walker?"

Ming-huà's expression sharpens. "No."

Pythia's hump emits a tight sequence of vibrations, controlled, directed, and deliberate. The agents remain composed, but their attention sharpens beneath the calm exterior. Something has shifted. They feel it. A disturbance too subtle to name, yet impossible to ignore. They do not move. They do not speak. But already, their judgment begins to narrow.

Dunlap speaks evenly, emotionless. "Ms. Walker was present in Baltimore on the night those men were dismembered. Until recently, we believed only you and the surviving victims witnessed the event. Now, Ms. Walker has come forward."

"Ain't true!" Jasmine snaps. "They posted a reward. I need the goddamn money."

Her voice is raw, her body jittery, her mind knotted with addiction and desperation.

"We also have testimony," Dunlap continues, "that you gave her money the night before. She lived in an alley. Carried a knife. Locals called her 'Crazy Jasmine.' And she had a child."

"She's dead!" Jasmine blurts. "I killed her. With my habit. But I'm clean now, swear it!" Her eyes gleam as she looks at Ming-huà. "You were kind. Gave us money. That's why I followed you."

Both Pythia and Ming-huà know Jasmine is clueless about the dismemberment. But she believes in witches and believes Ming-huà is one. Her testimony would dissolve in a courtroom, but that's not what the agents are after. They're circling. They want Ming-huà to stumble . . . just once.

Dunlap presses on. "Why were you on that street two nights in a row?"

"I couldn't sleep. I have a sensitivity to the suffering of others."

"And your husband?" Saunders asks. "He lost his arms. Same as those men in Baltimore. And you were there too."

"As I've said, I was doing charity work. The timing is a terrible coincidence."

"Could this be . . . military?" Ming-huà adds. "Some secret weapon, tested on the vulnerable?"

Jasmine cackles. "You tell 'em, honey!"

Unfazed, Dunlap says, "Ms. Walker claims you were being attacked when the injuries occurred. You were angry?"

"No, terrified."

Dunlap coughs. "Did you . . . ah . . . want your attackers to . . . ah . . . die or lose body parts? I mean, in your terrorized state?"

"What a silly question. As I said, I was terrified. Revenge played no role in my terror."

"Did you *want* them dead?"

"I wanted them to stop."

"Did you visualize their injuries?"

Ming-huà leans forward, her voice low but firm. "I do not believe in revenge, Agent. But I do believe in limits. Some things rupture the natural order. Unchecked violence often sows the seeds of its own undoing. And nature abhors unchecked violence. It answers, and it answers in ways we do not always understand."

"Mrs. Powers, do you have any idea . . . any guesses, how this might have happened to these men?"

"No. I've answered this many times. Perhaps it *is* a new weapon. Something invisible. Government conspiracy you aren't in on?"

Saunders shifts his gaze to Pythia. "Have you been to Mexico recently?"

"I have."

"Why?"

"Research. I'm continuing my mother's work. I share her condition. My father struggled with addiction. I need firsthand data."

"For school?"

"Partly."

"For Dr. Paine?"

"No."

"Does your research involve drugs?"

"Yes. And how they affect vulnerable women."

"Sex trafficking?"

"That too."

After a few more perfunctory questions, the agents leave, Jasmine shuffling behind them, still scratching. But before she exits, she turns to Ming-huà, eyes glittering.

"You, lady—you're a good witch. Devil or no, I say give 'em hell. Take the arms and legs off every goddamn man out there as far as I care."

~

When the house falls silent, Ming-huà and Pythia sit unmoving, speaking only through thought. Zookeeper soon slips in through the back, brushing twigs from his shirt.

"Saw the bastards pull up. Hid in the woods till they left. Is it bad?"

"Bad enough," says Ming-huà.

"Not that bad," Pythia replies. "They're guessing. They don't have blood. Just shadows, empty speculation, and superstition." She pauses, head tilting slightly. Somewhere, miles away, Jared is thinking of her. A flicker. A pang of confusion, concern. She feels it like a ripple in a deep pool. And then it's gone.

Ming-huà's voice is tired. "It's not about evidence. It's about pressure. They'll never let us rest. If not to arrest, then to contain. Detain. Study. We've become a national security riddle."

"They don't give a damn about the victims," says Zookeeper. "What's haunting them is *how*. How the impossible happened. That's their obsession."

"I'm not running," Pythia says. "Running makes us guilty. Makes us the mechanism they're hunting."

"Then we stay," says Ming-huà. "Until the child is born. Then we'll see."

Zookeeper's face tightens. "You think Lady Oracle and her shadow-men will stay out of this?"

"No," Pythia replies. "They'll come. One way or another."

"The cave again?" he mutters.

Ming-huà's face hardens. "The cave! My mother and father were born and died and were reborn many times in that mystical place where time and space are twisted and folded in a thousand different shapes. It is a carnival house of mirrors, easy to enter, hard to get out—and getting out exacts a cost."

Pythia nods agreement. "All of us have had our own experiences in that place. Sixteen years, Mother!"

Zookeeper frowns, his voice quieter now. "I think . . . I've been there too. Once. Maybe as a kid. I remember something. Cold light. A voice calling from behind a wall. I forgot it until just now."

Ming-huà turns to him, startled. "You never told me."

"I never remembered."

Pythia nods. "Sixteen years, Mother. Lost to cracks between dimensions."

Tears line Ming-huà's lashes. "Amnesia wrapped in echoes. Time bleeding inward."

"But that is where I learned," Pythia says. "I saw human evil laid bare, governments worse than criminals. I gained knowledge beyond physics, chemistry, biology. My abilities were shaped there. I became something new."

Zookeeper raises a brow. "Where'd you go?"

Pythia pauses. "Nowhere. Everywhere. The cave broke Plato's illusion. I stepped out of shadow and into dimension. I left behind the cave-dwellers, born blind and dragging their chains, and they will hunt me by scent alone in a world they cannot see. They will fail. They must fail."

Zookeeper pumps a fist. "Fuckin' A. Let's drink to that."

Pythia's gaze drifts to the window, to the gathering night. "Drink, Father. The cave is already opening. And this time, none of us will come back unchanged."

Chapter Thirty

Labor

More Steps

~ Approaching Birth ~

The demands of Jared's work leave him little time to dwell on his separation from Pythia. But as her pregnancy advances, he feels a mounting pressure to revisit the strange concepts that once disturbed his equilibrium: *sympatric evolution, saltation.* The woman carrying his child is, by all evidence, not entirely human. His fiancée, his lover, is a separate species. Try as he might, with all his training in the scientific method and its sacred empiricism, he cannot quite metabolize this truth. Much as he wants to believe his love for Pythia is pure, unburdened by ego or motive, he cannot deny what draws him like moth to flame: her knowledge, her power, the depth of mystery she embodies. He tells himself it is curiosity, a noble, intellectual curiosity. But beneath it simmers something messier. Possessiveness. Awe.

He has dismissed the notion that the cognitive depths of her kind lie beyond human understanding. Surely minds like his, descendants of Darwin, Newton, Einstein, can comprehend the architecture of such beings. Even so, he fears what lies at the core of this evolutionary leap. A single being with such power is remarkable. A population of them? Potentially apocalyptic. He finds himself agreeing, reluctantly, with Lady Oracle, Sy, and even Pythia herself: this experiment must be shielded from premature exposure.

As for *Homo sapiens*? He has faith in the minds of the educated and the rational. But humanity as a whole? He is, increasingly, without hope. Which leaves him dangling on the prongs of a paradox: can he love what he also fears? Can he defend what he does not entirely trust? *My child,* he thinks. *How can I be the father of an alien species?* The absurdity of it delights him—and terrifies him.

"You wanted to ask me something?" Professor Frank Rutledge's voice cuts through Jared's spiral, pulling him back to the here and now.

They sit in a quiet campus café, paper cups steaming between them.

"Yes. Thanks for meeting me. I have a few questions. Genetics-related."

"Oh?" Rutledge's gray hair is a storm cloud above his wrinkled brow. "That's a bit outside your usual realm, isn't it?"

Jared shrugs. "Call it intellectual spillover. I've been thinking about sympatric evolution, saltation, and polyploidy."

Rutledge lets out a dry chuckle. "That's not spillover. That's a flood. What's sparked this new obsession?"

"Grad students, mostly. They were speculating on how humans might evolve rapidly, within a generation or two."

Rutledge sighs. "The younger generation loves to imagine *Homo sapiens* obsolete. Still, it's a worthy thought experiment."

"Is it biologically feasible?" Jared leans in. "Could a species like ours evolve into something recognizably different within a handful of generations?"

Rutledge straightens, voice more serious. "It's wildly improbable. Not impossible, but vanishingly rare."

"But not impossible," Jared repeats, gripping the thread.

"Well, consider polyploidy. In most vertebrates, an extra chromosome leads to death or disability. Humans, especially, don't tolerate chromosomal irregularities well."

"But it *has* happened."

"Yes. Rarely. There are studies showing rapid chromosomal shifts, like the chromosome 2 fusion between chimps and humans. There's the Australopithecus pelvis, too, 3.5 million years old, yet strikingly human. Some evolutionary biologists propose saltational leaps during periods of environmental stress. The theory goes that in rare instances, multiple beneficial mutations can occur at once."

"I hear rare, I don't hear impossible."

Rutledge rubs his forehead. "There's a phenomenon called *chromothripsis*—where chromosomes shatter and reassemble in a single catastrophic event. Usually seen in cancer cells, and mostly fatal. But it proves the genome isn't always gradual. Sometimes, it breaks and reforms in strange ways." He pauses, then adds, "There's also increasing interest in the idea that non-coding DNA, what used to be called junk, might carry dormant regulatory codes. Under enough environmental or biochemical stress, whole systems of genes could switch on. It's speculative . . . but not insane."

"And sympatric evolution?"

"Possible—more common in plants, less so in higher animals. But under the right conditions, sure."

"And the resulting changes could be substantial?"

Rutledge laughs. "You're not going to sprout wings, Jared. But yes, under extreme pressure, speciation can leap. Nature is a chaotic sculptor."

Jared hesitates before asking for reading material. "Any chance you could send me some papers?"

"I'll email you a few. Might warp your physicist brain a bit."

"Thanks. I'll take the risk."

~

Later that night, combing through the articles Rutledge sent, Jared comes to a tentative, and unsettling, conclusion. The extraordinary traits exhibited by Ming-huà and Pythia are unlikely the result of natural processes alone. Some guiding hand has shaped them, and done so selectively, deliberately, and with purpose. But whose? The answer, as always, circles back: Lady Oracle. Sy. Altan. Architects of a hidden lineage.

They are not simply *observing* this evolutionary shift. They are conducting it. And like any experiment, it carries with it the hazards of miscalculation.

What if this child is a monster? Jared wonders. *What if it cannot be reasoned with?*

Then again—*what if it carries a deeper intelligence? What if empathy evolves in step with power?* Surely it must. Otherwise, the future will burn itself out before it begins.

He seldom permits himself to dwell on the physical memory of Pythia. When he does, it is not desire that returns to him, nor even the ache of absence, but something closer to reverence. Their moments of intimacy held a charge he could not explain, an intensity that moved through him with purpose, precision, and force. It was not mere physical response, but a deeper synchronization, as if her presence, her intelligence, and something greater than either of them had converged for a brief and undeniable union.

He remembers feeling—no, *knowing*—the equations beneath the skin of reality. The scaffolding of stars. The quiet breath of galaxies.

"Ridiculous," he mutters aloud. "Romantic delusion."

But still, a shiver runs down his spine.

The birth draws near, and with it, a paradox wrapped in flesh: ecstasy and terror in equal measure. A child of two worlds, born of fear, love, and something that has no name.

~ *Nearer* ~

One day, during the seventh month of her pregnancy, Pythia walks with her mother through their favorite forest path. Their communion unfolds across layers: verbal, telepathic, ambient. Birds chime in at the edge of thought; squirrels leap with a kind of joyful commentary. Even the slow, patient respiration of the great trees seems to ripple through the soil, stirring the air like benevolent earthquakes.

Pythia halts mid-step, hands on her stomach.

"What is it?" Ming-huà asks, instantly alert.

Pythia's face is radiant. "I heard the baby."

"And?"

"It said, *I am become.*"

She gasps. "Again. It says it again: *I am become.*"

The two women exchange a glance, brimming with ancient expectation.

"Quiet now," says Pythia.

Ming-huà lowers her voice. "Do you think this will be a typical nine-month gestation?"

"I don't know."

"Any pain?"

"No. But my hump is sharing its signals with a new tenant, just moved in. Quite harmoniously."

"I've picked up nothing yet," says Ming-huà.

"Curious. With this announcement, I suspect we'll be hearing more."

"Let us hope it bears no resemblance to Oppenheimer's ominous quote from the *Bhagavad Gita*."

Pythia lifts a fallen madrone leaf. "I hope not, Mother."

"Do you know where wisdom lies, daughter?"

"Not in explosive power, but in the expansion of executive function and the restraint of the limbic throne."

"Yes. We'll see which path this child follows."

Still gazing at the leaf, Pythia murmurs, "Sooner than we think. What follows *I am become*?"

She is right. Two weeks later, another message arrives: *I am become. Becoming, I am become.*

Mother and daughter spend hours parsing its layers, tracing meaning in each fragment, as if deciphering a long-buried code. Great-grandmother Child of Buddha had once read the taps of the Precious Object.

Now they do the same.

Zookeeper, in his usual blunt manner, breaks the spell. "Shit! It's Shakespeare. The kid means, 'I'm conscious now, and I'm still waking up.'"

Ming-huà and Pythia exchange a knowing grin. They had considered that.

"You may be right, Zookeeper," says Pythia.

"Damn right."

"Never known you to be wrong, husband," Ming-huà jabs.

"Self-love, my lady, is not so vile a sin as self-neglecting."

"The empty vessel makes the loudest sound."

Zookeeper howls like a wolf. The women fall silent, agreeing (via hump) that further banter is unnecessary. Still, a shadow lingers. They cannot crack the code of the unborn.

More messages follow, stranger each time.

By the ninth month, the messages have grown nearly incomprehensible.

Despite the rising mental chatter, there is no sign of labor. The due date passes. Concern deepens.

Jared, Lady Oracle, Sy, and Altan arrive. Jared stays with Pythia, while the rest lodge in town.

The baby's thoughts now arrive in torrents, incomprehensible flares of sound and symbol. Interpretations fail. A pall settles over the household.

Something has gone terribly, perhaps fatally, wrong.

~ *Birth* ~

A month overdue, Pythia's water breaks. Lightning, then thunder: a contraction slams into her. Pain spreads like wildfire. The household stirs into motion. The old midwife, stern and enigmatic, arrives in a jeep driven by Altan.

Lady Oracle bars Jared from the birthing room. "No guarantee you'll be safe."

As contractions grow, the womb becomes an amphitheater of shrieking speech, as if the child is speaking in tongues which are alien, volatile, and urgent. Pythia, wracked with pain, struggles to endure. The midwife cries out in disbelief. Ming-huà tries to reach her daughter telepathically, but finds only a wall of pain. Sy paces and flails; Zookeeper rocks beneath a tree, muttering. Jared is a clenched fist of fear.

Pythia's suffering stretches across two days. The midwife, pale and trembling, finally calls the others.

"I've never seen anything like this. The mother and child may die. Evacuate her to the mainland."

Jared fumbles for his phone. Lady Oracle stops him.

"No. That is not possible."

"Let go! They could die!"

"Put the phone away. Neither will die."

"How do you know?"

She turns to the midwife. "Return. The child is coming."

Moments later, the midwife cries from the room, "The baby is crowning!"

Jared lowers the phone and waits.

~

Silence follows the birth.

The midwife emerges, haunted. "A girl. I think."

"You think?"

"Yes, but . . ."

Jared bolts into the room. The others follow. Zookeeper trails, whispering prayers.

Pythia lies pale, unmoving, but breathing. The baby, large-eyed and upright, leans against the headboard.

Jared recoils. Lady Oracle steadies him. "Go slowly."

"She's not a cobra," he mutters, but hangs back.

Altan reaches to lift the child. Pythia bolts upright.

"No! I am now fully become, but still becoming. Leave me with this one. Wait."

"Pythia? Are you okay?"

"Becoming," she says. "Wait."

"The child is speaking through her," says Lady Oracle.

"Leave them," says Ming-huà. "She asks for time."

Jared hesitates, steps forward.

"No, Jared!" cries Pythia. She collapses. "Please go."

He flees the room, stricken. "What have we done?"

Lady Oracle laughs. "All is well. Necessity's child is here."

"Yes," says Altan.

"Agreed," adds Sy.

Ming-huà nods. "Yes, Jared. All is well."

"What is this *becoming* business?" asks Zookeeper.

"It is business," says Altan.

Sy twirls. "She's in the becoming business! Soon, a multinational!"

"When does she stop?" asks Jared.

"Never," says Lady Oracle.

Jared laughs nervously. "She looked like she might hurt me."

"She won't," Lady Oracle replies. "But you must also become someone new. Don't overrule her."

"Especially physicist males," Jared says.

"Take my word for it," says Zookeeper. "Push these ones too hard, you're fuckin' toast."

Lady Oracle shrugs. "Gene expression is unpredictable. We must be patient."

"Not a human strength," Jared mutters.

"Then be more than human," says Altan.

The midwife dons her coat. "I'm leaving. You know where to send payment. I'll stay quiet, but . . . whatever came out of that room was not entirely expected."

"What do you mean?" Jared asks.

"Thank you," says Lady Oracle. "Altan will drive you."

"No, wait—what did you mean?"

The midwife hesitates. "Internally, the mother's anatomy . . . it was different."

"Thank you," repeats Lady Oracle.

The midwife follows Altan out.

Jared runs after. "How was she different?"

"Don't worry, Jared. She's strong, and she's safe. Yes, there are differences. Just remember—she is not your species."

Altan, from the driver's seat, calls back,

The jeep drives away.

Chapter Thirty-One

Terra Incognita

Stages

~ *Becoming* ~

Defying all prenatal expectations, especially after months of cryptic, unceasing chatter from the womb, the newborn enters the world with eerie composure. She rarely asserts her presence. Her eyes are pools of liquid light, her head oversized, her hump pronounced. But what lingers most is the way she locks onto novelty—whether spatial, symbolic, or abstract—with unblinking intensity. Nothing escapes her notice. Despite this silent, unsettling vigilance, she remains in constant telepathic dialogue with Pythia. Whenever someone, even Ming-huà, asks what the baby has said, Pythia tightens. Her lips flatten. She says nothing.

Naming the child becomes the first open clash of wills between Pythia and Jared. He wants something sturdy and safe, something American, something forgettable. A name to help her "blend in." Pythia insists it must arise from the child herself.

Jared scoffs at the idea. "How can an infant choose her name?"

Yet the stalemate drags on. Days pass, then weeks. The child offers nothing, though Pythia asks again and again.

Then one dawn, the answer comes:

I know you as Mother. You are Pythia.

Yes.

I am Tara.

Pythia's heart leaps. *A name that honors your ancestor, Child of Buddha, my great-grandmother. She could read the riddles of the Precious Object.*

I am aware, the child replies.

When Pythia tells Jared, he grits his teeth and bites back whatever sarcasm rises to his tongue. "That's a goddess, right?" he says, trying for neutrality.

"Yes. But it's more than that. In our history, it began with great-grandmother Child of Buddha, in war-torn China. Though even earlier, in the silence of a mental institution."

"I've heard bits and pieces," Jared mutters. "You and your mother."

Though kind by nature, Jared feels quietly exiled from any recognizable role as father. Species aside, he is the restless outsider—watching, excluded, and feeling unwanted. And worse: unable to access the thread of consciousness that connects mother and child. Already, the dark seed of resentment, until now a vague discomfort, begins to grow.

Thank God we're not married, he thinks for the first time. *An alien child who sees me as some lesser species? That's unbearable.*

Still, he clings to the two lifelines that make this bearable: sex and science.

When Pythia takes him to bed, he loses himself completely in the strange, ecstatic forces she channels. For a few brief moments, he feels lifted, fused into something greater than himself, cradled in the rapture of her power.

"I can read your mind, Jared," she says one morning. "I know what you're struggling with. But I can't soften the truth for you. Soon, Tara and I will return to the cave as I once did. By your reckoning, years will pass before you see her again. When you do, she'll be what you would call an adolescent. I can't change that, and neither can you."

Jared stares at her. "And what exactly happens in that cave across all those years?"

"Many things. But not in the cave. It's not something most humans can grasp. Still, you're a physicist, so you've entertained the notion of multiple dimensions. Use that."

"My God," Jared says, suddenly alert. "You're finally saying something real. Okay. Dimensions. That's something I can understand. String theory, or some version. I am familiar with the concept of multiple dimensions beyond our four. Explain it. Give me something."

"Jared—"

"No. No evasion." He grabs a sheet of paper. "You want me to stay sane? To feel *part* of this? Then give me something. Anything."

With a sigh, Pythia sits at the kitchen table. "I'll need more paper."

Jared brings her a stack. She begins writing, scrawling page after page of dense equations. Jared stands behind her, watching, breath caught somewhere between awe and despair.

"These are basic field equations," she says at last. "Simplified, incomplete. But enough to give you a glimpse."

Jared takes them, flipping through. The notation is alien. Entirely unfamiliar.

"This may as well be hieroglyphics," he says bitterly. "I don't recognize a single system."

"Yes. They're not human. Each one carries a whole substrate of internal fields. But even taken together, they're inadequate. Because you face an obstacle no equation can solve."

"Which is?"

"You cannot *see* a fifth dimension. Or a ninth. Or a hundredth. Not the way you see length, width, height. You can model them, but you cannot inhabit them. I can."

"Can't you teach me?"

"You already know the answer," she says gently. "The maths are nothing. It's access in the *physical* world that matters."

And then, before his eyes, the papers vanish.

"Protecting your superiority?" he snaps.

"Protecting *you*, Jared. From yourselves. From this planet's others. You're not ready."

Misery overtakes him. Even his most private thoughts are open to her now. He can't even sulk without being read.

Maybe I really am no better than a beloved dog, he thinks. *Maybe worse.*

Pythia offers no consolation. Harsh truths are part of survival. Natural selection is not a kind teacher.

Jared says nothing. Instead, he turns inward, deciding to study, observe, endure. He will treat Tara as a specimen, a marvel. And perhaps, through sheer persistence, find some bridge. *Even gods appreciate affection,* he reasons. *Even a human feels the loyalty of a dog.*

The sting softens. With self-deprecating humor, he shrugs off his humiliation. Mostly. Yet the bitter kernel remains. And on certain nights, when it sprouts again, he wonders—just briefly—if he could betray them. Report everything to the authorities. But then he remembers: Ming-huà, Pythia, Tara, clairvoyants all. He shudders and chokes the thought.

Instead, he watches.

Tara's face is impossible, a stunning and uncanny projection of something not quite human. Her responses are unlike anything he's studied. She speaks in words he cannot decipher. Pythia translates what she can.

Despite everything, Jared feels love. Awe. And the scientific hunger to understand the unprecedented. She is beyond him, yes. But she is also his daughter.

And that, whatever else she becomes, is the one thing he clings to.

~

Amid the fragile peace of their temporary life, Tara's capacities unfold at a pace that astonishes even Pythia. Daily, she stretches her mind into dimensions unreachable by ordinary cognition, mapping territories of being that defy human language. After a brief interlude with Ming-huà and Zookeeper, Pythia and Jared return to San Francisco—she to the old Victorian house, he to his Berkeley apartment to resume his lectures. Lady Oracle, Sy, and Altan disperse without ceremony. Their withdrawal is quiet, but charged with expectation.

They are waiting.

And Pythia knows what for. Soon, Tara will enter the cave just as she once did with Ming-huà. Sixteen or more human years will pass while they journey across realms not governed by time. And though the "great forgetting" may again extract its cost, stripping memory from both mother and child, it is part of the pattern she now accepts. Ming-huà and Lady Oracle have prepared her for this trial.

It is Jared she pities most. Like Zookeeper before him, he will remain earth-bound, left behind not just in space, but in meaning.

Even before entering the cave, Tara evolves at a pace that eclipses even Pythia's own rapid maturation. She walks at six months, speaks in lucid sentences by her first birthday. She has never once wept. Her focus is unrelenting, piercing and tireless; it never falters.

Jared is delighted. He can speak with his daughter. But Pythia senses unease stirring beneath the marvel. There is an edge to Tara, a cold rationality masked as clarity. Her mind is already working toward transformation: disappearing objects, rehearsing interventions. She speaks often of improving the world, of following in the footsteps of her mother and grandmother. But Pythia hears, in the background, a subtle hunger for command.

One morning, as fog drapes the windows in spectral folds, mother and daughter sit quietly in the anteroom. Pythia works at her laptop. Tara watches her in silence, as she often does, her gaze sharp, unblinking. They've been conversing telepathically, but now Pythia speaks aloud.

"Did you enjoy your father's visit this weekend?"

"Yes," Tara replies. "He's funny. But dull."

"Dull?"

"Yes. His cognition is slow. He overlooks much."

"Such as?"

"There was a spider in the corner above his chair. He didn't notice, even when it caught a fly. He missed the hiss of its feeding, the increase in breath after the meal. Even within his three spatial dimensions, he's inattentive."

"Your father sees different things, Tara."

"Like what?"

"Small things. Quiet things."

"Name one."

"He's a physicist. They're trained observers."

"But you understand physics far better."

Pythia sighs. "He notices *you*, Tara. Often. He calls you brilliant. He speaks of your attentiveness, your light. I remember when we bathed you together; he was mesmerized by your hump, by the shifting symbols across your skin. He said he could watch for hours, but didn't want you to wrinkle. He was spellbound."

"Yes, compared to him. But he knows only you and grandmother. That's not a representative sample."

"Tara. Do you feel this superior? Even to your own father? Even to the spider?"

"That is different."

"How so?"

"The spider possesses skills I do not. Father does not."

"He produced the sperm that helped create you. A singular act you cannot replicate."

Tara pauses. Then offers her habitual refrain for what lies beyond her frame-work:

"Excuse me. I am become and still becoming."

"Soon," Pythia says gently, "we'll return to the cave. But before then, you must deepen your empathy. You must learn compassion for humans."

"All of them?"

"Yes."

"But you and grandmother have killed some."

"Yes. Out of necessity."

"And how is necessity known?"

"Only by those who've been properly raised. Who have *become*."

"But killing is wrong."

"Yes. Killing *can* be wrong."

"When?"

"Was the spider wrong to kill the fly?"

"No. It was necessary."

"Then you understand the concept."

"But you didn't need the humans you killed to survive. You didn't eat them."

"No. But their deaths preserved the lives of others."

"Then if we are to replace humanity, wouldn't that be comparable? They are the flies. We are the spider."

"No," Pythia says, firmly now. "That metaphor contains a fatal error. You reduce humans to resources. That is the first step toward extermination. Toward genocide."

"Then what? Should we allow them to continue even if they damage the planet, harm each other, and resist our protection?"

"That is not the question. The question is whether power gives you the *right* to decide."

"But humans make such decisions all the time. They protect lions, ele-phants—species they've displaced. Could we not do the same?"

"They protect those species only when it suits them. But even that protection is riddled with violence. Do not inherit their moral confusion."

"If humans resist, wouldn't necessity demand their removal?"

"Necessity is not a blunt instrument, Tara. It must be tempered by conscience."

"Is the line drawn at sentience?"

"No. Sentience is not enough. The lion is sentient. The elephant, too. Yet humans kill them. You must go deeper. To *intention*, to *relationship*, to the possibility of transformation."

"Then killing is wrong, except when it's right. I'm confused."

"You *should* be confused. Morality without confusion becomes dogma. Cer-tainty is the birthplace of cruelty."

Tara furrows her brow. "Like grandmother and the fawn?"

"Yes. She acted rashly, out of anguish. She regrets that now. She's learned . . . she would not repeat it."

"She could have just removed their hands."

"Yes."

"I can remove as much or as little as I want."

"And you must never forget *why* you do it. Power used without reflection is tyranny. No matter how noble the goal."

Tara is quiet, then speaks with sudden solemnity. "Mother, do we have a religion?"

"No. We have no doctrine, no fixed code. We believe in harmony with the living world and all its forces. That is not religion. It is relationship."

"But humans have moral systems like religions and philosophies, yet they still kill. By the millions."

"Yes. That is the tragedy of abstraction. They kill for purity, for heaven, for progress, for reason. We must not follow that path."

"Then . . . do we believe in God? Or Goddess?"

"Not yet. That question is too large. You must live into it. Perhaps the cave will guide you."

"I want to understand now."

"You cannot. Some truths cannot be inherited. They must be *borne*. For now, it is enough to know that not understanding is a form of wisdom."

Tara nods slowly. "I am becoming."

~

Conversations like these leave Pythia uneasy. She remembers herself at Tara's age—more pliant, more cautious, perhaps less intellectually acute, but also less inclined to challenge the ethical scaffolding she was given. Where might Tara's sharpened will lead? When she shares her concerns with Ming-huà, her mother is gentle, unconcerned. She views Tara's probing questions not as warning signs, but as the natural turbulence of early becoming. But Pythia pushes back. If Tara is left entirely free to construct her own moral code, where is the anchor? What is to prevent a logic of utilitarian brutality?

"Exactly," replies Ming-huà, softly but firmly.

And so Pythia is left with irony as her companion. She, who once broke from her own mother's caution, is now disturbed by her daughter's widening gyre. She, who has dared more than Ming-huà ever would, is now the one tightening the reins. Yet Tara, even as she mirrors Pythia's boldness, exceeds it, more unbound, more certain. Still, Pythia monitors her daughter's mind daily, trying not to intrude too forcefully. But the very act of constant surveillance carries its own dangers. Will Tara eventually chafe? Rebel? And if so, how might that rebellion manifest? Her genetic code, after all, still carries vestiges of human emotional volatility—evolutionary remnants not easily overwritten. She recalls Rogelio's final thoughts, his terrified longing for his mother in the seconds before death, and wonders whether anything lasting was gained by his execution. Some girls were freed, yes, but others would inevitably be caught in the same nets. The power she exercised felt righteous in the moment, but its legacy is uncertain. *Or perhaps*, she thinks, *incomplete.*

It taught her something sobering: only deeply wired, innate compassion for all living things—not selective or situational—can prevent even her kind from becoming monstrous in turn. But therein lies the deeper paradox. For if the emergence of her species spells the decline of *Homo sapiens*, how can such a transition avoid becoming yet another catastrophe? How does one species replace another without inflicting mass suffering?

Perhaps Tara will be the one to solve this. Perhaps her cold precision is not callousness, but clarity—the kind needed to face the most difficult equation: When is doing good inseparable from doing harm? And when must it stop? Since the incident in Mexico, Pythia—despite her access to cosmological knowledge—has been haunted by a more primal dilemma: if one has the power to alleviate suffering by confronting those who inflict it, but those inflictors are themselves writhing in their own inner agony, is the exercise of power not simply the multiplication of suffering? Is the logic of retribution always self-defeating?

Will replacing humankind improve the fate of the planet? Or will the same cycle, wearing a different mask, resume? Her sixteen years in the cave, immersed in simulations of epochal violence and world-ending events, provided no definitive answers. Only more refined forms of uncertainty. What will prevent her kind from misusing their power under the guise of eradicating suffering, only to create more? Even humans, with their cognitive limits, have produced rare sages who discern the only real path: empathy and compassion, unmarred by ideology. But knowing is not the same as being. External wisdom means little without internal compulsion.

Have Tara's genes evolved far enough to embed that compulsion at the core? Or do old patterns still hide in the roots?

~ *A Preparatory Visit* ~

One crisp spring morning, Lady Oracle arrives with Sy and Altan to discuss the approaching return to the cave. Jared, adamant about being included, is present.

As they enter, Lady Oracle takes Pythia's arm and asks quietly, "How is she progressing?"

"Very well," Pythia replies.

Behind them, Tara chimes in, "I am becoming."

Lady Oracle turns with a faint smile. "Tara, Sy is going to take you for a long walk while we speak privately."

"Yes, I know," Tara replies. "The street noise makes my hump chatter too much, but I understand you wish to talk freely." She points a mock-scolding finger at Sy. "But listen, Sy. The walk must be *long*. Otherwise, I'll pick up everything from here. My range is considerable, and I'm too curious. You must distract me—and jam my sensors, too. Privacy is important. For *your* sake and mine."

She glances at Lady Oracle. "Correct?"

"Correct," says Lady Oracle, without blinking.

Sy takes Tara's hand, but she halts at the threshold and turns back. "Before we go, I know what you're thinking. That I'm ahead of where Mother was at my age."

"Correct. In some ways," Lady Oracle answers. "But there's a word the ancient Greeks coined. You should meditate on it."

"Yes, I know. *Hubris.* I'll reread *The Iliad.* You fear I have too much?"

"Yes."

Jared interjects, brow furrowed. "Sweetie, every adult in this room has too much hubris. Don't let it ruin you as it may ruin us."

"Thank you, Father," she says seriously. "But I will heed Lady Oracle's warning. I am still becoming."

~

Once Tara has disappeared with Sy into the thickening mist, Pythia lingers. The atmosphere in the house lifts slightly. Their absence is palpable. The tension relaxes. Still, Jared remains acutely aware of his outsider status. Always the human among post-humans. Always the one who must *speak* to be heard. He sips his tea pensively.

"We must verbalize for Jared," Pythia says, having read his discomfort.

The others had already agreed silently, but Lady Oracle confirms aloud, "Yes. Jared is the father."

The remark stings. Yet Jared is grateful for the inclusion.

Lady Oracle continues briskly. "Jared, since my tactlessness caused offense, let me begin with you. You are aware that once the journey begins, you will not see Pythia or Tara for several Earth years?"

Jared straightens. "Yes. I'm ready. I have my own life, my own work."

"But you're also aware," she presses, "that your students—and their children, and grandchildren—will eventually be replaced. Their education, even your research, will become obsolete."

Jared responds sharply. "We *Homo sapiens* are still capable of full lives. Without education, we sink into ignorance. You haven't replaced us yet."

"No," Lady Oracle admits. "Not yet. And this experiment may still fail. But if it does, Jared, I'm not sure you comprehend how bleak the world will become."

"I don't accept that inevitability."

"It is as inevitable as the billions of barren planets where sentient life once tried and failed."

Jared has no response.

"But that's not why we're here," she says, softening. "You know Pythia will forget these years with Tara?"

"I've been told. I still don't understand why."

Lady Oracle turns to Pythia. "And you understand, Pythia, you will not be permitted to assist Tara—unless disaster strikes."

"Yes," Pythia says evenly.

Jared sits forward. "What kind of disaster would justify intervention?"

"She will know, if and when it comes," Lady Oracle replies.

"And . . . is it true," he presses, "that they will be traveling in time?"

Lady Oracle laughs softly. "Don't worry, Jared. No laws of physics will be violated. Think of it as . . . a dream."

"A sixteen-year dream," he mutters. "A long one."

"You know they can travel in ways you do not yet comprehend."

"I don't 'know' unless you *tell* me."

"Then let me tell you this," she says, more serious now. "We are being watched. By the FBI."

"What?" Jared sits bolt upright.

"Yes. Drones, wiretaps, there are multiple channels. But not minds. Not yet."

"But . . . they need warrants!"

"They have them."

"Which means probable cause. . . . "

She nods.

"How long has this been happening?"

"Months."

"They'll follow you to the cave."

"They may see us enter," Lady Oracle replies. "But they won't see us emerge."

"Not unless they wait sixteen years or so."

"Closer to ten, in Earth time. Still, while they wait, you will be innocently teaching."

That final remark lands strangely in Jared's heart. A part of him welcomes the return to the mundane: lectures, students, a rational world. But another part, a larger part, mourns the loss of awe, of danger, of cosmic proximity.

He nods, caught between relief and longing.

~ *Coda* ~

Jared shifts in his chair, pretending interest in his untouched tea. Lady Oracle is silent. Time, which has bent and curled around this house so many times before, now prepares to fold once more. But not gently. In a matter of days, the child will vanish. And with her, the fragile chord that has bound three beings together—mother, father, daughter—across the impossible distance between species.

Pythia will forget.

Jared will remember.

And Tara will become.

Outside, a raven lands on the iron railing, cocking its head once before launching itself into the deepening mist. It does not return.

Chapter Thirty-Two

Official Interest

No More Secrets

~ On the Edge ~

Pythia has just given Jared a final, lingering embrace. Then, without a word, she turns and walks into the mouth of the cave, little Tara at her side and towering Altan ahead, his rugged paperbirch staff stirring up thick shadows as if stirring sediment in dark water. As the darkness deepens, she glances back. Lady Oracle, Sy, and Jared stand haloed in sunlight, waving. She lifts her hand in farewell.

As you know, we are being watched, comes Lady Oracle's voice, cool and amused, threading through Pythia's mind. *So foolish they are. See you in a few human years. Let's see how patient they are.*

A sharp pang catches in Pythia's chest, an ache for the years about to be lost. She wishes she could stay behind to face the inevitable scrutiny, to dismantle the systems that will surely try to tighten their grip in her absence. But another, more primal discomfort twists beneath: the early whisper of instinct, the biological urging to diversify her lineage. That too will have to wait. Tara tugs her hand impatiently, eager to begin. Altan, who needs no light, glides forward as if skating on the bones of time. His walking stick parts the air like Charon's oar, steady and effortless. The cave takes them in.

They have gone only a little way when Altan pauses. From somewhere ahead, a woman's siren voice, smooth and resonant, floats toward them, neither echo nor hallucination but something woven of both.

"Welcome, little Tara. A long human time ago, I once asked your great-great-grandfather, John Powers, how one justifies a life without cruelty, and therefore without the distilled beauty of cruelty. What do you say to that question?"

Tara peers into the void, her eyes shimmering with interior light. "The spider's web is beautiful, and the taste of captured flies—exquisite. Is that what you mean?"

"Is that what *you* mean?" the voice responds, and from the gloom, a radiant figure emerges, elegant, impossible, lit from within like Pythia.

Tara blinks. "I'm still becoming."

"Yes," says the woman. "You are still becoming, and becoming leads to more becoming, until you have become."

"Become what?"

"What your ancestors died for."

Tara tilts her head. "Yes. The Chosen Ones of the distant past."

"Come," the woman says, gesturing gracefully. "Speaking of your great-great-grandfather, we will visit him soon when he was young, in a human war. But first, in human terms, you have many years of becoming ahead."

"Like school?"

"Yes and no. Definitely not like any school you know. It will be very hard, but not as hard as what comes after."

"I look forward to it. Who are you?"

"Who do *you* think I am?"

"A teacher."

"Yes and no."

"An alien intelligence? From some advanced civilization?"

"Yes and no."

Tara turns to Altan. "Do you know who she is?"

He shrugs without answering.

"Mother?"

Pythia smiles faintly. "Yes and no."

Tara presses, her tone suddenly urgent. "Then tell me what you *do* know. Who is she?"

"I don't know. I've never known. And we've met many times. Your grandparents didn't know. Nor did their parents. Nor did theirs."

"But they're old. Or dead. And she's young. And beautiful."

"Yes," says Pythia. "There you are . . . your first riddle."

The radiant woman smiles, her whole body pulsing with light.

"Almost right, Pythia," she says. "But Tara's first riddle was mine—the one about cruelty."

"Did I answer it right?" Tara asks eagerly.

"Yes and no. Now come. We must go deeper. There are many tunnels, many times, many places. Eventually, you'll meet all the ancestors your mother spoke of, and many more."

"Will they see me?"

"Sometimes. That depends. You'll discover how."

They continue deeper. Then the woman points, and a side tunnel bursts into a clear and beckoning light.

"Go there."

Tara pulls her mother forward. Altan leads the way.

The tunnel is familiar to Pythia. She recognizes every bend, every silence. And when they finally emerge into their destination, Tara gasps, just as Pythia had, eons ago.

As the tunnel blinks shut behind them, Altan turns and begins to speak, not in riddles now, but in curriculum. He offers a preview of what's to come: courses on the physics of multidimensional manipulation, standard and non-standard singularities, hypermutability, hominin accelerated regions, evolutionary rescue, and other subjects no human child has ever imagined.

Thus begin the beginning years of Tara's education, the journey toward what she is, and what she will one day become.

~ *On the Trail* ~

A week has passed since Pythia, Tara, and Altan stepped into the desert cave. None have returned. In a glass-walled conference room in San Francisco, Agent Lance Romellian studies the morning's intel. Two names flash red on every screen: Ming-huà Powers and her daughter, Pythia. The mother remains isolated on her coastal island, tending quietly to her armless husband. But the daughter, along with her child and an unidentified man, vanished into a fissure in the Mojave. A cave, ancient and unremarkable to most. But not to Lance. He's known of it since childhood.

His uncle, Emile Ruska, once a homicide detective, used to tell strange bedtime stories. Disappearances. Impossible murders. A cave that warped time and memory. Back then, Lance thought they were fables. Until the patterns began again.

Two hunters vanished on a northern island—no bodies, no signs of struggle. A crackhouse in San Francisco's Tenderloin district: every addict found alive, their limbs gone, cleanly removed. In Baltimore, a near-identical scene—same silence, same clinical mutilation. Another in San Francisco: a hate crime halted mid-act. The skinhead, identified as "Rocket," found conscious on the pavement, missing one arm and a hand. Most recently: a trafficking ring in Mexico collapsed overnight. Same result.

Each case leaves the same residue: bloodless amputations, no witnesses, no forensic trail. Just rumors. And a figure with a curved back, glimpsed only briefly.

Sometimes it's Ming-huà. Sometimes, perhaps, her daughter.

Too many patterns for coincidence. Too little evidence for a charge. Romellian has reclassified all five. Same technique. Same vanishing point. Same modus. The vanishing point: always the cave.

Now, seated at a metal table under hospital-bright lights, he listens to the reports.

"They entered the cave?" he asks.

Agent Duffy nods. "Three of them, Pythia, her kid, and a male companion. Still working on an ID. Goes by Altan."

"And they haven't come out."

"No. Drones, long-range optics, night-vision. Almost a week. Nothing."

"The perimeter?"

"Holding. No breach."

Romellian looks at the satellite image, an oval shadow in the sand, as if the Earth had blinked.

"Then unless there's another exit. . . . "

"They're still inside."

The room falls into quiet.

"Do we go in?" Agent Lorenz asks.

Romellian doesn't answer immediately. He's looking not at the cave, but at the silence surrounding it.

"Not yet. Everything on record says one way in, one way out. Keep watching. We'll wait."

~

That evening, Romellian drives north through fog. He carries no illusions about what he hopes to find. Just questions. His uncle, Emile Ruska, now lives in a faded care home near the coast. The old detective, once a force of law, now just bone, bourbon, and whisper, meets him in the lobby. His eyes, though dulled by age, still hold the tension of unsaid things.

In his small room, they speak with little prelude.

"I've reviewed your old case files," Lance begins. "Michael Powers. Tamara Chu. Ming-huà. I know Powers was institutionalized. Suicide. Three psychiatrists dead under unclear circumstances. You tracked him to the same cave I'm now surveilling. But your notes . . . they read like code. Missing pieces. Riddles. Am I close?"

Emile smiles thinly. "You're skimming foam and calling it the sea. Want the depths? Be careful what you breathe down there."

"I want what's real."

"You sure?"

"I don't have the luxury of doubt."

"Good," Emile murmurs. "Then start asking. I'll give you what time I have."

Lance leans forward. "Did you ever encounter mutilations like these? Dismemberment without trauma. Victims in pieces, but no blood. No violence."

"No. Not then. Michael Powers didn't lose limbs, or cause others to. He lost boundaries. Said he heard two voices—God and Goddess. Always arguing."

"You believed him?"

"I believed he heard something. Whether it was madness or intrusion, I couldn't say."

"What did they argue about?"

"Goddess was trying to cure God's addiction."

"To what?"

"Suffering."

Lance stares. "That's metaphor."

"Is it?" Emile's gaze sharpens. "Or is it the last truth we dare admit?"

Silence. Then Lance shifts tack. "Was Michael schizophrenic?"

Emile's voice lowers. "Something else. Something I couldn't write in reports. I saw things. Did things. And the cave—" He stops, collecting breath. "That place doesn't just swallow people. It folds them. Disassembles them. Reassembles them."

Lance frowns. "Telepathy? ESP? Hypnosis?"

"All of it. Thought moved like light in a mirror maze. At first I thought it was a con. But the patterns didn't crack."

"What about Tamara Chu?"

"She was no mere mother. And then there was Buandelgereen."

"Lady Oracle's grandmother?"

"Maybe. A Mongol woman. She bent steel with her mind. And even she answered to something stronger."

Lance is quiet. "You think someone . . . or something used Michael to kill those psychiatrists?"

"I think something passed through him. What it was . . . it was not human. Not quite."

"And this . . . *thing*—what does it want?"

Emile closes his eyes, opens them slowly. "Wrong question."

"Then what's the right one?"

He stares hard at Lance, as if searching for a doorway in his face.

"Not what they want. *What they are?*"

Lance doesn't respond.

Emile exhales like someone surrendering a long-held breath. "If you go into that cave . . . beware the young one. She isn't what she looks. Not even close."

"What do you mean?"

"You'll see. Goddess doesn't play with straight cards. You might end up in Vietnam like I did."

"What?"

But Emile only smiles, a tired, sideways grin.

"Conversation's over. Go find your truth. Just don't expect it to resemble anything you were trained to recognize."

~

Driving back under sodium lights and low fog, Lance tells himself the stories are just that: warped memory, grief dreams, myth dressed as testimony. But part of him knows better. The facts remain: most of the victims were criminals. The violence was surgical. Deliberate. Someone—*something*—is drawing lines around human depravity and cutting it off at the joint. He builds theories. Black ops. Foreign tech trials. Rogue AI. Radical justice movement. Government conspiracy. Each falls apart before it coheres into something solid.

The cave remains. Cold. Watching. Not a place, but a problem. A wound in the skin of the world. Romellian doesn't believe in prophecy. But he does believe in pursuit. And something is moving beneath the fabric—too organized to ignore, too vast to understand. He will follow it. Even if it leads to silence. Even if it leads to her. Even if, at the end, it leads to the answer he was warned not to ask.

~

Back at the office, Lance tries to clear his head. He dismisses most of his uncle's claims about Goddess, aliens, Vietnam, and the rest, as the embellishments of an old man too long inside unsolved cases. Powers with supernatural abilities? No. He won't go there. But something persists. Why dismemberment? Why only criminals, except for the missing hunters? If these are targeted hits, what's the motive? Revenge? Message? Market control? And the psychiatrists—why them? He sketches out theories: cartel warfare, rogue justice, foreign psy-ops, domestic extremism. Each sounds plausible until it doesn't. The dots refuse to align. Too scattered. Too surgical.

And then the cave.

He wants to believe this is just an operation—illegal, sophisticated, containable. But he doesn't, because underneath all the data, something festers. Not strategy. Not ideology. Not routine.

Intent—cold, precise, and without identifying signature. He shudders. It is a malevolence that doesn't shout, but meticulously selects.

And that, more than anything, is what keeps Lance awake.

~ *Deeper into Disbelief* ~

A few days later, Lance Romellian stands before the cave's jagged mouth, flanked by two agents and a Forest Service guide. All are equipped for a descent into darkness. The guide, Edward Golden, offers a clipped overview of the cave's geology, but as he shifts into local history, the tone changes. Anecdote seeps in. Superstition follows.

"White Thunder, a Native guide who worked thirty years for the Service, refused to go inside," Golden says. "Said it was haunted. Got written up for insubordination when he wouldn't accompany a cop in. Swore the guy came back . . . different."

"What was the officer's name?" Lance asks.

Golden shrugs. "Too long ago."

"Do you have a problem going in?"

"Not really. Just never had reason to."

Lance raises a brow. "Not even once?"

"Back when the rumors started—escaped mental patient, serial killer, weird disappearances—this place got attention. But even before that, nobody wanted to come here. You still can't pay folks to."

"Why not?"

"Stories."

"What kind of stories?"

"Ghosts. Demons. Aliens. Take your pick."

Lance nods, then gestures. "Let's go."

Their flashlights slice into the gloom as they enter. The air thickens. The cave swallows sound.

"Watch for exits," Lance says. "There are side tunnels and, farther down, a chasm. Duane—first tunnel. Carl—second. I'll take the third. Golden, stay on the main path and monitor movement."

As they split up, Lance approaches the third tunnel. "That's me," he tells Golden. "Wait here. Let me know if you see anything—or anyone."

He steps inside. The tunnel begins broad, then narrows. The walls tighten around him. He spots a narrow seam, investigates, finds it leads nowhere. Turning to retrace his steps—a face. A woman, inches away, haloed in the beam of his flashlight.

"Shit—" he gasps, stumbling back.

She is young, composed, and unmistakably beautiful. A backpack hangs from one shoulder, and a snug cap frames the quiet radiance of her face. Her presence settles into him with unexpected force, dissolving the residue of confusion and strain. Something within him steadies, as if a long-held tension has quietly released.

"Hello," *she* says, smiling gently.

"What . . . what are you doing here?"

"Exploring," *she* replies.

He flashes his badge. "I'm with the FBI. Investigating."

"What sort of investigation?"

"Missing persons. Have you seen anyone?"

Her eyes remain fixed on his. "Just the cave. Some bats. Nothing worth reporting."

"No people at all?"

She tilts her head, her gaze unblinking. "People? I hope not. I told your uncle Emile long ago—this cave is meant to remain pristine. I was surprised to see him. I'm even more surprised to see you."

The name hits him like a blow. "My . . . uncle?"

"You must be careful, Lance," *she* says softly. "There are shadows darker than darkness."

Before he can speak, *she* vanishes.

He swings his light in all directions. Empty. Cold stone. Breath catching, he reaches the tunnel's terminus—a blank wall. He stands there, stunned, replaying her words. Emile's warning, as clear and ominous as tolling bells, rises in his mind.

What the hell is going on here?

He calls out, "Come back!" but only silence responds.

When he rejoins Golden, his composure has partially returned. *Must be a relative,* he tells himself. *A lookalike. There's a rational explanation.*

Golden glances up. "See anything?"

"Did you?"

"Nope."

"Not even a flicker, a sound?"

Golden shakes his head. "Nothing."

Lance stares into the dark behind them. "Let's keep moving."

Duane and Carl soon report. No signs. No findings. Just more empty tunnels. They press deeper.

At the next set of shafts, Lance repeats the assignments. Golden eyes him warily.

"You sure everything's okay?"

"Just stay alert."

Lance's second tunnel stretches wider. He advances slowly, scanning for seams, splits, odd textures. Nothing. He reaches the end: another rock wall. Almost without thinking, he presses his palm against it.

Then a voice behind him.

"My, my. You are thorough. But I wouldn't push too hard. Be careful what you wish for, Lance."

He turns.

She stands there again, smiling, undisturbed by logic.

"Who *are* you?"

"Your uncle helped us once. Perhaps you're similarly inclined."

"Help with what?"

"One never knows."

She studies him with the air of one observing an intelligent pet. "Tell me, Mr. Romellian, how do you justify a life without cruelty, and therefore without the distilled beauty of cruelty?"

"I'm not here for riddles. Who—what—are you?"

"I am not a who. Nor a what."

He grits his jaw. "We're searching for—"

She lifts a hand. "Spacetime is curved. So are answers."

He presses again. "Do you know Pythia Powers?"

She doesn't answer.

He tilts his head, encouraging a response.

"In this cave," *she* says, "space and time twist so tightly, you may arrive before the beginning or return where you started. Better to go back to chasing your 'bad guys.' Leave this to those who can bear it."

"Or else?"

"There is no 'else.' This isn't a threat. Others need your attention more than we do."

"But you said I might be needed."

"If that time comes, you'll be summoned. And you will remember."

She dissolves in a shimmer of light, leaving no sound and no farewell.

Lance stands alone.

Eventually, he rejoins the others and says nothing.

They continue through side tunnels. Nothing. No signs, no passageways. Only deepening silence.

Then they come to the bridge.

A narrow rock span arches over a black chasm. One by one, they cross. On the far side, something shifts. The air grows denser. The dark presses in, thick as tar.

His flashlight dims against it. The tunnel he draws next is vast, hollowed as if by an ancient hand. He walks forward. The light flickers. The shadows feel viscous, almost alive. His thoughts lose order. The last of his rational mind slips. He falls to his knees. The flashlight clatters. His breath shallows.

Suddenly, *her* hand is on his shoulder. Warmth spreads through him like liquid fire. Muscles melt. Control vanishes.

"You seek the unseekable to find the unfindable," *she* murmurs. "Let me help."

She squeezes gently. His strength returns.

"Follow me."

He does.

They walk through the bog of darkness. *Her* steps leave no sound. At the tunnel's end, *she* points to a seamless wall of stone. "Now place your hands here. Push."

He does. Nothing.

"Again, Lance," *she* says. "With all that famous determination."

He braces. Pushes harder.

And what happens next will haunt Lance Romellian, not just because it defies explanation, but because somewhere deep inside, he realizes it was not an anomaly, not a glitch in reality, but the beginning of something vast, final, and inevitable.

It will be a new scripture written in silence, with humanity itself as the fading text.

Epilogue

The Stillness

Defeat is not the end, only a gate through which something unseen begins to rise.
The survivors will soon learn that what rose to replace them is stronger, stranger,
far more empathetic, and far less hurtful than humankind.
The Voices yield.
End the ending.
The Stillness listens,
And humanity moves down its long, final path.

www.ingramcontent.com/pod-product-compliance
Lightning Source LLC
Chambersburg PA
CBHW021439310726
48971CB00005B/1431